Drowning

in the

Sea of Cortez

John Turner

REGULATOR
PRESS

Also by John Turner

The Wicked Kind

Dodging Bullets

This novel is dedicated to James Lee Burke, a superb wordsmith, and a genuine American icon

And some memories you wish you never had
—Stephen Kellogg

We're all criminals
—Jay Farrar

Drowning

in the

Sea of Cortez

Prologue
Loose Ends

The man took the turns at high speed, the Corvette's perfor-
mance-tuned suspension and six hundred horses barely
breaking a sweat. He'd wanted to put the top down if only to
drown out the woman's incessant whining, but the evening air
had a bite to it, so he kept the top up and the radio loud. The
woman was undeterred.

God, she was a bore, going on about this thing and that,
none of it worth hearing once, let alone set on repeat. She was
hammered already—problem number two. When he picked
her up she'd already plowed through a bottle of red, and at dinner she threw back three glasses of Chivas, neat. She could
drink like a longshoreman, and talk like one too. He used to
find that attractive, in a slumming sort of way. Now it was just
tedious.

The man wondered about his plan, if he should move up
the timetable. He had two viable options, either one foolproof.
But still, it was tricky business with multiple ways to go wrong.
He had to be sure. There could be no loose ends, no overlooked
details. He looked at the woman and thought, Baby, you have
no idea what's coming.

She was ranting now. He'd lost the thread ten minutes ago
and he wasn't about to pick it back up. A U2 song came on the
radio; it wasn't very good. Whatever happened to those guys

anyway? They used to be great. He spun the dial, stopped on the Stones, *Gimme Shelter*. Wicked.

He thought about the woman. She wasn't always like this. Time was, she had her head together and she was good for some laughs. How long ago was that, a year now? Damn, had it been that long? The minute she started harping on the future he knew he was done. There was never going to be a future. Not with her at least. A saying came to mind: don't shit where you eat. Man, he sure screwed the pooch on that one.

"You're sure about it, right?" the woman said.

The man sighed. "Yes, I'm sure about it." They'd been over it ten times already.

"Because it has to happen. Just like you said it would."

"It'll happen. Trust me."

"That sanctimonious bastard isn't going to win this time." The woman was seething. "Him and his holier-than-thou bullshit. I'm sick of it."

"I told you, it's going to happen. How many times do I have to say it?"

The woman shot the man a steely look and he had half a mind to smack her. Instead, he shook out a cigarette, steering with his knees as he lit it. He blew out a stream of smoke. She hated it when he smoked, especially in the car. He knew it and didn't care. For being such a lush, she had no tolerance for cigarettes, cigars even less. Maybe when they got to the hotel he'd break out a fat stogie, just to piss her off.

"Can you not do that?" the woman said.

"Do what?"

She rolled down her window and pouted.

Ortega Highway was clear, the moon full, and the man gassed it on the straights, easing into the curves with the grace of a seasoned driver. He loved his car, got off on the feeling of power, the sensual vibration coming up through the seat, straight into his loins. Power, lust, and sex—it all came together when you drove a fast machine.

He probably loved his car more than any woman. More than his wife. Certainly, more than the mewling shrew sitting next to him. Did he ever love her? He wasn't even sure he liked her, outside of the sex. And *that* had turned to shit fast. If it wasn't for his hatred of her husband, he would've cut her loose a long time ago.

But he didn't cut her loose. And then things happened, unintended consequences as they say, and the man was forced into his plan. Too late to turn back now, he thought. In for a penny, in for a pound. He would see it through, just like any number of unpleasant tasks he'd been forced to undertake in his life.

The man backed off the speed at Ortega Oaks. The moon cast spooky light through the canopy of trees over the highway, the ribbon of asphalt bathed an ethereal blue. The woman stared straight ahead, her face hard in the glow of the dashboard lights. She looked old and haggard—hell, she was only forty-six. Booze will do that to you. At least she'd stopped her yapping.

He accelerated at the switchback, two-handing the steering wheel. Decker Canyon Road flew by. Maybe this weekend he'd take the bike out and make the run to Lake Elsinore. Just past Hells Kitchen he saw road flares. The man checked the time: ten forty-five. The flares angled from right to left, forcing the man to drive onto the shoulder on the opposite lane. Up ahead he saw an Orange County Sheriff's cruiser parked with the running lights on, the light bar dark. What was this?

No cars came in either direction and there were no houses along this stretch of road. The man and woman in the Corvette were alone on Ortega Highway. The man pulled even with the cruiser. There was no one inside. The woman was about to speak when there came a tap on the driver's side window. The man and woman looked to their left, immediately blinded by a bright light. Irritated, the man eased the window down. He was about to tear into the fool when a white-hot muzzle flash ended all that. The woman screamed. At the same moment, another flash turned her world black.

***

THE MAN with the flashlight shut off the Corvette's engine. The woman was still breathing. He looked at her curiously, and then put two rounds into her face.

He reached behind the seat and lifted the driver's briefcase, snuffed the headlights and rolled up the window, left the keys in the ignition. He walked to the rear of the Corvette, reached under the frame and removed a small black box about the size of a deck of cards and placed it in the glove box of the cruiser. Then he picked up the road flares, swept away the ash, and put the spent flares into a container in the cruiser's trunk. He pulled a disposable cell phone from his pocket, dialed a number from memory. A tired voice came on the line, sounding booze-slurred.

"Yes?"

"It's done," the man with the flashlight said.

"Completely?"

"Yes."

"Good. Make sure it looks right. Did you get the brief-case?"

"Yes, I got it."

"That's good."

The line went silent, followed by a deep sigh.

"Was it quick?" the tired, boozy voice said.

"As quick as these things go."

"Did she suffer?"

The man with the flashlight stifled a yawn. "I don't think so," he said.

"Good. That's good."

"Is there anything else?"

"No. I suppose that's it."

"Then I'm out."

"Yes, well goodnight. And Godspeed."

Chapter 1

Jake Donahue woke up on the couch. The television was on with the sound turned down. He'd been watching the Angels get clobbered by the Yankees when the lazy summer day finally got the best of him and he closed his eyes for just a minute. That was two hours ago.

The house was hot and Jake noticed the floor fan had crapped out. Must've been that damned frayed wire. He'd have to get a new fan; the June heat had been brutal and the old house in the canyon had no air conditioning. He'd considered installing a window unit but so far hadn't gotten around to it. But air conditioning was the least of Jake Donahue's concerns. Little did he know; his world was about to tilt on its axis.

The afternoon newscast was on. Jake rarely watched the local news. Whenever he did, he got that song stuck in his head, the one by Don Henley. News as entertainment always rubbed Jake the wrong way.

He sat up and stared unfocused at the television, his head foggy from sleep. The news anchor cut to a live shot of a press conference outside the county courthouse in Santa Ana. A well-dressed man faced a crowd of reporters, a young woman standing at his side. The woman was very pretty, with straight blonde hair past her shoulders, intelligent eyes behind black-rimmed glasses, and a posture of confidence as she spoke.

Jake considered the man, thinking the guy looked familiar. He leaned his head back and closed his eyes, thought about laying back down for a while longer. Then something clicked, a jolt of awareness shooting through the fog, and Jake reached for the remote and turned up the sound, his heart beating fast at the realization he knew the man on the TV. The blonde woman was speaking, a trace of anger in her voice.

"My father came down here in good faith to answer the district attorney's questions. It is my fervent hope that his co-operation today will put to rest whatever unfounded notions there are regarding the death of my mother. Frankly, the idea that anyone would suspect Bruce McAlister of such a heinous crime is incomprehensible, and I'm appalled beyond words. There's a killer out there, a ruthless monster who tore our family apart, and he must be caught. That's all I have to say."

The blonde woman turned and whispered something to the man, reporters shouting questions over one another, and seconds later they disappeared behind a row of stern-faced men wearing black suits and sporting crew cuts. The row of men closed ranks and guided the man and woman to a waiting SUV.

The reporter came on then, some dapper-looking dude affecting an air of journalistic seriousness as he gave his recap before sending it back to the station. The news anchor thanked his colleague for the fine reporting and he moved on to another story.

Jake clicked off the TV.

He sat in the silence of the old house, the heat of the room stifling. A lot of thoughts hit him at once, an emotional chain reaction that was unstoppable.

Jake thought about the man on the television.

What in the hell have you gotten yourself into now, Bruce?

Chapter 2

What Jake Donahue remembered most about that summer was the heat. Unrelenting waves of it settling over Southern California like a wet blanket, the record-breaking temperatures accompanied by higher than normal humidity. Not Deep South humidity—Jake knew *that* kind of heat—but enough discomfort to fray nerves and set people on edge, a general meanness charging the air like the static electricity from a Santa Ana wind.

Jake had recently returned to Orange County after a long absence. His father died and Jake inherited the Silverado Canyon house, and he was living in it while he figured out his next move. The house—more of a cottage really—was built in the early 1920s, allegedly by a Mexican bandit who once rode with Tiburcio Vásquez. Jake's father bought the place for a song after the deadly flood of 1969 washed away a portion of the house and spooked the owners into selling.

The house sat vacant for a long time before Jake's father realized its full potential as a love nest for his trysts, and a boys' club for weekend poker bashes that were notorious throughout the canyon for the large amounts of money wagered. Jake's mother knew of the trysts, and while she tolerated them in the manner of women of her generation, the humiliation led to a slow-burning rage that manifested itself in drunken blowouts.

Jake was thirteen when his parents divorced. After, he divided his time between his mother's house in Orange and the Silverado Canyon house, where his father took up residence. As he moved through his teen years, Jake spent more time living with his father than with his mother, her long slide into alcoholism necessitating survival measures.

But living with Ed Donahue was hardly a healthy alternative.

Jake's father was a larger-than-life, self-aggrandizing man with insatiable appetites and no moral compass. He'd made a fortune selling used cars—Big Ed's House of Sleds, formally known as *Reliable Motors*. Half the illegals in Southern California drove a beater from Big Ed. His five dealerships were strictly low-rent, catering to a very specific clientele; easy financing and no credit checks was the pitch. Ed repossessed a lot of cars because of his pitch, but the law of averages worked in his favor, and exorbitant interest rates insured that Ed Donahue made bank. He pissed most of it away when he embarked on a second career as a professional gambler.

By middle age Ed had grown tired of the used car game and he yearned for something new. After watching the World Series of Poker one weekend he found his calling. Ed became a self-professed cardsharp, teaching himself Texas Hold 'em and honing his craft at the canyon house poker parties. Soon, he was hanging out in Las Vegas, staying up for days on end, stoking his dream of winning a gold bracelet.

When in Vegas, Ed only played Binion's Horseshoe Casino. The Horseshoe was old school. The Horseshoe was ground zero in the quest for a title. The trouble was, Ed Donahue had no head for cards. Sure, he had the ego, but not the gravitas needed to succeed. The losses mounted, and before long, Ed's dream of poker stardom turned into a money-draining habit akin to that of a common street junkie. But still the good times rolled; the parties got wilder, the women younger, and the stimulants stronger.

Big Ed Donahue finally stroked out at midnight on Halloween night while playing in some low-level poker tournament at the Commerce Casino down in the industrial part of Los Angeles. He was seventy-four years old with two hundred thousand in the bank, one dealership in Santa Ana, and the house in the canyon. The sum total of a lifetime spent selling used cars.

When Jake got the phone call from his father's attorney informing him of his inheritance, he was surprised there was anything left. He sold the dealership for taxes, rolled the cash into a couple of high-yield funds, and moved south three weeks ago to take possession of his father's house in the canyon. So far, Orange County hadn't gotten to him, but Jake knew it was coming. It always did whenever he returned home. Old bones lie buried but not forgotten.

He'd come down from Truckee, where he'd been living for the past three years. Jake had enjoyed living in Truckee, but circumstances had conspired against him—as they always seemed to do whenever he stayed anywhere too long—and it was time to move on. The call from the attorney was opportune, and Jake wasted no time in tying up his loose ends and hitting the road.

It was a pattern started long ago, a nomadic lifestyle born of tragedy; a stint in the Navy followed by stops in Seattle, New Orleans, Galveston, Bismarck, Las Cruces, and a smattering of small towns throughout the West. Jake had worked as an oil roughneck in the Great Plains, a logger in the Pacific Northwest, crewed fishing boats in the Gulf of Mexico, and built houses in the desert.

Because he was a big man, with the broad back and strong hands of a laborer, Jake was drawn to physical work. He loved being outdoors, deriving great pleasure from good pay for an honest day's work. He was not an ignorant man, although many treated him so, and Jake was fine with that. He preferred to keep to the sidelines anyway and quietly go about his business. Taciturn and fiercely honest, Jake would speak his mind when necessary, but most often he adhered to the notion that actions meant far more than words. Having been raised by one of the world's great bullshit artists, Jake figured there was more than enough of that nonsense to go around. Nose to the grindstone, that was Jake Donahue's way.

So now he'd returned to Orange County, to the place of his birth. Just to take care of business. That's what he told himself. But in truth, Jake was going through a major upheaval, a complete reevaluation of his life. Maybe it was the onset of middle age, or maybe his nomadic ways had simply lost their allure. Regardless, Jake Donahue sensed a sea change coming. He'd felt it for months, an intuitive awareness that could not be ignored. The death of his father would be the impetus, a match flame that would torch everything Jake had ever known or thought to be true. It would reshape him as a man, and lay bare his secrets for all the world to see.

Chapter 3

There was work to be done on the canyon house. Jake had compiled a long list of repairs prioritized by importance, divided by interior and exterior. He was an orderly man—a habit he'd formed while in the Navy—and he approached every task in a measured way, breaking it down to its basic components before settling on the best approach. The old house had been in disrepair for some time and Jake was eager to get busy and put things right. He hadn't yet decided if he would sell the place or hang onto it as a rental property, but either way, the work needed to be done.

Before starting on the work, Jake had some surfing to do; Bruce McAlister's press conference had intrigued him and he wanted to know more about it. He took his laptop and a tumbler of iced tea to the sun deck at the back of the house and set up at a redwood table in the shade of an oak tree. Evening was coming on fast, as it always did in the canyon, a warm breeze blowing from the east.

The house backed up to Silverado Creek. The creek was usually bone-dry in the summer, but come the winter rains it could turn deadly. The house used to extend to the end of the deck, but the flood of '69 washed it away along with a concrete retaining wall. A new wall was built, the deck replacing the damaged portion of house.

Jake enjoyed sitting on the deck. It was peaceful, more so when the creek ran. Fall was the best time of year; Indian summer giving way to shorter days and cool evenings, fire smoke scenting the canyon, a nostalgic feeling in the air. Jake wondered if he would still be here come fall.

He recalled times spent here in the years after his parents' divorce. They were both the best and the worst times of Jake's life. His father was mercurial and life with him was a crapshoot. In his most settled moments, Big Ed was a caring and compassionate man. But when that unknown thing tugging at his guts got the best of him, he was hell on wheels. At those times, Jake would seek refuge with his mother, although Mary Donahue had her own demons, and many were the times Jake felt he had no real home to call his own.

Jake turned his attention to the computer. The house wasn't wired for Internet so he relied on his wireless card for connectivity, although the narrow confines and remoteness of the canyon made for dicey reception; cell phones didn't work here either. After logging on, Jake navigated to the news channel website. A few clicks later he located the full video for the press conference. He turned the sound up and hit play. The video kept lagging while it buffered, but Jake Donahue was a patient man, and after making a few adjustments to the computer's settings he simply waited out the delays.

While the video buffered, Jake allowed his mind to wander, to a time and place in the past. Memories hit him from all sides, firing in his brain like signal flares: memories of high school and the squad; memories of Bruce; memories of Mexico in '84. Jake had spent a long time locking those memories down and he usually didn't indulge in reminiscing. Too much hurt there. Too much water under the bridge.

The video finally loaded and Jake got through it in one pass. Seeing it again, he was struck by the thought that time had been kind to Bruce McAlister. He looked good, better than good. But then again, Bruce had always looked good. Sure, it seemed like he might've had some work done, but it was obvious the slow creep of middle age had gone easy on the man Jake Donahue had once considered his best friend.

Jake and Bruce were three months apart in age—they were both forty-eight now—but Jake's lifetime spent working outdoors had given him a rugged and weathered look, whereas Bruce clearly took an easier path in life. There was a time Jake did all the heavy lifting for his friend, as Bruce McAlister wasn't the type who got his hands dirty. He seemed to have a knack for it, and it looked like nothing had changed in that regard.

The video finished and Jake considered what he'd seen.

Bruce McAlister, founder and head pastor of the Canyon New Life Ministry, had been questioned in the death of his wife. Susan McAlister was shot on a Thursday night in April, on a remote section of Ortega Highway, deep in the Santa Ana Mountains. Also killed was Orange County Supervisor Richard Lawson. Lawson represented District 3, which included the area of Silverado Canyon, and Susan had worked for him as a consultant.

Lawson and McAlister were shot in Lawson's Corvette, the bodies discovered Friday morning when a bicyclist stopped to fix a flat tire and he became curious about the vehicle parked alongside the road. The coroner placed the time of death as sometime between 10:00 p.m. and midnight on Thursday. It was unclear what Richard Lawson and Susan McAlister were doing on Ortega Highway so late at night. Lawson owned a vacation home in Idyllwild, but it was unlikely he was heading there, as staff members said he was expected at an early board meeting on Friday.

The news report characterized the questioning of Bruce McAlister as routine. Officially, he had not been named a suspect. The tall woman who spoke at the press conference was Bruce's daughter Paige. She was an attorney for a Newport Beach law firm. When asked if she was representing her father in an official capacity, Paige McAlister had no comment.

Jake restarted the video from the beginning and then paused it on Paige. He studied her features, thinking she didn't look much like her father. He sensed familiarity there, a deep sense of knowing. He hit play and closed his eyes, listened to the young woman speak, faint stirrings tingling at the cadence of her voice, the firm yet lilting tone. She was a confident woman, proud too, that much was clear. Jake supposed in *that* way she was very much like her father.

But the physical appearance had him stumped, and the more he watched, the more he realized that Bruce and Paige McAlister looked nothing like each other. He became curious about Paige's mother, figuring the family resemblance must reside there. He Googled Susan McAlister, clicked over to the images. Jake sat upright when they loaded, a flush of nerves rising inside him, his face suddenly hot. He scrolled through the images, his world becoming smaller with each click of the mouse.

Chapter 4

The old man pulled the '72 Chevy pickup into the driveway. It was a workingman's truck, mechanically sound if not aesthetically lacking. He got out of the truck, fitted his wide-brimmed straw hat and walked bow-legged to the front door of the canyon house, his shoulders slightly stooped. He wore a long-sleeved shirt buttoned at the cuffs and neck, tucked into blue jeans faded from use, a dusty pair of western boots scuffing the pavement.

Jake heard the truck from the sun deck and he arrived at the front door as the old man knocked. When he swung the door open, the old man beamed a dazzling smile; perfect teeth set in a wizened face, laugh lines at the corners of sky-blue eyes—eyes that exuded kindness and compassion.

"The prodigal son returns," the old man said loudly.

"Returns, yes. Prodigal is highly doubtful." Jake shook the man's hand vigorously. "How are you, Hector?"

"I am good, *mi hijo*."

Jake blushed; Hector Santiago had called him that since Jake was a child.

"You had a good trip down?"

"Yes," Jake said.

"I am sorry for not visiting sooner, but other matters needed tending."

"No worries, Hector, I understand."

"No, I will not hear of it. Proper form dictates amends. And to that end."

Hector walked to the truck, hoisted something out of the bed. He shuffled back to the house, a portable air conditioner resting on his shoulder. Hector's gait was not indicative of his age—he would be eighty-one in July—but more an economy of motion; he saw little reason to expend energy needlessly.

"Let us find a spot for this."

"I'll get that," Jake said, taking the air conditioner from Hector's shoulder.

"I will not argue the point," Hector said jovially. He tilted his hat and dabbed his brow with a folded bandana. "I knew this old place would be hot, and we cannot have the prodigal son feeling uncomfortable."

"Will you please knock that off?"

"As you wish." He winked at Jake.

Hector was renowned for his devious sense of humor and sharp wit, and he'd been a fixture in the canyon for as long as Jake could remember. He'd worked for Ed Donahue for many years, becoming one of his most trusted friends. As Jake's parents battled and their marriage disintegrated, Hector provided a calm port in stormy seas, and many were the nights Jake stayed at his house at the far end of the canyon.

Hector's house was ancient, older than the one Jake had inherited. In fact, the house was one of the oldest in a region once known as *Canyon de la Madera*, or Canyon of Timber. Hector could trace his family lineage to the original Spanish land grant that settled the area of Silverado Canyon.

He was a man of contradictions: a Stanford graduate with a degree in philosophy who'd made his living performing manual labor; a pacifist who was a Korean War hero; a civil rights advocate who was staunchly anti-illegal immigration.

Hector Santiago had always walked his own path, adhering to his own code, one of honor and discipline, of compassion and consequences. He'd fathered seven children, three of them now dead, and been married for fifty-three years to the only woman who'd ever stolen his heart. Eighteen grandchildren and seven great-grandchildren rounded out the family, and Hector still remembered and acknowledged every birthday, every graduation, every milestone of note.

Jake supposed that Hector Santiago was possibly the greatest man he had ever known.

The two men entered the house and Hector surveyed the front room. He then moved to the bedroom, the bath and the kitchen, and finally the small guest room. When he came back to the front room, Hector said, "I believe this place is the best. I will retrieve my tools and we will begin our work."

AN HOUR later the air conditioner was perfectly installed in the sash window at the east side of the house, humming pleasantly as it filled the room with cool air. Hector was a true craftsman, the window modified expertly, the unit blending in as if it had come with the house. Jake gave whatever help he could, but mostly he just watched as Hector did his thing. Later, the two men shared an iced tea on the sun deck.

Jake was preoccupied by thoughts of Bruce McAlister. They were jumbled thoughts, old feelings mixed with the things Jake had read online, and he felt like talking about it. Hector was always a good listener, possessing an endless well of patience. In the confused years following his parents' divorce, it was often Hector who Jake turned to for guidance whenever his dad was MIA and his mom was off the rails.

"Have you heard of the Canyon New Life Ministry?" Jake said.

"Yes."

"Where is it?"

"You pass by it every time you come and go from the canyon. It is near the fire station. Why do you ask?"

"No particular reason."

"Do you know who runs that place?"

"Yes, I do."

Hector nodded, and he sipped his tea. A silence settled between the two men. Jake was comfortable with silence, as was

Hector. Darkness had fallen, the lights of houses twinkling through the branches of the trees lining the creek.

"Have you seen him since your return?" Hector asked.

"No, I have not."

"How many years has it been, *mi hijo*?"

"Too many."

"I see."

More silence. The breeze stiffened, shaking the big oak tree alongside the sun deck. Hector gazed at the tree with a look of wonderment. "God's work is fine, is it not?" he said. "How can one look at such a majestic old tree and not believe this is true?"

Jake did not respond. He was lost in thought. Hector was an intuitive man, and he took note.

"The past is a wicked mistress, Jake. She will pierce the heart of those who trample blindly. But denial of the past is equally foolish. Time cannot heal our wounds if we do not allow it."

"Some wounds cut deep, Hector. Far too deep to heal."

"This is true. I will not argue the point."

Hector knew of Jake's history with Bruce McAlister. He was the only person outside of McAlister who knew *everything*. Hector Santiago had never judged Jake for the things that had happened; indeed, Hector was a man haunted by his own misdeeds, and he knew all too well the frailty of man in his weakest moments. Jake would forever love Hector for his kindness and compassionate discretion.

"Your old friend has done well for himself," Hector said. "And for others. He does good work through his church, helping those in need. Yes, he is a bit of an egomaniac, but I think all men of significance possess this very same character trait."

"What do you know about Limestone Canyon?"

"Ah, Mr. McAlister's grand vision to transform his ministry. This is a tricky question, Jake."

"Do you think it's right, to take county park land to build a church. Don't we have enough of those already?"

It was something Jake had read online. Bruce McAlister was currently negotiating a deal with the Orange County Board of Supervisors to secure sixty acres of land in Limestone Canyon Wilderness Park, where he had plans to build a new megachurch. The wilderness park was in Richard Lawson's district, and Lawson had gone on record as being against the land grant. The other four supervisors were in favor of Bruce's plans, citing what they called an environmentally sensitive design and the church's extensive work in the Hispanic immigrant communities of Orange County.

Critics of the plan railed against what they called backroom negotiations to give away land that was supposed to be protected against any form of development, and they'd taken to calling the project the Limestone Land Swindle. Supporters pointed out that the Canyon New Life Ministry wouldn't own the land, they would merely be given a conditional use permit, with strict requirements regarding design features intended to integrate the campus into the natural surroundings.

An unnamed source in the Sheriff's Department had hinted at a connection between the murder of Richard Lawson and the Limestone Canyon negotiations; with Lawson gone, there was talk of allowing a vote on the matter before his successor was named. While no one had publicly said outright, or even implied, that Bruce McAlister had a part in Lawson's death, privately there were whispers. The whole situation was a mess.

"It is not for me to say," Hector said in answer to Jake's question. "Too many churches, not enough churches, or just the right amount, take your pick. I do not know the answer. I no longer worship in those places, ever since my beloved Magdalena passed to the other side. My spirituality has taken a different course."

Jake laughed. "You missed your calling, Hector. You should have been a politician."

"Have I not been specific enough for you?"

"You're fine. I respect your opinions. I always have. I'm just not sure how I feel about this. With Bruce, anything is possible."

"But it has been many years since you two have spoken. Perhaps he has changed."

"Not likely."

"Not likely, or not possible?"

"There's a difference?"

"Why certainly. The second precludes the first. But the first indicates hope. Without hope, all is lost, and nothing is possible."

"Are you trying to confuse me, Hector?"

The old man laughed. "I would never think of such a thing."

Jake laughed with him. He was grateful for Hector Santiago's company. The breeze stiffened, the temperature down twenty degrees from earlier in the day.

"Perhaps the heat will subside," Hector said.

"It'd be nice."

A silent moment passed. The two men sipped their tea. Hector gazed again at the old oak tree, its branches enveloped by darkness.

"Will you see him, Jake?"

"I don't know."

"Perhaps it is time."

Jake considered Hector Santiago's words. "You might be right about that, old friend."

Hector reached out his hand and placed it on Jake's knee.

"Yes, I might be."

Chapter 5

The next day Jake entered the parking lot of the Canyon New Life Ministry at nine o'clock in the morning. It was already eighty-five degrees, any hope of a break in the heat wave gone with the sunrise. Jake parked his Jeep Rubicon at the far corner of the lot in the shade of a sycamore tree. He'd bought the vehicle used when he moved to Truckee, a four-door model fully outfitted for off-road use.

Jake sat in his Jeep, taking a moment to gather himself, unsure of what he was doing. On the drive over, he told himself he was just going to check things out. But he knew that was a lie. A hook had been set, and Jake had allowed it to pull him to the doorstep of a man he hadn't spoken to in thirty years.

Don't borrow trouble.

The thought kept recurring, and Jake swatted it away like an annoying insect.

Surveying the church layout, he recalled driving by this place countless times in his life, yet he never once stopped, never even gave it a thought. His was not a religious upbringing and Jake was not a churchgoing man. But while he adhered to no specific belief system, that's not to say Jake wasn't spiritual. He believed in a higher power, he was just reluctant to call it God. Jake bore no grudge against organized religion, even if he did recognize the inherent absurdity and blatant hypocrisy couched in it.

Bruce McAlister had grown up in one of those religious homes, although he was never a true believer. So it was strange seeing his name inscribed in bold script at the bottom of the large monument sign at the front of the church. Jake figured Bruce more for a business mogul or high-powered real estate agent, maybe a politician; a mover and shaker, someone important. He certainly had the personality for it. And he was smart too, probably too smart for his own good. Jake wondered if that had changed.

He recalled spirited religious debates with Bruce's father. Bill McAlister was a hardcore evangelical, a hellfire and brimstone believer who'd driven himself to great success in business by preaching the virtues of the gospel and clean-living, touting the great rewards awaiting those who walked the straight line of God. During his high school years Jake spent a lot of time at the McAlister house, and often Bill would invite Jake to have a seat and get schooled in the ways of God.

Bruce openly mocked Jake for indulging his father and for encouraging what Bruce derisively called "all that God nonsense". There was a lot of friction between Bruce and Bill McAlister. Bruce had four older sisters and his father went hard on him while the sisters skated. Bruce got the full brunt of his father's unyielding ways and harsh spare-the-rod philosophy of child rearing.

The aggressive discipline only served to alienate Bruce, and once he'd gone through a mid-teens growth spurt and towered over his father, he started using his size to intimidate the man. A standoff ensued, and while the abusive behavior stopped, Bruce and his father never healed their relationship. But then again, Jake hadn't seen or spoken to Bruce McAlister since 1984, so things might have changed. For all he knew, Bill McAlister was dead.

A hot breeze blew down the canyon, shaking the limbs of the sycamore, and Jake had half a mind to fire up the Jeep and split—head for the beach, or maybe just crank the tunes and drive. Anxiety fired his insides and he wondered again what he was doing. Hector's words came to him. The old man had a point; maybe it *was* time to confront the sins of his past. Because that's what Bruce McAlister represented, the sins of a tortured past.

To hell with it, Jake thought. Just go see the man.

He stepped from the Jeep and started walking, a murder of crows cawing from high in the trees.

JAKE ENTERED the church office located at the rear of the building. It was a medium-sized room with padded chairs along one wall, a rack holding pamphlets along another, and two desks at the far end, both unoccupied. Sitting on a rectangular table in the middle of the room was a scale model of Bruce's proposed church in Limestone Canyon. Jake stared at the display, impressed by its detail. The design was Mission Style, with subtle Craftsman elements blended in, understated yet quite elegant. He wondered about the controversy surrounding the project, what it was that had people lined up against it. Perhaps it was just the usual gadflies and malcontents at work, unhappy for the sake of being unhappy. But then again, maybe it was Bruce McAlister they were pissed at, a distinct possibility to be sure.

After a few minutes a man entered the room through a rear door. He was tall and well-built, handsome with a crew cut and a tailored suit. He looked like a cop, carried himself like one too. Jake recognized him immediately as one of the men he'd seen in the news video of Bruce's press conference.

"Impressive, isn't it?" the man said.

"Looks like it," Jake replied.

"Bruce is truly a visionary. What can I do for you?"

Jake hesitated a moment. He looked at the man, caught something behind his blue eyes. Before he could speak, the man held out his hand.

"I'm Jason Stafford. And you're Jake Donahue, right?"

"Uh, yeah, I am," Jake said uncertainly. "Do I know you?"

The man laughed. "Probably not. But I recognized you right away. El Modena, class of eighty-four, right? You were the starting tight end on the CIF championship team that year."

23

Jake shook Stafford's hand. "You've got the facts right."

Stafford laughed again; something inside it irritated Jake.

"I was three years behind you, freshman squad. We sucked that year. I gotta say, I idolized you. You and Bruce McAlister, damn, what a combo you guys made."

"Thanks," Jake said. "Speaking of Bruce, is he here?"

"No, he isn't. Can I help you with something?"

"I just stopped by to say hello. It's nothing important."

"You want me to tell him you came by?"

"If you don't mind."

"I don't mind," Stafford said, his unblinking eyes fixed on Jake.

Over the man's shoulder, Jake saw a row of framed portraits hanging on the wall. He moved forward a few steps and stared at the third from the left. It was a photograph of Bruce, Susan, and Paige McAlister. Seeing Susan and her daughter resonated deeply within Jake, and he felt his breath catch, his eyes watering.

"It's a shame what happened."

Stafford's words startled Jake, and he quickly wiped his eyes and turned around. "Excuse me?" he said.

"Susan McAlister's untimely death. Such a beautiful person. It's a real shock to everyone here."

Jake thought it an odd choice of words—her *untimely* death.

"Yes, it's a real shame what happened," Stafford went on. "Did you know they were high school sweethearts?" He chuckled oddly. "What am I thinking? You went to school with them." He stared at Jake, a probing, almost clinical light in his eyes.

"Yes, I was friends with them," Jake said awkwardly.

"Bruce absolutely worshipped Susan. Almost as much as he worships the Lord. I'll tell you what, it really pisses me off to think that anyone would suspect him in her death."

Jake stepped back to clear some space between himself and the bigger man. He felt a sudden urge to leave; something about Jason Stafford unnerved him. "You'll let Bruce know I came by?" he said.

"Sure thing. Anything for a former Vanguard."

Jake turned and left the room. He felt Stafford's eyes on him, and he knew that if he turned around he'd catch the man staring.

Chapter 6

Jason Stafford moved to the front window of the church office, pulled back the blind and watched Jake Donahue as he left the Canyon New Life Ministry. He noted the make and model of the vehicle Jake drove. Though the distance was substantial, Stafford could easily make out the plate number. He closed his eyes and repeated the number three times out loud, committing it to memory.

Jake seemed to hesitate before leaving the parking lot, and Stafford stood completely still as he watched, his mind calibrating, calculating, assessing. He could stand like that all day if necessary. Whatever it took.

Finally, Jake started his Jeep and drove out of the parking lot, pausing at the driveway before making a left turn onto Silverado Canyon Road. Stafford moved away from the window. He took a moment and stared at the framed portrait on the wall, the one Jake had looked at. He felt nothing as he looked at Susan, his mind erasing her from the picture. He felt a swell of pride when he looked at Bruce, combined with an odd sense of pity. Then Stafford's eyes settled on Paige McAlister, and he closed them, sending up a silent prayer for her soul in these times of trouble.

He retrieved his cell phone from a back room, dialed a number from memory.

"He was here."

"When?" the man on the line said.

"Just now."

"What did he want?"

"He said he wanted to see you."

The line went quiet. Stafford felt no urge to speak. He knew that conversations with Bruce *evolved*, and it was best to stay patient and wait the man out. After another minute, Stafford heard a car pull up outside the church office, followed by a car door being slammed shut.

"Someone's here," he said. He moved to the window and looked out. He saw Ricardo Salazar leaning against his dusty sedan, smoking a cigarette.

"Who is it?" Bruce said.

"What?"

"You said someone was there. Who is it?"

Stafford yawned. "I'm not sure. I'll have to go check on that."

"Okay. Hold down the fort until I get in later today. I have a job for you."

"Whatever you need, Bruce. I'm here for you."

"I know you are, Jason. You're a good soldier. A man of God. Remember, the greatness of man has only been achieved through the sacrifice of those like you, the foot soldiers of the Lord, the—"

"Hey listen, Bruce, another car just pulled up outside. I got to jump." Stafford cut Bruce off. He was in no mood for a damn sermon.

"Sure. Okay, Jason, go take care of business. By the way, did you get some particulars on our friend Jake Donahue?"

"Yes, I have what I need."

"Good. We need to keep tabs on the man. I'll see him when I'm ready. For now, we don't need any snooping around. We're too close for that. Clockwork, Jason, that's what we need. No surprises."

"Got it."

"Good. I'll see you in a few hours."

Jason Stafford put his cell phone in his pocket, and he walked outside to meet Ricardo.

Chapter 7

Before leaving, Jake took a moment to think over his encounter in the church office. He couldn't get the image of Susan and Paige McAlister out of his mind. Seeing them together tugged at Jake from a deep place. He sensed a swirling of energy surround him, closing in on him. Suddenly he felt watched, and he turned abruptly toward the church office.

Did the window blind just move?

Jake stared across the distance, his eyesight not what it used to be. He thought about Jason Stafford. A weird guy. A very intense guy. Jake let out a chuckle at his jumpiness; he wasn't normally like this, seeing ghosts, getting creeped by people upon first meeting them.

He started the engine and put the Jeep in gear, backed out and swung wide, looking at the church office as he passed but seeing nothing out of the ordinary. He stopped at the driveway, looking both directions on Silverado Canyon Road. He knew he should go back to the house and get some work done, lose himself in the repetitiveness of physical activity, but other forces had his mind now. He turned left and headed out of the canyon.

On his way out, Jake passed a car going the other direction, a silver Crown Vic. A cop car, he thought. In the rearview mirror, he saw the sedan turn into the church parking lot. He thought again about Jason Stafford. The guy looked like a cop.

One cop going to meet another, at a church? Something about that seemed unusual.

After a mile, Jake stopped alongside the road. He felt a strong urge to run, and not look back until enough miles had piled up between him and the past. But that was surely a fruitless endeavor, as Jake had known for a long time now. Indeed, it was *that* knowledge that had brought him to this uncertain place in his life. He was tired of running, tired of remaking himself every time he felt the claustrophobic crush of that thing in his gut closing in. Maybe Jake was a lot more like his father than he wanted to admit. Big Ed had fought his demons with booze and smokes and reckless living. Jake fought his in retreat, telling himself for far too long that he was a together dude.

But it was a lie, an enormous deception perpetrated by Jake upon himself. He knew that regardless of what he did right now—if he turned around and went home, or if he bolted with the wind—he was going to have to answer for that lie. It was his destiny. It had been his destiny for thirty years.

Jake looked at his reflection in the rearview mirror.

"Stop being a gutless asshole," he said out loud.

And then he smiled, confident in the knowledge that he couldn't screw his life up any more than he already had. He cranked some tunes, put the Jeep in gear and tore down the canyon road, his destination Newport Beach.

JAKE TURNED off Jamboree Road and drove to Fashion Island. He'd taken the long way—Santiago Canyon to Jamboree, straight through to Newport—marveling at the never-ending construction of homes and strip malls and office buildings. Business was clearly booming in Orange County. It seemed every time Jake returned home the population had doubled, to the point he wondered just how many people you could cram into one geographical area.

He was going to see his father's attorney to sign the last of the paperwork associated with his inheritance. After that, all the legalities regarding Big Ed Donahue would be complete, leaving nothing but memories of a man who continued to hold sway over his only son. Jake could have handled the paperwork through the mail, but he had another reason to see Lucas T. Summerfield, and it had nothing to do with Big Ed's House of Sleds or the house in the canyon. What it had to do with, Jake couldn't say for certain. I'm just checking things out, he told himself more than once on his way to Newport.

Summerfield had been Ed Donahue's personal and business lawyer for more than thirty years. A regular at the canyon house poker parties, he was a genuine character befitting Big Ed's inner circle. For years, the attorney ran his law practice out of a forty-foot sloop moored in Newport Harbor, until he either lost it in a poker game or it was seized by the IRS, depending on which story you believed. Jake tended to believe the poker story, as Lucas Summerfield was only a marginally better player than Ed Donahue, which wasn't saying much.

Jake hadn't seen Summerfield in a long time, but the minute he heard the lawyer's booming voice over the phone informing him of his father's death, a flood of memories came roaring back. Turning off Jamboree onto San Joaquin Hills Road, Jake found himself smiling at the prospect of seeing the man who had been one of his father's closest friends and confidants.

He followed the road around Fashion Island and turned onto San Miguel Drive, located the office building and pulled into a crowded parking lot. He found an empty spot at the rear of the lot and parked the Jeep. Ten minutes later Jake exited the elevator at the seventh floor and made his way to Summerfield's corner office. He thought of what he would say to the attorney; he was only mildly interested in the affairs of his father's estate. Jake had other things on his mind, although his focus was scattered and he had trouble putting it all together. Information is what he wanted, that much he knew. He also knew that Lucas Summerfield was plugged into the pulse of business and politics in Orange County on a deep level, had been for a long time. Lucas knew where the bodies were buried, and he didn't mind talking.

Jake entered an empty waiting room. There was a reception desk at one end next to an inside door, the desk unoccupied. Music played at a low volume—the radio station KROQ—and it took a moment for Jake to realize the sound was coming from speakers attached to the computer on the reception desk. It seemed an odd choice of music for a law office. The desk was cluttered, with a half-filled cup of coffee and a fashion magazine on the blotter.

Jake sat in a padded chair and waited. After five minutes a young woman came through the inside door carrying a file box. She dropped the box on the floor next to the desk and straightened her skirt—a skirt more suited to nightclub attire than a law office—and she turned, noticing Jake sitting across the room.

"Oh, hi. How are you?" she said casually.

"I'm good," Jake said. "Are there more of those to bring in here?" He pointed to the file box, figuring he'd help the girl out if she needed it.

"That's the only one. You here to see Lucas?"

"Yes. Is he in?"

"He had an errand to run."

She sat down and drank some coffee. Then she turned the music up and started pulling files from the box she'd dropped on the floor, stacking them on the desk. Green Day came on, *American Idiot*, and the girl tapped her foot in time with the music. After a minute, she looked up.

"Is that too loud? I can turn it down if it is."

"It's fine," Jake said. "Can you tell me when Lucas is coming back? I was hoping to see him this morning."

"He's out running an errand," the girl said.

"I know, you already told me that."

"Ha! I guess I did, didn't I?" The girl giggled. "I'm new here, so I'm still figuring things out." She laughed again. "I used to work at Starbucks but I got tired of it, so now I'm here."

The girl smiled at Jake and he wondered how old she was. He guessed just a year or two out of high school. "What time is he coming back?"

"Who?"

Jake groaned inside. "Lucas Summerfield. You know, the guy you work for?"

"Ha! Are you trying to be funny?"

"Something like that."

Jake forced a smile. The girl smiled back and Jake wondered what kind of operation Lucas was running. He knew that Summerfield was a character, but he also knew that he was a sharp lawyer, cagey in a streetwise way. Maybe he'd hit the skids. It usually happened with gamblers. It didn't matter if they were attorneys or doctors or used car salesmen—eventually the house always won.

The girl went on with her work and Jake retreated into his head. He thought about Jason Stafford. Something about the man bothered Jake on an intuitive level, and he recounted the scene in the church office, trying to put a finger on it. Aggression is what he came up with, an animal-like heat that seemed to radiate off Stafford.

Jake was used to random male aggression directed at him. Because he was a big man he seemed to draw that kind of attention; tough guys wanting to mark their territory, some kind of primal instinct gone haywire. Jake was certainly able to handle himself, and when challenged he would stand his ground, but as he got older he found the high road was usually the best recourse. Let the badasses blow their steam. Jake had nothing to prove and he had no desire to be the king of the hill. He'd been at the receiving end of one too many beatings for that nonsense.

Jake was about to say something to the receptionist when he heard loud footsteps and talking from outside the office. A few seconds later Lucas Summerfield entered through the door. He was talking on his cell phone.

"You tell that son of a bitch that he either gets with the program or I'm cutting him loose. I don't have time for this, Jerry. There's a legal shit storm brewing and I'm not getting caught in the middle of it, you got it? Good, so make it happen."

Lucas disconnected from the call and slid his phone into an inside pocket of his suit coat. He looked at the girl sitting behind the desk. She was rocking out to a tune on the radio, thumbing through her magazine.

"Come on, Janine, turn that off and get those files taken care of. This is a law office, not your living room."

The girl pouted and complied. Lucas turned and saw Jake, broke into a big smile.

"Jakey! How are you, boy?"

Jakey was a nickname that only Lucas used, one that Jake never particularly cared for. He smiled at the attorney.

"I'm okay. Nice office."

Lucas grimaced. "If you say so." He jerked a thumb over his shoulder. "Follow me." He turned and went through the inside door.

Jake got up and followed, giving the receptionist a smile on his way. As he went through the door, he heard the radio turned up and a Social Distortion song blaring. Something about that made Jake laugh.

Chapter 8

M y sister's kid," Lucas said as he took a seat behind a cluttered desk.

He was a tall, thin man with hawk-like features and probing eyes. He wore his gray hair pulled back into a ponytail, with neatly trimmed sideburns and a small chin beard, giving him the appearance of a university professor or a sixties hippie gone mainstream.

"Who?" Jake said.

"The girl out front. My receptionist." Lucas laughed. "I've been trying to teach her the meaning of that word for six months now."

"She seems like a good kid. Maybe a little distracted."

"I'll say. All she wants to do is go across the street to Fashion Island and shop. I keep telling her work comes before play. But she doesn't get that concept."

"Did any of us when we were that age?"

"Point taken." Lucas straightened some papers on his desk. "Anyway, my sister's been hounding me to help Janine out, so I hired the kid to answer the phone and whatnot. It's supposed to be temporary while she figures things out, but I got a bad feeling about that. I think the kid's nesting."

Lucas went on tidying his desk. Jake looked out the window behind the attorney, at a perfect view of Newport harbor and Catalina Island beyond. It was a view made for daydreaming, something Jake had been prone to since he was a kid. His thoughts drifted to memories of places he'd visited in his life, a warm feeling coming over him. He wondered if maybe it was time to move on, see what the horizon had to offer. Was a man a coward if he never put down roots? Was he weak for never confronting his past? Or was it all just another way of taking the easy way out? These were questions that came to Jake Donahue regularly, questions he had no answer for.

"By the way, did she offer you some coffee?"

Lucas's words startled Jake out of his reverie.

"Huh?"

"Janine. Did she offer you some coffee? That's one of the things she's supposed to do when we get clients."

"Uh, yeah, she did," Jake fibbed, figuring he'd help the kid out on that one. "I told her I was good though."

"Well, I'm not. I was up all night playing in some two-bit poker party out in Anaheim. I went over there to see a client of mine and got sucked into his regular game. When will I learn?"

"How'd you do?"

Lucas gave a disgusted look. "I lost my ass, to a bunch of hillbillies. Good thing I'm a better lawyer than card player, that's all I got to say about that."

Jake smiled inside, thinking about his father and how the same sentiment surely applied. Lucas got up and opened the door, asked Janine to fix him a coffee. He eased the door shut and walked back to his desk, stopping to look out the window.

"You remember the boat, Jakey?"

Jake remembered it more for the stories his father told. He might have been on it once or twice when he was a kid.

"Dad used to talk about it," Jake said. "He got a kick out of telling his friends he had an attorney who worked out of a boat. Kind of like that movie with Matthew McConaughey."

Lucas turned to Jake with a bemused expression. "He got that idea from me, you know."

"Who did?"

"Connelly, the guy who wrote *The Lincoln Lawyer*. He used to sit in on a game I frequented up in Brentwood. This one time he was asking me a lot of questions about my work, and the boat. He dug the name *Legal Tender*. A few years later he wrote a book about it. Except he changed the boat to a Town Car. It was a big hit for him too, especially after the movie came out. I figured the guy owed me some royalties or something, for giving him the inspiration."

"You should have sued him," Jake said with a smile. "Isn't that what lawyers do?"

"Very funny, Jakey."

Lucas eased onto his chair. Janine came into the office with a mug of coffee and set it on the desk. She looked at Jake. "You want anything?"

"No thanks. I'm all right."

The girl giggled and turned to leave. Lucas asked her to bring Jake's file. Janine left the room and Lucas sipped some coffee.

"Jesus this tastes like shit," he said, grimacing. "How hard is it to make a cup of coffee?"

"C'mon, go easy on the girl. She's just a kid."

"Kids gotta learn, Jake."

"To make coffee?"

"Good point. You hungry? Let's get the hell out of this dump and go grab a bite. This place depresses me. I miss being on the water."

"Shouldn't we take care of business first?"

"We can do it over lunch."

Jake checked the time. It was a little early for lunch and he wasn't very hungry anyway, but he figured he'd indulge Lucas. He'd already written off the day as far as any productive work went.

The two men left the office. Out front, Janine was thumbing through her magazine with the radio turned up loud. She'd completely forgotten about the file Lucas had asked for. The attorney took a deep breath as if to calm himself and the girl hopped to, handing over a thick file with a giggly apology. He told her to take an hour off and go shopping or something. Janine collected her things and left without a word. Lucas gave Jake a shrug, and the two men followed Janine out the door.

***

TWENTY MINUTES later, Summerfield parked his Jaguar in a public lot on Ocean Avenue in Laguna Beach, and the two men walked across the street to Hennessey's Tavern. It was a beautiful summer day and Lucas had put the top down for the drive on Pacific Coast Highway. He regaled Jake with stories of his father and their crazy times spent together. That was the thing about Ed Donahue; people who were close to him had stories to tell, many of them so outrageous they seemed made up. Jake had long ago grown tired of hearing about his father's antics, but something in the way Lucas spoke made the tales seem fresh, or at least mildly amusing.

He was a natural orator, and once he got rolling it was easy to get swept up in his narrative. Ed Donahue used to call Lucas Summerfield the "best damn attorney I ever knew". He certainly got Big Ed out of a lot of jams over the years, although Jake knew their friendship went deeper than that. Lucas was ten years younger than Ed and he held a genuine affection for the man, trying in vain to get Ed to slow down and take better care of himself. But men like Ed Donahue know only one way to live—drop the hammer and grind the gears, consequences be damned.

Inside the restaurant, Lucas ordered fish and chips and a Guinness. Once the smell of food hit Jake he realized he was hungrier than he thought, and he ordered shepherd's pie and a salad, passing on a beer in favor of iced tea. Lucas thumbed through Big Ed's file while they waited for their lunch. There were several documents Jake had to sign, one of them pertaining to a mutual fund that deposited another forty-two thousand dollars in Jake's bank account.

"Don't be surprised if there's more."

"And here I thought Dad was flat broke," Jake said as he signed the documents.

"You and me both. Turns out that old bastard had dough stashed all over town."

"Do I need to worry about taxes on this?"

"It's already taken care of."

"That's why Dad loved you so much, Lucas. You're a true maestro."

"Just taking care of business. Besides, I have a special interest in sticking it to Uncle Sam when it comes to taxes. That's how I lost the boat, you know. Goddamn IRS seized it over some bogus tax bill."

"I thought you lost it in a poker game. That's what Dad said."

"Don't believe everything you hear, Jakey," Lucas said with a laugh. "Especially when it comes to things said by Big Ed Donahue. The man had a flair for exaggeration."

The waitress brought the drinks and Lucas took a long pull of his Guinness. He fished some more documents out of the file, explained their meaning, and Jake signed them where indicated. In fifteen minutes the business was done. Lucas leaned back in the booth.

"So, what's really on your mind, Jake?"

"What do you mean?"

"We could have handled this through the mail. I know I'm a charming dude and all, but you must have better things to do than hang out with an attorney."

The waitress came with the food then, giving Jake a moment to sort his thoughts. He knew the reason he chose to see Summerfield in person, he just didn't know *why*. It was something he felt deep inside, starting with the news video yesterday, seeing Bruce and Susan and the memories they dredged up. But it was more than that, and it centered on Paige McAlister. The fact that Bruce and Susan had a daughter triggered a deep curiosity in Jake, and it resonated on an emotional level that he found both strange and disturbing.

To say that Jake Donahue had a lot of catching up to do was an extreme understatement. He had thirty years to account for, from the day he turned his back on Orange County—and more importantly, his family and friends—to now, when fate brought him back home to what Jake increasingly began to see as a reckoning.

Jake was the type of man who believed in standing by the choices you made in life, and answering for the things you've done. And there was no time limit on that. When fate came calling, you answered, whether you wanted to or not. From the moment he left Truckee and headed south, Jake couldn't escape the feeling that his time had finally run out. He'd long known that a piece of him was missing. And although he never gave it words, Jake had also known for a long time where to find that missing piece. It was here, in Orange County, the place of his birth.

"What's your take on this thing with Bruce McAlister?" Jake said.

"The church thing, or the murder thing?" Lucas replied, dousing his fish and chips with vinegar.

"Both, I guess. Let's take the murder thing first."

Lucas took several bites of food, washing it down with beer.

"I don't know much more than what's been in the papers," he said. "The fact they questioned McAlister is no surprise. The husband is usually the prime suspect whenever a wife is murdered. Granted, McAlister's position dictated kid gloves, but it was only a matter of time before they formally questioned him."

"What about Lawson?"

"What about him?"

"Could he have been the target?"

"Lawson was a first-class dirtbag, and a more corrupt bastard you've never met. I suppose he could've been the one. Probably a jealous husband."

"Why do you say that?"

"In addition to putting the arm on every developer and businessman in his district, that son of a bitch was probably banging half their old ladies. Some of the stuff he's rumored to have done would make Bill Clinton blush."

"Do you credit the rumors?"

Lucas drained his beer and took a bite of food. He smiled at Jake.

"Who really knows? But when it comes to politicians—and lawyers, I might add—rumors generally add up to truth."

The two men ate in silence for the next few minutes. A warm breeze blew in through the open front windows of the restaurant, and a steady stream of pedestrians passed by; some shopping, some on their way to the beach, others just enjoying the day with no real purpose in mind. After a moment, Jake went on.

"What about Bruce's church? Do you think that played a part in it?"

"Ah, the Limestone Land Swindle." Lucas chuckled. "You got to love our local press. The OC Weekly has been all over that one. I guess they've grown tired of beating on the Great Park."

He ate the last few bites of his food and pushed his plate out of the way.

"It's intriguing to think about. Prominent pastor proposes new megachurch and the philandering county supervisor cockblocks him every step of the way. That's the stuff of TV movies. One thing's for certain though. With Lawson off the board, the coast is clear for a sure-fire yes vote on McAlister's land deal."

Jake considered the information. Lucas laughed.

"What's so funny?" Jake said.

"Rumors. He was supposedly nailing McAlister's wife."

"Richard Lawson was having an affair with Susan McAlister?"

"Yes. I have that on good authority too. A client of mine knew them both and he swears it's true. So, add that to your list of motives. The cuckolded husband seeks revenge by blowing the adulterers away. And as a bonus, he gets to build his new church so he can continue to preach the virtues of godliness to his myopic flock."

Lucas gave out a booming laugh.

"You can't write a better script than that. Not even that son of a bitch Connelly."

"What do you know about their daughter?"

"Paige? She's a damn sharp attorney by all accounts."

"Have you met her?"

"Never. But I know people who know her. Why the curiosity? She seems a little young for you." He gave a lecherous grin.

"Come on, Lucas. Ease up on that."

"Just a little humor to lighten the load. Seems like you're wound a little tight. What gives?"

"Sorry," Jake said. "I guess this thing with Bruce has gotten under my skin. I only found out about it yesterday, but for some reason it's dug in deep. I knew her."

"Susan?"

"Yeah. She was my first crush. Third grade. Kid stuff, you know? I remember the first time she saw Bruce, when he transferred over from another school. We were freshmen then, and Bruce already had a reputation. She fell hard for him. Bruce and I became friends and Susan was always there, hanging in the background, waiting her turn. Bruce finally noticed her the summer before our senior year. After that, they were off to the races."

Jake paused a moment to reflect. He'd given Lucas the sanitized, thumbnail version of events. The truth was much deeper, and darker. But there was no need to go into all that now.

"So anyway, I'm just curious about things. I didn't really keep up with anyone from school after I joined the Navy."

"You've been a wanderer, no doubt about it. Your dad missed you because of it. Did you know that?"

Jake considered the statement. Whenever he came home, he never sensed much of anything from his father. Granted, he only came home for specific reasons, like when his dad had bypass surgery or his mom passed away, and that was only when he could be reached. There were long stretches of time where he went off the grid, and that was by design. Solitude had always served Jake best, and that was how he'd built his life. The only problem, it's an endless cycle; the more you iso-late, the harder it is to integrate. Did his dad miss him? That was a question Jake couldn't begin to comprehend.

"I never really got that from him," he finally answered. "Dad wasn't exactly an emotional man, and nostalgia wasn't really his thing."

"This is true. Your father was a paradox to be sure. But trust me when I tell you he missed you. It's a shame you two never reconciled that."

"Thanks, Lucas. I appreciate the sentiment."

Jake reached across the table and touched the attorney's hand. Lucas seemed warmed by the gesture.

"So back to Paige McAlister," Jake said. "What's the story with her?"

Lucas gave a brief bio and Jake made a few mental notes. And then Lucas said something that piqued Jake's interest.

"Chapman University?"

"She teaches a law class there. Bruce's old man is a big contributor to the school. In fact, Bill McAlister bankrolls a lot of politicians and organizations in the county, all of them ultra-conservative, the kind that give Orange County a bad name. You ask me, the guy is a religious nut. But he's got money, so that makes him an important religious nut."

Jake thought about Bruce's father. He'd always liked Bill, even if the man could be intense at times, and more than a little over the top when it came to religion.

"It's a family thing," Lucas went on. "Bill McAlister grad-uated from there back when it was Chapman College. Bruce went there too, but there was a scandal his senior year, so I'm not sure if he graduated. Paige got her degree there as well."

Lucas gave some more details about Paige McAlister, along with his theory regarding the murder of her mother. He credited a vengeful husband, Richard Lawson's philandering ways finally catching up with him. He figured Susan's death to be merely collateral damage; she was simply in the wrong place at the wrong time.

Lucas said it was time to get back to work. He had a couple of client meetings scheduled for later in the afternoon, and he wanted to get back to his office to see what Janine was up to. He paid the bill and the two men took the coast route back to Newport Beach. There was little conversation on the ride. Lucas took a couple of business calls and Jake retreated into his head.

The men said their goodbyes in the parking lot. The inland heat had made its way to Newport, the sun high in a cloudless sky, and the Jeep was an oven when Jake slid inside. He started the engine and cranked the air conditioner, checked his phone and saw a missed call. Keying over to voicemail, he saw a familiar number. A tingle went through Jake as he listened to the message. He closed his eyes and leaned his head back, the words blending into a toneless drone.

The call was from Amy Watson, the woman Jake had been involved with in Truckee. He was never very good at goodbyes and this one had been especially difficult. When Jake broke the news to her that he was leaving, sitting in a booth at Jax at the Tracks, he knew that he'd torn the heart out of the woman. For that he would never forgive himself.

He set the phone aside and pulled the Jeep out of the parking lot. He'd have to deal with Amy eventually, but not right now. Right now, Jake had other things on his mind. He turned onto Jamboree Road, a sense of anticipation pushing him forward.

Chapter 9

Jake pulled up to Chapman University in the city of Orange. Lucas had said that Paige McAlister gave a lecture on campus every Tuesday afternoon, and while Jake had no legitimate reason to be here, he knew that his curiosity would not be satisfied until he saw Bruce and Susan's daughter in person.

Driving down Glassell Street, Jake recalled scenes from Old Towne Orange: eating dinner with his father at the counter in Watson's Drugstore; going to Sunday matinees at the Orange Theatre; the time he broke his arm trying to jump the fountain in the traffic circle on his skateboard. The sleepy streets with their pre-war homes and grand shade trees evoked another time and place, the pace just a little bit slower down here. The neighborhood reminded Jake of similar places he'd visited around the country, the hamlets and small towns along the blue highways, far removed from the chaos of the big cities.

The campus had changed over the years and Jake tried to remember the layout, thinking of summer basketball tournaments held here when he was a kid. He drove once around and then parked on Center Street, left his cell phone in the console and locked his car, and headed toward the middle of campus.

Jake saw a group of students nearby and he casually approached them, asking for directions. A few minutes later he found the lecture hall but hesitated before entering. A girl came out, and through the open doorway Jake heard the amplified voice of a woman speaking.

"Have they already started?" he asked the girl.

She turned. "Excuse me?"

"The lecture," Jake said. "Has it started?"

"Yeah, it has." She smiled and turned to leave. "Sorry, I gotta pee."

Jake entered the lecture hall, easing the door shut and taking a seat in the back row. It was a medium-sized room full of students. Paige McAlister stood at a lectern, speaking in the same clear, strong voice Jake remembered from the news video. She exuded poise and confidence, and Jake imagined Paige being a persuasive litigator. Even from a distance the resemblance to her mother was startling, and images of Susan McAlister quickly came to mind: Susan as a young girl skipping down the street in her polka dot dress and cowgirl boots; Susan as a blossoming high school sophomore, giggling with a group of girls at the homecoming dance; the indelible image of Susan that fateful summer down in Mexico.

Jake eased back into his seat and closed his eyes. He had no idea what Paige was speaking about, but her words mattered little. The mental imagery of Susan combined with the sound of Paige's voice tapped into Jake's psyche. A powerful moment was at hand and Jake didn't question it, he simply rode the wave.

Paige brought the lecture to a close and Jake snapped back to the moment. She confirmed the schedule for next week and then fielded questions from her students. Jake slipped out and circled the building until he found the rear door. He spent a minute weighing the odds, and then decided Paige would exit the building from the front. He had no intention of approaching her outright, although the possibility of that intrigued him.

Students began exiting the lecture hall, chatting and laughing as they splintered off in various directions. Paige was the last to leave, engrossed in conversation with two students. They flanked her on either side as they walked slowly in the direction of the parking garage. Jake waited a moment and then followed, being careful to hang back a good distance. He felt a little creepy, following them like that, and he tried to keep his demeanor and body language loose so as not to draw attention to himself.

At the parking garage the two students broke off and went down a flight of stairs to the lower level. Paige continued walking toward Glassell. Jake followed. She went north on Glassell and crossed the street at Walnut, entering the Chapman Coffee House.

Jake stood on the corner and thought, Do I follow her inside, or give up on this foolishness? He was sure he could pull it off—just go inside and casually order a cup to go, and linger long enough to...do what, exactly? Act creepier? Introduce himself as her father's long-lost friend? Tell her that he had a crush on her mother in high school and that he was sorry she died?

The longer Jake stood there on the sidewalk thinking it over, the more conspicuous he felt, until finally the moment of indecision passed. He turned abruptly and started walking to his car. Maybe next week he'd come back and make contact then. He felt that it was inevitable.

Back inside the Jeep, Jake retrieved his cell phone from the console. He saw a missed call from Amy Watson and grunted his frustration, tossing the phone aside. He knew that Amy would keep calling until she reached him. And if Jake continued to dodge her, it was entirely possible she would drive down to Orange County and confront him directly. The fact that she didn't know where Jake lived would not deter her. She would find a way. Amy was *that* kind of woman.

He checked the time. He had errands to run but if he got to it, Jake figured there'd still be enough time left in the day to get some work done on the house. He started the Jeep and pulled out onto the street. While stopped at the light in front of the coffeehouse, he saw Paige McAlister sitting at an outside table reading a newspaper. She lowered the paper and seemed to stare off into the distance, a look of sadness on her face. Something about the scene touched Jake deeply.

***

WHEN HE finally turned into Silverado Canyon, Jake was glad to be home. It had been a long and emotional day and he felt fatigued. Passing by Bruce's church, he glanced at the empty parking lot and dim lights burning in the dusky twilight, feeling an immediate tightness in his stomach. He rolled the window down for some fresh air.

A few minutes later he turned off the canyon road and onto a narrow street, the lights of neighboring houses twinkling through the canopy of trees shrouding the road. Turning into his driveway, Jake stopped short. Hector Santiago's truck was blocking the driveway, a sheriff's cruiser parked behind it. Jake looked at the front of the house, a jolt going through him when he saw Hector handcuffed on the porch.

Chapter 10

Paige McAlister had a lot on her mind as she walked to the coffeehouse near the campus. The lecture had gone well today. She had a good group of students—engaged, energetic kids. Yet despite that, she felt burned out. The death of her mother had hit her hard. To have her father under suspicion only made it worse. It was true that her parents had issues and their marriage was in serious trouble, Susan had even confided as much to Paige one night at dinner, alluding to the possibility of another man in her life. But murder? It was absurd to even consider that her father was involved in something like that.

While Susan didn't come right out and say there was another man, Paige could read between the lines. Her mother was drunk that night and it broke Paige's heart. Susan McAlister's descent into alcoholism was subtle at first, but once she hit her stride she never looked back. Everything that was good about her began to fade, replaced by bitterness and sarcasm, and hopelessness. Paige had always sensed that her mother suffered from some great emotional hurt, one that ate at her soul. Alcohol was the spark that ignited that hurt, generating a white-hot flame burning Susan from the inside out.

Her father seemed helpless in the face of her mother's decline. Paige adored her father and she believed in him, and she wanted so badly for him to reach that place of hurt inside her mother, to soothe her ache and ease her soul, to *heal* her. But he couldn't. He simply could not be that man. And Paige didn't love him any less for it.

The coffeehouse was crowded and Paige waited her turn in line, her mind momentarily drifting from her troubled thoughts. She checked her cell phone, saw that she had a text message from Jason Stafford. It was the third one today. She was going to have to do something about that. Somehow Jason had gotten it into his head that Paige had eyes for him. It started at church with her just being nice, not in any way flirty. Paige was careful that way; men so often misconstrued that kind of stuff.

Jason was nice enough, but something about his handsome features seemed off to Paige. And those eyes—cold and un-blinking, like two shiny blue marbles revealing absolutely nothing—my God they were unnerving. A lot of women would go for a guy like Jason Stafford. Paige McAlister was not like a lot of women.

She knew that Stafford was a trusted member of her father's inner circle, and her grandfather, Bill McAlister, hired him for security jobs on a regular basis. The two of them sang Stafford's praises constantly. If Paige didn't know better, she'd say they were intent on a little matchmaking. She'd made it clear to her father that she had no romantic interest whatsoever in Jason, but it seemed the message wasn't getting through.

So lately he'd been texting her, suggesting they get to-gether for coffee or lunch, or a walk in the park. Who goes for a walk in the park these days? Paige wasn't currently involved with anyone and that suited her fine. She'd suffered a bad breakup just a year ago, and those wounds were slow to heal. The last thing she wanted right now was a relationship. Be-sides, Jason was too old for her. The man was middle-aged, nearly as old as her father. Paige was certainly capable of fall-ing in love with an older man, but he'd have to be an excep-tional man. Jason Stafford was *not* an exceptional man.

Paige got a coffee and a pastry and took it outside. She found a table in the shade and sat down. It was still warm but the breeze was up, making for a pleasant afternoon. She read through a discarded newspaper, saw a follow-up article to her mother's murder. After a few paragraphs, she set the paper down and recalled the last time she saw her mother alive. It was a week before Susan was killed and it didn't go well. They'd met at a café in Newport Beach for an early lunch. Susan was tipsy when she got there and she drank red wine throughout lunch, and the more she drank, the more she railed about her husband. After trying her best to listen and not judge, Paige finally lost it. She condemned her mother and implored her to get help. Susan was unmoved, her booze-fueled indignation overriding any sense of reason. Paige gave up. She told her mother that she loved her, gave her a hug, and then left the café for work. The following week Susan McAlister lay dead in another man's Corvette on Ortega Highway.

Paige sighed deeply at the memory. And then she noticed a Jeep Rubicon stopped at the light on Walnut Street. She recognized the man behind the wheel; he'd come in at the end of her lecture, looking out of place among her students. The man turned left on Glassell. Paige gave it a moment of thought before passing it off as inconsequential. She leaned back in her chair and sipped her coffee, and let the lazy afternoon carry her away.

Chapter 11

Jake shut off the engine, adrenaline coursing through him, and he literally jumped out of the Jeep, running to see Hector. The old man's eyes stopped him short. They seemed to say: *Hold steady and don't be foolish.*

"Inside the house," Hector whispered.

Jake kneeled and put his face close to Hector's. "Are you okay? What's going on?"

"I am fine. There is a policeman inside. Be careful, he is a dangerous one. Perhaps a little crazy in the head." Hector nodded toward the house.

Jake stood and hesitated, assessing the situation. The porch lights were on, casting Hector's face in shadow as he sat perfectly still, leaning against a wood post with his legs outstretched. He looked small and vulnerable, and Jake felt rage at what was a clear abuse of authority, because no way in hell would there ever be a legitimate reason to handcuff Hector Santiago like he was some common criminal.

"I'll be back," Jake said as he turned to leave.

"I will be waiting," Hector replied. When Jake looked at him, he saw his old friend smiling in that way of his.

Jake walked around to the back of the house, stopping at the stone retaining wall near the creek to compose himself. The door off the back deck was open and Jake heard movement from inside the house. The cop's radio went off, the dispatcher's voice distorted and inaudible. Jake stepped carefully onto the deck and was about to enter the house when Jason Stafford came through the open door and nearly knocked him over.

"What are you doing inside my house?" Jake said as he stepped back.

Stafford stared at Jake. In his uniform, he looked every bit the cop that Jake pegged him for at the Canyon New Life Ministry. The man exuded malice, his posture coiled tight like a predator ready to attack.

"Hello, Jake. It's good to see you again."

Stafford smiled. He had good teeth, straight and white. He was a handsome man and he carried himself like he knew it, and Jake imagined him leveraging his good looks to achieve whatever ends he desired. He decided there and then that Jason Stafford was a bad dude.

"I asked you a question," Jake said firmly.

He wasn't about to get chummy with this guy, not with Hector cuffed on the front porch. Stafford continued staring, and Jake felt heat come off the man, a fuse inching its way to a powder keg.

"I got a call," Stafford finally said, his posture easing slightly. "Witnesses saw a man trying to get inside your house. I came to investigate."

"That man is my friend. He has a key to this house."

"Then why was he trying to jimmy that window over there?" Stafford pointed to the sash window by the back door, the jamb splintered badly.

Jake was about to call Stafford a liar when Hector's words came to him. *Don't be foolish.* He took a breath and changed course.

"Take the handcuffs off him. I'm vouching for the man. I can't explain the window, but I can assure you Hector Santiago is my friend and he's welcome in my home whether I'm here or not."

"Normally I wouldn't condone a tone like that," Stafford said, the intensity in his eyes implying a deeper meaning. "But I'm going to let you slide, being as you're a friend of Bruce's."

Stafford walked to the front of the house and Jake followed. He wondered if he could take the man, if it came down to that. Something in the back of Jake's mind told him this was just round one with Jason Stafford.

Up on the porch Hector appeared to be sleeping, with his hat pulled down over his eyes. Stafford kicked his feet, not hard, but enough to send a message to Jake.

"Wake up, old man."

Hector leaned his head back against the wood post, knocking his hat off. "I am awake," he said pleasantly. "Have we resolved the situation?"

"Sure, it's resolved." Stafford reached down and roughly jerked Hector to his feet, got behind him and unlocked the handcuffs. "Just don't go around opening windows that aren't yours."

"Hey," Jake said. "Enough of that."

"Sure thing, partner," Stafford said as he stepped away from Hector. "The thing is, we get a lot of wets out here in the sticks causing all sorts of trouble, and it isn't easy keeping them in line."

"What did you call him?"

"A wet. You know, wetback. You have a problem with that, Jake?"

"Show some respect. I told you, Hector is a friend."

"You aren't one of those politically correct types, are you?"

Jake was about to kick it up a notch when Hector reached out and held his arm.

"It is okay, Jake, I am not offended. Mr. Stafford has a job to do and we must respect that. It is best to let this matter end here."

Hector smiled at Stafford, a smile brimming with sincerity and not a hint of irony. It was classic Hector, diffusing a situation with grace and ease. Yet Jake could see the truth behind the old man's eyes; this was far from over.

"I think I'll skip the paperwork on this one," Stafford said, his smile completely at odds with the intensity of his stare. "You okay with that, Jake?"

Jake felt an immense pull to escalate the situation, but he knew that would only end in disaster. He tamped down those feelings and took the high road. "Yeah, I'm okay with that," he said.

Stafford offered his hand, turning his back to Hector. It was a blatant act of disrespect, and Jake felt like knocking the cop out right there on the porch. He glanced at Hector, who nodded slightly, and Jake gritted his teeth and accepted Stafford's hand.

"Just so you know," Stafford said, holding onto Jake's hand with a tight grip. "I routinely patrol this area on the swing shift, so I'm sure we'll be seeing more of each other. I also do some work for Bruce McAlister and his church. Just so you know."

Stafford released Jake's hand and walked to his cruiser. Hector and Jake watched silently as the cop backed around the Rubicon and onto the street, kicking up gravel and dust as he sped away.

Jake turned to Hector. "Tell me what really happened."

"Let us go inside and sit down."

Inside the house, Hector told the story. He'd come by to help Jake install a new water heater, as they'd agreed to the day before. An agreement that Jake completely forgot about. When he found that Jake wasn't home, Hector decided to get started on his own. He was inside the house using the bathroom when Stafford let himself in.

"He just came into my house unannounced?" Jake said.

"It would appear so. I came out of the bathroom and there he was. He seemed to be looking for something."

"I'm sorry, Hector, for forgetting about the water heater. I got sidetracked and I guess it slipped my mind."

Hector raised his hand. "No need to apologize."

"I should have been here."

"Nevertheless, it is done. Shall I continue?"

"Sure. What happened next?"

"The officer seemed surprised to see me, which is quite odd since my truck is parked in the driveway. He accused me immediately of breaking in."

"Did you tell him differently?"

"You see how that one is. Do you believe it would have mattered? I have learned from other such encounters to say nothing and let things run their course."

"I understand. And then what?"

"He handcuffed me and put me on the front porch. Then he went back inside your house."

"How long were you there before I showed up?"

"Perhaps twenty minutes, maybe a little longer."

"I see."

"Do you know this man, this police officer?"

"No, I don't. But I met him this morning at Bruce's church."

"Did you see Mr. McAlister?"

"No, just that cop. He was dressed in a suit and seemed to be working at the church."

"This is interesting."

"Listen, Hector, I'm tired and need to rest. We can work this out later. Are you okay to drive home?"

"Yes, I am fine. Perhaps tomorrow we can change the water heater."

"Absolutely."

Jake saw Hector to his truck. Then he inspected the damaged rear window of the house. It was a clumsy attempt at staging a break in. Once inside, Jake sat in his recliner and took in the room, the silence of the old house seeming to close in on him. He walked through the incident in his mind, trying to grasp its meaning. *What were you doing inside my house?* He scanned the room, looking for anything out of place, a clue to Jason Stafford's purpose here. And there *was* a purpose, of that Jake was sure.

He thought about what he should do. Report the incident? No, that wouldn't fly, he'd just be opening a can of worms if he did that. Cops had a lot of leeway when it came to manipulating facts to suit their version of the truth, and Jake had no desire to go up against the Orange County Sheriff's Department and Jason Stafford. He'd just have to let this one go for now.

The events of the day played on Jake's mind. He tried to sort it out, compartmentalize it, boil it down to a problem to be solved. He was always good at that. But this one had him stumped. The sequence of events made no clear path to *this*. Did it start with Jake's visit to the Canyon New Life Ministry?

After a while Jake shut it down. For him, clarity of thought often came from an extended period of no thought at all. He turned off the air conditioner and opened all the windows of the house to let in the cool canyon breeze, turned off the lights and put some music on. He stretched out on the couch and took in the moment. Jake felt his father's presence inside the old house, and he rode that feeling until he fell into a deep sleep.

Chapter 12

Jason Stafford turned onto Silverado Canyon Road and headed toward the church. He was supposed to meet Ricardo and now he was late. He reached for his cell phone, saw there was no reception. He thought about what he would say when he made the call.

McAlister didn't like complications. The old Mexican was a complication he'd have to explain. Or not. Jason could just say that everything went as planned. The situation was merely an inconvenience and no way would it come back on him, Jason was sure of that. That old dude knew the score. Most wets did.

Jake Donahue might cause problems, but Jason wasn't too concerned about that possibility either. Donahue didn't look like the type who would run to the cops. No, he'd keep it to himself, deal with it in his own way. Which was fine with Jason. It might make things more interesting.

He thought about the old Mexican, Hector Santiago. Jason knew of him, had seen him around the canyon and heard others talk about him. Santiago seemed like a decent old guy, although Jason didn't care much for Mexicans either way, good or bad. He saw plenty of the bad ones in his line of work—gangbangers, shiftless layabouts, drunk day laborers who beat on their wives and girlfriends, you name it. These days Mexicans were all the rage, barging into our country like they owned the place, demanding legal status, and the politicians fall all over themselves to accommodate them. It was ridiculous. Sickening really.

Bruce had a thing for the Mexes, that's for sure. Bruce's old man even more. Jason didn't get it. There were too many of them, who couldn't see that? They were overrunning the country and no one wanted to do anything about it.

Bruce was bent on saving the poor and downtrodden. Not downtrodden Americans, mind you, but poor Mexicans. He set up that church way down there in the sticks, on the Gulf of California—the Sea of Cortez they used to call it. Jason went down there regularly on church business and he hated it. Dirt-poor Mexico. One step removed from the Stone Age. Houses with no running water, no indoor toilets, flies, dust and heat. They weren't even houses, just shacks built out of whatever scrap the people scavenged. Bahia de Cortez was two hours south of San Felipe and it was a righteous hellhole, a backwater village if ever there was one. *Village*. The word made Jason laugh. Who lived in villages anyway? Peasants, that's who.

Bruce said he felt a connection to the place, ever since he started going down there on surfing expeditions when he was in high school. What the hell, the waves at Huntington or San Onofre weren't good enough? Bruce was determined to show those people the way of God. A zealot, that's what he was. Jason didn't get it; most Mexicans are Catholic anyway, so what's the point? But Bruce went at it hard, saving souls one stinking peasant at a time. He was good at it too, and he'd converted thousands of them, and now his church in the canyon was filled to the brim with dirt-poor Mexicans. Jason understood it was the by-product of that other operation they had going on down there, but why couldn't Bruce leave well enough alone? Get them over here and let them stay among themselves, over there in Santa Ana or whatever barrio their kin lived in. He wondered if once the new church was built the riffraff would be shown the door.

Even though Bruce was a little nutty when it came to God, Jason still looked up to the guy. What a ballplayer he was. Too bad college didn't work out for him. Jason always wondered why Bruce didn't try for a walk-on spot on an NFL team, or even the Canadian league. Maybe it's because he went nuts for the Lord. Anyway, Jason never asked Bruce why; some things he just didn't feel right talking about.

Like when Susan was alive. What a raving bitch that woman was. It was hard to believe she was actually Paige's mother. Jason always wondered why Bruce stuck with a woman like that. Well, at least that situation is over now. And good riddance, too. Sure, it was a little brutal the way it went down, but it had to be done. Same thing with that asshole Richard Lawson. What a corrupt piece of garbage that guy was. Good riddance to him too.

Jason thought about Paige McAlister. Damn, she was so fine. What Jason wouldn't give to have a woman like that. Sure, she was a little too headstrong for his tastes, but that could always be worked out. As far as Jason was concerned, everything could be worked out. *If* you had the will, and the stomach for it.

So, Paige had gotten under Jason's skin. He'd made a few subtle moves but so far, they hadn't worked. Bruce and Bill McAlister seemed to be in his corner, but that didn't amount to anything. Jason wasn't used to being the pursuer and he wasn't sure he liked it. Sometimes it made him crazy, the way he felt about Paige.

He tried the cell again but the call rang through to voicemail. He left a message, telling Bruce the job was done and everything was a go. He wondered about Bruce's fixation with Jake Donahue. Jake seemed like an okay guy, although Jason could tell he rubbed Donahue the wrong way. Comes with the territory, he told himself. Someone's got to be the alpha dog and Jason's always been it. That's the reason he was a cop. It was the perfect job for a physical guy like himself. Sure, he went over the top every now and then, and it had jammed him up a few times, but he'd learned to keep a lid on it. Or at least cover it up better. Ricardo had been a good mentor that way, and Jason hoped to eventually become a detective like him. But he'd make damn sure he was a better detective than Ricardo Salazar. The guy knew the ropes, and there wasn't a rule he didn't know how to bend, but he was a lazy bastard and completely unmotivated when it came to solving crimes. How he kept his gig was a mystery Jason had yet to figure out. He probably had dirt on someone.

Regardless, they'd caught a big break when Ricardo was assigned to investigate the murder of Susan McAlister and Richard Lawson. It made it a lot easier to keep tabs. And with Ricardo's stellar work ethic, Jason knew that hell would freeze over before the case was solved. Funny how things work out. You plan and scheme and obsess, but in the end, it usually comes down to a lucky break.

Speaking of lucky breaks, Jason owed a big one to Bill McAlister for getting Jason out of that scrape a few years ago. That was back in the days before Jason learned to keep a lid on things. Sure, he had leverage over Bruce's old man; Jason had busted Bill McAlister for DUI back in '06 and he'd swept the whole thing under the rug, including the part with the half-naked woman in the back seat of Bill's car. Bill owed Jason because of it, and when Jason got crossed up with that crazy bitch down in San Clemente, he called in the marker. McAlister made the whole thing go away, like magic. Magic Bill McAlister was an actual nickname that Jason hung on Bruce's father for a time. He stopped using it as his admiration for Bill grew. The man had his program dialed in, and he knew how to make things *happen*. No messing around, just clear, decisive action. That was Bill McAlister's way. That, and the Lord. Bill was gone for the Lord, and he attributed everything in his life to his belief in God. Including getting out of that little incident back in '06. Divine intervention is how Bill saw it; God was looking out for him by having Jason Stafford pull him over that night and not some dumbass with scruples.

Bill started hiring Jason for odd jobs, security stuff mostly, and it was good too because the county had cracked down on overtime and Jason was feeling the pinch. Through his work with Bill McAlister, Jason got hooked up with Bruce. He never knew Bruce in high school and it was kind of a trip to get to know him all these years later. They were only four years apart in age, but to Jason it seemed more substantial than that. He looked up to Bruce, and when Bruce preached the gospel, Jason listened. He would never be a zealot like Bruce, or Bill for that matter, but Jason Stafford was a believer, albeit in his own way. You see, some of the work he did for the McAlisters was a little shady, falling into what could rightfully be called a spiritual gray area. It required a certain amount of rationalization on Jason's part. But it was important work, and it was a universal truth that all great men needed someone like Jason Stafford behind them. Or in front, as the case may be.

So, Jason did what he was asked to do, did it willingly and with great purpose. And it wasn't for him to know the big picture. It was enough to know that he had a seat at the table. Bruce was shooting for the stars, and with his father's backing, the sky was the limit. The Limestone project was just the next step in the establishment of Bruce McAlister as a leading light among evangelicals in America. There was talk of political aspirations as well. Jason knew that he'd hitched his wagon to the right train, one that would pull him from his humble, somewhat tragic beginnings, to a place of power and respect, a member of the inner circle.

Those thoughts pleased Jason Stafford as he approached the Canyon New Life Ministry. He saw Ricardo leaning against his dusty sedan, smoking a cigarette. The guy looked shifty, lazy, *corruptible*. Ricardo had taught Jason a lot and he'd served a valuable purpose, but Jason knew the time was coming when he'd have to cut him loose. Great men evolved, and as they evolved, as they took each successive step in their journey to greatness, they were forced to cast off the old as they reached for the new. Ricardo represented the old Jason Stafford.

"Times change, Rico," Jason said to himself as he pulled into the church parking lot. "It's nothing personal."

Chapter 13

Hector came by on Wednesday to help Jake install the new water heater. By agreement, they didn't talk about what happened the night before. Hector seemed none the worse for wear after being clearly humiliated by Jason Stafford. Certainly, he'd been disrespected, and it made Jake's blood boil to think about it. The two men worked in silence and in short order the job was finished. Afterwards, they walked to the Silverado Cafe for lunch, and after returning to the house Jake continued his work while Hector left to run some errands.

While trimming a hedge near the stone retaining wall at the creek, Jake discovered an access panel cut into the siding under the deck. It was well-fitted, its seams barely visible. He removed some dirt under the bottom and pried the panel loose, saw that it was attached by clips on the inside, with a handle on the inside face. The area under the deck was excavated a few feet lower than outside, deep enough so a person could sit upright, with wood planks laid as makeshift flooring. Nothing was stored in the space, and the cobwebs and thick layer of dust said that no one had been down there in a long time. Shafts of thin sunlight filtered through gaps in the decking, and Jake could see the crawl space under the house.

He fitted the access panel back into place and took a moment to consider why someone would build what appeared to be a hiding place under the deck. He knew that the old house had a storied past, including a stint as a stash house for illicit booze during Prohibition. At least that's what Big Ed used to tell people back in the day. Jake always thought his father made that stuff up, but who knows, maybe it was true. Of course, the deck was built in the late 60s, long after the days of bandits and booze runners. Hell, maybe Big Ed built it himself, to hide out from Jake's mom whenever she came looking to tear his head off for his latest transgression.

Jake chuckled at the thought, thinking that maybe someday he'd get under there and clean the area out. With a little work, he could turn it into a good storage area.

ON THURSDAY Jake had to pick up some supplies from Home Depot down in Orange. He took Santiago Canyon Road to get there, stopping on the way to have a look at the site of Bruce's proposed church in Limestone Canyon. About a half mile past the bridge over Santiago Creek he turned off the road and pulled up to a locked gate. He got out of the Jeep and approached the gate, saw a sign affixed to a post: *If you can read this you have already been photographed.*

Jake looked around and wondered where the camera was. He doubted there was one, the sign merely a deterrent, meant to scare off trespassers or kids goofing around. He'd done a fair amount of that sort of thing himself back when he was a teenager, riding his dirt bike all over this area. Bruce was his sidekick on a lot of those excursions, and they'd spent many hours together riding the canyons and hills throughout the Santa Ana Mountains.

Jake looked in the direction of Black Star Canyon, recalling the time he and Bruce dared each other to ride out there one Halloween night. Black Star is said to be haunted by the spirits of Indians massacred there in 1831, and tales of paranormal activity and a host of urban legends have been passed down through the years. The night Jake and Bruce made their midnight ride they didn't encounter any spirits, although the pint of Jim Beam they shared before heading out likely had something to do with their fearlessness. They had a hell of a time, tearing ass down the trails in the full moonlight, hooting and howling like fools, doing their best to draw out the ghosts of the canyon.

There were many times like that in the years Jake was close to Bruce, and it seemed like they would last forever. Youth is funny that way; the inability to imagine a time beyond the now, the absolute belief in your own sense of purpose and immortality, the idea of death never entering the picture. It just doesn't occur to a young person that things can change. That things *will* change.

These were the thoughts that filled Jake's mind as he gazed out at Limestone Canyon. He pictured the scale model of Bruce's church superimposed over the bucolic landscape in front of him, tried to balance the Bruce McAlister he once knew with the man capable of envisioning such a thing. Jake was no environmentalist—he'd once worked on a fracking crew in the Dakotas, and he believed there was a time when economics took precedent over conservation—but something about Bruce's plans felt wrong. He recalled Hector's words about churches. Did civilization need more? And when does it become less about God and more about man's ego? After all, Saddleback Church was just down the road, wasn't that mega-church enough for this area? He wondered if Bruce's grand plans for the canyon were the result of a genuine desire to serve mankind, or simply a reflection of that part of Bruce that said what was good for *him* was good enough for the rest of us.

Jake snapped a few pictures on his cell phone. A sheriff's cruiser sped by and a tense moment passed as Jake wondered if it was Jason Stafford. The feeling angered him. He had no reason to fear Stafford—hell, he didn't even know the man— but now, through two separate encounters, he'd become a thing in Jake's life.

Resolving to keep a lid on the situation, Jake got into his Jeep and fired the engine. Enough messing around, it was time to get back to work.

* * *

LATER THAT evening Amy Watson called.

Jake had been avoiding her but he knew he couldn't keep that up forever. It wasn't so much that he didn't want to talk to Amy, he just didn't know what to say to her. He'd broken the woman's heart, and truthfully, he didn't know why. Jake only knew that he'd felt hemmed in during his final months in Truckee, and Amy's talk of marriage and settling down only made it worse. He tried to let her down easy but his efforts failed miserably.

Jake stared at the phone in his hand as it continued to ring. And then he breathed deep and answered the call.

"Hello, Amy."

"Jake, is that you?"

"Yes, I'm here," Jake said through the bad connection.

"I can't hear you. Jake, are you there?"

Jake pinched the bridge of his nose. He'd felt a headache coming on for the last hour, and now this. He disconnected from the call and briefly considered not calling back. Instead, he got in his Jeep and drove down the street to the Silverado Canyon Market, where he knew he'd get a stronger cell signal. He made a mental note to call the phone company first thing tomorrow morning and arrange for service to the house. There was a landline in place but it had been disconnected when Jake's father died.

Before calling Amy back, Jake went into the market and bought a six pack of Coors. Back inside the Jeep he rolled all the windows down and twisted the top off a bottle. He drank deeply, and set the bottle in the cup holder. Darkness had fallen, a floodlight near the Jeep casting shadows across the hood. The heat of the day had dropped to a tolerable level and a nice breeze blew through the open windows. Jake dialed the phone.

"It's me," he said after she answered.

"I thought you'd hung up on me."

"Sorry about that. I had lousy reception when you called earlier."

65

Neither of them spoke for several seconds. Crickets chirped nearby and a car passed on the canyon road. Jake's mind drifted and he drank some more beer.

"I've been calling you," Amy said. "I guess you're still at your dad's place, huh?"

"Yes, I'm still down here. Tying up loose ends." Jake sighed. "I'm aware you've been calling, Amy. I haven't called back because I don't know what to say."

"I know it's hard for you, Jake. Really, I do. I only called to say that I miss you, so much."

More silence on the line.

"Did you hear me?"

Jake killed the bottle and opened another. A coyote crossed the road and Jake watched as it trotted behind the post office. They've been getting bold, he thought, coming down in broad daylight, snatching pets from backyards. Whatever it takes to survive, right?

"Jake?"

"I heard you, Amy. What do you want?" Jake grimaced at the edge to his words. "I'm sorry. I don't mean to be short with you. I'm just tired. It's been a long day."

"I just thought it would be nice to talk, you know? It's been a few weeks since you left and I guess I'm feeling lonely. Maybe a little sorry for myself."

"I understand how you feel."

"Really? Maybe I could come down there, keep you company. Just a short visit. A friend of mine from high school lives in Tustin, I could stay with her."

"Come on, Amy, you know that's no good. We've been over this already. What's the point?"

"The point? Does there have to be a point?"

"You know what I mean." Jake felt anger rise, and he took a long pull on the beer.

"Yes, I know what you mean," Amy said bitterly. "But why do you have to be so cold about it?"

"That's not fair."

"You know what your problem is, Jake? There's a hole inside your heart big enough to drive a truck through and you don't want anyone to fill it. You won't let anyone in. I don't get it. We were good together. But here we are, miles apart. I don't understand you at all. I…"

Amy's voice trailed off and Jake leaned his head back and closed his eyes, put the cold beer bottle against his forehead. She's right, you know, Jake thought. You're damaged goods, buddy. There's not just a hole in your heart, there's a hole in your soul. A cavernous void that swallows anything good that touches your life.

"Are you done?" Jake said, his voice whispered.

"Yes, I am. I guess I'm done."

Amy's voice sounded so small it almost hurt to listen. Jake was at a loss for words. He was about to throw out some line when he saw a sheriff's cruiser come down the canyon road and turn into the parking lot. His pulse quickened.

"Listen, Amy, something just came up here and I have to jump."

"You don't have to lie, Jake. Just say goodbye and hang up."

Jake took in a breath.

"Okay, have it your way. Goodbye, Amy."

He ended the call and put his phone in the console. That went well, Jake thought cynically. It's always nice to talk to an old friend.

He turned his attention to the police cruiser. It was parked by the entrance to the market. The cop wasn't inside the car, and a quick scan around the parking lot revealed nothing. Jake rolled up the windows and turned the engine over. Before he could back out, someone tapped on the passenger window. It was Jason Stafford.

"Hey, chief, what's cookin'?" Stafford said when Jake rolled the window down.

"Officer."

"I like that. Officer. Sounds respectable."

"Is there a problem here?" Jake said, keeping his tone even. He felt heat rise up his neck, the feeling of adrenaline building. He'd known guys like Stafford his whole life, guys who could turn things ugly in the blink of an eye.

"I was going to ask you the same thing. You seem a little tense, Jake."

"I'm fine. But thanks for asking."

Jake forced a smile. Stafford stared back with those weird eyes.

"I got a call from old man Critchfield over there in the market. He said there was a coyote roaming around. I came out to have a look."

"Cops investigate coyote sightings now?"

"Well, you know how quiet it is here in the canyon. Makes for a boring shift. Anything to break up the monotony. With any luck, I'll be able to roust some teenagers drinking up there at the trailhead. Maybe catch some Romeo parked in his car with his pants down."

Stafford gave out a creepy laugh.

Or you could just fabricate a break in, Jake thought as he looked at the man who was quickly becoming his nemesis. That ought to spice up your night.

The two men said nothing for a long moment.

"Is that an open beer you got there, Jake?"

"Just finishing it."

"I'd hate to have to haul you in for DUI. That would righteously jack up your day."

The implied threat was clear; Stafford was marking his territory. Jake took the high road. "Sorry about that," he said. "I was on my way home to have a cold one and I guess I got a little ahead of myself."

"I guess you did. You'll want to watch that. Like I said the other day, I cover this area, so I'm sure we'll be seeing a lot more of each other."

"I'm sure we will," Jake replied.

He pulled out of the parking lot and onto the canyon road. Through the rearview mirror, he saw Jason Stafford standing ramrod straight, watching as Jake drove away. It took all the way to his house before Jake's heart stopped pounding.

Chapter 14

On Friday, Jake made another step into the past when he sought out a high school friend.

It started when he was going through some boxes he'd brought with him on his move from Truckee. Jake always traveled light, ever since his Navy days, and whatever he couldn't fit inside his Jeep was left behind. He'd stored the boxes in the garage at the canyon house and had forgotten about them. Outside of the odd memento and a handful of family photos, tax returns and various legal and financial documents, the remainder of the items were of negligible importance. Be that as it may, Jake couldn't bring himself to throw *everything* away.

That was always the way of it; each time Jake pulled up stakes and moved on, he lost a little more of his past, to the point his entire life's history could fit inside four bankers boxes. A sad situation, if you chose to look at it that way.

Sorting through the items Jake came across a polaroid photograph of the squad from El Modena High School. It was taken the summer after they graduated, down in Mexico in a little town called Bahia de Cortez, located on the Gulf of California. It was a place Bruce used to surf with a group of guys Jake didn't know, guys from Bruce's old neighborhood who were a few years older. He was always amazed that Bruce's parents would let him drive down to Mexico like that, unaccompanied by adults. But that's how Bill McAlister was. He was a very take charge kind of guy, and in his mind, boys only became men by doing masculine things. Take risks, that's what men did. Jake supposed that made a certain amount of sense. Besides, back in those days Mexico wasn't anywhere near as violent and dangerous as it is today.

The trip was Bruce's idea, one last blowout for the squad before the realities of life after high school took over. Looking at the photograph, Jake was instantly transported to that time. He remembered it all so clearly, could picture the very moment the photo was taken. There was Susan, tan and full of life, with her long golden hair and million-dollar smile. Jake stood between Bruce and Susan, as he always seemed to do, catching Susan as she fell backwards. They were a thing then, Bruce and Susan, and they looked like they belonged together. But looks can be deceiving, as Jake knew so well, and the way the three of them were posed in that photograph spoke volumes.

Bruce was a stud, the team captain, all-county quarterback two years in a row. And he looked like it too. He looked like a movie star, as clichéd as that sounds. His arms are up and flexing in the picture, a bodybuilder's pose, and the look on his face said it all: *I'm the best, and don't you forget it.*

The rest of the squad was there, some of them with their girlfriends, some flying solo. There was Danny Shaffer, Scott Newman, Mark Davis, Eric Johansen, Alex Brady, and there at the end, Tom Cook. A good group of guys, if maybe a little on the crazy side. The core group of an undefeated team three years in a row. 1984 CIF champions. *The Squad.*

Jake wondered where they'd all gone. He literally had no idea. He didn't plan on it being that way, and in the summer of '84 he had every expectation that the squad would stay together, in some form or another, well into the next phase of their lives. But it was not to be. Because Jake chose to make it so. He turned his back on the guys, his family, Bruce and Susan—especially Bruce and Susan—and marched headlong into what would prove to be a long and solitary journey.

The memories coming at him now were the bad ones, and Jake forced his mind clear of them. Remember the good times, he told himself as he looked at the photograph in his hand. His eyes settled on Danny Shaffer. Outside of Susan McAlister, he'd known Danny the longest. They met in sixth grade, and for years Danny was Jake's closest friend. When Bruce came along and Jake gravitated toward him, Danny felt hurt by it. A lot of things changed when Bruce came along. Out of all the guys on the squad, Danny was the one Jake thought of most often, although he never sought Danny out whenever he came back to Orange County. Holding onto the photograph, Jake felt a little ashamed by that.

An idea formed in Jake's mind, and he decided to act on it. He knew that Danny Shaffer's father owned an automotive repair shop in Garden Grove, or at least he used to. A quick internet search showed that Shaffer Auto Repair was still in business. Riding a wave of good feeling, Jake decided to drive out there and see if he could find Danny. At the worst, he'd waste an hour of his day. And if Danny was still around? Well, then Jake would just take it from there.

THE SHOP was located on Trask Avenue near the Garden Grove Freeway. Jake left his house at one thirty and it took him about twenty-five minutes to get there. Shaffer Auto Repair looked exactly as Jake remembered it. All the guys on the squad got their cars fixed there. It was a long shot that Danny would have anything to do with the family business—if it was still a family business—because the one thing he always said back in school was that he would never make his living as a grease monkey. He used to work summers in the shop and he hated it, and by his own admission he was anything *but* mechanically inclined. He would tell hilarious stories about his various screw ups when making repairs to cars or doing simple tasks such as changing oil or rotating tires. Danny Shaffer always had a great sense of humor.

Jake parked his Jeep and walked to the office. He noticed only one out of the five service bays was in use and the parking lot was empty. Maybe business wasn't so good at Shaffer Auto Repair these days. Back when they were in school, it seemed Carl Shaffer was always struggling to keep the shop afloat.

Danny's grandfather started the business in the 1920s, constructing the building himself with the help of his three brothers, and Carl worked there and inherited the shop upon his father's death. He went through boom times and lean times, almost losing the property when the Garden Grove Freeway was built in the 1960s, but he always managed to make it through.

Danny didn't have a lot growing up, but what he had in abundance was the love of his family. Carl was a gregarious man, and whenever one of the guys on the squad came by the shop to have their car worked on, he took the time to shoot the breeze and make them feel at home. He usually didn't charge for the repairs or service work, and if he did, it was at a reduced cost. Jake spent the night at Danny's house on occasion and he always had a good time, the love and affection he witnessed there so different from the emotional disorder he experienced in his own home.

Entering the office, Jake heard a bell jingle above the door. He turned and laughed; it was the same brass bell that hung over the door thirty years ago. He could tell by the dent in the side and the word "ouch" written in black marker. The dent was the result of an errant shot Danny fired from a BB gun when he was screwing around one day in the shop with some guys from the squad.

"Can I help you?" the man behind the counter said.

"Does Carl Shaffer still own this place?"

"He died fifteen years ago."

"Who owns it now?"

"His son, Danny."

So far so good, Jake thought. He was saddened to hear about Danny's father, and he pictured Carl's gap-toothed smile and booming laugh.

"Can I help you with anything?" the man said. The name Larry was stitched on his work shirt.

"I'm an old family friend," Jake said. "I recently moved back to town and wanted to get in touch with Danny. Is he here?"

The telephone rang. "Hold on," Larry said.

While Larry spoke on the phone, Jake looked around the small office, amazed at how little it had changed. It wasn't just the dented brass bell that was familiar, and it was nice to see that some things in this world stayed the same.

Larry finished the call. "Danny's in his office, down at the end of the service bays. You can go back there."

"Thanks," Jake said.

When he got there, he found the door open and the office empty. There was a wood ramp covering the concrete steps leading into the office, and Jake noticed there was no chair behind the desk. He was looking at some family photos on the wall when he heard a voice from behind.

"Who are you?"

"I'm sorry," Jake said as he turned around. "The door was open and I—"

He stopped short, momentarily speechless.

Danny Shaffer was in front of him, and he was sitting in a wheelchair.

"Jake?" Danny said. "Jake Donahue? Are you shitting me?"

"Hey, Danny. What's shakin'?"

Danny did a wheelie as he rolled toward Jake.

"Bend down here and give me a hug, bro. I'd stand, but I can't."

Danny laughed and Jake leaned down and awkwardly embraced him. Danny wrapped strong arms around Jake, patted his back hard. He smelled faintly of motor oil and liquor. When Jake stood upright, Danny just stared, his face beaming.

"Damn, I can't believe what I'm seeing. Jake Donahue, in the flesh. Where in the hell have you been for the last, oh, I dunno, *thirty years*?"

"It's a long story. How are you, Danny?"

"Doin' all right. Considering."

Danny wheeled around behind the desk. Jake took a seat in the chair in front. Neither of them said a word, the silence of the office broken only by the sound of an impact wrench coming from the service bays. Danny lit a cigarette from a pack on the desk.

That was strange. Danny had always hated cigarettes, tried for years to get his dad to quit, said they'd kill him some day. Jake remembered one time at a beach bonfire when Danny got all over Scotty Kincaid's ass for lighting up, calling him a dumbass while taking the smoke out of his mouth and crushing it between his fingers. Scotty lit another and kept right on smoking, but at least Danny had made his point.

"So, go ahead and ask," Danny finally said.

"Ask what?"

"How I got my wheels."

Jake chuckled inside. Typical Danny, blunt and to the point. Speak once and think twice was always his motto. Danny used to handle a lot of things with humor, but when necessary he could be deadly serious, and he'd usually cut right to the chase.

"Okay, buddy. How'd you get your wheels?"

"Car wreck, back in eighty-nine. But it's a long story. Kind of like yours, I suppose."

"I suppose," Jake said.

"I'll tell you what, Jake Donahue. I've got a boatload of paperwork to get through right now and if I don't get to it, I never will. But I sure don't want to go another thirty years without talking to you. Before you disappear again, let's get together and swap our long stories. What do you say?"

"Sure, Danny, I'd like that."

"You know the Rail Bar?"

"Never been."

"It's down there by the Santa Ana train station. Meet me there at seven and I'll tell you all about it."

"You got it."

"See you then, Jake."

On the way home, Jake thought about Danny Shaffer and the passage of time. I guess we all have a long story to tell, when you get right down to it. He was looking forward to hearing Danny's. When the time came to see Bruce, Jake wondered if he'd feel the same way.

THE RAIL BAR was located near an abandoned railroad spur on Santiago Street, a few blocks from the historic French Park district east of downtown Santa Ana. It was a drinker's bar, with no effort made at respectability. Jake got there early, but even so, Danny was already inside.

"What're you having," he asked as Jake approached the corner booth where Danny had rolled his wheelchair up to the edge of the table.

"Make it a beer."

"Sure thing, boss. Coors?"

"Always," Jake said.

Danny held up his empty bottle, flashing two fingers to the bartender. Jake slid into the booth and noticed three empty highball glasses next to a couple of dead soldiers. The ashtray was filled with butts and Danny had one burning in his left hand. It looked like he was settled in for a long one.

Danny stared at Jake, a glint in his eyes.

"What happened to you?"

"What do you mean?" Jake said.

"One minute we're down in Mexico, the next you're gone. We thought you died or got yourself kidnapped. I wanted to go to the cops, but Bruce said he talked to you. He was weird about it too. To this day, he's never said what happened."

The last time Jake saw Danny Shaffer was on their trip to Bahia de Cortez a few weeks after they'd graduated high school. Jake had left Mexico without telling anyone. Only Bruce knew the truth about what happened. When Jake got home he went straight to the Navy recruiter's office and signed up, asked to be fast-tracked to basic training but still had to wait three months. He spent that time working on his uncle's ranch in Colorado. His parents didn't balk when he told them his plans; they were so deep in their own drama, Jake wasn't sure they even heard him.

"You still see Bruce?" Jake said.

Danny dragged on his cigarette. When he exhaled, the smoke curled around his face.

"Oh yeah, I still see him," he said, irony in his tone. He stubbed out his smoke, and immediately lit another. "I heard rumors about you joining the military, but I figured it for bullshit. It wasn't until after I talked to your old man that I found out it was true. My mind was completely blown."

Jake thought about what to say. He wasn't prepared to talk about it, but he couldn't just lie. Not completely at least.

"I had some family stuff going on," he said, carefully choosing his words. "Between my parents. I couldn't talk to anyone about it. Finally, I had enough, so I bolted."

"Kind of extreme, isn't it?"

"Desperate times call for desperate measures."

"How many years were you in?"

"Five."

"And after that?

"I drifted. Just trying to figure things out."

"Thirty years is a long time to figure things out. Did you have much luck with that?"

Jake laughed. "What do you think?"

"Amen to that, brother." Danny raised his beer in a toast. "Here's to figuring shit out."

Jake raised his beer and the two men drank.

"You never came home, in all those years?"

"A few times. But I never stayed for very long."

"And it never occurred to you to look up your old friends?"

The question wasn't accusatory and Danny's smile was genuine. Jake could only shrug and offer a blank expression. "I'm here now," he said.

"Yes, you are, in the flesh. So, tell me, you ever been married?"

"Never."

"Any special lady friends?"

"Here and there. How about you?"

Danny shrugged and dragged on his cigarette.

"C'mon, Jake, who wants half a man?" He blew out the smoke and hit his beer. "I had a girl back when the accident happened, but she dumped me before I was out of the coma. Ain't that a bitch?"

Danny laughed, but there was no humor there. Jake finished his beer and the bartender brought two more. Someone punched up some tunes on the juke. The room was nearly empty, just a few guys sitting at the bar and a couple huddle deep in conversation over near the front door.

"Tell me about it," Danny said. "All that time you spent drifting."

Over the next thirty minutes Jake recounted an abbreviated version of his wandering years. He felt oddly disconnected as he told it, like it was someone else's story. He felt like he was being evasive with Danny. Somewhere in the story Jake switched to bourbon and water. The mellow buzz felt good, like a warm emotional buffer against his discomfort. He was glad he'd sought Danny out, yet an undercurrent of doubt flowed below the surface. Thirty years is a long time to go without talking to someone, and to try and catch up in any meaningful way feels unnatural, the whole exercise lending itself to superficiality. It was hard for Jake to picture himself establishing a relationship with Danny, despite his eventual words to the contrary. He meant well, he just wasn't sure if he could deliver.

"So now I own a house in Silverado," Jake said. "I'm not quite sure what to do with it though."

"You think you might want to stay here a while?"

"You know, up until a few months ago I would've told you I wasn't sure I wanted to stay anywhere for a while."

"What happened?"

"I don't know," Jake said. "Something changed I guess. Maybe it's age. Maybe it's my dad passing away. Who knows?"

"I hear you. I went through some stuff when my old man died. I still have my mom, but she's got Alzheimer's and it ain't easy. My brother and sister live on the east coast, so it's like I'm alone."

"I know the feeling."

They ordered another round and Jake got up to use the restroom. When he came back, he asked the inevitable question. "So how'd you end up like that?" Jake pointed to the wheelchair.

Danny smiled.

"That *is* the question on everyone's mind, isn't it?" He broke out into a laugh, like he'd just said the funniest thing ever. It made Jake feel uncomfortable. When he stopped laughing, Danny said, "Before I get into that little tale, let's do a shot. How about some Patrón? I think this dump has a bottle back there behind the bar somewhere."

Danny waved the bartender over and ordered the shots. Jake was feeling the liquor and wondered if maybe he should stop. The shots came and he ignored that thought, downing the tequila and slamming the glass on the table.

"Good, eh?" Danny said. "Just like old times, Jake."

"Sure, Danny. Just like old times."

Pink Houses came on the juke, an instant flashback to those old times. Jake rode a boozy wave of nostalgia, the years falling away like so many dead leaves.

"I've been in this chair since November thirteenth, nineteen eighty-nine," Danny said, his voice nearly drowned out by the music.

Jake stared at him. "How did it happen?"

Danny looked at Jake and his eyes watered. He lit a cigarette and took in some smoke. "Bruce McAlister put me in this chair," he said, blowing out a long stream.

The words settled between them. Danny finished off his beer and slid the bottle across the table. It went off the edge and shattered on the floor.

"Sorry, Salvador," Danny shouted to the bartender.

Jake bent down to pick up the pieces of broken glass.

"Leave it," Danny said sharply. "Sal doesn't give a shit. He'll get to it when he gets to it."

Jake sat up, startled by the sudden change in Danny's tone.

"So yeah, our good buddy Bruce got me my wheels."

"How?"

"We were coming back from Vegas. Bruce had just gotten a new Camaro. My dad helped him soup it up. Can you believe it? Car could go a hundred twenty-five easy. Anyway, Bruce was drinking the whole way home. I tried to get him to stop, but you know how he could be. Hell, I was drinking too, so who am I to talk?"

Danny paused and dragged on his smoke.

"He lost control coming down the Cajon Pass and rolled the car off the freeway. I was ejected out the windshield."

Danny exhaled the smoke, stubbed out his cigarette, and looked at Jake.

"And there you have it. That's how I got my wheels."

Jake sat motionless, stunned to silence by the story. "I'm sorry, Danny," he said after a long moment. "I don't know what to say, except I'm sorry."

"What's there to say? Shit happens, and then you deal with it."

"What happened to Bruce?"

"He got cut up a little from the broken glass, but other than that, the dude was okay. Thing is, he stayed inside the car. He had a roll cage installed in the Camaro, so he survived getting launched off the freeway. Who the hell puts a roll cage inside a car anyway? A crazy person, that's who. The bitch of it is, if I'd been wearing my seatbelt I probably would've stayed in the car too."

Danny laughed bitterly.

"What's so funny?" Jake said.

"Bruce's old man. You know what he said? He said it was divine intervention that saved Bruce's ass. I guess pagan worshipping heathens like myself aren't worthy of God's good grace. Anyway, fuck that guy and his God bullshit. Bruce made it through because he put his seatbelt on. I didn't. It's as simple as that."

Danny stared at an empty beer bottle on the table, started peeling the label off. The bar had gotten crowded, the music louder. Jake felt dizzy from the liquor, Danny's empty stare rattling his emotions, forcing him to look away.

"So anyway, there was an insurance settlement but my folks didn't think it was enough. They made a lot of noise about suing Bruce. I was still living with them when all this went down. It got pretty ugly, until finally Bill McAlister offered to invest a sizable amount of money in my dad's business if he dropped all the lawsuit talk."

"What?"

"Oh yeah. He knew, Jake, he knew that my dad was barely hanging on, maybe one more year and he'd lose the shop. Bill just wanted the whole thing to go away. He had plans for Bruce, and they didn't involve a scandal. He'd been trying to get him on the straight and narrow since high school. He bought that church in the canyon and he wanted to make Bruce the pastor. Isn't that some crazy shit?"

"Did your dad settle?"

"Yeah, he did."

"How'd that make you feel?"

"Honestly? I didn't care. It wasn't gonna give me my legs back. And my dad needed the money. I didn't hate Bruce for what happened. I was a drunk fool that night too, so how can I blame him? But I'll tell you what, that whole sorry episode sure straightened Bruce's ass out."

"How?"

"He turned to God, just like his daddy wished for. He became an insufferable holy roller. And he finally married Susan, after years of treating her like crap and banging every skirt in sight. Made an honest woman out of her."

"That bad, huh?"

"Oh yeah, he was hard on her. I could never figure out why. Susan was always cool. And damn was she a looker. Well, until the end at least."

"What do you mean?"

"She was living hard, drinking, maybe a little coke here and there. There were other men too, although I could never blame her for that. Bruce always loved himself more than he loved Susan. She and I stayed close. It seemed like the higher Bruce climbed, the lower Susan got. She used to come by the shop sometimes and we'd share a bottle in the office. She knew how I felt about Bruce, and I think that was the attraction. Misery loves company, eh, Jake? I probably shouldn't have encouraged her bad habits, but I'm nobody's keeper. She'd get hammered and I'd call her a cab, have one of my guys drive her car home."

"Where'd they live?"

"Bruce has a place up there in Cowan Heights. Funny how all those big shot preachers have nice pads. How does that work, anyway?"

"They'd probably tell you it was God's work," Jake said with a laugh.

"That's a good one. And true too. But anyway, Susan was a real mess. It broke my heart when I heard what happened to her."

"You think Bruce had a hand in it?"

"Man, I honestly don't know. Is he capable? Sure, I'd say there's a part of Bruce that could do something like that, if the stakes were high enough. You know how he is, Jake. Dude's a narcissist times a hundred. And he's always been a little twisted. Maybe she was a threat to those big plans of his and he needed an easy solution to the problem."

"I was thinking that maybe he'd changed."

"Sure, he changed a lot after he crippled me. But at his core he's still the same old Bruce McAlister. Don't you forget that."

"You still see him? Are you friends?"

"Friends? I guess you could say that. I still tap him for loans every now and then, whenever the shop ain't doing so good. It's kind of an arrangement we have. I wouldn't call it blackmail exactly, but I make sure to go every Sunday to hear him preach, and I roll my wheels right up front so he can see me, and know that at any time I could spill the beans on what that prick is really like."

Danny's eyes watered.

"He's quite the sensation these days," he went on. "You know he's written a couple of Jesus books? Big bestsellers too. He even has a radio show for the Jesus freaks to geek out on. And those big plans for Limestone Canyon? That's gonna put him over the top. Bruce McAlister, the king of OC preachers. Don't you love it?"

Danny laughed so hard he started coughing—a phlegmy, smoker's cough. Jake felt numb from the booze and the conversation. It was late and he was tired, and he had the feeling Danny could go on all night, pounding drinks and smoking cigarettes, talking about the old times. He decided to end it there.

"I'm gonna hit the road," Jake said.

Danny put his hand on Jake's arm.

"I'm really glad you came to see me, Jake."

His eyes were unfocused, his skin chalky, and Jake wondered what the emotional toll was for all this, for the present, and the past. He wondered if he would ever see Danny Shaffer again.

"So listen up. I want you to come out and see Bruce do his thing. It's quite a sight, let me tell you. I'll be right up front, like I always am. You'll do it, right, Jake? You'll come out and see Bruce preach?"

"Sure thing, Danny. I'll do that."

"You always were a good dude, Jake Donahue. It's kinda fucked you were gone for so long."

"Yeah, it is. I'm sorry for that, Danny."

Chapter 15

Hector Santiago woke early on Saturday morning. He showered and shaved, put on pressed black jeans and a pearl-snap shirt, added his silver and turquoise bolo tie—the one he bought at that roadside stand in Raton, New Mexico—and black Tony Lama boots, and he went out to see his deceased wife.

It was a fine morning to visit with Magdalena. The sky was clear, the heat of the day still hours away, the canyon redolent of oak and chaparral, stone and earth. Hector's house backed up to the Maple Springs trailhead, a fire road that snaked its way over the Santa Ana Mountains. He'd lived in the house since 1953, when he and Magdalena moved in as newlyweds. The house was a gift from Hector's uncle, whose own father built it in 1915.

Hector went into the backyard and gazed out at Silverado Creek. He remembered times when the creek ran full from its headwaters on the north slope of Modjeska Peak. It was the second year of drought in California and the creek was bone-dry, the entire canyon a tinderbox. Hector knew the rains would eventually come, they always did. Patience, he told himself. In times of trouble, man must rely on patience to get him through.

Hector watered his garden and swept the front walkway, stopping long enough to gaze at a golden eagle. They were fine birds, with their broad wingspans and graceful speed of flight, and Hector never tired of watching them. When the eagle soared out of view, Hector finished a few other chores, and then he drove out of the canyon.

At eight thirty he pulled his pickup truck into El Toro Memorial Park. He came here once a week without fail, usually on the weekend but occasionally on a Thursday or Friday afternoon. He'd laid Magdalena to rest here eight years ago, and while Hector believed life to be sacred, at times it seemed that the years since his wife's death were nothing more than a marking of days until he could be reunited with the only woman he had ever loved.

He followed the road around to the back of the cemetery and parked in the shade, took a small tool bag and folding chair from the back of the pickup and walked to Magdalena's headstone, being careful not to step on the graves. It bothered Hector to see others trample around the cemetery carelessly, stepping on gravestones with no regard for the sanctity of such a place. Disrespectful, that's what it was. In Hector's opinion, the world had gotten far too disrespectful.

He found the granite marker and stood looking for a moment.

"Good morning, *mi querido*."

Hector opened the tool bag and removed some grass clippers. For the next ten minutes, he trimmed around the headstone, brushed and cleaned the smooth granite, and placed a bouquet of flowers he'd bought on the way to the cemetery. Then he unfolded his chair and sat to the side of Magdalena, on the plot that would be his when the time came.

"It has been quite a week, my love. Let me tell you all about it."

He recounted his week, speaking in a clear, strong voice, laughing at his humor, gesturing with his hands as if his wife were sitting right there in front of him. Sometimes people would pass by when Hector was talking to Magdalena, and he knew they likely thought he was just some crazy old man sitting there talking to the dead. The thought made him smile.

"So you see, *mi querido*, your husband has been dutifully tending to all that must be done, despite the efforts of those who would stand in his way."

Hector let out a jovial laugh. He treasured these chats with Magdalena, his heart bursting with love for all that has been and all that would be. Yes, life is good, Hector thought contentedly.

When he was finished, Hector said goodbye to his wife, collected his things and walked back to his truck. The heat was on the rise, and Hector wondered if today it would finally subside. His old truck had no air conditioning but that was all right. Hector could certainly afford to buy a new truck, one that was outfitted with all the modern conveniences, but he saw little reason for that when his faithful old Chevy got him where he needed to be.

He planned on getting some breakfast at that little café on Fourth Street in Santa Ana, and then he would go see Father Ramón over at Our Lady of Guadalupe. Hector was not a churchgoer, and he had mixed feelings about the Catholic Church in general, but Father Ramón was doing good work in the immigrant communities of Santa Ana. Hector had known the priest for a long time, and he volunteered at the community center sponsored by the church.

Hector did not condone people coming from Mexico into this country illegally, although he certainly understood why they did it. He knew that the journey north was a dangerous one and that many of those who came were victimized by the ones they paid to get them over. It angered him to think of the *coyotes*, most of them working for the drug cartels, taking advantage of these people. Enforce the immigration laws and save everyone the trouble. But Hector knew that would never happen, and therefor the problem would never cease, so he did what he could to be of service, to lend a hand to those in need. The way Hector looked at it, once they were over here, they couldn't just be ignored.

He'd been hearing disturbing stories lately of a human smuggling ring with ties to a church in Orange County. The information came in bits and pieces, and people were afraid to talk about it. Father Ramón had been putting the story together with the hope of involving the authorities at some point, and Hector was helping in any way he could. Today there were interviews to conduct with several day laborers who were willing to come forward. They were *campesinos*, peasant farmers from the state of Baja, abandoned and left to die in the desert south of Yuma, Arizona. And they would have died too, if one of them had not managed to make it to Interstate 8 and flag down a van carrying members of a church affiliated with Father Ramón's. It was an act of providence to be sure, one of those events that made Hector believe there just might be some justice in this cruel world after all.

Hector would hear their stories, he would comfort and not judge the very people whose actions he did not agree with, and he would do his best to be of service, for he knew that is what Magdalena would want.

Chapter 16

Jake walked out to the canyon road to collect his mail. When he got there, he stood at the row of mailboxes feeling lousy. It was early on Saturday and already it was warm. Jake was hungover from last night and he wondered how Danny was faring. Probably a lot better than Jake. Danny was an old hand when it came to drinking, that much was obvious.

Jake sat on a tree stump in the shade and rested, his head aching. He looked to the east and saw a golden eagle soaring high in the canyon, and he wondered how the bird felt this morning. He thought about last night. It was good to see Danny Shaffer, even though it was obvious the guy was a mess. While Jake fought the urge to judge Danny based on one night of drinking, it was clear to him that his old friend needed help. Maybe he just needed someone to talk to, someone who understood the pain that comes from stuffing things so far inside they make you sick. Jake knew about that kind of sickness.

Even though Jake had stayed way later than he intended, and he drank more than he should have, he was glad that he'd met with Danny. He thought about seeking out some of the other guys from the squad. Maybe they could have a reunion, do it at the canyon house, recreate one of Big Ed's poker blowouts. The thought amused Jake. The fact he was even thinking that way surprised him.

Hector Santiago drove past and honked his horn. Jake smiled and waved. He was probably on his way to the cemetery. Jake admired Hector for his devotion to his wife, even in death. He was truly an honorable man. Maybe later he'd invite Hector over for dinner, talk to him about Danny Shaffer and the things that were said at the Rail Bar. Jake needed a sounding board and Hector was the best one out there.

After ten minutes Jake hoisted himself off the tree stump and walked back to his house. He made a pot of strong coffee and got to work, figuring physical activity was the best cure for his hangover, sweat the poison out of his system.

He worked all day Saturday and slowly started feeling better. When he stopped late in the afternoon for lunch, Jake sat on the back deck and soaked in the essence of the canyon. In the shade of the trees the small breeze felt nice. He let his mind wander, recounting the turn his life had taken since receiving the news of his father's death. For the first time since coming back to Orange County, Jake envisioned staying put for a while. He had no idea what the house would bring if he sold it, and he wasn't very motivated to find out. Keeping the house for a rental sounded like a good idea at first, but the more Jake thought about it the more he realized he didn't want to be a landlord.

Jake liked living in the canyon. It was peaceful here, rural, far removed from the hectic pace just down the road in the suburbs. If he was going to live anywhere in Southern California, this would be the place.

After finishing his lunch, Jake eased back in his chair and closed his eyes. He was awakened twenty minutes later when a neighbor's cat jumped into his lap. He smiled and spoke to the cat, scratching behind its ear. Jake liked cats, much more than dogs. Cats were independent. Cats were loners. Cats didn't give a shit. Jake identified a lot with cats.

He was surprised his neighbor let his cat roam outside. Most people kept theirs indoors because of the threat of coyotes. You must be a pretty tough guy, Jake thought as he picked the cat up and set it on the deck. Either that, or you're just lucky. Maybe you're both, and the predators leave you alone because of it. We should all be so lucky, Jake thought as he stood and prepared to get back to work.

Later in the afternoon a technician from the phone company came by to install the telephone line. Jake had requested a change in phone number from the one his father had used; the last thing he wanted was his dad's cronies and gambling buddies to start calling the house, asking where the hell Big Ed was. Jake also had high-speed Internet brought into the house and he expanded his cable service. He wasn't much of a TV watcher but the cable company was running a promo and Jake figured what the heck, might as well go for it.

Later, he flipped through channels and laughed to himself; it would appear he *was* settling down after all. It was an interesting turn of events, these last few weeks, and Jake wondered if this is what it was like to finally grow up.

He'd used a lot of excuses over the years to justify his choices, to rationalize his refusal to put down roots, to minimize his inability to develop lasting relationships. But ever since returning to Orange County those excuses had broken down, crumbling under the weight of truth and the cold realization that the life Jake had been living for the past thirty years was no life at all.

Seeing Danny Shaffer was part of it, and Hector too, but more importantly Jake began to see that the void he'd been trying to fill since the summer of 1984 was one of his own making, and the way he'd been living only served to deepen that void, to ensure that Jake would never find comfort and stability, and ultimately, peace of mind. It's a sobering reality to know that your entire life has been built on a foundation of sand, and a daunting task indeed to try and rebuild that life from the ground up.

Jake clicked off the television and made himself something to eat. The neighbor's cat returned and Jake opened a can of tuna and put it on the sun deck. Maybe I'll go full tilt, he thought with a laugh, and get a cat of my own. What better way to establish permanence than to have a pet?

The cat finished the tuna and split, and Jake wished it well out there on the mean streets of Silverado Canyon. Then he washed the dishes and started a load of laundry. He tested the phone with a call to Hector, but he got no answer. He thought about calling Danny but decided against it. Jake was determined to nurture a friendship with Danny, but he knew that he'd have to take it slow.

After a while Jake got bored and he considered going to Cook's Corner, a biker bar located a few miles away on Santiago Canyon Road. They had bands playing there on the weekend and Jake thought it'd be a nice change of pace. It was coming up on eight o'clock, a little early for the music to start, and Jake figured he could kill some time by taking a drive out to Irvine Lake.

The alternative was to stay at home and flip through cable channels.

Jake opted for the biker bar.

He took a quick shower and got ready to leave. He thought about Jason Stafford coming into his house, and he made sure to secure all the windows and doors, and to turn on the porch light and the flood light over the sun deck. If the guy was fool enough to try it again, Jake wanted to make it as difficult as possible.

Leaving the canyon, Jake passed by Bruce's church. He noted the service times listed on the sign out front. Maybe tomorrow he'd go and see what all the hoopla was about.

Chapter 17

B ruce McAlister sat in a back room at the Canyon New Life Ministry, preparing himself for the ten thirty service. The early service went well, the church packed to overflowing. That was a good sign, a very good sign indeed. While he hadn't expected attendance to drop because of recent events—his was a devoted flock, after all—you can never be certain how people will react to a perceived scandal. Thankfully, everything seemed to be going along as usual.

The vote on the land deal for his new church would come soon, after one final public hearing scheduled for next week. There was a lot of talk about delaying the vote until Richard Lawson's successor was chosen, but Bruce didn't put much stock in that talk. The other four supervisors were firmly on board, there was no question about that, so even if someone made a good argument for waiting on the vote it could rightfully be argued that it didn't matter. No, Lawson's seat would remain empty until the election next year, and Bruce would get his land grant, of that he was sure.

It was a lucky break when Lawson was killed. As cold as it sounded, Bruce knew it was true. He was amused that investigators suspected him, because Lawson had a list of enemies a mile long and if anyone needed killing, it was *that* bastard.

As for Susan, Bruce was truly saddened by her passing. But the truth is, he'd cut her loose a long time ago. At least now she would know some peace. Bruce believed Susan was with the Lord, for she had accepted Christ a long time ago, truly accepted Him into her heart, and even though she'd let sin overtake all that was good about her, she was saved.

It was probably for the better, Bruce thought as he studied his notes for the upcoming sermon, making a few minor tweaks here and there. Once the new church was built the sky would be the limit, and it just wouldn't do for the pastor's wife to be some bitter alcoholic who had grown old before her time, consumed by her grievances. After a respectful mourning period, Bruce would start looking around for a new partner, someone who shared his ambition and understood the mercurial nature of great men like himself. She would have to be immune to petty jealousy, understand her place in things. In short, she would have to be the perfect—

Jason Stafford came into the room, cutting off Bruce's thoughts.

"Did you see who's here?" Jason said.

"Yes, I saw him."

Bruce had gone for a cup of coffee earlier and saw Jake Donahue talking to one of the ushers at the literature table out front. Bruce went out of his way to avoid Jake. The time for meeting would come later.

"What's with you two anyway?" Jason said.

"What do you mean?"

Aren't you the coy one, Jason thought.

"Come on, Bruce," he said. "You know what I'm talking about."

Bruce sighed deeply.

"Jake Donahue represents past sins, Jason. I suppose that's all you really need to know."

"That's it?"

The two men looked at each other. The worship band could be heard from the other room. Bruce thought about the new church; it would be state of the art in every way, far removed from the thin walls of this tired old building.

"The Lord forgives sin, Jason, but man does not. It would be a shame if all the good work we have done, all the plans we have made, are negated by the narrow-mindedness of those who are unable to forgive sin."

So, Jake has some dirt on you, Jason thought as Bruce closed his eyes and bowed his head as if in prayer. He did that a lot, usually after saying something he perceived as profound. Jason figured he'd have to investigate this great "sin" that Jake Donahue represented. Information like that could be useful. Jason was fully on Bruce's side, although he never stopped looking for an edge.

"Danny Shaffer has been talking," Bruce said, his head still bowed.

"To who?"

"Jake Donahue."

"How do you know?"

"Does it matter?"

"He's a weird guy," Jason said, ignoring the question.

"He drinks too much, and when he drinks he gets emotional, starts talking about the old days." Bruce looked up. "Danny's my friend, Jason. Far be it for you to judge."

Jason felt a flash of anger. If things were different, he'd smack the shit out of Bruce McAlister. But things weren't different. At least for now.

"What do you want from me," he said, keeping his tone even.

"I just wanted you to know, that's all. I trust you'll do the right thing." Bruce stood. "I have to get ready now."

That was Jason's cue to leave.

"You'll join us later for lunch?" Bruce said. "Paige and myself. I think my father is coming along as well."

Jason stopped at the door. "Sure, Bruce, that would be nice."

After Jason left, Bruce McAlister stood in front of a mirror and adjusted his tie. The worship band was cranking it now, and he could hear parishioners singing and clapping. It sounded joyous. It sounded like the future.

***

THE CHURCH was filled, the parishioners hanging on every word. Bruce usually hit his stride at the second service and today he was knocking it out of the park. He spoke in a strong and unwavering voice, modulating his intensity, pushing and pulling his congregation, leading them to the edge of tears and then bringing them back with laughter. He was so good at this. This was his gift.

Bruce loved preaching the word of God. And yes, he loved the adulation of his congregation, his people. Vanity was a sin and Bruce fought mightily against it, but he was a rock star and he knew it. Certainly, God would forgive him this one transgression in return for all the good he'd done, the souls he'd saved, and would continue to save once his new church was built and Bruce took his place alongside the world's religious greats. Yes, he was a rock star. An evangelical superstar.

He noticed Jake Donahue in the back row, down at the end, trying to blend in, to not be noticed. Poor, lost Jake Donahue. Soon the time would come for Bruce and Jake to meet, and to reconcile the past. It was tricky business though, and it took a subtle hand and great intuition to see it through. It would have been best if Jake had not returned when he did. A year or two from now, after the church was built and all was said and done, would have been better. But Bruce knew that he had no more influence over the course of events than he had wings to fly. And besides, he knew that God had brought Jake to him at this critical juncture to test him, to steel his nerve against those who would endeavor to destroy him, to derail his path to greatness.

Bruce had absolute faith in God, and in himself. But just to be sure, he'd been careful to cover his bases. He had Jason Stafford for that. And his father. Bill McAlister probably had more at stake than his son, and that old bastard would make sure he came out on top no matter who he had to step on to get there.

Bruce brought his sermon to an end. He always liked to finish big and today he tried something new, leading his congregation in prayer as the worship band played behind him, subtly at first before building to a crescendo, Bruce's voice rising with the music. And then the band stopped cold, and in the silence that followed, in a voice whispered yet strong, Bruce spoke.

"In Jesus' name, we pray."

Chapter 18

Bill McAlister turned off the radio after Bruce's sermon. The boy really nailed it today, he thought with pride. He could only imagine how it sounded in person. My God, it must have been impressive.

The radio program was Bill's idea, a way to extend Bruce's reach beyond his small church in the canyon. Two years ago, he bought time on a local AM talk station and started broadcasting the second service every Sunday. The response was immediate and overwhelmingly positive, and there was talk in the works of adding a mid-week worship program. And once the new church was built, a deal was already in place to broadcast the early service on television.

It pleased Bill McAlister to see his son's rise as a leading light among Orange County's clergy. It was a role intended for Bill by his own father, but one that never took. Isaac McAlister was a hardline Southern Baptist who preached at tent revivals throughout the Gulf Coast from Baton Rouge to Pensacola, until mental illness made him join the Pentecostals and take up serpents. Isaac lasted a year doing that before succumbing to a snakebite when Bill was fifteen years old.

Bill had tried to pick up the torch, but he had a head for numbers, not preaching, and that's the direction his life took. He moved to California, and after graduating college he entered the insurance business. Success came early, and soon Bill branched out into real estate and mortgages, and as his wealth grew he began to dabble in politics, financing the campaigns of men who shared his vision for California. And for America.

Every business venture Bill McAlister embarked on was a huge success, something he attributed to his unwavering faith in God. When Bruce was born, Bill saw an opportunity to fulfill his destiny through his son, to make him into the preacher Bill could never be.

It was a tough road though, shaping Bruce into the man he would eventually become. Bruce fought his father tooth and nail, and if it wasn't for Bill McAlister's iron will and determined focus, character traits that had served him so well in business, the job might never have been accomplished. Thankfully, those troubled years were behind him now, and the future held nothing but promise, and that pleased Bill McAlister greatly.

He'd wanted to be at church this morning but he just couldn't get it together. It wasn't any one thing that held him up, just a general malaise that seemed to overtake him lately. Getting old was a bitch. Bill would turn seventy-nine in two months, and at times, he felt like he was ninety-nine.

His mind was still sharp as ever and the fire still burned in his belly, but the sad truth was, his body was breaking down. The doctor said he was as healthy as a seventy-eight-year-old had a right to be, but Bill was convinced the guy was lying to him, and he wondered if he'd even live long enough to see the new church built.

Bill had invested so much in setting that deal up, and he'd used a lifetime of political capital to make it happen. Things almost went haywire when that turncoat Lawson started scheming behind Bill's back. What a double-dealing snake that guy was. But the threat had been neutralized, and the other four supervisors were firmly on board now, so barring any last-minute complications the land deal approval should come soon, maybe as early as next week. What a glorious moment that will be.

He thought about Susan McAlister. It was a shame the way things turned out. But the truth of the matter was, she'd let her inner demons turn her into a threat. Bill had heard through back channels that Susan was having an affair with Richard Lawson and that she had been making a lot of noise about "getting even" with her husband by derailing the Limestone deal. When confronted with the situation Bruce hedged and equivocated, and he made excuses for his wife. Bill was gravely disappointed by that. He had spent many years trying to shape Bruce into a man of decisive action, and it was the one area where work remained.

But it's all taken care of now, Bill thought as he went into his bedroom to change clothes. He had a lunch date scheduled with Bruce and Paige, and possibly Jason Stafford. Now there's a man of action, Bill thought with a smile. Stafford never equivocated, never wavered, never shied away from the task at hand. He'd be a nice addition to the family, should things turn out that way.

Chapter 19

Jake left the church service before the band finished playing. It was an impressive performance. Bruce was really in his element up there, moving gracefully in his tailored suit, punctuating his words with subtle hand gestures, music swelling behind him. It was, in a word, mesmerizing.

The place was packed with hundreds of enthralled folks hanging on Bruce's every word. When Jake first heard of the plans for Limestone Canyon he wondered what the fuss was about. Now he understood a little more. Now he could see that Bruce McAlister was a big deal.

On his way into the church Jake had stopped to look at items displayed at a table set up in front. Books and DVDs and CDs, flyers announcing various retreats and conferences, bible study schedules and pamphlets—all of it prominently featuring Bruce. The usher working the table welcomed Jake to the church and encouraged him to sign the newcomers' list. He told him that Bruce had a popular radio program, so if Jake was ever unable to make it here in person he could still listen to the sermon in the comfort of wherever he happened to be. He gushed about the new church in Limestone, suggesting that Jake go to the public hearing and make his voice heard. It was quite a sales pitch. The man made no mention of Susan McAlister and her recent death.

Jake felt something after seeing Bruce preach, and while he couldn't quite put his finger on it, he knew it was there. He'd certainly gotten swept up in the moment. Maybe it was the music, the way it was choreographed with Bruce's sermon. Maybe it was simply the good feeling that coursed through the church like an electrical current. Whatever it was, Jake knew that it was real. It made him feel...what, exactly? Uplifted? Connected to a roomful of strangers in a way that made him want to reach out and hug every one of them?

The more Jake considered it, the more he realized it was a sense of humanity that he felt. It was hopefulness, a lifting of his spirit beyond the chaos and triviality of daily life, the self-inflicted wounds that drive a wedge between us all. It was an interesting phenomenon. But more than that, it was contagious, and Jake found himself wanting more.

HE WENT home and put in a full day of work on the house. Gradually the good feeling began to fade, but even so, he felt energized, his head full of ideas for the house and for the future. It was an odd turn of events, as Jake had never been one to think about, let alone plan for the future.

After finishing his work Jake went out for a run. It was late afternoon and a good time for it, the canyon road shaded and the breeze up. Since moving south to settle his dad's estate, Jake had fallen off his workout regimen and he was eager to get back into it. He'd been thinking about getting a mountain bike. It seemed everyone around here had one, and Whiting Ranch Wilderness Park was nearby, a popular biking area. He'd had a road bike when he lived in Truckee but it was stolen six months before Jake moved. It was probably just as well; the thing wouldn't fit in the Jeep and likely would have been left behind.

He put in five miles at a good pace. When he got back home he saw a new Range Rover parked in his driveway, a *Jesus saves* sticker on the rear window. He'd seen the same vehicle parked at the Canyon New Life Ministry that morning.

Jake did a few stretching exercises to cool down, his chest thumping in anticipation, and then he walked to the back of the house. When he rounded the corner, he saw Bruce McAlister sitting at the redwood table on the sun deck, drinking a bottle of Dr. Pepper.

"You're looking a little worn out," Bruce said as Jake came up the steps to the deck.

"Just out for a run."

"I know. I passed you on my way up here."

The two men stared at each other without speaking.

"You want some ice for that?" Jake pointed to the bottle in Bruce's hand.

"No, I'm good."

"How about we go inside and talk?"

"Let's stay out here," Bruce said. "It's a pleasant evening."

"That it is. I'll be right back."

"Take your time."

Jake went inside the house. His heart beating fast, he leaned against the kitchen counter to steady himself. He could see Bruce through the window, eased back in his chair, casually drinking his soda. He was dressed in blue jeans and an untucked polo shirt, and a beat-up pair of black Converse high tops. He looked like a regular guy. He looked like an old friend eager to reminisce.

Jake toweled the sweat off and changed clothes. He poured a tumbler of iced tea and took it outside, sitting in the chair opposite Bruce. The breeze kicked up, shaking the limbs of the trees shading the deck.

"Tell me, Jake. What is the nature of man?" Bruce said.

"What are you, a philosopher now? That doesn't fit your style."

"That's just the cynic in you talking."

"I have good reason to be cynical."

"Just answer the question."

"I'm tired, Bruce, and I don't feel like riddles. So why don't you get to it, tell me why you came here."

"A little touchy, aren't we?"

"With you? Yeah, I'm a little touchy."

"I saw you at church today."

"Yes, I was there. Impressive, I must say. You nearly had me believing."

"Susan used to talk about you."

"Did you kill her?"

Bruce looked at Jake, his face expressionless.

"That's a little random, isn't it?"

"Did you?"

"No, Jake, I didn't kill my wife. Nor did I have her killed. That's a little incongruous, isn't it? A murdering pastor? How does that work exactly, preaching the gospel with that kind of skeleton hanging in your closet?"

"You tell me, buddy. You're the one into forgiveness."

Bruce sighed deeply.

"It seems life has not been kind to you, Jake. Why is your heart so hard?"

"My heart isn't hard. I just believe in owning up to the wrong you've done. And that doesn't mean saying some prayers at night before you go to bed, pretending it makes everything all right."

"Prayer works, if you let it."

"Save it. We're not in church right now and I'm not a believer."

Bruce stared off into the distance. Jake had rehearsed this moment countless times but he couldn't remember his lines. He wasn't even sure what he was looking for from Bruce. The things Jake felt were so old he wondered why he even carried them around anymore. He couldn't tell if his anger was real or just something he expected from himself, a performance he was supposed to give. Bruce didn't seem like such a bad guy, and Jake had to admit, when it came to preaching, he was solid gold. If things had played out differently, they might have stayed friends to this day.

"You wouldn't have a mind to cause trouble for me, would you?"

"Are you worried about that?"

"I'm sure you're aware of my plans for Limestone Canyon."

"I've heard."

"Susan's death was tragic. And I know this will sound cold, but it's true—her murder came at a bad time. That's just a fact. I don't know that I can survive another scandal."

"You're right, that sounds cold. In fact, that's pretty fucked up."

Bruce seemed to grimace at Jake's obscenity.

"Be that as it may, it's the truth. Susan and I did not have a good marriage. I'm sorry she's dead, but the fact is, I had not loved her for a long time. Yes, I feel the loss. But not in the way I should."

Jake looked at Bruce, saying nothing. Images flashed in his brain; Susan and the schoolboy crush he had on her, and the way it all changed when Bruce came on the scene. The memories brought a surge of anger, and more than a little shame.

"You're afraid I'm going to spill your secrets, is that it?" Jake said.

"I'm not afraid of anything. My soul is redeemed. Is yours?"

"I'd say probably not. In fact, I'd say I'm headed straight to hell the minute my ticket is punched."

"I'm sorry to hear that. Really, I am. Salvation is a glorious thing, and not something to be dismissed so cavalierly."

"I'll take my chances."

Bruce sighed again. It seemed like a practiced move. He looked off in the direction of the creek, his expression difficult to read. Up close, Jake could see that Bruce had lost none of his youthfulness, the small amount of gray at his temples lending him a measure of sophistication befitting a man of his age. His skin was smooth, his jawline strong, and Jake was reminded of what a heartthrob Bruce was back in high school. They were tight back then, and even though they looked nothing alike, people often mistook them for brothers. But like Cain and Abel, their friendship was doomed to tragedy.

After a pause, Bruce spoke, his head turned.

"We live in strange times. Social media and the Internet, a twenty-four-hour news cycle and reality television, all of it conspiring to feed the public's insatiable appetite for life's dirty little secrets. As a society, we have an almost pathological desire to build someone up just to tear them down. It's a sickness really, eating us from the inside out."

Bruce turned and looked at Jake earnestly, the power of conviction in his green eyes. Jake knew that if he looked long enough into those eyes, he'd probably believe just about anything Bruce McAlister told him.

"It's human frailty, plain and simple. The flesh of the enemy rotting us from the inside. But I know you're not interested in hearing about that, so I'll get to the point. God has great plans for my ministry, plans that will benefit us all. It would be a shame if they were destroyed because of some mistakes I made a long time ago."

"Mistakes? Is that what we're talking about here? Because as I recall it, what happened between us was a lot more than a mistake."

"Let's not argue semantics. The point is, the past cannot be changed. The question is how we deal with the future. I've made my amends. Clearly, you haven't. It would be—"

"Shit happens, huh, Bruce?" Jake said disdainfully.

"Don't be so callous."

There was contempt in Bruce's voice. Up to that point he'd been keeping it in check, tamping down the arrogant, self-serving part of his personality that time had clearly not erased.

"Is that why that cop is following me around, leaning on me?"

"What cop?"

"Come on, you know who I'm talking about. Jason Stafford. The guy who works at your church. What is he, your enforcer?"

"He's a member of my church. And yes, he does volunteer work for me. I believe he also does security work for my father, but I don't get involved in that."

"Is he keeping tabs on me? Making sure I don't do anything to torpedo your land deal?"

"You've been watching too many movies, Jake. Real life doesn't work that way. I'm sure whatever Jason Stafford is doing is simply part of his job. There's no grand conspiracy here."

"That remains to be seen," Jake said spitefully.

He was being antagonistic now, for no other reason than to get under Bruce's skin. Jake was unsettled because he'd wanted to meet Bruce on *his* terms. There could only be one first meeting between them, one shot to make it mean something. Everything after that wouldn't matter.

"I've always known," Bruce said. "Every time you came home, I knew. And each time you came back I wondered, will this be the time? Will this be our chance to resolve the past, to say the things that should have been said thirty years ago? I understand why you left, Jake. I just didn't expect you to be gone so long."

"What do you want me to say?"

"I used to come see your dad sometimes," Bruce said, ignoring Jake's question. "He'd give me little bits of information about you. He missed you. He didn't understand why you turned your back on him."

"I never—" Jake held his tongue, determined not to succumb to anger or give in to Bruce's manipulations.

"He became a believer at the end. Did you know that? He was a sick man and I think he knew the time was near. I was there for him. I witnessed to him, counseled and comforted him."

Jake looked at Bruce.

"What are you trying to do here? Why are you telling me this?"

"I just wanted you to know how it was," Bruce said. "How your father's last days were spent repenting his sins, and accepting the Lord into his heart."

"I don't believe you."

"Why?"

Jake didn't know why, he just knew that it wasn't true. Bruce was playing an angle, running a game. Jake didn't believe for one minute that Bruce had had anything to do with his father, let alone in his last days.

"Look, Bruce, why don't we just stop here. I don't want to talk about my father and I don't want to talk about the past. To be honest, I don't want to talk about anything with you right now. Maybe later that will change. But today, right now, I'm done. I've dragged you around for a long time and I don't want to do it anymore."

"I understand."

"Do you? Do you truly understand? Because I've got this sense that you just say whatever you think needs to be said."

"Are you staying, Jake?"

"What do you mean?"

"Are you here permanently? Here in Orange County?"

"I haven't decided yet."

"Well before you leave again, give me another chance to reach you. That's all I ask."

Bruce smiled. For a moment, Jake pictured him from high school. They'd had some good times together, there was no denying that. Jake felt a storm of emotions. He looked at Bruce. "Sure, buddy. I'll give you another chance. Someday. But for now, get off my property."

Chapter 20

On Monday Jake drove out to Ortega Highway to see where Susan McAlister was murdered.

It wasn't something he'd planned on doing, but he woke before dawn that day, unsettled after a fitful night's sleep and dreams of Susan, and the more Jake thought about her, the more compelled he was to see for himself where the crime took place. Bruce's visit was still fresh in his mind, the things that were said weighing heavily. Jake felt a range of scattered emotions—anger, frustration, regret—and a deep, unrelenting sadness that tugged at his guts and made him quite literally unable to sit still.

After showering he ate a light meal, brewed a thermos of coffee, and hit the road, thinking that at the very least the long drive might serve to clear his mind and ease his spirits. He took Santiago Canyon Road south and picked up the 241 Toll Road east, exited at Oso Parkway and took surface streets the rest of the way. Ortega Highway is a scenic roadway that cuts through the Santa Ana Mountains, connecting Orange and Riverside counties, and it is considered one of the most dangerous highways in the state due to its narrow width and winding turns. There are a lot of accidents on that road, but not a lot of people are shot to death there.

Jake knew from reading the news stories that the murders took place near Ortega Oaks. He had no trouble finding the spot due to the makeshift shrine erected to honor the victims.

He parked the Jeep alongside the road and left the motor running, taking a moment to scope out the area. It was hot out, the dashboard reading ninety-two degrees. A steady stream of cars came westbound on the highway and Jake figured them for morning commuters heading to their jobs in Orange County. He pictured the scene here late at night. There'd be little traffic at that time of day.

The crest of the highway was just east of here, the road descending rapidly in a series of sharp, treacherous turns before reaching Lake Elsinore. There was a campground and fire station nearby, but the closest houses were to the west, clustered around Hells Kitchen, a roadside diner popular with bikers. It didn't seem like a very remote area for killing someone out in the open. It was a bold act to be sure.

Jake shut off the engine and got out of his vehicle, crossing the hot asphalt to the roadside memorial. It was set up at the base of an oak tree, and Jake wondered if this was the exact spot where it happened. It sent chills to think he was standing where Susan had died. He shook off the feeling and knelt to look at the assortment of items piled and covered in dust. A picture of Susan was stapled to the tree. Most of the items were inscribed to Susan. Jake wondered if Bruce had left anything here.

The stream of cars began to thin out. It was coming up on nine-thirty, about time for the morning rush hour to start subsiding. Jake scanned the campground and saw no tents or vehicles there. He felt a peculiar energy in this place, and his intuition told him there was something to be found here.

He walked toward the El Cariso fire station, the heat enveloping him. There was no breeze to speak of, the trees and shrubs still, dry as old bones, just waiting for a spark to ignite the entire landscape into a fireball. Jake had worked for a time on a fire crew in Idaho and he knew all too well the danger that existed from conditions like this.

Approaching the station, he saw a large building that housed the fire trucks, and several smaller structures, a visitor's center, and a monument for firefighters killed in the line of duty. The visitor's center was closed, and there were no fire trucks to be seen. Jake stopped at the monument and read the inscription. He'd known some guys from a Montana hotshot crew killed back in '94. Firefighters are a tight group, and even though Jake was just a volunteer for a summer he felt the loss like a seasoned veteran.

Turning to scan the layout, Jake saw an older man walking a dog alongside the highway. He went in that direction. "Howdy," he said as he neared.

The man stopped and looked at Jake curiously. He was tall and lanky, and quite a bit older than he appeared from a distance. He was dressed in faded khaki trousers and a flannel long-sleeved shirt, the cuffs rolled up, and he wore a sweat-stained bush hat. The dog was an Australian shepherd and it came right up to Jake and started sniffing until the man pulled back on the leash.

"They're out on a call," the man said, pointing to the fire station.

"That's what I figured," Jake said.

The man started walking away.

"Can I ask you a question?" Jake said. "About what happened here in April."

The man turned and looked at Jake with a wary expression. "What business is it of yours?"

"I knew the woman."

"The preacher's wife?"

"Yes. The preacher's wife."

"You her kin?"

"No," Jake said. "Just someone who knew her."

He choked up a little, a sudden flush of emotion coming over him. The reality of the moment hit him then, about Susan and the finality of what took place on this very highway. He looked at the old man, unsure of what to say next.

"Are you some kind of investigator?" the man said, his manner brusque. "We've had a lot of them traipsing around here lately. Reporters too. A disrespectful lot, you ask me."

Jake nodded sympathetically. "No. Like I said, I knew the woman. I heard about what happened and wanted to come out here and see for myself."

"There's not much to see."

The man looked steadily at Jake, his eyes probing. The dog pranced around a bit, and then came closer and nuzzled Jake's leg.

"He's friendly," Jake said, reaching down to scratch behind the dog's ear.

"It's a she. Her name's Maggie." The old man smiled.

"Can you tell me anything about that night?" Jake said.

"There's not much to tell, from my end of it. I live down the road and didn't see what happened. I might've heard it though."

Jake stood upright. "What do you mean?"

The man explained that he'd been awakened that night by the fire crew going out on a call. He couldn't get back to sleep so he took Maggie out for a walk. He figured this was a little after ten o'clock. He'd walked as far as the fire station when he saw an Orange County Sheriff's cruiser drive slowly past. The man continued his walk, and a short distance later he saw the cruiser parked alongside the road and the officer standing at the open trunk. The man watched the officer for a few minutes before Maggie got restless and tugged on her leash. Back at his house he had a glass of warm milk before going to bed. He was standing at his kitchen window when he heard several muffled pops.

"My kitchen faces in this direction. At night, sound travels straight down that ravine over yonder. Sometimes you can hear the smallest noises clear as can be. It didn't register with me until I'd read the story of the killings in the paper. Now I'm fairly sure that what I heard was gunshots."

"Interesting."

"It's a curious thing though, about that sheriff," the man said, scratching at his bearded chin.

"How so?"

111

"This here is Riverside County. We don't get a lot of law around here anyway, outside of the Highway Patrol. What was that Orange County sheriff doing up here?"

"That's a good question. Did you get a good look at the cop?"

"Not really. Like I said, he was standing at the open trunk of the car. His back was turned. He was a big man, I can tell you that. A little bigger than you, I'd say. He was built pretty good too, like one of those weightlifter types."

"What about that campground over there? Do you think anyone might have seen something?"

"We don't get many campers that time of year. As I recall, the place was empty the night of the murder."

"And there was no one at the fire station because they were out on a call?"

"That's right. Normally one or two fellas will stay behind, but there was a brush fire south of here and it was all hands on deck."

"I guess that's about it, then?" Jake said.

"Pretty much," the man replied. "I told all of this to the investigator. He was from Orange County too. When I asked him about that he got a little huffy with me, said to mind my own business."

"Really? That sounds odd. Can you describe the man?"

"He was a Mexican. Ricardo something or other. Medium height, slight build. He had a mustache and he wore a cheap suit. He seemed lazy to me, didn't have much interest in what I had to say. Until I mentioned the jurisdiction thing, and then he started puffing out his chest."

"Has he been back?"

"No. And I don't expect he will. A Riverside County investigator was here last week. He was friendly. He told me there was a bit of a pissing match going on between the two counties, seeing how one of the victims was that supervisor fella. Politics is a lot of horseshit, you ask me."

"I hear that," Jake said with a laugh. "I appreciate your time. And thanks for the information. I think I'll be moving along now."

"Glad to be of help," the man said. "And I'm sorry about your friend. This is such a peaceful place, outside of those damn motorcycles tearing ass up and down the highway. It's a shame what happened here. You take care."

The man turned and walked away, Maggie leading the way back home. Jake stood for a moment and pictured that night, how he imagined it going down. From what he'd read, he knew that Richard Lawson's car was found parked on the wrong side of the road. What would make him stop like that? Something or someone blocking the road? A cop, perhaps?

Jake let that thought settle as he walked back to his Jeep. While it seemed completely implausible, Jake was certainly not naive enough to think that cops never committed murder. He'd always believed that given the right set of circumstances and enough motivation, human beings were capable of just about anything. Jake was living proof of that. Cops were no exception.

Chapter 21

Hector came by the house on Monday evening and he brought homemade enchiladas and a pot of tortilla soup. Jake made some rice and fixed them both salads, and they took their dinner out on the deck. It was a perfect evening for eating outdoors. The air was cool and the weather forecast was finally calling for a break in the heat, maybe even a few scattered showers. Monsoon-like conditions had been developing all day.

The two men ate in silence. Crickets chirped in the creek and a pack of coyotes gave out high-pitched yelps from somewhere up on the hillside. The neighbor's cat had returned and was sniffing around the table, but as soon as it heard the coyotes it wisely scampered off in the direction of home.

"I saw you drive out Saturday," Jake said. "Did you go to the cemetery?"

"Yes."

"How was it?"

"It was nice."

Hector poured some tea and drank from his cup. He seemed unusually subdued. Jake had plenty on his mind and he wanted to share it, but he was careful to allow Hector the time to speak first. Throughout Jake's life, Hector had always been so strong and steady, so patient with other people and their problems, that sometimes it was easy to forget he was still a human being like the rest of us, given over to his own disappointments and emotional lows. If Hector Santiago had something on *his* mind, then Jake would just sit and wait until his friend was good and ready to tell it.

"Yes," Hector said, "Magdalena is doing well. For a dead person."

Jake did a double take and Hector winked, accompanied by a sly little grin.

"And here I thought you were bothered by something," Jake said with a laugh.

"Do I seem bothered?"

"You seem quiet, Hector. Are you bothered by anything?"

"Life ebbs and flows, does it not? But like the ocean tide or a sunrise, there are some things you can always count on. One of them being the regular occurrence of bothersome things. Yes, I have something on my mind tonight."

"Do you want to talk about it?"

"I am not sure you are the person I need to speak to about it."

Jake immediately thought of Jason Stafford, and he wondered if maybe Hector had again crossed paths with the rogue cop. He felt a jolt of anger that made his skin tingle. He forced down the feeling and spoke in an even tone.

"Why don't you just put it out there, see where it goes?"

"Let me ask you a question first. Have you seen your old friend, Bruce McAlister?"

"As a matter of fact, I saw him yesterday, at his church."

"I see," Hector said. "How was it?"

Jake thought for a moment. "It was uplifting," he said. "The man has a definite flair for the gospel."

"I have heard others say the same thing." Hector smiled and touched Jake's hand. "I am glad you went, *mi hijo*. It was long overdue. Perhaps now you two can repair the past, and move into the future."

"Perhaps," Jake said, deciding not to mention Bruce's visit later in the day yesterday. Jake was still processing *that* encounter. "So why are you asking me about Bruce?"

"His church does missionary work in Mexico."

"So?"

"Mr. McAlister has built a church in Bahia de Cortez."

"Go on," Jake said.

"From what I have heard, he does good work helping the poor. For that he deserves much praise."

"But there's another side to that story, isn't there?"

"Why do you say that?"

"When it comes to Bruce—at least the Bruce I once knew—there's always another side to the story. I don't imagine that's changed much."

Hector laughed. "You are getting wise in your old age."

Jake nudged Hector's chair with his foot. "Get to the point, old man."

"As you wish." Hector smiled and collected himself. "I was speaking with some men recently who came over the border."

"Illegals?"

"Yes, illegals. These men are *campesinos*, and they have come here for work. I do not condone their actions, but that is another matter. They are here now and they need help."

"I understand," Jake said. He held no strong views about illegal immigration. If pressed, he would say it's wrong and something should be done about it. But he knew that it was a deeply complex problem with no clear solutions. "What does this have to do with Bruce?"

"I do not know, exactly. But the men told me a very interesting story about their crossing, of the arrangements they made through an American church in the town of Bahia de Cortez."

Jake stared at Hector for a moment. "I don't get it. Are you telling me that Bruce is running illegals across the border?"

"The men I spoke to did not know of Mr. McAlister. They told of another man, a gringo they called *diablo de ojos azules*. The blue-eyed Devil. They described him as a big man, a hard man. He was the one in charge of making the arrangements.

The actual crossing was done by *coyotes* working for the Tijuana Cartel."

"What the hell?"

"This is how it works, Jake."

"Go on."

"The *campesinos* came from their hometown to the church at Bahia de Cortez. There were people there from all over Baja California. They spent one month at the church, and during that time they took English and religious classes, and they learned how it would be when they arrived. They were promised safe passage and documentation in return for their payment, and they would have jobs waiting for them."

"How much?"

"Four thousand dollars. Some paid more, some less."

"How many were in this group?"

"Thirty-six men.

Jake did some quick math. At four thousand a head, the take was nearly a hundred and fifty grand to run one group across the border. A lucrative business by any measure.

"So outside of the fact that Bruce's church might be fronting a profitable smuggling business, what's the concern?"

"The men I spoke to were abandoned in the desert. Left to die when the *coyotes* got spooked by the border patrol. It was a miracle they survived. This kind of thing happens frequently. Once they have their money, the *coyotes* do not have much interest in seeing the job through. At the first sign of trouble they will abandon their cargo and save themselves."

"It's kind of hard to get repeat business that way, isn't it?"

"No one hears the stories. Or if they do, they choose to ignore them. These are desperate people, willing to risk death to have a better life. You cannot create a more perfect opportunity for exploitation."

Jake considered the story. It was hard to fathom such a thing. After all, churches are supposed to help people, not profit from them. Then again, organized religion has always been a profitable venture, has it not? Taking money from those who can ill afford it, dispensing hope and salvation like some traveling salesman peddling patent medicine guaranteed to cure.

But Jake knew that was just the cynic in him talking, and it wasn't reflective of any deeply held belief. Sure, religious charlatans have been fleecing mankind since the dawn of time, trading on fear for personal gain. Yet it was also fair to say that religion has provided a bedrock of stability and serenity for countless believers, and we'd likely be far worse off without it than we are with it. The truth, Jake thought, is probably somewhere in the middle.

"What does this mean?"

"I do not know," Hector replied. "There are more questions than answers, and it is difficult to get to the truth in these matters."

"I think Bruce is capable of lots of things, but what you've described is on a whole different level."

"Perhaps he thinks he is helping these people."

"Perhaps," Jake said.

Hector finished his tea. He set the cup on the table and smiled at Jake.

"Now you know what is troubling me. But this is not for you to worry about. I believe you should continue your path of reconciliation with your former friend. Whatever he may be involved in will be revealed in its own time. Try not to judge him, and make no assumptions. That kind of thinking will only poison your mind, and it will not change the outcome no matter what the truth may be."

"Is that your nugget of wisdom for the day?"

"Certainly. If it pleases you, *mi hijo*."

Hector gave out a bellowing laugh. The two men cleaned up from dinner and afterwards they took a walk along the canyon road. At the market, they bought ice cream cones and ate them at a picnic table out front. On the way home, they spoke of things that had no meaning, and they laughed at their own jokes.

Chapter 22

Danny Shaffer wheeled into the kitchen to get another beer. It was Tuesday morning and he was pissed. He'd been pissed since Sunday. Danny grabbed two bottles and wheeled back into the living room, turned off the television and popped the top on one of the beers, drinking deeply.

Yeah, he was pissed all right.

He set the bottles on the coffee table and listened to the rain. It had started way before dawn, blowing against the windows of the house like a hurricane. Not that Danny had any idea what a hurricane was like, but he imagined if he did, it would be like this.

After a few minutes, he felt like some tunes. He wheeled over to the stereo system set on a credenza across the room and perused the vinyl. Danny was completely disorganized in every aspect of his life except one; his record collection. His vinyl—and Danny only listened to vinyl, make no mistake about that—was organized alphabetically, divided into genres. He had over two thousand records in his collection. It was the only thing he spent money on, outside of liquor and smokes.

He thought about Bruce. Damn, that guy had pissed him off.

Danny eyed the heavy metal collection, knew exactly what he wanted to hear. He pulled Deep Purple's *Machine Head*, slapped that bitch on the turntable and raised the volume. *Highway Star* blasted from massive speakers suspended from the ceiling, and Danny played air guitar, banging his head in time with the music. He wheeled over to the coffee table and killed his beer. He opened the other bottle, laughing out loud. *Highway Star* was playing on the stereo the night Bruce launched his Camaro off Interstate 15 and crippled Danny.

Life's a bitch and then you die, Danny thought spitefully as he lit a cigarette and chugged his beer. And then he stewed some more.

Bruce had taken Danny aside after church on Sunday and said he wanted to speak to him in his office. He kept it short and sweet; he'd heard that Danny had met with Jake Donahue and he wanted to know what they'd talked about. Something about the way Bruce asked pissed Danny off. What business was it of his who Danny talked to? Bruce went on about loyalty and keeping confidences, couching the whole thing in God-talk, like he was preaching some universal truth.

Danny kept his temper under control, nodding his head, smiling and telling Bruce what he wanted to hear. After all, he was planning on hitting Bruce up for a loan soon and there was no sense upending that by getting into it with the guy. But still, the whole thing pissed Danny off. Bruce could be such an insufferable asshole.

Danny went into the kitchen and got two more beers. He wheeled over to the turntable and put the needle back at the start of *Highway Star*. That was the bitch of vinyl—you couldn't repeat songs easily. Danny hated CDs, but at least they had that going for them.

He chugged the brew. He knew he should slow down, but these things tasted so good. It was eleven thirty in the morning and Danny had no shame about slamming beers so early in the day. He polished off the bottle and opened the other. And he stewed some more.

The worst part was, Bruce had sent that goon Jason Stafford to the house. Danny hated that guy; he reminded him of a Nazi, one of those Aryan storm troopers you see in old black and white movies. Danny had hated Stafford since high school, when Stafford used to bully Danny's younger brother. At least until Danny put a stop to it.

It happened during Danny's senior year. Stafford was a freshman. A pretty decent football player too, even though the freshman squad sucked hard that year. Danny cornered Stafford in the weight room one afternoon and knocked him on his ass. Granted, he'd coldcocked the guy, but that was necessary since Stafford was a lot bigger and he would have destroyed Danny in a fair fight.

Anyway, Danny did what he had to do and Stafford got the message loud and clear: lay off my brother or there's more of this waiting for you. Stafford didn't balk. He knew that if he did, he'd have to answer to the entire squad. That's just how things went at El Modena High in 1984.

Danny drank some beer and laughed.

They were something else back then, the guys on the squad. Everyone respected them. Some even *feared* them.

Danny didn't see much of the guys these days. Most of them were married with kids, settled into their suburban middle-class lives. Tom Cook was the only one he kept in touch with. Tom was a cool dude and it was always a good time whenever they got together. He was divorced with two grown kids, and he worked as a set builder for the movie studios. Tom lived in Los Feliz, and even though the drive was a bitch, Danny tried to get up there once a month or so, or Tom would come down to Orange County and they'd go to a ballgame or see a band at the Coach House. Tom Cook was cool.

Jason Stafford was definitely *not* cool.

Danny couldn't figure out why the guy was so tight with Bruce, and Bruce's dad too. Dude was a Neanderthal. Danny was pretty sure that Stafford did some dirty work for the McAlisters. He was just that type of guy.

So, Bruce sent Stafford around to talk to Danny. Threaten was more like it.

Keep away from Jake Donahue. Mind your own business, Shaffer, or else.

Danny laughed.

Or else what, tough guy? You'll beat my ass? A guy in a wheelchair? How about you just kill me, put me out of my misery.

Stafford had pulled up to Danny's house driving a new BMW 5-Series sedan. *How does that work, anyway? Dude is a cop and he can afford a ride like that?*

The visit was a short one. Stafford puffed out his chest, made his threats, and then split. Danny figured it for some half-assed, good cop, bad cop play. First, Bruce laid his smooth rap on Danny after church, going on about loyalty and the future, hinting that there might be a job waiting for Danny once the new church was built. That was a hoot. Danny knew he'd die at Shaffer Auto Repair. That shit was written in the stars.

And then here comes Stafford, the bad cop, squeezing Danny like he was some two-bit crook. Danny could only laugh at how it went down. He'd played Stafford like a cheap fiddle, telling the fascist what he wanted to hear, acting all scared of the big bad wolf. After Stafford left, Danny hit the beers. And he stewed about it. That was two hours ago. And still he stewed about it.

He called the shop and told Larry he wasn't coming in today. Then he hit a shot of Patrón. *Damn, that's good. And why shouldn't I knock back shots at noon on a Tuesday? What the hell do I have to live for?*

He wheeled up to the stereo and put his headphones on, set the needle at the start of *Highway Star* and cranked the volume. *Yeah, baby!*

Danny grooved to the music, thinking about Bruce and the Camaro. Thinking about flying through the windshield. That's the only part he remembered, flying out the windshield. And then everything went black. When Danny woke up nine days later, he was a cripple.

"Ooh it's a killing machine, it's got everything."

Danny sang the lyric out loud, the riff pounding in his brain. He cranked the volume higher. Dark thoughts filled his mind.

I should have died in that wreck.

But I didn't die, and now I have to deal with Bruce and his bullshit, and assholes like Jason Stafford leaning on me. Screw you, Bruce McAlister. You don't want your business on the street, that's fine by me. But show some respect. You took my legs, you ain't getting my dignity too. I know some secrets all right. All those times Susan came by the shop and got hammered? Well, she talked, about all kinds of things.

The music drove a wedge between Danny's eyes, mainlining to his brain.

Respect, Bruce, that's all I ask. And since you can't hear, I'll have to teach you.

Danny ripped the headphones off and threw them at the turntable. The needle skidded across the vinyl in a rasp, ruining the record. Screw it, he thought. I'll buy another. He laughed; he'd worn out four copies of that damn record already.

Danny slammed another shot and grabbed his cell phone. His ears were ringing. He thought about Bruce, his heart racing.

"I'll show you bastards!" he screamed, as he dialed Jake Donahue's number.

Chapter 23

Jason Stafford drove away from Danny Shaffer's house in Anaheim. He checked his watch; this little errand for Bruce had left him short on time.

It was more Jake Donahue nonsense. Jesus, Bruce was fixated on that guy. Jason knew it was a tricky time and that the Limestone deal could go south at any moment, but he'd yet to figure out what threat Donahue posed. Hopefully, things would return to normal soon. Jason was keeping tabs on so many people he needed a scorecard to keep track.

He didn't mind leaning on Danny Shaffer. He'd hated that dude ever since high school, when Shaffer coldcocked him in the weight room. There wasn't anything Jason could do about it back then, and now…well, now Shaffer was a cripple, and there wasn't much point in beating up a guy in a wheelchair.

Truth is, Jason hadn't thought about Danny Shaffer at all since high school. And then Jason hooked up with Bruce and started going to his church, and boy was he surprised to see Shaffer there, wheeled right up front. Seeing him in a wheelchair was a trip, and Jason did a little detective work on that, found out how it happened. *That* was a mindblower.

It didn't take long for Jason to figure out there was something going on between Bruce and Danny. He figured Shaffer had some dirt on Bruce, just like Jake Donahue had some dirt on Bruce, Jason was convinced of that. He'd figure it out eventually, you could bet on it. And when he did, he would file the information away until the right time to use it.

The rain was really coming down and the freeway was backed up. Jason had a stop to make at the courthouse in Santa Ana, and after that he had to drive out to Corona Del Mar and deliver a package to an aide of Orange County Supervisor Frank DeMarco. While he never asked, he had a pretty good idea what was in the package. He'd been delivering a lot of them lately, always to some snot-nosed flunky at a Starbucks or a strip mall parking lot. It was Bill McAlister's way of greasing the wheels. You had to hand it to the old man, he knew how to make things happen, and he wasn't queasy about it either. Jason didn't mind being Bill's bagman—or his muscle—for he knew that it served a valuable purpose. Just as long as Bill understood that Jason's ambitions went further.

He got off the freeway at the next exit and took surface streets to the courthouse. He thought about Paige McAlister. Maybe later today he'd meet her for coffee near the college. He considered calling her first but decided against it. Better to just show up and see what happens. His last few attempts at setting something up had fallen flat and Jason had been reconsidering his approach.

He wasn't a very subtle guy to begin with, and despite his good looks he wasn't the smoothest dude walking around. The thing is, Jason had always gone for a lower class of woman— easy prey, you might say—and Paige intimidated him. She was intelligent and accomplished, and Jason always felt a little dumb when he was around her. Okay, a *lot* dumb. And that pissed him off. It threw him off his game, made him feel unsure of himself.

Lunch after church on Sunday had gone well enough, but Bruce and Bill were there to smooth the way. Jason wasn't sure how it would have gone over if they hadn't been. He just couldn't get a handle on Paige and he was starting to obsess over it. He knew he would eventually figure it out and get what he wanted. He always did.

And if Paige didn't come around?

Well, that just wasn't an option. Failure was never an option.

Jason had learned that the hard way at the hands of an abusive father who had never gotten over his own shortcomings and who carried himself like a big man, when he was really just a coward and a fool, one who took his angst out on those least able to defend themselves. Jason's father was a straight-up asshole, that's a fact, but he taught his son some valuable lessons—like how to take a punch, for instance. His father was dead now and Jason rarely thought about the man, which was just as well, because when he did his anger burned like a flare gun and it triggered feelings inside him that were impossible to reconcile, feelings that could rightfully be termed pure evil.

Jason had confided in Bill McAlister about those feelings, told him of the rage boiling just below the surface, of the shame and despair he felt when he looked in the mirror and saw his father looking back. Bill counseled Jason and he never judged, never made him feel like anything less than the man he was. He showed Jason the power of prayer and how to use it to channel all that bad energy and turn it into something good, something useful. It never once occurred to Jason Stafford that Bill McAlister might have been using him.

He pulled his BMW into the courthouse parking lot. The rain had eased to a light drizzle, the sky the color of slate, and Jason hoped it would clear by the time his shift started. He liked working the swing shift but he didn't like working it in the rain. He checked his watch and did a quick calculation, laying out his stops in his mind and allocating the time required for each one. He figured he should have plenty of time to get his business done and go see Paige before the start of his shift. Jason liked to keep things orderly, to run his program tight. Things just worked better that way. The more analytical he kept things the less apt he was to get emotional, and thus lose control.

Control was key. Lose it, and things go to shit fast.

Jason saw Ricardo getting out of his car and he hustled over there to talk to the detective. He'd heard that the Riverside County district attorney was making a big push to take back the investigation into the murder of Richard Lawson and Susan McAlister. That was no good. They needed the investigation to stay right where it was, in the hands of the Orange County Sheriff's Department, and more importantly, Ricardo Salazar.

Jason wasn't overly concerned about it, knowing full well that Bill McAlister was on it, the man at the top of his game. Bill's influence ran deep, and he had his hands on a lot of levers. But even though their bases were covered, Jason had learned long ago not to take anything for granted; if you didn't see the whole playing field, you were likely to get blindsided. He wasn't going to let that happen. Not now, not ever.

JASON LEFT the courthouse a short time later and headed to his next stop. Driving to the freeway he passed by the Catholic church located a few blocks from the courthouse. He'd been keeping an eye on that church for the last few months. A priest there had been making a lot of noise lately about the treatment of illegals crossing the border, and the purported abuses they endured at the hands of the smugglers. Jason didn't think anything would come of it. After all, there were countless activists and organizations and media outlets going on non-stop these days about the plight of the illegals, all of them calling for amnesty, and the situation remained a stalemate. But still, you have to remain vigilant.

That was one area of exposure Jason didn't understand. Sure, the operation down in Mexico brought in a lot of money, but compared to the risk it seemed like a foolish endeavor. It was strictly Bill McAlister's deal and Jason often wondered how much of it Bruce knew. The way he figured it, Bruce had to know and he simply chose to look the other way. Willful ignorance. Jason had the feeling that Bruce had been operating that way for a long time.

Bill had a separate crew that handled the operation down in Mexico, under the guise of missionaries doing the Lord's work. Jason's job was to keep everyone in line, and to shore up their defenses whenever a risk was detected. The new church was being heavily funded by the proceeds from Mexico, and Jason hoped that once it was built, Bill McAlister would come to his senses and scrap the whole thing.

A delivery van blocked the street just past the church and Jason had to wait a few minutes until it moved. He glanced in the rearview mirror and something caught his eye. He turned in the seat and looked through the back window, saw a familiar Chevy pickup turn into the church parking lot. It looked like the same truck that old man who was friends with Jake Donahue drove. Jason was about to back up for a better look when a car pulled up behind him. Frustrated, he tapped impatiently on the steering wheel while waiting for the van to clear.

The delivery van finally lumbered out of the way and Jason accelerated up the street, turned right at the next corner and made his way back around to the church. He parked at the curb where he had a clear view of the rear of the pickup, and he closed his eyes and read the plate numbers silently, matching them up with what he remembered from the night he cuffed Hector Santiago on Jake Donahue's front porch. Outside of his steely nerve and stomach for violence, Jason Stafford's powerful memory was his most valuable asset.

Once he was convinced it was the same truck, Jason knew he had a situation on his hands. He watched the church, saw no one moving about, the parking lot empty save for the old man's truck. He checked the time. He couldn't afford to sit on the church, not unless he blew off his meeting in Corona Del Mar, and he knew that wouldn't do. Take care of the money first, Bill McAlister always told him, just like coach Holmes used to drill into their heads to take care of the football.

The decision made, Jason pulled away from the curb and went on his way. Later, if he could fit it in, he'd come back here and poke around, see if he could find out what Hector Santiago was up to.

He merged onto the 5 Freeway south and gassed the BMW, his thoughts turning to Paige McAlister. If he hustled, he'd have time to stop by the Chapman Coffee House. The thought both thrilled and unnerved him. Get ahold of yourself, he thought spitefully. She's just a challenge, that's all. And Jason had never shied away from a challenge, not since the days when his dirtbag father used to knock the hell out of him for sport.

Chapter 24

Jake drove past Chapman University and turned right at Walnut. He drove slowly, found an empty spot at the curb on the opposite side and U-turned into it. He had a clear view of the coffeehouse, and the intersection Paige McAlister would cross if she came this way.

Water fell from a tree overhead, tapping on the Jeep in a hypnotic pattern. It had rained all morning; heavy, wind-blown rain that swelled the creek behind Jake's house and whipped the trees into a frenzy. Jake had taken his morning coffee out on the front porch, sitting in a comfortable chair under the deep eave, just watching the rain come down. It was one of his favorite things to do. That was one drawback to living in Southern California; it didn't rain much, and when it did, it didn't last very long. If Jake decided to stay, it was something he'd have to get used to.

Watching the rain that morning, Jake considered what he'd heard from Hector the night before. The idea of Bruce McAlister fronting an illegal alien smuggling operation seemed too fantastic to be true. He didn't particularly care if it was true or not, it bothered him only because it bothered Hector. And because it bothered Hector, Jake felt there was legitimate cause for concern.

He checked the time, figured he had maybe twenty minutes before Paige arrived at the coffeehouse. He almost didn't come today, blaming it on the rain. But Danny Shaffer had called and he told Jake some things, and now there was an urgency to all of this. Jake knew that he had to see Paige McAlister *today*, rain or not.

Danny was upset when he called but he wouldn't say why. Jake suspected that he was drunk too, and for that reason he'd made up an excuse when Danny said he wanted to meet for lunch. He felt bad lying, but he couldn't deal with a repeat of the Rail Bar scene. When Jake clicked off the line there was an uneasy feeling in his stomach, spurred by an irrational fear for Danny Shaffer's well-being.

On his way to the coffeehouse, Jake had rehearsed some lines in anticipation of meeting Paige, but everything he came up with felt awkward, or somehow disingenuous. While he knew that he had no ulterior motives in wanting to meet Paige, Jake couldn't say exactly why he felt compelled to do so. The best he came up with was the sense of a puzzle piece being fitted into the picture of his reawakening, his reemergence, as it were, into a life he'd rejected long ago.

The Jeep got stuffy and Jake rolled down the front windows to let the breeze in. The rain had dropped the temperature but the humidity was up, and Jake knew that once the sun came out it would be unbearable.

PAIGE McALISTER got a coffee and a scone and took a seat out on the patio. She felt remarkably at ease, a welcome change from the seemingly endless turmoil since her mother's death—the night sweats and mid-day panic attacks, the difficulty concentrating, the horrifying recurring vision of her mother's last moments. It had been a difficult time and Paige was under no illusions that she'd gotten over the hump emotionally, but when the good days came, she was determined to enjoy them.

She watched the clouds and let her mind wander. Sunlight peeked through in the west, painting the gray-black sky with splashes of golden light. It was a wondrous sight and it filled Paige with the hope of better days ahead. Hope. It was important to always have hope. Without it, you set yourself adrift. Her father had taught her that and Paige truly believed it.

Granted, her faith had never been tested in any meaningful way, but if the last couple of months were any indication, Paige's spirit was strong.

Something caught her eye and she turned to look. She saw a black Jeep parked a short distance down Walnut Street, a man sitting in the driver's seat. Despite a glare coming off the windshield, Paige recognized him; it was the same man she saw on campus the previous week. She turned slightly in her chair, surreptitiously watching the man. Her heart began to race, not with fear, but with a heightened sense of awareness. The man seemed to be watching her, and the longer it went on, the more curious Paige became.

The man exited the Jeep and walked toward the coffee-house. Paige had the distinct thought that she should get up and leave. But she ignored the thought, something deep in her mind telling her it would be all right. She turned to watch the clouds, sipping her coffee, a feeling of peace enveloping her.

JASON STAFFORD sat in his car parked across the street from the Chapman Coffee House, listening to Ricardo drone on about some point Jason had tuned out five minutes ago. He saw Paige at the patio and he was anxious to get over there, try out his new approach.

It had come to him earlier in the day, what he was doing wrong in his efforts to woo Bruce's daughter. He was being too wishy-washy, too soft, too *indecisive*. That wasn't what he was about, and acting that way was like wearing an ill-fitting suit—it gave off an entirely wrong impression, one that a woman like Paige McAlister would never find attractive. Jason needed to be himself, be assertive, show Paige the kind of man he truly was.

Ricardo went on, and Jason realized that he'd stopped caring a long time ago about what his former mentor had to say. Watching Paige, Jason felt his heart do a little dance of anticipation. Damn, she was a fine woman. It came to him all at once; he couldn't lose this one. No way in hell was he letting Paige McAlister get away.

Jason was about to cut Ricardo off when he noticed a man walking on Walnut Street. He stared intently, not believing what he saw. It was Jake Donahue and he was going inside the coffeehouse. Jason told Ricardo he had to go and he ended the call. He leaned forward, arms on the steering wheel. What the hell was this about?

Jake entered the patio and he took a seat at the table next to Paige's. All other thoughts left Jason's mind as he watched the scene unfold. A flash of jealousy hit him, and he fought the urge to bolt across the street and confront the situation head-on. Irrational emotion had always been Jason's undoing, and he breathed deep, forcing himself to think and not react. He knew this couldn't be just a random, innocent occurrence. Not with Bruce's fixation on Donahue and the steps he'd taken to keep tabs on the man. Something was clearly going on, and it was Jason's job to find out what it was.

JAKE TOOK his cup of coffee outside to the patio, sat at a table near Paige. His heart jackhammered and coffee was probably the last thing he needed, but he sipped it anyway, trying not to appear conspicuous. He considered different approaches, some way to initiate contact, but his thoughts were scattershot and clouded by an odd emotional energy—nerves mixed with anticipation, and the sense of something bigger at play.

Paige eased her purse off the back of the chair and set it at her side. She didn't sense a threat from the man, but knowing her Springfield 9mm was in easy reach certainly evened the odds if he meant her harm. He was turned sideways, and she studied his features. He was a big man, a couple of inches over six foot at least, and he had a strong build. He was dressed in jeans and a flannel shirt rolled to his forearms and well-worn hiking boots. He looked like he should be chopping wood at a mountain cabin.

The man sipped his coffee in a way that said he didn't want a cup of coffee just then, and Paige found herself intrigued by his intentions. He didn't give off a predatory aura, and she was certain this was no pickup attempt. The man glanced once at Paige. He had a nice face, tanned with a strong chin, and sandy brown hair cut above his ears, a little gray showing in the curls. He gave a crooked smile and quickly looked away.

"I saw you the other day," Paige said, blurting it out on impulse.

The man said nothing. He looked nervous.

"Should I be concerned about that?" she said.

The man gave his crooked smile again. It was a nice smile, endearing. He took in a breath, and then spoke.

"I knew your father." He smiled again, and Paige sensed his awkwardness. "Your mother too. I'm very sorry about what happened."

Paige had been approached before by random strangers expressing their condolences over her mother's passing, and each time it was unsettling. But this was different.

"Thank you," Paige said. "What's your name?"

"Jake Donahue."

He extended his hand and Paige accepted. His was calloused and rough, hers soft, with long fingers and well-manicured nails. She held Jake's hand for a moment, looked into his eyes, and something passed between them. All at once Jake felt calm, settled, and he breathed an inner sigh of relief, knowing that he'd made the right decision coming here today.

A moment of silence ensued as Paige released Jake's hand and stared at his face, a look of curiosity coming over her. Rain had started to fall, dripping off the patio awning onto the sidewalk a few feet away. Traffic was light on Glassell, the occasional sloshing of car tires blending with the sound of the wind swaying nearby trees.

"I didn't know I was so interesting," Jake said, breaking Paige's stare. She smiled and let out a small laugh.

"I'm sorry. That's rude of me."

"You're fine. I'm the one who barged in on your afternoon, remember?"

"That you did, Jake Donahue."

It was Jake who did the staring now. He saw Susan in Paige's eyes, in the high cheekbones and defined chin, the perfectly shaped button nose that Jake used to tease Susan about when they were kids. There was something else too. Looking into Paige's eyes, Jake had the sudden and distinct impression he was looking at himself. What he didn't see was any trace of Bruce McAlister.

That's when Danny Shaffer's phone call from earlier that morning came back to him, and what Danny had said about Susan confiding in Danny not long before she died. It was hard to follow along, Danny was so upset and talking fast, slurring at times, but the gist of it was that Susan had said that Bruce might not be Paige's father.

Jake asked for an explanation but Danny got sidetracked and started talking about the time he coldcocked Jason Stafford in the gym, and wasn't that a goddamn hoot, and the more Jake tried to get him to focus on the other thing the more Danny rambled incoherently. Finally, Jake just gave up on the call.

Danny Shaffer's call brought to mind Jake's own secrets, the things he'd been carrying for years, things only Hector Santiago knew, and Susan McAlister, but she was dead now and Jake would never get the chance to reconcile with her. At the heart of it he supposed that was why he was sitting here now, what it was that drove him forward, through the rain, through his own self-doubt and emotional discomfort.

"Hey, are you there, Jake?"

Paige's words startled him, and Jake wondered how long he'd spaced out.

"Sorry," he said, "I got lost there for a moment."

"You knew my parents?"

"We went to high school together. Your father and I played football. I grew up with your mom, had a crush on her in third grade."

Jake smiled awkwardly at the memory. Paige seemed to study him before her eyes lit with recognition. She laughed. It was a good laugh. An honest laugh.

"So, you're the one," she said.

"The one what?"

"The one who got away." Paige thought for a moment. "How was Mom put it? She used to call you the road not taken."

"She did?"

"More than a few times. I used to wonder about this mysterious boy she knew in high school, the one who stole her heart. And now I know."

Paige smiled again and sipped her drink. Jake's head swam with thoughts, his heart filled with emotion. Danny's call came to him again, along with a nagging thought that had been in Jake's mind all morning. He blurted out a question.

"When were you born, Paige?"

She seemed surprised by the question. "You don't know?" she said. "I thought you were friends with my parents."

"I was, but I lost touch with them when I joined the military, not long after we graduated."

"For how long? I mean, how long were you out of touch?"

"Too long," Jake said.

Paige looked at Jake as if contemplating what he meant. And then she said, "I was born in nineteen eighty-five. March twenty-first."

"And you have no siblings?"

"Sadly, no. My parents tried to have more children, but they were unable."

JASON GREW impatient watching the scene unfold across the street. Bruce called and Jason hesitated with the phone in his hand. He was about to answer when he thought better of it, and he set the phone aside and checked the time. His shift was scheduled to start soon, and even though he could be late he decided against it. His work for the McAlisters had been interfering with his cop work far too much lately, and if he wasn't careful, someone would start noticing.

The wheels turned in Jason's mind. Before he pulled the plug, he wanted to go over there and make his presence known, if for no other reason than to set the ground rules, make Donahue understand clearly where he stood. Scanning the street, he saw Jake's Jeep parked on Walnut Street. An idea came to him.

"Time to fix your wagon, Jake Donahue," Jason said out loud, as he picked up his cell phone and made a call.

JAKE GAVE Paige a snapshot history of his high school years and his relationship with her father and mother. There was so much that he wanted to tell her but he couldn't pull it all together, and he wasn't sure if he was ready for that anyway. Paige listened with genuine interest, the two of them settling into a comfortable rapport more indicative of lifelong friends rather than complete strangers.

Jake steered clear of talk of Susan's death. There would be time for that later, he was sure of it. He knew there would be more talks with Paige McAlister, more time to peel away the years, more time to heal that part of himself that he'd allowed to atrophy through neglect and cowardice. For now, he kept the conversation light, his intuition telling him that Paige needed an afternoon of happy reminiscence in what was surely a difficult time for her.

Sunshine broke through the clouds, bathing the coffeehouse patio in warm light. The rain had stopped and the breeze had settled, a sense of calm following the stormy weather. It was turning out to be a fine afternoon, and Jake found himself thinking that his meeting with Paige had gone so much better than he'd anticipated, reminding him once again that most things he worried about never came to pass.

The good feeling was stopped cold when Jake saw a man crossing the street at Glassell. The man walked with purpose, with coiled intensity, and Jake's heart raced. It was Jason Stafford crossing the street, and he was headed straight for the coffeehouse.

Chapter 25

Amy Watson stopped to eat lunch in Minden, Nevada. She'd gotten a late start and wasn't sure if she'd make it to Orange County today. She didn't like to drive at night, and she began to consider stopping points. Maybe she could make it to Bishop before dark.

It had taken Amy a long time to leave Truckee, her indecision acting like an anchor, her anxiety clouding her thinking. It took her nearly an hour just to decide which route she'd take. She finally settled on Highway 395, figuring the slower pace on the mostly two-lane road would better suit her mood.

Sitting in the roadside café, Amy fingered a well-worn piece of paper. She'd paid two hundred dollars to a private investigator for the information on the paper, and no matter how hard she tried, she couldn't get over her guilt about that. It held the address of Jake Donahue's house in Orange County. It was the house he'd inherited from his father.

Amy knew very little about Ed Donahue. She knew that he was a car salesman and that he had some money. She knew that he was a gambler. More than anything, she knew that Jake had a complicated relationship with the man. But beyond that, she knew nothing, for Jake was not one to talk about the past, and he kept the details of his family life and his youth carefully guarded.

Try as she might, Amy could never break through the wall that Jake had built around himself. Fortress was more like it, for it was an impenetrable barrier that stood in the way of all who endeavored to reach Jake's heart. Amy was always perplexed by Jake's reluctance to open up, for he was a deeply caring man capable of genuine intimacy, and he was fun-loving too, with a subtle yet wicked sense of humor. But step near those walled off parts of his soul and alarm bells went off, resulting in a full emotional shutdown that could take days to lift. Amy Watson loved Jake Donahue, there was no question about that. The fact that she couldn't reach the whole of him troubled her deeply.

They had met in February of 2013 at Squaw Valley, where Amy was a ski patroller and Jake had recently hired on as a snow cat operator. Jake's shift would start as Amy's was ending, and for the first month he was there she only saw him in passing.

Amy was immediately smitten by Jake's rugged good looks—he was not pretty boy handsome in the way most women go for, but Amy had never been interested in that type of man anyway—and she was drawn to the quiet, determined way he went about his business. Whenever Jake was near, Amy felt an attraction that was undeniable. She asked around but no one seemed to know anything about the new snow cat operator. Jake seemed oblivious to female attention, and Amy's initial attempts to break the ice went nowhere. She finally got a chance to meet him when he came into the Truckee restaurant where Amy waitressed part-time. It went nothing like the various scenarios she'd imagined.

It had been a tough day for Amy. In the afternoon, a skier caught an edge dropping into the Palisades and crashed into the rocks. It took three patrollers to get the guy down. He was airlifted to Reno, his injuries too extensive to treat locally. Despite having been a ski patroller for five years and witnessing just about every scenario imaginable, Amy was deeply rattled by the incident; the injured skier looked so much like her younger brother, they could have been twins. Tim Watson committed suicide in 2004, and Amy had never reconciled the loss. Seeing the injured skier who looked just like Tim brought it all back, and even though she was able to put her emotions aside and act with the detached, professional focus that came from years of experience, when it was over she fell apart.

Amy left the mountain early that day and she was unsure about going to her second job that night. But she went anyway, thinking it would be better than sitting home all night brooding over the past. The work helped to keep her mind off things, the pleasant conversation with her regular customers a salve for her hurt. Jake came in for a late dinner near the end of Amy's shift. At first, he paid no attention to her, but after a while he introduced himself and asked Amy how she was feeling after what had happened on the mountain. Apparently, he'd heard about it from another snow cat operator.

Amy was flattered that this man she didn't know would care about how she was doing. Sure, they worked together, sort of, but that didn't amount to much. That he asked indicated to Amy that Jake Donahue was a good person, something she'd intuitively felt from the moment she first saw him. When she told Jake that she was okay, and gave him a brief rundown on what had happened, she noticed that he listened with genuine interest, waiting for her to finish speaking before asking questions or voicing his thoughts. That was a refreshing change from the caliber of men Amy had been dating recently. She'd had so many negative experiences that she'd come to believe her picker was broken. That's what her therapist called it, her picker. In short, Amy Watson seemed to have a knack for picking bad apples.

But all that changed when she met Jake Donahue. Or so she thought. Time would eventually prove otherwise, but *that* night was magical. Amy stayed on after her shift ended and had coffee with Jake at his table. And then they went to Rusty's and had a few beers and shot some stick. When Amy drove home late that night, she truly believed she was on the cusp of something wonderful, and she harbored no doubts about Jake Donahue.

Sitting in the café in Minden, holding onto the piece of paper with Jake's address, the memories of that first night came back like a bitter aftertaste. Amy and Jake had indeed enjoyed what was at times a wondrous and thrilling relationship. They made it nine months before the cracks started to show, and by their one-year anniversary the dam had broken. And then one day, seemingly out of the blue, Jake said he was moving south. Amy knew it had something to do with his father's passing, at least on the surface. But like a lake frozen over in winter, what's visible on the surface belies the true nature of things.

Amy always felt that Jake just needed time to work through his issues, and she desperately hoped he would change his mind and stay in Truckee to do it. She believed in her heart that they belonged together. She would end up bitterly disappointed in his decision to leave.

After living in a fog for a couple of weeks, Amy decided to act. Although her phone calls to Jake had not turned out as planned, she took comfort in the fact that he had not changed his number. Undeterred by Jake's tepid response, Amy hired the private investigator. It always burned her that she didn't know where Jake lived. She felt she deserved better than that. But once she had the information, Amy froze with indecision, and it took her a lot of soul searching to muster up the courage needed to travel to Orange County.

The waitress came by and refilled Amy's coffee. It was getting late, and once again Amy worried about the time and driving at night. She stared at her cell phone, debated calling Jake. She fought against her sense of fair play, knowing that if she told him she was coming, the information would not be received well. She finally relented and dialed the number, feeling relief when the call went to voicemail after several rings. Her conscience clear, Amy got into her car and resumed her trip south.

Chapter 26

Jason Stafford moved quickly, crossing against the light at Glassell. A car blared its horn and Stafford stood in the middle of the street, holding up traffic as he stared down the driver. Then he continued his walk to the coffeehouse.

When the car horn went off, Paige looked in the direction of the street. Jake saw something cross her face, some undetermined emotion, and his nerves tensed as he waited for Stafford to appear.

He came into the patio then, pulled up a chair without a word and sat. The chair was reversed and Stafford leaned forward, his muscled forearms extended across the back of the chair. Jake felt aggression come off the man.

"Jason, what are you doing here?" There was a catch in Paige's voice, a note of apprehension that made Jake feel immediately protective.

"I was in the area and thought I'd stop by and see you."

"But you didn't call first," she said matter-of-factly.

Stafford's jaw tightened. "How's it shakin', Jake?" he said, ignoring Paige.

Jake was about to speak when his cell phone rang. The phone was face down on the table and he tilted it slightly to see who it was. The phone continued to ring.

"You gonna answer that?" Jason said. "Might be a friend of yours."

Jake muted the phone, sending Amy Watson's call to voicemail.

"Speaking of friends, I saw one of yours today."

Stafford stared at Jake. Paige shifted uncomfortably in her chair, and Jake wondered about the relationship between the two.

"Who?" Jake said, meeting Stafford's eyes with a steady gaze. He was determined to hold firm, to give up nothing, having learned over the years that it was the only way to deal with guys like Jason Stafford.

"Danny Shaffer. Remember him?"

"Sure, I remember Danny."

"Did you know he's crippled?"

"I heard about that," Jake said, resenting Stafford's disrespectful tone. He wondered if Paige knew about that part of her father's life. "Didn't he knock you out in high school?"

Stafford's posture stiffened, his jaw working like he was crushing marbles back there. Then he smiled, a joyless smile on par with those unblinking eyes.

"Something like that. Kid stuff. Right, Jake?"

"Sure, whatever you say."

"Save it for later," Paige said tersely, looking directly at Stafford. "I asked you a question, Jason."

"Was that a question?" he said lamely, seeming to shrink at her words.

"A question, a statement, take your pick. The point remains, you didn't call."

"I...uh...didn't know I had to."

"It's common courtesy. I'm sure you would expect the same in return."

Jake felt a swell of pride at the way Paige put Stafford in his place. She was a strong woman, unafraid to speak her mind. It was strange seeing Stafford react so meekly, and Jake wondered again about his relationship with Paige. Did he have a romantic interest in her? Is that why he was here now, attempting to assert himself in Jake's presence?

And then Jake thought about Danny Shaffer's phone call, the way he rambled on about the time he'd coldcocked Jason Stafford in the gym. It made sense now why he was talking about that. Was Stafford leaning on Danny too?

"Isn't that your Jeep parked down the street there?" Stafford said.

"What?" Jake said.

"The one they're hooking up," Stafford replied, a smirk crossing his face.

Jake turned and looked down Walnut, saw a motorcycle cop and a tow truck at his Jeep.

"That's your Jeep all right. I noticed your tags were expired. I guess you haven't had a chance to fix that since you moved from Truckee."

Jake stared at Stafford. No one in Orange County, outside of Hector and Lucas, knew he had been living in Truckee. He cursed himself for not renewing his registration; he'd been meaning to get to it but got sidetracked with the move. It was unlike Jake to forget such a thing, and now he would pay for it.

"Looks like they're impounding your rig."

"What did you do, Jason?" Paige said, her tone accusatory.

"I didn't do a damn thing," Stafford shot back. He nodded in Jake's direction. "Better go take care of that."

Jake stood to leave.

"Is there anything I can do to help?" Paige said, her face worried.

"No, I'll handle it," Jake replied. "It was good to meet you, Paige. Maybe we can do it again."

She glanced at Jason as she pulled a business card from her purse. "Call me whenever you like," she said, smiling warmly and handing over the card. Jake pocketed it and left the coffee-house.

Chapter 27

Jake turned off the canyon road and made his way home. Jason Stafford had righteously burned him, no doubt about it. The motorcycle cop had just finished writing a citation and the tow truck was pulling away with the Jeep when Jake got there. He tried to reason with the cop but it was no use; the guy was polite, but it was obvious he had no interest in letting Jake slide. Standing there staring at the cop, Jake had the sense that he'd seen him before.

When it was over, he looked up the address of the impound yard on his phone. It was two miles away, and he decided to walk there in hopes of getting the Jeep back. He could have gone back to the coffeehouse and asked Paige for a ride, but that would have meant another encounter with Stafford, and he didn't want to put her through that.

The female clerk working the front desk at the impound yard said the vehicle would be held for thirty days. Jake was incredulous. He showed her the citation for the expired vehicle registration and promised that he'd go to the DMV first thing tomorrow and take care of it. The Jeep was literally just impounded, couldn't she cut him some slack? The clerk expressed sympathy for Jake's plight, but rules were rules. The vehicle would not be released for thirty days.

Jake looked at the clerk, wondered if she was in on Stafford's scam. After a moment of silence, he forced a smile and politely asked about rental car locations nearby. She said there was one on Katella Avenue, about a mile away. He thanked her and left.

He rented a late-model Mustang. He would have gotten a Jeep but they only had Japanese sedans, a couple of oversized SUVs, and the Mustang. Jake opted for something with a little muscle behind it.

Inside his house, Jake opened all the windows. The rain had sweetened the canyon air and the coming of evening had cooled the temperature. He called Lucas Summerfield on the landline. The call went to voicemail and Jake left a brief message about the Jeep, hoping the attorney could pull some strings and resolve the matter quickly.

He opened the refrigerator to survey dinner options, grabbed a beer instead and took it to the sun deck. An owl hooted from high in a eucalyptus tree and Jake listened as he drank deeply from the bottle. Then he removed Paige McAlister's business card from his shirt pocket and studied it, feeling pride at the fact she was an attorney. He recounted their meeting at the coffeehouse. Jake felt an undeniable connection to Paige and it confounded him. There was no reason he should feel so strongly about someone he didn't know. Granted, Paige looked like her mother, and even after thirty years the memory of Susan Young—her name before her marriage to Bruce—stirred feelings in him. Maybe that was it. Maybe Jake was transferring his long-ago feelings for Susan onto her daughter.

But on a certain level he knew that wasn't all of it. There was something else going on, some deep emotional switch that had been flipped upon meeting Paige. He drank some more beer and pondered a question; why has this young lady affected me this way? He got to the end of the bottle with no answer.

He went inside the house and got another beer and his laptop, brought them out to the deck. The machine booted and Jake did a quick search on impound laws in California. He was glad he'd gotten the high-speed Internet, the web pages loading quickly. After a few minutes of sorting through random information he gave up, figuring he'd let Summerfield handle it.

Jake let his mind wander as he sipped his beer. He thought about the cop who wrote him the ticket, and the feeling that he knew the guy or had seen him somewhere before. After a minute, it hit him, where he'd seen the guy. He clicked on a webpage he'd bookmarked and played Bruce's press conference from last week. He stopped the video at the point where Bruce and Paige turned to leave, and they were surrounded by security men. He stared at each of the faces on the screen, and saw the cop standing next to Jason Stafford. I'll be damned, he thought with a flutter of nerves, maybe this *is* a conspiracy after all.

He finished his beer, went into the kitchen and dropped the empty bottle into the trash. Standing at the kitchen counter, Jake remembered the phone call from Amy Watson, the one that came through when he was with Paige. Amy was a complication he couldn't come to terms with. He'd hoped for a clean severing of ties. Now that she'd made contact, self-doubt plagued Jake, fueled by his guilt over the way he'd handled things in Truckee.

He briefly considered letting Amy back in. Not in any romantic way, but just as friends, someone she could count on in a bind. Maybe he could invite her down for a visit, mend fences and set them both on the path of forgiveness. He would have to lay out some clear ground rules and make sure that Amy understood it was to be a short visit with no guarantees attached.

But the more Jake thought about it, the more foolish the idea became. It would never fly. Jake would just have to find a way to get Amy to stop calling and torturing herself with futile dreams of a happily ever after.

He took another beer from the fridge and walked outside with it. He'd landed in the middle of a real shit pile, no doubt about it. He started walking, hoping to clear his mind. At the canyon road, he stopped and finished the beer, dropped it into a neighbor's trash bin. He considered going left or right. His empty stomach said to go left, to the Silverado Cafe. He called Hector on the cell to invite him to dinner, but he only got voicemail. Which was probably just as well. Jake wasn't sure he'd be very good company tonight, and it seemed unfair to constantly dump his problems on his old friend.

Chapter 28

Paige McAlister sat at her vanity brushing her hair. She'd removed her makeup, washed her face and brushed her teeth, and now she was ready for bed. A James Lee Burke novel lay on the nightstand, but Paige wasn't sure if she was up for some reading.

She was tired after her long day, and the afternoon encounter at the Chapman Coffee House weighed heavily on her mind. The part involving Jake Donahue made her smile. That was a nice surprise. She looked at a photograph of her mother taped to the corner of the vanity mirror. Susan was smiling, the bright light of life in her eyes. The picture was ten years old and Paige kept it there as a reminder of better times. She stared at the photo and conjured scenarios of how it might have been between Jake and her mother, back when they were young and carefree, the innocence of youth on their side.

And then thoughts of Jason Stafford crept into the picture and anger took hold.

Paige didn't like feeling angry; it was not an emotion she was familiar with. She'd always had an even temperament, not given over to mood swings or rampant emotion. But Jason pushed her buttons and made her feel so uncomfortable at times that she doubted her own self-control. When he barged in on her afternoon, getting aggressive with Jake, pulling that stunt with Jake's car, she knew beyond a doubt that there would never be anything between them. Not that she'd ever harbored any doubts in the first place.

And speaking of the incident with Jake's car, Paige was certain that Jason was responsible. Which only reinforced her feelings that much more; how could she ever love a man like that? A man capable of such pettiness. The fact that she even suspected him spoke volumes.

After Jake left to deal with his car, Jason tried to shift gears and act as if nothing had happened. He seemed oblivious to Paige's discomfort, her one-word answers and lack of interaction, her obvious disdain for his mere presence. He was a blockhead of the first order. When it became clear that Jason was incapable of grasping just how irritated Paige was, she simply got up and left. She didn't like to be rude—not even in the heat of legal battle would she act that way, when opposing counsel would try every trick in the book to get under her skin—but Jason was a different situation altogether. Paige had no qualms about stepping on his feelings.

Jason acted nonchalant about it, but Paige could tell he was seething inside, and that frightened her. For the first time, standing there looking at him as she collected her things and prepared to leave, Paige saw something in his eyes that scared her. She always knew there was something a little off about Jason Stafford, but she'd never *felt* it.

She picked up her cell phone, considered calling her father. It would be a difficult subject to bring up. But she had to get the message through to Jason. She hit speed dial.

"Hey, Dad, how are you," she said when Bruce answered.

"I'm good, honey. What's up?"

"I'm just getting ready for bed."

"A little early, isn't it?"

"I have court in the morning. You know how I get when I'm tired."

Bruce laughed. "That I do."

"I need your help with something. It involves Jason Stafford."

"What about Jason?"

150

"I know that you and grandpa Bill have been promoting him lately, and I would like you to stop."

"What do you mean, promoting?"

"Maybe that's the wrong word. It just seems like you two have been pushing the idea of a romance between Jason and me. I wanted you to know that I'm not interested in a relationship with him."

"I wasn't aware that we were pushing him on you. Why do you think that?"

Really, Dad? Paige thought, her frustration building.

"So you're denying that you have been trying to get me and Jason together?"

"Paige, honey, how can I deny involvement in something I know nothing about?"

"Dad, please."

"Please what?"

Paige took a deep breath.

"Okay, let's try it this way. What if I told you that Jason was becoming a nuisance? That he was harassing me? Would that register with you?"

"I have a hard time believing he would do such a thing."

Her father's tone of voice was irritating. It wasn't exactly condescending, but it was close. He was minimizing her feelings and playing dumb about it, and that offended her. Paige revered her father, but right now he was pissing her off. It was time to put an end to it.

"I'm getting really frustrated, so I'm just going to cut right to it. He scares me, Dad. Today when I was having coffee with Jake Donahue, Jason showed up uninvited. He acted belligerent with Jake and he didn't seem to care how I felt about it. I want something done about him."

"You had coffee with Jake Donahue today?"

"Yes, I did."

"When?"

"After my lecture at Chapman. Dad, did you even hear what I just said?"

"Of course I did."

"Do you have anything to say about it?"

"I'll talk to Jason, find out his side of it."

"Do you believe me? That he scares me?"

"If you say so, then I believe you."

Paige bit her tongue. "Thank you," she said, choosing the high road.

"What did you and Jake talk about?"

"What difference does it make what we talked about? I was telling you about Jason and how he makes me feel. *That's* the point behind this phone call."

"Listen to me, Paige. I want you to use caution with Jake, and be careful what you say to him."

"Why? Isn't he a friend of yours?"

"I haven't seen Jake Donahue for a very long time. I don't think he's someone you should be involved with."

"Why?"

"I have my reasons. They're complicated and I don't want to get into it right now, but I would appreciate it if you didn't see him anymore."

Paige didn't understand her father's reaction at all. She had been looking forward to telling him about meeting Jake. She regretted mentioning it in the context she did, but regardless, why did it elicit such a reaction? It was almost as if he wanted Paige to feel guilty about seeing Jake. It made no sense.

She decided to end the call. The last thing she wanted was an argument with her father before she went to sleep. His attitude about Jake troubled her, as did his evasiveness regarding her problems with Jason. She needed time to sort it out.

"I'm going to hang up now, Dad. I need my rest and this conversation isn't doing either of us any good. I hope you understand. I love you so much. Goodnight."

Paige hung up the phone before her father could respond. She held it in her hand for a moment as she recalled the conversation, her thoughts jumbled. Then she put the phone aside and looked at the photograph of her mother taped to the mirror.

The emotion coming to her now was sadness, and a deep melancholy ache for the pain and disappointment she knew her mother felt in the last years of her life.

"What happened to you, Mom?" Paige said out loud.

She did that sometimes when she was alone, blurting out questions, having small conversations with herself. She wondered if other people did it too.

The photograph didn't answer, and Paige considered how her mom might answer the question if she were still alive and sitting here right now with her daughter. It was a sad thing to think about.

She finished getting ready for bed, and then went through the house and turned off the lights and the air conditioning and opened her bedroom window, preferring fresh air when she slept. She wasn't afraid of intruders; the windows were alarmed and her handgun was within easy reach of the bed. Paige knew that if she ever had children she'd have to change her habits, but for now she took comfort in knowing that someone entering her house uninvited wouldn't get very far.

A call came in on her cell phone. She looked at the caller ID and saw it was Jason Stafford. It was the third call she'd received from him since their afternoon encounter at the coffeehouse. She'd also received four text messages, which she'd ignored along with the calls. This was getting ridiculous, and Paige was determined to put a stop to it. If her father wouldn't make it happen, then she would get a restraining order. That would be an extreme move to make, but something had to be done.

Paige shut her phone off. She had a landline if anyone wanted to reach her. Thankfully, Jason did not have that number. Or at least she thought he didn't. Whatever, it was all going to stop soon anyway.

She picked up her book and started reading, but gave up after a few pages, unable to concentrate. She set the book aside and turned out the light. From the bedroom window, she had a perfect view of Newport Harbor, and she lay on her side and stared at the lights in the distance, trying her best to clear her mind of troubling thoughts. A breeze blew into the room, bringing with it the sound and smell of the ocean, and Paige imagined herself sailing away to a place of peace and tranquility. It was a meditative technique she employed whenever her mind was busy and sleep was elusive, and it usually did the trick. It took a little longer tonight, but soon Paige was drifting off to a deep, dreamless sleep.

Chapter 29

Bruce McAlister pulled up to his father's house in Cowan Heights, the phone conversation with Paige weighing on his mind. The part about Jason Stafford was inconsequential; if she had no romantic interest in Jason, so be it. It was the part about Jake Donahue that troubled him. What the hell was that guy up to now?

The serpentine driveway was lit by Malibu lights, the turnaround at the top affording an unobstructed view of Saddleback, the landmark formed by the two highest peaks in the Santa Ana Mountains. Bruce shut off the engine and stepped out of his Range Rover, taking a moment to soak in the view. It was a beautiful evening, the rain from earlier having washed the sky clean, the moon illuminating clouds hovering over the mountaintop. Bruce thought about Jake sitting alone in his house, down there in the darkness of Silverado Canyon, ensconced in the cobwebbed embrace of his memories. He laughed disdainfully.

Jake could be a royal pain in the ass. Like right now.

Sure, they'd had some great times together, but that was a long time ago, and the truth is, Jake had always gotten under Bruce's skin. When he disappeared after the Mexico trip in '84, Bruce was secretly relieved. And not just because of what went down between them. He needed a break from Jake's judgmental attitude, from the way he continually sucked up to Bruce's father, from the snickering behind Bruce's back that he wouldn't have been half the quarterback he was if not for his star tight end, from the glances Susan gave Jake whenever she thought Bruce wasn't looking, and the way she always stuck up for him at the slightest provocation.

Yeah, there was a lot about Jake that bugged the hell out of Bruce.

He thought about it from time to time, how it might've been if Jake had stayed in Orange County. He knew that Jake's conscience would have eventually gotten the better of him. What he would have done about it is anybody's guess. Luckily, things didn't turn out that way. Still, Bruce never imagined that the guy would stay gone for so long.

It wasn't true, of course, what Bruce had told Jake about knowing whenever he returned to Orange County. Just like it wasn't true about witnessing to Big Ed. Bruce didn't feel bad about lying to Jake. It was just a little innocent gamesmanship. His conscience was clear on that score.

Just like his conscience was clear about what happened in Bahia de Cortez back in 1984. Yes, it was tragic and it was preventable, but life is made up of tragic and preventable events, and when heavy shit goes down you either learn from it and move on, or you let it define you and ultimately destroy you. Bruce chose the former, and he was convinced that he was a better man for it. Besides, the point was moot; Bruce had long ago repented of *that* sin.

He turned and looked at his father's house. It was no small fact that Bruce's own house was a few streets down the hill from here, and try as he might, he could never seem to get out from under his father's shadow. Things would change as soon as the new church was built, Bruce was sure of that.

The first change would be the easiest. Bruce had his eye on a choice lot in Newport Coast, one he was set to make an offer on. Once the groundbreaking took place in Limestone Canyon, Bruce would set about designing a home that would put his father's house to shame. It would truly be a joyous moment when he finally broke free of Bill McAlister's grip and transcended the old man's accomplishments.

But first things first.

Bruce still needed his father's help for the final push down the homestretch. Despite his lifelong contempt for Bill's domineering personality, Bruce knew that he could never have gone it alone. It started with his salvation at the hand of his father's unwavering faith, which led to a spiritual path taken lightly at first, but soon consumed by genuine zealousness. Bruce's journey had truly been amazing, and it had led him to the doorstep of greatness. They were so close now, and Bruce could not afford to let his pride and ego get in the way of success. He loved his father, but more importantly, he needed him to achieve his destiny.

And once he had achieved that success, Bruce wouldn't love his father any less. He just wouldn't take any more of his crap. Like now, being summoned like he was some lackey. Bill had been doing a lot of that lately, calling Bruce at odd hours, telling him to drop everything and come right over. Usually Bill was tipsy, if not outright drunk, whenever he made those calls. Bruce would dutifully respond, and listen as his father ticked off yet another list of tasks deemed critically important.

The drinking didn't necessarily bother Bruce, for he knew it was his father's way of coping with his declining health. And the truth is, the booze took the edge off Bill McAlister's overbearing personality, making him prone to nostalgic reflection that was oftentimes amusing to Bruce.

Bill had a way of glossing over the past, making it seem all *Leave it to Beaver*. Well, Bill McAlister certainly was no Ward Cleaver, and his mom was no June. And as Bruce remembered it, the TV show didn't feature any Cleaver sisters getting all the love and attention while Beaver got a daily ration of shit. His life had been no fifties sitcom, that's for damn sure, no matter how nostalgic his old man wanted to make it.

But all that was in the past now. Fences were mended. His father was reconciled. His mother passed on. And now they were on the cusp of something great.

Bruce took a last look at Saddleback, sighed deeply, and turned for the house.

***

HE KNOCKED on the door and waited. He had a key but preferred not to let himself in. He knocked louder. Finally, he unlocked the door and entered the house. It was dark inside. Bruce called out for his father but got no response. He moved through the downstairs rooms, found them dark and unoccupied. The house looked in order, although the air was stuffy with the heat of the day and the faint smell of discarded food coming from the kitchen. Bruce noticed the windows were closed, and he checked the thermostat, saw that the air conditioning was turned off.

When Bruce's mother died several years ago, Bill let the full-time help go. Since then, he'd grown more reclusive, his demeanor more erratic, and the upkeep of the property seemed to become less important. The house hadn't gone to seed necessarily, but Bruce knew that his dad could use some help running things, maybe even provide a little companionship.

Back in the front room, Bruce looked up the stairs, saw a thin shaft of light coming from the end of the hallway. He walked up the stairs. The rooms were dark, except for his father's study. He approached the door, opened about three inches, no sound coming from the room. For a moment, Bruce had the expectation of finding his father dead inside the room. The moment came and went like a jolt of electrical current. He took in a breath and steadied himself.

"Dad?" he called out softly.

There was no response.

Bruce pushed on the heavy door and entered the room. It was a large room, wood-paneled with bookcases and stout furniture and portraits of biblical scenes hanging on the walls. The desk sat in a far corner, massive and untidy. A floor lamp lit an opposite corner, the rest of the room dark but for the bluish moonlight seeping through the slats of the Cherrywood window blinds.

Bill McAlister sat sleeping in a stuffed leather chair, his feet propped on a footstool, a book in his lap. Bruce moved closer and saw it was the Bible. He also noticed a bottle of High

West whiskey and a half-full rocks glass on the side table next to a reading lamp that was turned off. In that moment, Bill looked insignificant, like a sad caricature of a once great man. Bruce nearly pitied him for it. But he knew it was merely an illusion; his father might be getting old but his influence still ran deep, his indomitable will a force to be reckoned with. He was not a man to be underestimated.

Bill McAlister stirred. Bruce stepped back behind the door to the study and waited for his father to awaken. He heard rustling and the sound of weight shifting on leather, followed by the sound of ice tinkling in glass, his father no doubt freshening his drink.

"Dad, are you in there?" Bruce called out.

"Yes. You may come inside."

Bruce reentered the room. His father told him to sit. Bruce took the matching leather chair next to the one Bill occupied. The liquor was between them, the Bible resting closed on the table. The reading lamp was turned on now, the low-wattage bulb casting shadows across the two men. Bill drank deeply from his glass. He did not offer his son a drink.

Bruce McAlister had not touched a drop of alcohol since the night he drove his Camaro off Interstate 15 and crippled Danny Shaffer.

"How are you, Dad?" Bruce said, making it an honest question, with no hint of sarcasm or judgement. The last thing he wanted tonight was a fight with his father.

"I'm okay," Bill said. "Better than okay, to tell the truth. I'm right as rain, Bruce, and it's only getting better." He finished off his drink and set the glass on the table. "I've been reading some scripture tonight. The Book of Job."

Of course you have, Bruce thought derisively. Sitting in a half-dark room, drinking yourself stupid, reading violent tales of God's wrath.

Bill McAlister loved the Old Testament. Whenever he sermonized—or ranted as Bruce liked to think of it—Bill invariably invoked what he believed to be the true Word of God. He derided the current crop of evangelical preachers and their focus on the New Testament, dumbing down Christianity to a feel good, user-friendly form of self-help—if you believe you can achieve.

Bill had no use for that nonsense. The world was not a place of unicorns and rainbows. It was a cruel and violent place, full of heathens and fakers and non-believers just waiting to drag mankind into a cesspool of filth. There was only one way to fight that kind of evil—the true Word of God. The stakes were too high to allow for anything else.

Bruce knew this all too well. It was the reason he stopped seeking his father's advice when putting together his sermons. He was constantly at odds with Bill over the content and tone of the message, and more importantly, the direction of the Canyon New Life Ministry. He learned how to insert just enough of God's dark side to appease his father, without driving away those who drifted through his door in search of something they didn't even know they were looking for. Once the new church was built, Bruce knew he would finally be free of his father's unyielding shackles.

Rather than indulge him, Bruce chose to stay on point. "You had something you wanted to talk about?" he said, careful not to appear insolent.

Bill stared at his son for a long moment. In the past, he would have admonished Bruce for the perceived slight. But things had changed over the last few years, the balance of power shifted significantly. They both knew it, although Bruce was careful never to openly acknowledge it. He wondered if his father ever admitted it to himself.

"Things are moving along as planned," Bill said. "The final vote is scheduled for next week. While you can never be certain until the ink has dried, I expect we will prevail."

"I wasn't concerned about it," Bruce said.

"Nor was I," Bill replied.

Neither man spoke. Outside, a breeze blew against the trees near the house, distorting the moonlight coming through the window blinds, the effect ethereal. Bruce thought of his deceased wife. He looked at his father and wondered, Are you responsible?

It was a question that came up occasionally in Bruce's mind, one he was incapable of reasoning with. He'd satisfied himself that Richard Lawson was the real target. That's what the police thought, and it made sense. It could have been one of the unsavory characters Lawson was connected to through his political shenanigans, or it could have simply been a jealous husband looking to even the score. Bruce knew all about Lawson's philandering ways. He even knew about Susan's affair with Lawson. He never let on to anyone that he knew, and frankly, he didn't care anyway; he'd long ago moved past the point where Susan could hurt him emotionally. True, there were other ways she could hurt him, but that didn't matter anymore.

The key question, whether Bill McAlister was capable of engineering murder, was one Bruce could not answer. Which was probably answer enough. Regardless of all that, Bruce was content to satisfy himself with the results; a major impediment to his Limestone plans was off the board, and the problem of what to do about his wayward wife was rendered irrelevant. All in one fell swoop. As if intended by the Lord himself. Bruce could hardly be faulted for not asking questions, especially when the answers wouldn't change the outcome anyway.

Back to the business at hand.

"It seems there's not much left to do but wait," Bruce said.

"There's plenty to be done," Bill replied. "A million little details that must be worked out. But you needn't worry about that. It's all being taken care of."

As it should be. Because that's what you do, Dad, you *handle* things. You plan and you scheme, moving your chess pieces so expertly, your stratagem flawless. So be it. This is the way of the world.

"Do you need anything from me?" Bruce said.

"Just keep believing."

"I will, Dad."

As Bruce left the house, he wondered why he was summoned here when they could have just as easily spoken over the phone. But of course, he knew the reason. Bill McAlister needed reassurance that he was still in charge, that he was the master of *his* universe. In service of the Lord, of course. Always in service of the Lord. But the master nonetheless.

Chapter 30

Jake exited the 15 Freeway at Cleghorn Road in the Cajon Pass. He turned left under the freeway and then south onto Cajon Boulevard. He was driving along old Route 66—the Mother Road—although that fact was lost on Jake as he scanned the roadside for Danny Shaffer's Dodge van.

He saw it after a few miles, parked alongside the road below the freeway embankment. He parked the Mustang and turned off the engine, hesitating before exiting the vehicle. Danny had called earlier in the evening and asked Jake to meet him here, said he had some important news but he wouldn't tell it over the phone. Jake's curiosity was just strong enough to override his sense of caution, and his increasing irritation with Danny's erratic ways. The location of their meeting was not lost on Jake.

He stepped from his vehicle and approached the van. The lights were off and all the doors shut. After a moment, Danny wheeled around from the far side of the van.

"Sorry, dude. I had to take a leak."

Jake looked at Danny in the wheelchair and wondered how that worked. He wasn't sure he wanted to know. Then he thought about the van, how it was setup so Danny could drive.

"You want a beer?" Danny said. He wheeled up to the sliding side door and opened it, pulling two beers out of a cooler. He tossed Jake a bottle, not waiting for an answer.

Danny drained his bottle in one long pull, threw the empty into the nearby bushes and pulled another from the cooler. From high above the embankment came the drone of freeway traffic, thousands of cars coming and going, the constant flow of humanity in motion. Like time itself.

"Nice wheels," Danny said, nodding at the Mustang. "Red is a badass color. What happened to your Jeep?"

"It's a long story."

"I got time."

"Let's talk about what I'm doing here instead."

"You gonna drink your beer? If not, give it to me."

Jake opened the beer and took a drink. Danny smiled.

"That's my boy. Just like the old days, eh, Jake?"

"Sure, Danny. Just like the old days."

Danny lit a cigarette. When he got to the filter, he said, "This is where it happened."

"I figured that."

"Hell of a place to lose your legs. Not that I can think of a better one. Funny thing is, I must've driven by this spot a hundred times before it happened. Funny how life works out."

"Life is strange."

"Strange and fucked up."

"I'll drink to that."

Jake sipped his beer. Danny finished his and belched loudly, then he lit another smoke.

"So, why am I here?" Jake said.

Danny smiled. "You're here for the truth."

"The truth about what?"

"About us."

"That makes no sense."

"Why'd you shine me on, Jake?"

"What do you mean?"

"This morning, when I called you. I needed to see you, and you shined me on."

"I'm sorry about that. It wasn't a good time for me."

"Welcome to the club, pal. It's never a good time for me."

Jake looked away, unable to meet Danny's eyes. He had to see this through, but his growing discomfort made it difficult. He decided to approach it straight on.

"Listen, Danny, I'm sorry about this morning. I know that Jason Stafford came to see you today. What was it about?"

"He's an asshole."

"Yes, he is. But why did he come to see you?"

"Bruce is an asshole too," Danny mumbled, staring at the end of his burning cigarette. He looked at Jake. "How did you know Stafford came to see me?"

"Because he told me. I saw him today when I was having coffee with Paige McAlister."

"She's a good kid."

"You know her?"

"A little bit. From church. She came by the shop one time when Susan was there and the three of us went out to lunch. It was nice."

"Stafford has been leaning on me. He does some kind of security work for Bruce. He showed up today at the coffee-house and he mentioned that he'd seen you."

"He came to my house this morning. He threatened me, Jake."

"Why?"

"Because of you."

"Me? What have I done?"

"You came home."

"Why would anyone care about me coming home?"

"He doesn't want his secrets out."

"Bruce?"

"Bingo!"

Danny yelled and sailed his empty bottle onto the road, the pop from the shattering glass sounding like a gunshot. He wheeled around to get a couple more. Jake wondered if Danny knew the truth about Mexico. If he did, he would have heard it from Bruce. But it was hard to picture Bruce telling that story to anyone. He might have confessed it to a clergyman, or maybe to his father, but Jake doubted that he'd ever told it to one of the guys on the squad.

"What secrets are you talking about?"

"Remember the other day, when I told you that Susan used to come by the shop and drink with me?"

"What about it?"

"She used to go on about all kinds of stuff. Mostly about what an asshole Bruce was. But one time she was talking about Paige, and how it went down when she got knocked up."

"And?"

"Bruce denied he was responsible, told everyone that Susan was a slut and that she was getting it on with a couple of dudes from Foothill High School. Remember that running back they had? He was one of them."

Jake stared blankly.

"Come on, you must remember those dudes. We tangled with them down in that dump Bruce took us to after we graduated, Bahia de…what the hell was it?"

"Bahia de Cortez," Jake said.

"That's it. Anyway, those Foothill dudes were there, you remember that? Damn, *that* was a scene." Danny laughed and drank some beer. "So yeah, it was a big soap opera. Happened a couple months after we got home from Mexico. Bruce accused Susan of all kinds of nasty shit. And then he broke it off with her and went on a tear, like a man on a mission."

He killed his beer and started on the next one.

"You would have known about all this if you'd stuck around."

There was a hint of sarcasm in Danny's voice. Jake ignored the comment and pressed on.

"What does any of that have to do with Paige?"

"I'm getting to that. So fast forward five years or so. I'm in this chair, courtesy of our good friend Bruce McAlister, and that prick has had a spiritual awakening on account of what he did to me. He married Susan and all was forgiven. He said he made everything up, about Susan sleeping with other guys and getting pregnant by one of them. He accepted that Paige was his daughter and the three of them had a nice little family."

"That's an interesting story. Tell me why I should care. You're going over ancient history and it's got nothing to do with me."

Danny laughed. "Oh, trust me. It's got everything to do with you."

"Listen, Danny," Jake said wearily. "It's been a long day and I'm tired. I want to go home. Can't you just—"

"What if I told you I know?" Danny said abruptly, cutting Jake off. "Would that keep you here?"

"What do you mean? What is it you know?"

"See, now you're interested."

"Knock it off, man. Just say whatever it is you have to say."

Jake's words came out sharp and Danny stared at him bewildered. Jake felt nervousness rise, anticipation over what Danny was about to reveal. It came to him all at once.

"You know who Paige's father is."

"Yes, I do."

Danny wheeled his chair close and he touched Jake's hand, looked at him with watery eyes, a sheen of alcohol sweat on his unshaven face.

"And now, so do you."

Chapter 31

An hour later, Jake sat at Cook's Corner nursing a Maker's and water. He'd left Danny Shaffer at the Cajon Pass and gone straight home, the drive a blur, the things Danny said clouding Jake's mind and his heart. He couldn't come to terms with it. *He* was Paige McAlister's father.

He repeated it to himself out loud, the words sounding foreign to his ears.

He cursed Danny Shaffer; why couldn't he leave well enough alone? For a moment, Jake tried to convince himself that Danny was wrong, that what he'd said was just a product of his alcoholic delusions. But deep in his heart he knew it was entirely possible that he was Paige's father. But was it true?

If so, it would explain the way Jake had been feeling. The subconscious, almost cosmic connection he felt to Paige. Jake knew about a mother's natural instincts to nurture and protect her offspring. He wondered if a father's paternal instinct was just as strong. From the time he became aware of Bruce and Susan's daughter, Jake felt a pull, some sort of emotional gravitational energy that drew him to Paige. And now Danny had laid this...*thing* on him. Jake knew that his life was irrevocably changed.

If it was true.

Danny wanted to hang out and he tried to get Jake to go with him to the Summit Inn and have some rounds. He seemed oblivious to Jake's feelings, as if he hadn't just laid some heavy news on his friend and Jake might need some time to sort it out. Danny got belligerent about it and then he got emotional, and Jake wondered if he wasn't on the verge of a nervous breakdown. When Jake finally drove away, leaving Danny sitting in his wheelchair by the side of the road, he wondered if he'd ever see him again. He shouldn't have abandoned him like that, but Jake was incapable of dealing with Danny Shaffer any longer.

When Jake got home and turned into his driveway, he nearly rear-ended Amy Watson's Subaru Outback. He stared in disbelief, wondering if this day would ever end.

Amy was out of her car as soon as Jake pulled up, the expression on her face in the Mustang's headlights uncertain. Jake wasn't about to let her off easy.

"What are you doing here?" he said through the open window. He'd left the motor running, the car still in gear. He was ready to bolt.

"Hi, Jake. How are you?"

"How am I? Are you serious?"

"I know this is a surprise and all, but I—"

"A surprise. This is a fucking ambush."

Amy seemed to shrink into her skin and Jake felt a flash of guilt. He fought the feeling, knowing he had every right to be angry.

"I…uh, I thought it would be okay. I tried calling you earlier today to let you know. I'm sorry I didn't leave a message. I just…I thought…" her words trailed off.

"You thought it wouldn't go over very well, that's what you thought. Just be honest about it. How'd you find me, anyway?"

"I paid someone," she mumbled.

"Who? A private detective?"

Amy nodded.

"Terrific. Did he dig up some dirt on me as well, or just my address?"

"Please, Jake, you know I would never do something like that."

"Really, Amy? Do I know that?"

"Please stop. I feel bad enough already."

"You brought it on yourself. Why the hell did you come here in the first place?"

Jake put the car in reverse and backed out of the driveway. He drove too fast down the canyon road. When he passed Cook's Corner he hit the brakes and pulled into the lot. It was after midnight and last round would be called soon. Jake wasn't normally the type to lean on alcohol to solve his problems, but tonight was different. He parked the Mustang next to a piece of crap Chevy and a couple of bikes and went inside.

The place was a ghost town. Jake took a seat down at the end of the bar and ordered a drink. No one approached him and the bartender seemed uninterested in loose chatter. That was fine with Jake. The thoughts in his head were company enough.

Soon his anger ebbed, and feelings of shame over his treatment of Amy took hold. He had no reason to be so hard on her. Hell, just earlier that evening he was entertaining thoughts of letting her back in. But that would have been on *his* terms. What she did tonight was clearly out of bounds. Jake didn't like to be forced into things. He didn't like to be boxed in.

He finished his drink and ordered another.

He put Amy Watson aside and considered Paige McAlister. He still had her business card in his shirt pocket. He pulled it out, turned it in his fingers. He thought of Susan and the one time they'd been together. One time, so damn long ago. It seemed incomprehensible that he could have fathered a child and gone his entire adult life without knowing it. The emotional enormity hit Jake like a weight pressing down on him, building pressure with every agonizing minute that had passed since Danny revealed the truth.

If it was true.

The thought kept coming back to Jake.

Maybe Danny made the whole thing up. Or maybe Susan had lied to Danny just to spite Bruce. Anything was possible, and Jake had no way to know for certain. It's not like he could go to Paige McAlister and ask for a DNA test. That would be crazy. Jake supposed he could completely rock Bruce's world by confronting him with it, making a big noise publicly until Bruce had no choice but to compel Paige to submit to a test to determine who her real father was. But that would be grossly unfair to Paige. No way would Jake ever put her in that position. She had just lost her mother. Jake couldn't take away her father too.

The bartender asked Jake if he wanted another drink. He was about to close for the night so it would have to be a quick one. Jake declined, the mellow warmth of the whiskey numbing his brain sufficiently to calm his anger. He didn't want to be drunk. He still had Amy to deal with. She might be gone when he returned home, but Jake doubted it.

It wasn't fair to leave her like that and Jake knew he had to make it right. Amy was a good person at heart and she'd always treated him with kindness and respect. It wasn't her fault she'd fallen in love with a broken man. Maybe he should have warned her, saved her the heartache. But he didn't warn her. Just like she didn't warn Jake that she was coming. He supposed they were even on that score. He finished his drink, paid off the bartender and walked out to the Mustang.

Chapter 32

Later that night, Jason Stafford gave into his anger.

He'd been seething ever since Paige's rebuke. It burned inside him in a way he hadn't felt for a long time, his tightly wrapped self-control in danger of failing him. He tried reaching her several times but couldn't. And each time he couldn't, each time he pictured Paige ignoring him, he grew more desperate and angry. It took tremendous willpower just to control himself as he patrolled his shift. He was glad that he did, for he could not afford another disciplinary report in his file.

The night was a quiet one, providing little temptation for wrongdoing, nor opportunity to vent the fire burning inside. When Jason left the station at midnight he was ready. He fired up the BMW and went on the prowl.

First, he drove by Jake's house. He saw a Subaru Outback parked in the driveway and figured it for a rental. That was a nice play with the Jeep, a real stroke of genius, and Jason gave himself a pat on the back for it. He considered going up to the door, see if he could stir up a second act with Jake, but decided against it. Tonight, he was looking for something different.

The dome light came on in the Subaru and Jason saw a woman sitting in the driver's seat. What's this? Does Jake have himself a little lady? Jason took note of the plate number so he could run it later, and then he headed out of the canyon. When he got to Santiago Canyon Road he stopped and considered options. There were a few dive bars in Orange and Santa Ana he could try, or he could head over to Cook's Corner and see what kind of lowlifes were hanging around. He decided on Cook's, turned left and gassed the BMW.

Ten minutes later he drove past the bar and realized it was the wrong choice. The lot was nearly empty; just a red Mustang parked next to a beater Chevy and three motorcycles. Pickings would be slim. He turned around and headed for Santa Ana. It was probably just as well—someone in Cook's likely would have recognized him.

He tried Paige's cell phone again and it went right to voicemail. The fire burned hotter in his gut, fueled by the thought of her rejecting him. He went straight to the Rail Bar, a place notorious for its clientele; outlaws and hard cases, gun-runners and hitmen, lowlifes of all stripes. It was there he would seek release.

He drove slowly past the parking lot. It was full of shitty cars, which meant a room full of shitty people. Perfect. He parked a short distance down the street, locked his handgun in the glovebox along with his wallet. He had enough cash on him for a couple of rounds, but he didn't plan on staying that long. He grabbed a trucker cap from the back seat and pulled it low on his head. The cap had *White Power* embroidered across the front. He added wraparound shades and he was ready to go.

Inside the bar the action was heavy. Ranchero music played loudly from the jukebox. Jason drew stares as he entered. His shades allowed him to scan the crowd at will. He had no doubt he could take anyone in the room, but he wanted to choose carefully. He didn't want this to come back on him.

He ordered a bottle of beer at the bar and took it to the pool table in the corner. A couple of Mexican dudes had a game going. They looked like good candidates. One had jailhouse tattoos on his arms and neck, the other Jason knew about from a friend of his that worked the gang detail. He studied the two, noted their cocky swagger, the way they stared at his trucker cap and shot him hard looks. They were the ones. Jason knew they wouldn't report anything to the cops, no matter what happened tonight.

He leaned back and drank some beer, got himself primed. He focused on his afternoon encounter with Paige, felt the aggression rise. He thought of Jake Donahue, pictured beating him senseless. Before long Jason was gripping the beer bottle so tight his knuckles were white. He wondered if he could crush the bottle if he squeezed hard enough.

The two men playing pool racked another game. They kept staring at Jason, making comments to each other, laughing while doing it. They were disrespecting him, sizing him up. One of them stepped close to make a shot. The guy with the tats. Jason crowded him.

"Back off, motherfucker."

"Sorry," Jason said, keeping his tone friendly.

"Damn right you're sorry, bitch," Tattoo Man said. His friend laughed. Tattoo Man made his shot, banked the three ball into the corner. "That's how it's done, esé," he said to his friend, taking a long pull from his bottle of beer.

"That was a good shot," Jason said. He walked up and put a couple of quarters on the table.

"What the hell you doing?" Tattoo Man said.

"Calling the next game. I'll take the winner."

"Fuck that, white boy. You be takin' this cue up the ass you keep hanging around this table."

Jason felt the adrenaline rush. "I got the next game," he said evenly.

"You got shit. Take those glasses off so I can see your eyes."

"No."

"What?"

"I'm not taking them off. The light hurts my eyes."

"*I'm* gonna hurt you, you keep standin' there lookin' stupid."

"I usually don't let wets talk to me that way. But I'm willing to let it slide. I got the next game."

"What the fuck?"

Both men crowded in close to Jason. Some people took notice. The bartender shot a look, whispered something to the heavyset man standing at the end of the bar. Jason figured the guy was the bouncer. It didn't matter, he was ready to take the action outside.

"I'm going to take a leak. Hold my game for me."

He headed down a long hallway toward the restroom. Tattoo Man and his friend looked at each other and laughed. Words were passed between them, and then they followed. Jason ducked out the rear exit door and stood in a shadowed corner. The two guys came through the door, looking confused.

"Where is he? He said he was goin' to the can," Tattoo Man said.

"Fuckin' pussy split."

Jason stepped out of the shadows and laughed. The two Mexicans seemed surprised. They split up and circled Jason. Tattoo Man pulled a switchblade, snicked it open.

"Time to die, white boy."

He came at Jason straight on, the knife held low. His friend came in from the left. Jason timed the friend's approach and he spun quickly, snapped his elbow into the man's face with enough force to destroy his nose. He spun back around as Tattoo Man jabbed the blade. The other guy was on his knees, holding his hands to his face, moaning as his blood poured out onto the filthy asphalt of the parking lot.

Tattoo Man had no technique, his jabs with the blade slow and telegraphed, and Jason was able to weave and dodge with ease. He saw his opening and took it. He feigned right, Tattoo Man followed, and Jason viciously throat-punched him with his left. Tattoo Man dropped his knife and gasped for breath. Jason could have taken him out with the blow, but he'd held back just enough. Now he went to work.

He threw a quick series of punches to the man's face and stomach, and then kneed him in the balls, dropping him like dead weight. The other guy was still moaning, down on his knees. Jason spun around and kicked him in the face, knocking him flat. He kicked him in the side, breaking ribs. He stopped kicking when the man stopped moving.

With every blow Jason delivered he felt the rage leaving his body. He was focused on the pure act of physical cleansing, bleeding the aggression from his insides, exorcising the hurt and shame from his soul. The two men he was beating represented every wrong ever done to him, and Jason did not see them as human beings deserving of compassion, but rather agents of evil to be dealt with in the harshest way possible. Jason knew he was committing a grievous sin, but that did not deter him. He was forgiven in the eyes of the Lord.

The whole incident took less than five minutes, and Jason had not even broken a sweat. He looked at the two men lying at his feet. And then he started walking. He tossed the cap and shades onto the passenger seat of his BMW. Later, he would throw them out the car window as he sped down the 5 Freeway. He retrieved his wallet and handgun from the glove box, started the engine, and rolled down deserted Santa Ana streets. It was one forty-five in the morning and Jason Stafford was calm. He was at peace. He was ready for whatever tomorrow would bring.

Chapter 33

Amy Watson looked at Jake earnestly. He glanced away, unable to meet her eyes. They were inside Jake's house, an uneasy truce declared between them.

When Jake returned home from Cook's Corner, Amy was still parked in his driveway, asleep inside her car. Jake felt tremendous guilt about that. He roused her, collected her things and invited her into his home. He set her up in the spare bedroom, and while she showered and settled in, Jake went for a walk to clear his head. Later, they sat down to talk.

"I'm sorry for not telling you I was coming," Amy said. "That was wrong of me."

The living room was dimly lit, the scent of the canyon coming in through the open windows. Jake's whiskey buzz had worn off. So too had the emotional shock from his meeting with Danny Shaffer, and in a small way, he was glad for Amy's company. His normal ritual of solitude seemed inappropriate for a day like today. Amy triggered mixed feelings in Jake, but deep down he knew that he did not want to be alone.

"I was going to spend the night in Bishop, but I was too wound up to sit in a hotel room alone."

"What happened with your friend, the one who lives in Tustin? When we spoke last week, you said you could stay with her. Or was that a lie?"

"No, Jake, it wasn't. I called Stephanie and tried to arrange things, but she had to leave town on business. I didn't feel right asking to stay at her place if she wasn't there."

"But you felt right just showing up at my front door?" There was accusation in Jake's voice and he regretted it immediately.

"I said I was sorry for that. Look, I can get a hotel for the night, okay? Just don't be mad. I didn't come here to upset you. I came here because I love you. Can't you see that?"

"You can stay here tonight," Jake said, ignoring Amy's question. "And I'm not mad anymore. I'm sorry for earlier. It's been a long day and I've got a lot on my mind. Seeing you here tonight was the final straw."

He grimaced inside. His words were coming out wrong, his mind too jumbled to think straight. Jake didn't want a reconciliation with Amy, but he didn't want to crucify her either.

"I'll leave tomorrow, I promise."

"Let's just get through tonight," he said, softening his tone. "Tomorrow we'll see where we're at. I don't mind taking it one day at a time. But you have to understand, it comes with no promises."

She let out a breath, as if she'd been holding it in anticipation.

"I get it. I have to be back in Truckee by the weekend anyway, so you don't have to worry about me becoming a nuisance."

"You're not a nuisance, Amy."

"Nonsense. I'm a pain in the ass. Be honest."

She smiled awkwardly and brushed the hair out of her eyes, and for a moment Jake saw her as he did when they first met in Truckee, that night at the restaurant, and later when they had beers at Rusty's. They'd had chemistry, there was no denying that, and Jake had always found Amy attractive. There was a time he thought she might be the one. But all that changed.

"You're not a pain in the ass," he said, giving out a small grin. "You're just a woman."

"Touché, Mr. Donahue."

They both laughed and it felt good. They fell into an easy silence, something that had always come naturally for them. Mark that in the plus column, Jake thought. Truthfully, there were a lot of pluses with Amy, and when Jake thought of it that way, he lost track of his reasons for breaking it off with her. Tonight, he allowed himself to be in the moment, to experience Amy's presence without judgment or expectation.

Gradually the storm quieted in Jake's head, although Danny's revelation remained constant in the background. It seemed there should be a next step, somewhere to go from here. Or should he just ignore the whole thing? Jake was well-versed at ignoring things, focusing on the mundane repetition of day to day life as a way of denying emotional truths that were simply too difficult to cope with. Some would call that cowardice. Jake would not disagree.

"This was your father's house?" Amy said, breaking the chain of Jake's thoughts.

"Yes," he replied, his head tilted back on the sofa, his eyes closed.

"Did you live here with him?"

"For a time, when I was younger."

Amy was treading cautiously. Jake had never shared his story, and it was a glaring hole in their relationship that she had struggled to come to terms with. Sure, he shared plenty of anecdotes, and he told wonderful stories of his travels, but his life story, the one about his family of origin, he never told. There was much about Jake that Amy didn't know.

"It's a nice house. And the canyon seems wonderful. I'm looking forward to seeing it in the daylight."

Jake nodded but did not respond. His eyes were still closed and he was deep in thought. The day had been an emotional roller coaster, a jerky, careening ride that had left Jake exhausted and at odds with himself. The past had crashed headlong into the present, and as Jake wrestled with the aftermath, he felt a great pull to unburden himself.

"Are you tired?" Amy said. "We can call it a night. I don't mind."

Jake opened his eyes.

"Do you believe in karma?" he said, staring at a spot on the ceiling.

"I'm not sure. I never gave it much thought. Do you?"

"For most of my life I would have said no. Now that I'm older, I'm not so sure."

"I believe our actions have consequences that go beyond what we can see or understand. I suppose you'd call that karma."

Jake did not reply. He was weighing a heavy decision. In all his life, he had told only one person—Hector Santiago—what happened in Mexico in 1984. He came close to telling a woman he'd been involved with in Belle Fourche back in '92, when he was working in the Black Hills, but he lacked the courage to do so. He'd always lacked the courage to tell that story. He'd wanted to tell his father many times over the years, but emotional honesty was never Big Ed's thing.

So, Jake never told another soul after that October day in 1989 when he'd returned to Orange County for a short visit and reconnected with Hector, and he'd dragged that anchor around ever since. Sitting here with Amy Watson, on a day he'd received the most shocking news a man could ever receive, Jake wanted to snap that chain and lose that anchor once and for all. He took in a breath and steeled his nerves.

"What if I told you I had a daughter? Would that change how you feel about me?"

"I don't understand. You have a daughter?"

"You deserve to know the truth about me, Amy."

"I know you, Jake. I know your heart, and it's a good one. That's all that matters."

"No, it isn't."

Jake sat up straight and looked into Amy Watson's eyes, a world of haunted truth in his.

"What if I told you I've killed someone? A child. Would that change how you feel about me?"

The shock in Amy's eyes nearly stopped Jake right there. But he pushed on. It was time to unburden himself. It was time to tell his story.

Chapter 34
Baja California, Mexico
June 1984

It took the squad nine hours to get to Bahia de Cortez. They'd chosen the eastern route—Interstate 10 to highway 86, crossing the border at Mexicali. From there it was a straight shot down Mexican Federal Highway 5 to San Felipe, where they stopped for a late lunch and too many beers. They arrived in town nearly two hours later, just as the sun was sinking over a western horizon broken by a ridge of jagged hills.

The town didn't look like much to Jake, not after all the talk he'd heard from Bruce about it; Mexico wasn't his thing anyway and surfing was only a casual interest. But the squad had taken a vote and they'd settled on Bahia de Cortez for their summer blowout. Jake would have preferred Palm Springs or Lake Havasu, but the boys wanted to surf and Bruce pretty much insisted on Mexico. And there you have it. Bruce McAlister usually got what he wanted.

And who was going to argue with that?

No one, that's who. Not after Bruce had led the squad to their third consecutive undefeated season and a CIF championship. High school might have been over, but the euphoria of that night back in December was slow to wear off. Some of the guys still strutted around like the rest of their lives were set, nothing but a golden road ahead.

Jake could only laugh. Most of them would never play another down of football, and the ones who did go on to college would likely find the road paved with disappointment when they realized they were the king of a very small hill. It was a cynical attitude for an eighteen-year-old to have, but true nonetheless.

The town of Bahia de Cortez was a squalid and featureless place, with a badly potholed main street and ramshackle buildings housing restaurants and shops and seedy bars. Side streets branched off the main drag, leading to a residential area fanning out to the north and west, climbing the gradual slope of the low hills ringing the town. Two miles east was the shoreline of the Gulf of California, and a surf village made up of rental trailers, a bar, restaurant, and bait shop that catered mostly to gringo surfers and fisherman. Brightly-colored outboard fishing boats lined the shore near a short pier, and scattered up and down the sand were palm-thatched cabanas. There were two other surf villages located on that stretch of the gulf, four miles to the north and six miles to the south.

It was rumored that the squad from Foothill was in town. If true, it might spell trouble; Foothill was El Modena's archenemy in the Century League. In the final game of the season, the Vanguards' undefeated record on the line, Foothill nearly pulled off an upset, losing in overtime by a field goal. The game was notable for a dirty player from Foothill taking out one of the Vanguards' defensive backs with a brutal hit, which cleared both benches in a brawl that took ten minutes to quell.

The squad had rented five trailers at Reef Point 2, an informal name given to the surf village by American travelers over the years and adopted by the locals. The other two villages were known as Reef Point 1 to the north, and Reef Point 3 to the south. The trailers at Reef Point 2 were spread out from one end of the village to the other, situated on a small rise overlooking the beach. Jake was bunking with Danny Shaffer and Mark Davis. The guys who'd brought their girlfriends had their own trailers. Bruce McAlister and Susan Young had rented the nicest of all the trailers, located at the south end of the village.

Jake rode in Bruce's Chevy Blazer. Susan and Bruce argued nearly the entire trip, most of it petty nonsense that Jake tried to ignore. He would've hitched a ride with one of the other guys but all their vehicles were full. Whenever Bruce wasn't looking, Susan flirted with Jake, throwing him glances in that seductive way of hers, turning it on and off at will. She complained openly about Bruce, ragging him constantly on just about everything he said or did.

Jake loved Susan Young. He'd loved her since he was a kid. His love was unrequited though, and ever since she'd hooked up with Bruce, Jake had felt the sting of rejection. Although he fought against it, Jake was painfully aware that his feelings for Susan had kept him in a constant state of emotional limbo.

Driving to Mexico, watching Bruce and Susan's little love drama play out, Jake tried to ignore his truth, to pretend as if none of it mattered. He was determined to enjoy this time and to move on to the next chapter of his life with wide eyes and an open heart. Jake supposed he would always love Susan, but he knew he would never get the chance to *be* in love with her.

He'd fled a train wreck of a family life, his mother and father both spinning wildly out of control. They'd hardly said a word about his plans. When Jake left his father's house that weekend, he hadn't seen his mother in a week and his father was about to embark on another of his Las Vegas gambling excursions that might last a few days or a few weeks, depending on his luck at the tables. But regardless of how long he was gone, Big Ed Donahue would return home broke. He always did.

After settling into their various trailers and unwinding from the road, the guys wanted to go into town for some tacos and beer. There was a bar called *El Gato Negro*—The Black Cat—a place notorious for its anything-goes vibe and loose drinking age. They could cut loose there and kick off their trip in proper style. The girls preferred to stay at the village and drink margaritas. Jake sensed their reluctance to go into town—to even be in Mexico for that matter—and it added to the shaky vibe he'd been feeling since they'd left Orange County.

Was it a premonition?

Whatever it was, it left Jake feeling wary. But he went along anyway. Because he was one of the guys. And while Bruce might have been the de facto leader of the squad, Jake was arguably the most respected and admired member. Teenage boys being who they are, none of the guys would have ever voiced that sentiment, but it was true. And Jake knew it was true. And because of that he put aside his concerns and took his place alongside Bruce McAlister, just as he'd always done, a dutiful wingman to the end.

THE NEXT day they hit the surf.

The guys were hungover. They'd had an uneventful night at the bar, the Sunday crowd thin and subdued. All night they'd kept their eyes open for the Foothill squad, slamming shots and getting primed, hoping for a little action with their rivals, but nothing came of it. For Jake, it was just as well; he didn't come all the way down to Mexico to fight kids from Orange County. He could do that back home. Hell, for that matter, he could surf anytime he wanted back home.

Bruce seemed especially bent on some action, and inside the bar he kept watching the door, aggression lighting his eyes. Jake found out later that Bruce had a major blowout with Susan before heading out to the bar. One of the guys said that Bruce put his fist through a wall in his trailer. More of the same, Jake thought regrettably. He wondered if he should talk to Susan about it, make sure she was okay. He'd always watched out for her, from the time they first met.

The food at the Black Cat was very good, and Jake drank too much beer and tequila along with the rest of the guys, and after a while he'd settled into the flow of things and had himself a good time. Back at the surf village he stayed up late with Danny and Mark, walking the shoreline with a six-pack of beer, chucking the empties into the sea, laughing at Danny's relentless humor. When they finally sacked out for the night, Jake felt at ease.

Monday morning brought a cloudless blue sky and soaring temperatures. Jake rose early and got a steaming cup of coffee from the bait shop, and he stood with it on a steep bluff dotted with manzanita and blooming cholla cactus, the Gulf of California spread out before him in gradual shades of blue as it made its way to deep water. Some of the locals referred to it as the Sea of Cortez, and Jake remembered a book he'd read in high school, written by John Steinbeck about his time spent here.

The surf wasn't great but Jake didn't care too much about that. His plan was to soak up rays and forget about life for a while. He watched fishing boats leave the pier and head south, and he thought he might like to give that a try. Maybe he could hook something good to grill up on one of those barbecues they had in the beach cabanas.

After a while the rest of the squad straggled out of their trailers and started working their way down to the beach. They set up at one of the cabanas and a couple of them hit the water. Jake drained his cup and walked down to meet them. When he got there, he saw Susan sitting in a beach chair off by herself, putting sunscreen on. She smiled at him.

"Good morning," she said brightly, a glimmer in her eyes.

"Hey, Susan," Jake replied. "You girls have a good time last night?"

"The best. And you?"

"Considering where we are, I'd say I had an excellent time last night."

"I'll drink to that," Susan said with a laugh. "I just wish they had a coffeehouse here."

"They have coffee in the bait shop."

"Really, Jake? You expect me to drink coffee from a bait shop?" she said with mock haughtiness.

"Consider it slumming," he replied with a smile, enjoying the casual banter that came so easily to them.

"Well okay, then. Show me the way."

Jake looked to the water, saw Bruce paddling out. Then he turned and looked at Susan finishing up with the sunscreen, noticing the cut of her bikini and the way it worked with her toned body. He felt the usual stirrings, a tingle of arousal he tried to ignore. He didn't want another cup of coffee. What he wanted was Susan. Sadly, he knew he could never have her.

THE NEXT few days passed lazily. The guys surfed and the girls sunbathed, and they all drank too much. The Black Cat became a regular hangout for the guys, but the girls remained leery, preferring to stay at the village engaged in their girl-talk and margaritas. Jake fell into an easy routine of rising early and getting coffee from Esteban, the old man who worked the bait shop, and taking it to his vantage point on the bluff. He'd positioned a comfortable beach chair up there, the perfect spot to absorb the beauty of the new day and engage in his contemplation.

So far, the Foothill squad had yet to materialize. Jake doubted they would. Bruce wouldn't let it go, and one afternoon he and Alex Brady took the Blazer and drove to the other two surf villages, on the hunt for trouble. They returned hours later, hammered and driving out of control. The top was off the Blazer and you could hear them coming from a good distance away, whooping and hollering, Van Halen's *1984* album blasting from the tape deck. Bruce said the Foothill squad had booked Reef Point 3 for the upcoming weekend, and he asked the boys if they were ready to get it on.

On Tuesday Jake rented a fishing boat with a guide, and he and Danny Shaffer and Tom Cook went out for the day. They came back sunburned and drunk, with a boatful of fish. The guide grilled the fish and Esteban brought the fixings, and the squad feasted on fish tacos and bottles of beer. Alex's girlfriend had brought a polaroid camera and Esteban took pictures of the squad, one for each of them. They tried different poses, cutting up and acting goofy. In Jake's picture, he stood between Susan and Bruce, the picture snapped just as Susan fell into Jake's arms, the firmness of her body and the summer scent of her skin sending a charge through him.

As the week went on, Jake sensed a change in Susan, the tension between her and Bruce spilling out from behind closed doors. She seemed tentative around him, a harried look in her eyes. Bruce walked around agitated all the time, fixated on the Foothill squad, badgering Susan about this thing and that.

On Wednesday Jake thought he saw bruising on Susan's face that she'd tried to cover with makeup. She flirted more openly with him, a few times in front of Bruce, and Jake felt the screws tighten, the escalation of a situation that would turn ugly if not held in check. Bruce was too self-absorbed to take notice, but Jake knew that could change at any moment.

The others were not tuned into the drama playing out between Bruce and Susan. Jake was acutely aware that he was fixating on it, fueling a deep resentment of Bruce. Sitting on the bluff on Thursday morning, watching the sun come up in a blaze of golden light reflecting off the shimmering waters of the Gulf, he felt himself coming apart. His feelings for Susan had morphed into an obsessive sexual desire, mixed with the protectiveness he felt for her. The trip had been a good one and Jake was glad that he'd come along, but the thing with Susan was becoming untenable, and Bruce's erratic and aggressive behavior showed no signs of abating.

The plan was to leave Bahia de Cortez on Sunday, although Bruce and some of the guys had been talking about taking a boat across the Gulf to Mazatlán and spending a couple of days there. So far, the vote was split, mostly because some of the guys were running low on money. Outwardly Jake had remained noncommittal, but in truth, he was ready to go home.

Finishing his coffee on Thursday morning, Jake prepared to leave the bluff. He saw some of the squad staggering out onto the beach. Danny Shaffer was waxing his surfboard, laughing at something he'd said to Mark Davis. Jake liked Danny a lot, his good-natured personality and constant humor a nice counterpoint to Bruce's intensity. Mark was a good dude too, and the three of them had gotten along well.

Let the day begin, Jake thought optimistically as he walked down the pathway to the beach. He forced his mind clear of troubling thoughts, determined to wring as much youthful pleasure out of this day as he could.

***

ON FRIDAY, it all fell apart.

It began innocently enough, when Jake took his morning coffee on the bluff. Susan was there waiting for him, sitting in his chair, looking tired and unsettled.

"You wouldn't consider getting me one of those, would you?" she said, pointing to Jake's cup.

"Take mine. I'll get another."

He handed over the cup and walked back down the hill, returning a short time later with his coffee and a bag of *pan dulce*. He sat on the ground next to Susan, and they ate their sweet bread and drank coffee in silence.

"This view is incredible," Susan said. "Now I know why you come up here every morning."

"I didn't think anyone noticed."

"Bruce did."

"Hmm."

"He says you think too much. That's why you come up here."

"Sounds like something he'd say."

Susan smiled awkwardly, and silence settled between them. Jake waited out the silence, knowing the small talk was simply a precursor to what was really on Susan's mind. A stiff breeze swept across the bluff, and she reached for her floppy sun hat to keep it from flying away. Her blonde hair was pulled back in a long ponytail, her bangs touching oversized sunglasses, a turquoise cover-up over her bikini. Jake tried to stay cool, the ache of desire tingling his skin, clouding his thinking. He wondered if it showed.

"I'm afraid of him," Susan blurted out.

"I know you are."

"How?"

"Call it a man's intuition."

Susan laughed. "Is that even a thing?"

"Today it is." Jake waited a moment, and then said, "Seriously though, it's obvious enough. If you're looking."

"And you've been looking?"

He ignored the question. "Bruce might be my friend, Susan, but he's also a dick half the time. With you, he's just a plain asshole most of the time."

"You're biased."

"Maybe. But he's still an asshole to you. Why do you put up with it?"

She gave out an ironic laugh, and said in a dramatic tone, "Is this the part where I tell you it's because I love him?"

"This is the part where you tell me the truth."

Jake was losing patience. He was tired of the wordplay, and he was starting to think that Susan was playing games with him. Just like the times she would throw flirty glances his way when Bruce wasn't looking, or the way she would brush against him, giving him soft little touches that sent electricity coursing through him. She did it on purpose and Jake knew it, and he hated himself for the way he anticipated it, the way he longed for those moments when Susan's proximity—her scent, her *presence*—made him feel alive.

He took off his sunglasses and looked at Susan, anticipating her response. She stared down at the beach, turned in profile, and Jake felt the immediate urge to lean in and kiss the side of her face, to breathe in her essence. She spoke in a stiff voice.

"He's watching us. There on the beach."

Jake turned and looked. Bruce stood expressionless under the cabana, leaning against a support post with his arms folded. Some of the others were milling around, waxing their boards and setting up beach chairs. Bruce just stood there like a statue, with his deep tan and pumped biceps, staring at the bluff.

"He's wondering what we're doing up here."

"What's to wonder? You and I are friends. He knows he can trust me."

The words rang hollow in Jake's ear.

"Let's go," he said. "No point stirring up trouble today."

"You're right. We can talk later. Oh, and thanks for the coffee."

***

JAKE PUT the clampdown on his thoughts, refusing to consider what Susan might tell him later. Instead, he dove headlong into the day, eating and drinking too much, spending long sessions in the water, cutting up with the guys as they recounted the highlights of the season and their three years spent together.

Bruce showed no apparent animosity toward Jake, and if the incident on the bluff was bothering him, he hid it well. But as the day wore on and the alcohol flowed, he became more intense, challenging each of the guys in his own brand of hyper-competitiveness. Danny Shaffer noticed it when they were in the water.

"Bruce is amped today," he said after Bruce had cut off Scott Newman while jockeying for a wave.

"I didn't notice," Jake said, floating lazily on his board as he waited for the next set.

"The hell you didn't."

"He's just being Bruce, that's all."

"I guess. I don't get why he pushes all the time. Dude needs to learn to chill. I mean what the hell, high school is over, right? We had our time, now get off the stage."

"That's some deep thinking there, Shaffer."

"Damn straight it is, brother. The deepest."

They both laughed and said nothing for a while. Soon the waves diminished and lost shape, and it was time to go in.

"Did you notice the bruises on Susan the other day?" Danny said.

"Huh?" Jake said, caught off guard by the question.

"I think he's smacking her around."

"Bruce?"

"Who else?" After a moment, Danny said, "I'm assuming by your silence that you noticed."

"Yeah, Danny, I noticed."

"You think we ought to do something about it?"

"Like what?"

"I dunno. Beat his ass I suppose. That's not cool, what he's doing. I've noticed before."

"You have?"

"Here and there. I'm surprised you haven't."

"Why would I notice?"

"C'mon, Jake, you notice everything about Susan."

Jake felt embarrassed. He had no idea it was so obvious.

"These waves suck. You want to get a beer?"

"Sure," Danny said. "So, we gonna do it?"

"What?"

"Beat Bruce's ass."

"I'll get back to you on that."

"Cool."

They paddled to shore then. As they neared, Jake saw Bruce standing at the waterline, staring at them in a defiant pose. For a moment, he wondered if the guy could read lips.

AS NIGHT fell, Bruce started fixating on the Foothill squad, cooking up all kinds of plots to get even with them. The rest of the guys had pretty much written off any chance that they were even in Mexico, let alone staying in Bahia de Cortez. A Mexican kid approached Bruce on the beach and whispered in his ear. Bruce nodded, asked a few questions, nodded some more, and then handed the kid some cash. Then he gathered the squad together under the cabana. There was fire in his eyes. He was ready to get it on.

"Who's the kid?" Alex Brady said.

"My informant," Bruce replied, a devious grin on his face.

"Who's he informing on?" Alex said, playing along with Bruce.

"The kid's been keeping an eye on the other two surf camps. I told him to come running if he saw those assholes from Foothill."

"No shit?" Mark Davis said.

"No shit. And guess what he just told me?"

"There's a fish special at the Black Cat tonight?" Danny Shaffer said, laughing at his own joke.

"There's a special all right, but it ain't fish. It's us settling the score with those pricks. They're gonna be there tonight. And so are we."

Bruce looked at each of the guys. Nobody spoke. The girls had gone back to the trailers a few hours earlier, feeling low from too much sun and booze. The guys had tied one on too, so there was little enthusiasm for a rumble.

"I promised Monica I'd take her into town for dinner tonight," Scott Newman said. "Alex and Nancy are going with us."

"So cancel," Bruce said.

"I can't. She's been nagging me, says I don't spend enough time with her."

"You brought her with you, didn't you? Goddamn bitches are never happy."

Bruce looked at the squad.

"What about the rest of you? Are you in?"

There was some mumbling and shuffling of feet, but no takers.

"You guys are pussies," Bruce said in disgust.

"Why don't we take a vote later?" Danny said. "After we've had a chance to rest. I'm beat."

"Whatever," Bruce said, waving off the squad as he walked away.

THEY ENDED up going after all.

At nine thirty Bruce rounded up the guys and they drove into town. Alex and Scott took care of business with their girlfriends, just to keep the peace. Bruce ragged them hard for it. He seemed especially uptight, and there were whispers it was because he and Susan had gotten into it. Tom Cook said he could hear them yelling from inside his trailer. Bruce said nothing about it. Jake took note of the whispers and he secretly worried about Susan.

When they got to the Black Cat the joint was crowded and raucous, music pumping and booze flowing. But there was no Foothill squad to be found. Bruce was jacked and ready, and he kept insisting they would show. After an hour, Jake decided he'd had enough. He didn't want to fight and Bruce's antics were wearing thin. He slipped out a rear door and walked back to the surf village. Bruce would be pissed but so what. He'd get over it.

The night was sultry, the moon rising full in an ink-black sky. On his walk, Jake thought about Susan and Bruce and what was really going on between them. He never considered that it might be about him. They'd always had a volatile relationship, and Jake knew it was as much because of Susan as it was Bruce. She could be a handful, and she had a way of pushing buttons in a guy. She'd been pushing Jake's since the third grade.

Jake went straight to Alex Brady's trailer because that's where the girls were staying. He told himself he was going there to update them on the guys. In truth, he was going there to see Susan. He wasn't sure what he expected to happen and he didn't spend any time trying to figure it out. He just let emotional momentum propel him.

Monica and Nancy were tipsy and giggly when they answered the door. They said that Susan had left because she didn't feel well. They asked Jake why he was alone, and did they ever find those guys from Foothill. He gave them the lowdown and said goodnight. And then he started walking.

He approached Bruce and Susan's trailer and stood outside the door. He heard waves crashing on the shore, the steady rhythm of the ocean, and little else. The lights were out in the trailer, the shades drawn. Jake felt lightheaded with anticipation, a faint ringing in his ear. His mouth was dry and he knew it was nerves at play. He wondered for the hundredth time what the hell he was doing.

He was skating on thin ice, that's what.

Dancing with the Devil. Tempting fate. Pick your cliché.

He raised his hand to knock, held it there for a second, and then plunged in.

Susan answered the door almost immediately. She gave a forlorn smile and Jake's heart broke when he saw the black eye. He stepped into the trailer. Susan shut the door and Jake knew he was in trouble.

A CANDLE burned on a table in the corner, casting flickering light in the dark room. The windows facing the ocean were open to the breeze and the scent of the sea. Susan wore a long night shirt and panties. She was braless and Jake did his best not to stare. She reached out and embraced him, the charge immediate and all-consuming. He was sure that Susan could feel his pounding heart. They held each other for a long moment. She pulled him tight, her face against his neck. She looked up, warm breath on his cheek.

"I don't know what to do."

"Leave him."

"It's not so easy."

"Bullshit."

"Oh, Jake…why can't it be you?"

She kissed him hard on the mouth. Everything stopped in that moment, time itself ceasing to exist. Jake gave in to his deep, unending passion, the physical ache of his wanting. He touched Susan's breasts and felt himself harden. She reached down and caressed him there and Jake felt himself ready to go. She slid her hands down the back of his shorts, her touch electric. She eased his shorts down and they fell to his ankles. She held him in her hands and Jake felt the release, his orgasm the deepest, most intense sensation he'd ever felt.

Jake had never been with a girl before, not like this, and although he'd had his share of wet dreams, and he'd handled himself plenty whenever the need became too much, he had never experienced *this*.

And then embarrassment set in.

Before he could speak, Susan whispered, "It's okay."

She wet a towel with warm water and used it to clean him and the carpet where they stood. Then she led Jake to the bedroom where she finished undressing him. She undressed herself and they laid on top of the covers and held each other, not speaking.

Jake had no idea how long they stayed like that, the warm breeze and salt air combining with the heat of Susan's lithe, naked body to create a surreal, almost otherworldly experience. At some point arousal took control and Jake felt himself harden. Susan responded with soft kisses and hands that roamed his body, heightening his desire. When he entered her, Jake on top and Susan staring into his eyes, the feeling was so deeply passionate that Jake hardly believed the reality of it. They fell into a natural rhythm, his thrusts eliciting gasps from Susan and playful love bites on his neck and ears. They climaxed together, and when they did, Jake nearly cried.

After a short rest, they made love again.

Afterwards, as they lay together in the darkness, they both knew there had been a major upheaval in the natural order of things. But Jake's reasons for believing so were quite different than Susan's, and while he found himself dreaming of where this moment would lead them, fate had altogether different plans.

A low rumble sounded from the road outside the trailer, followed by the faint strains of *Eye of the Tiger*. Jake sat up in the bed.

"He's here."

"Hmm…what, baby?" Susan said sleepily.

"Bruce is here."

Eye of the Tiger was Bruce's fight song, the one he used to blast in the locker room before games. Jake jumped up quickly and dressed. Susan sat up, eyes widened.

"How do you know?"

"The song. Hear it?"

The sound grew louder and Susan nodded. In seconds the sound of Bruce's Blazer pulling up outside could be heard. The music stopped and a door slammed shut.

"Hold him at the door," Jake said.

"What are you going to do?"

"I'm going out the window."

Pounding echoed through the trailer. Susan put on a robe and moved cautiously toward the door. She'd dead bolted it earlier and the trailer was sturdy, so Jake had little fear that Bruce could kick the door in. But you never know what an angry man is capable of.

"Open the door, Susan! I lost my key!"

"Go," Jake whispered, pointing to the door. He moved to the window at the far end of the trailer. Bruce kept pounding and yelling.

"Goddammit, I'm not screwing around! Are you in there?"

"Go away, Bruce."

"Go away my ass. Open the damn door!"

Jake pushed out the window screen. He looked at Susan. He didn't want to leave her this way, but to confront Bruce right now would be madness. Jake mouthed the words *I love you*, and he went out the window. Outside, he crouched in the sand and listened.

"You're drunk and I don't want you here," Susan said, her voice muffled from the distance. "You can spend the night with one of the guys, or on the beach, I don't care. Just go away."

"Is Jake in there?"

"I don't know where he is. I haven't seen him since this afternoon."

"I don't believe you. Monica and Nancy said he came to their trailer and asked about you. He bailed out from the bar without telling anyone. Are you in there fucking him?"

"Go away, Bruce. Leave me alone."

Jake couldn't take it anymore. He turned and ran in the direction of his trailer, the voices fading. His heart ached, and he knew this wasn't the end of it.

LATER, BRUCE came for him. Whatever suspicions he may have had were left unspoken.

"What the hell happened to you?" he said.

Jake had made it back to his trailer without being noticed. Danny and Mark were gone. He'd tried to settle down but it was impossible, visions of his lovemaking and nervous anticipation over what would happen next firing his mind and charging his nerves.

"I got bored," Jake replied.

"Whatever."

Bruce eyed him uncertainly. A thought seized Jake: Do I smell like her?

"We found them," Bruce said with a wicked grin.

"Who?"

"Those Foothill assholes. The other guys are chasing them down now. We gotta go."

"Where?"

"Don't worry about that, I'm driving. You're taking shotgun. And then we're taking care of business, the Vanguard way."

Jake hesitated. If he didn't go along, Bruce would know something was up. In that moment, standing there at the door of the trailer, looking at Bruce McAlister all amped like he'd snorted a bag of speed, Jake could never have known the hard consequences that would come from his decision.

"Let me change clothes, and then we'll roll."

"Cool. I'll wait in the Blazer."

Ten minutes later Jake got into the passenger seat. He'd changed into jeans, sneakers, and a long sleeve shirt. He wore a ball cap pulled low so it wouldn't blow off as Bruce took off at high speed.

"What happened at the bar?" Jake said. He spoke loud to be heard over the rush of air passing through the open-topped vehicle.

"They showed up an hour ago. Once they saw us, the fuckers booked."

"So where are we going?"

"Reef Point three."

Bruce drove erratically, way too fast for the winding, unpaved beach road that connected the surf villages. *Eye of the Tiger* blasted from the stereo. Every time it ended, Bruce rewound the tape. Jake was ready to toss the damn thing.

"Slow down," Jake said. "I don't want to die in Mexico."

"We gotta get there."

"What's the hurry?"

"The other guys are on the way. They can't have all the fun."

Bruce turned and looked at Jake with a sadistic grin and nefarious eyes. Jake held onto the door handle as they took a sharp turn. He wondered how drunk Bruce was, because he was driving like an idiot. They hit a rise, followed by a steep dip in the road, and Jake felt it in his stomach. Bruce hit the straightaway hard, accelerating wildly. At the next turn, they went wide right, centrifugal force causing the Blazer to fishtail.

And then it happened.

As Bruce straightened the vehicle a boy appeared in the headlights. He was riding a bicycle. Jake screamed.

"Watch out!"

Bruce turned hard to the left. The Blazer's rear end slid out and tagged the boy, sending him flying. Bruce hit the brakes and slammed into a cactus tree.

"Fuck!"

Jake was out of the vehicle and on the run. He found the boy twenty yards down the beach road. When Jake got there, he gasped, the boy's broken body splayed in the dirt and rocks like a discarded rag doll. He knelt and felt for a pulse. Bruce ran up and stopped behind Jake.

"The Blazer's fucked."

Jake turned and looked at Bruce incredulously.

"What did you say?"

"I said the Blazer is—"

Bruce stopped speaking when he saw the boy.

"What were you saying about the car, *Bruce*?"

"My God. What happened?"

"We killed him."

"Bullshit!"

"Bullshit, my ass. Come see for yourself."

"What's a kid doing out this late at night?"

"Does it matter?"

"What the hell are we going to do?"

They were on a remote section of the beach road, eerie blueish light from the full moon washing the landscape. The nearest houses were a good distance away, as was the town. The boy might have been eight years old, maybe ten. There was no blood, and the boy looked like he might have been sleeping if not for his broken limbs bent at unnatural angles, and his head turned in a way not humanly possible.

"We gotta hide him," Bruce said.

"We can't 'hide' him, Bruce. What the hell are you thinking?"

"We can't tell the cops. This is Mexico, Jake. You know how it is down here. We'll never see home again."

Jake stared back, speechless. Bruce was crazy, but he was right.

"We gotta get off this road before someone comes," Bruce said. He paused as if thinking about it, and then he said, "We'll take him out in the desert and bury him." He said it like he was calling a play in the huddle.

Jake shuddered, unable to grasp it. Bruce started pacing, going on about how they could do it, how it was the only thing that made sense. The boy was gone and nothing would change that. Now they had to save themselves. Jake looked at the boy, consumed by desperation and guilt, and a crippling sense of panic. Acting on pure survival instinct, he spoke words that would haunt him for the rest of his life.

"Get the car."

Bruce turned and ran. Jake lifted the boy's broken body—he couldn't have weighed more than sixty pounds. He stood there with the boy in his arms, waiting as Bruce struggled to start the Blazer. Jake started toward him, each step an agonizing walk of shame. The engine sputtered and coughed and finally kicked over. Jake lifted the boy into the back seat and then he got into the passenger seat and Bruce drove slowly inland.

Ten minutes later he parked the Blazer on a sloping hillside, the lights of the town twinkling far to the north. He nodded and waited while Jake took the boy from the back seat. Before they'd left the beach road, Bruce had tossed the boy's bicycle—a purple Schwinn that reminded Jake of a bike he'd once owned—behind some boulders. As Jake lifted the boy into his arms, Bruce got into the back of the Blazer and took a folding shovel from a toolbox. He ran ahead and stopped at a random spot and started digging. He dug like his life depended on it, throwing rocks and dirt every which way, grunting with the exertion. Jake held the boy, refusing to help. They didn't speak, and a part of Jake hoped someone would see them and end this lunacy.

But no one came, and the digging went on.

Finally, Bruce said, "I think it's deep enough."

Jake stepped forward as Bruce scrambled out of the shallow grave. He was drenched in sweat, breathing hard through his nose, his bare arms and clothes covered with dirt, a feral look in his eyes. Jake set the boy into the ground. He stayed there for a long moment, absorbing what he'd done, unable to comprehend it. Then he stood and looked at Bruce.

"You finish it."

He walked away, and left Bruce McAlister to his work.

JAKE SAT in his chair on the bluff, the rising sun in his eyes. Sleep had finally taken him a few hours ago, and with it came unspeakable dreams. He craved some coffee, if only to wash the sour taste from his mouth, but he couldn't face Esteban.

Bruce had dropped Jake off at his trailer at one thirty that morning. They didn't speak on the ride back to the surf village, and nothing was said when they parted. Afterwards, Jake walked the beach for hours, his thoughts scattered, his anguish complete.

He couldn't go back to his trailer, couldn't face Danny and Mark. Instead, he walked aimlessly until he couldn't do it anymore. And then he went to his place on the bluff and sat in his chair and waited, coming apart at the seams. He thought of Susan and the time they'd spent together. It was the most complete human experience he had ever had, only to have it followed by the most depraved, horrific act imaginable. It was incomprehensible that both things could happen on the same night. Where he would go from here, Jake could not begin to know.

The answer came a few hours later.

The squad started arriving at the beach, one by one, laughing and planning their day, the course of *their* lives intact, unaltered by tragedy, their happiness and peace of mind secure.

And then Bruce and Susan arrived together. They were holding hands, strutting on the sand like the perfect couple at ease with the world. Jake stared, unable to compute. He watched them take beach chairs next to each other, Bruce putting sunscreen on Susan, rubbing it on the tops of her breasts. Susan was laughing, and she leaned in and kissed Bruce on the mouth. Jake's heart beat so fast he thought it would explode, his skin hot with shame.

Danny Shaffer looked up then, and he saw Jake sitting on the bluff. They locked eyes and Danny waved at Jake to come on down. Danny turned away for a moment to speak to Bruce, and when he looked back, Jake was gone.

Chapter 35

Jake rose early on Wednesday and walked outside to get the morning paper. Amy was inside the house, sleeping. They'd been up late, and after Jake finished telling his story they made love. Amy made the initial advance and Jake let it happen, despite the emotional minefield that came with it. It was good—sex had never been their problem anyway—and in a small way their intimacy helped to ease Jake's tremendous guilt.

Amy had said little as Jake told his story, and he wasn't sure if it was shock or merely patience on her part. When it was over, she didn't try to minimize it or explain it away with meaningless platitudes, or act as if the passage of time had rendered the whole tragic episode irrelevant. She simply said she was sorry for what happened, expressing no judgement for Jake's actions. When she embraced him, and then kissed him, it didn't feel like a cheap play for affection or some angle being worked to ease her way back into his life. It felt natural. It felt right. It was *real*. And now, in the hard light of morning, Jake wondered if he hadn't made a mess of the whole thing.

He sat on his tree stump in the shade and unfolded the newspaper, trying to put it out of his mind. He went to the local news section first, flipping through the pages until he saw something of note. It was an article about an incident that took place at the Rail Bar in Santa Ana.

Late on Tuesday night two men were found badly beaten in an alley behind the bar. No witnesses had come forward, although several bar patrons reported seeing a tall, muscular white man talking to the two victims at one of the pool tables. They remembered him because of the *White Power* trucker cap and dark sunglasses he wore.

Jake lowered the paper and he thought about Danny Shaffer. He wondered if Danny had made it home last night. He wondered why the hell Danny hung out in places like the Rail Bar, drinking himself to oblivion. He wondered if Danny was telling the truth.

Jake wondered a lot of things about Danny Shaffer, but mostly, where Danny would fit in his life. He couldn't just cast him off, and even if he decided to leave Orange County, he knew he should stay in touch. But would he? Danny was a mess, and from what Jake had seen, that train wasn't stopping any time soon. He wasn't sure he wanted any part of that.

Jake's stomach grumbled and he craved coffee; it was time to get the day going. The events of the last twenty-four hours had derailed his routine and he was determined to get back on track. He had the Jeep thing to resolve and there was endless work to be done on the house. Lucas had not yet returned the phone call from yesterday but Jake wasn't too worried about it; he kind of liked driving the Mustang.

Later, he would decide what to do about Paige McAlister. The shock of Danny's news had worn off, and in telling his story to Amy, Jake had lifted the weight that had been pressing down on him for so long. The weight wasn't gone, but at least it wasn't suffocating anymore. And for that, Jake was grateful.

The day would be a hot one, but for now the morning cool of the canyon held, the air sweet with the smell of oak and wildflowers. It was a fine morning for a walk and Jake thought of huevos rancheros and good black coffee at the Silverado Cafe. His stomach grumbled again, and he went inside the house to rouse Amy.

***

THEY TOOK their time getting there, and along the way Jake talked about his father and his years spent living in the canyon house. The words came easily after last night's confessional, and Jake was surprised how natural it felt to let someone in.

The food at the café was excellent as usual. After eating, Jake and Amy talked over coffee.

"What I don't get is, how does your friend know for certain that you are Paige's father."

"He doesn't," Jake said. "He's just repeating what Susan supposedly told him."

"It sounds like you're not convinced he's telling the truth."

"Who knows? Danny drinks, and from what I've seen, it clouds his thinking. He's erratic and emotional, and you combine that with the booze, you've got a bad situation. Susan might've told him some things, but it's anybody's guess what the truth is."

"How did she know?"

"What?"

"That you were the father?"

"I don't understand."

"Well, she was sleeping with her boyfriend during that trip, wasn't she? She would have no way of knowing which one of you it was."

"According to Danny, Bruce saw a specialist when he and Susan were unable to have more children. The doctor said he was infertile from some genetic defect he was born with. I guess that sealed it for Susan."

"That's interesting, but still not conclusive. Doctors get that kind of stuff wrong all the time."

"That's what I thought, too."

The waitress came by and poured more coffee. Amy looked out the window at several cars passing by on the canyon road. She turned and looked at Jake.

"I guess that's it, then."

Her face held an uncertain expression, her eyes pensive, and Jake wondered if all this was finally settling in. It was a messy, ugly truth he'd laid on her. At some point, Amy was sure to see Jake for the deeply flawed man he was.

"That's the story. Who knows if any of it is true?"

"Are you going to try and find out?"

The question hung between them for a long moment.

"I honestly have no idea," Jake said with a sigh.

Amy reached out and touched his arm.

"My advice? Take your time. You'll know when it feels right."

AFTER BREAKFAST Jake decided he would skip working for the day and spend some time with Amy. First, he took her to meet Hector. She fell in love with his quaint little house at the end of the canyon, and he charmed her with his wit and stories of old Silverado. As they got ready to leave, Jake put the top down on the Mustang.

"Did you buy a new car since I last saw you?" Hector said.

"I was going to ask you about that," Amy said. "What happened to your Jeep?"

"It's a long story," Jake said. Now was not the time to get into all that, and he gave Hector a practiced look, receiving a small nod in return. Hector chuckled jovially.

"I understand, *mi hijo.*" He turned to Amy and took her hand, his eyes sparkling. "Our friend tells such long-winded tales, and I am certain if he begins, your entire day will be spent here at my house."

Amy giggled. "*Mi hijo?*" she said.

"A term of endearment, my dear."

"Enough of that, old man," Jake said sternly.

"As you wish." Hector tipped his straw hat. "It was a pleasure to meet you, Miss Watson."

"Likewise, Mr. Santiago."

"Let's hit it," Jake said.

Before leaving, Hector pulled Jake aside and whispered to him.

"Can you see me later today? I have some information to share with you."

Jake nodded, and then he joined Amy in the car.

They cruised the length of Santiago Canyon Road—music playing loud, the sun in their face and wind in their hair—out past Irvine Lake and down to Old Towne Orange, where they perused the antique shops on Main Street and took pictures at the traffic circle. From there they went to Sunset Beach, ate lunch at the Harbor House, and then rolled north on PCH to Long Beach, over the Vincent Thomas Bridge and into San Pedro. They had beers and shot pool at a longshoremen's bar on Gaffey Street, and when they finally left the joint, the sun was low over Palos Verdes and the heat of the day had subsided.

They took the 405 Freeway home, settling into rush hour traffic, talking the whole way. Jake felt at ease and he wondered at the ways of life, the trouble we make for ourselves for no good reason. He'd dreaded the idea of seeing Amy again, having convinced himself that no good would ever come of it. He laughed inside at his own stupidity, realizing once again that he was as full of it as the next guy. Probably more so.

For her part, Amy said and did all the right things, never pressing, seeming to hold in check her feelings for Jake. She was cool, naturally in tune with the day and Jake's mood. Amy was a good woman, and Jake was thankful for the opportunity to take one little step toward making it right with her. He had no illusions about the future, and that was okay. Just for today, that was okay.

Chapter 36

Jason Stafford sat at his desk flexing his hands. They were sore from his workout last night but the knuckles were clean, no bruising. He'd been laying off the heavy bag lately and it had been a while since he'd tuned anyone up, so it was to be expected that he'd feel it today.

The afternoon heat was up and yesterday's rainstorm was a forgotten memory, the sun reflecting brightly outside the second-floor window of Jason's Aliso Viejo condo. The condo fronted the 73 Toll Road, with sweeping views of the Saddleback Valley and Santa Ana Mountains beyond. It was your typical nondescript beige stucco box, no different than countless others that sprang up like weeds all over South Orange County. Jason had paid too much for the place and despite an improving market, he was upside down on the mortgage. As soon as he had enough cash put away he was going to dump it for a major upgrade.

He flipped open the OC Register and perused the local news, smiling when he read the story about an assault at the Rail Bar. He lowered the paper and thought about it. The trucker cap was a nice touch. Very memorable. He'd bought that thing from a disabled vet at a flea market in Tustin. He should've bought a boxful. Maybe this weekend he'd go back and see if that dude was still selling them. That could be his trademark for future workouts.

The White Power Enforcer strikes again. Nice.

Of course, he couldn't overdo it or else he'd get caught, and that wouldn't do. Maybe he could mix it up a little, try a different slogan each time. After a few minutes thinking about it, he chucked the idea as pure nonsense and got down to work.

He took a memory card from his pocket and inserted it into an adapter plugged into the desktop computer, beginning a tedious task that he'd been putting off for too long—listening to hours of recorded conversations, eavesdropping on the lives of an endless list of people he was tasked with keeping an eye on. Tedious or not, it needed to be done, and Bill McAlister counted on Jason to do it.

Before diving in, Jason sat back and thought for a minute. He was a little steamed. Bruce had called earlier to go over some things. But it was a ruse, and Jason figured out quickly that something was up. Bruce played it smooth, like he always did, laying his well-practiced rap on Jason, completely unaware of how transparent he was.

Back in high school Bruce was a cool cat, no doubt about it. But now that he was a big-shot preacher, he'd turned into a tool. It had been a gradual change that lately had gone into overdrive, and while Jason used to only occasionally think about beating Bruce's ass, these days the thought was near constant.

After a long-winded preamble, Bruce got down to the real point of the call. It seems Paige was a little upset yesterday after she'd had coffee with Jason. The details didn't matter, and Bruce sure didn't think that Jason had done anything wrong or had stepped out of line or anything like that. But still, this was his little girl and Bruce was obligated to follow through, even if the whole thing was a simple misunderstanding. So, it would probably be best if Jason took a step back for a while and let things cool down.

Jason literally bit his tongue while Bruce spoke, tasting blood, and he summoned every ounce of his willpower to stem the rise of anger he felt at the obvious reprimand. He offered no argument or explanation, keeping his words short and contrite. After the call was over, he took a moment to compose himself, regulating his breathing with deep inhales followed by long exhales. It wasn't meditation exactly—Jason wasn't *that* evolved—but a habit he'd gotten into purely by accident and had held onto over the last few years. The idea was to clear his mind of aggressive thoughts. It usually worked. When it didn't, Jason knew he'd have to seek release. Like last night.

Paige had rejected him, and that stung worse than the condescending nature of Bruce's call. Stung wasn't even the right word—it burned a hole right through him. It made him feel insignificant, *weak*, and that would never stand. His head went foggy with malevolence, and more regulated breaths were needed to bring it under control.

After the moment passed and Jason was thinking clearly, he realized that Bruce had not mentioned Jake Donahue or the thing with his Jeep. Interesting. Was Paige holding back on her old man?

Jason would think more on that later. For now, he had work to do. He put headphones on, cued the sound file and hit play. He took notes as he went along, and later he would extract the important parts and compile them on a flash drive for Bill McAlister's review. It was boring stuff and a few times Jason nearly dozed off. And then Jake Donahue started speaking to a woman. He called her Amy.

Jason perked up and listened more closely. He hit pause and took a single sheet of paper from the desk. It was the information he'd received when he ran the license plate of the Subaru Outback parked at Jake Donahue's house last night. The vehicle was registered to Amy Watson, from Truckee, California. Five foot eight inches tall, one hundred twenty-nine pounds, brown hair, green eyes. She had a pretty face, for a driver's license photo. A nice little package.

He hit play and continued listening.

The first part sounded like a lover's spat; interesting, but not very useful.

And then came the part about having a daughter. Now we're on to something. When Jake mentioned killing a child, Jason knew that he'd stumbled onto the motherlode. He was fully plugged in now, jotting notes, underlining key parts. After an hour, he stopped for a break.

Now it made sense, why Bruce was so fixated on Jake Donahue. And didn't Jason know it all along? Didn't he know there was dirt there, just waiting to be found? Jason's instincts were well-honed and he trusted them without fail, but still, it was immensely satisfying whenever his faith was rewarded with actual proof.

It was almost time for his shift to start and he had to get moving. There was still more on the surveillance recording but Jason doubted it would top what he'd just heard. He considered the implications of the information, and the opportunities it provided. This was a game changer, no doubt about it. But how should he play it?

After a moment of thought, he grabbed his cell phone and dialed a number.

"We've got a situation," Jason said without hello.

Chapter 37

It was dusk on Wednesday when Jake and Amy returned to the canyon house. They'd had a full day and Amy was tired, and she went into the spare bedroom to rest while Jake puttered around the house taking care of a few small chores. When he went outside to collect the mail he ran into his neighbor.

"Hey, Bob."

"Hi, Jake. How's it goin'?"

"Same old."

"I hear that."

They stood at the row of boxes along the edge of the road, retrieving their mail. "The rain was a nice change," Jake said, as he flipped through his.

"It was, but this heat is a bitch. I hope it breaks soon."

"Me too."

"Have you decided about the house?" Bob said.

"Not completely, but I'm leaning toward staying."

"It's a nice place. You can probably get a good price for it."

"Probably."

"I miss having your dad around. He was a character."

"That he was."

They made more small talk as they walked back to their houses. When they got to Jake's driveway, Bob said, "Say, Jake, you haven't been having any trouble with the cops, have you?"

It seemed an odd question, and Jake was thrown a little by it. "Uh…no, not that I know of," he said awkwardly. "Why do you ask?"

"Wait here a minute. I have something to show you."

Jake nodded, his curiosity piqued. After a few minutes, Bob returned, holding a folded sheet of paper. "What's that?" Jake said.

"It's a picture from my security camera."

"Which one?"

Bob Jenkins owned a security consulting firm and his house had more cameras and security devices than a high-priority government facility. He was always showing Jake the latest and greatest stuff on the market, trying to sell him on a system. He was never pushy about it though, and Jake always indulged him because Bob was a genuinely nice guy.

"I have a few, that's for sure," Bob said with a chuckle. "This came from the camera on the garage."

"And?"

"There was a fella poking around earlier today, along the side of your house."

"What do you mean?"

"I'm not sure exactly. I only caught a glimpse of him from my side window. He was turned away from me so I couldn't tell what he was doing."

"You sure it wasn't the cable guy? I recently had service put in. Maybe he was here adjusting something."

"I thought it might be something like that. But when I checked the camera feed I knew that wasn't it."

Bob went on to explain that his cameras took pictures at regular intervals and recorded them on a hard drive. The garage camera's point of view included the side of Jake's house. He handed Jake the folded sheet of paper.

"I printed that earlier today."

Jake took the sheet of paper and stepped closer to a yard light mounted on a pole next to the driveway. He unfolded the paper and angled it in the light to better see. The photograph was a little grainy but the man's face was clear enough. It was Jason Stafford, captured just as he was turning to walk away.

"Isn't that the sheriff who patrols the canyon?" Bob said.

Jake looked up from the paper. "I believe it is."

"What do you suppose he was doing at the side of your house?"

"I have no idea. But I'll try and find out."

"Let me know when you do."

"Sure thing. And thanks."

AMY WAS still sleeping when Jake entered the house. He put the photograph of Stafford in a drawer and sat down at the kitchen table to reason it out. Anger and confusion muddled his thinking, and he couldn't organize his thoughts. And then something shot through the fog. Jake rose quickly and went outside.

A hedge extended the length of the house in the area where Stafford was photographed. "Let's see what you were up to," Jake said to himself, staring at the hedge.

He got down on his hands and knees and started crawling, looking under the hedge. About halfway down he saw it—a rectangular plastic box attached to the house with Velcro strips. He pried it from the clapboard siding and stood to examine it. There was a hinged cover and Jake opened it, saw a circuit board and frequency indicator, and a memory card inserted into a slot. Jake didn't know anything about spy gear, but he'd seen enough movies and TV shows to recognize a surveillance device. He pulled the memory card and put it in his pocket, and then went inside the house to find the transmitter.

He eased open the door to the spare bedroom to make sure Amy was still sleeping; he wasn't sure he wanted her to know about this. She was out cold and Jake went to work. He stood in the middle of his living room and considered possible hiding places. It was probably small enough to be placed just about anywhere in the house, so he was basically looking for a needle in a haystack. He thought about the movies he'd seen, and he

checked the obvious places; the cordless telephone, the two table lamps, the baseboards, the stereo equipment and flat screen
TV. Nothing.

Jake figured that Stafford had installed the device on the
day he surprised Hector, and Hector had said that Stafford was
in the house for only about twenty minutes, not a lot of time to
plant the bug and install the receiver outside. He briefly considered getting Bob Jenkins's help in finding it—being in the
security business, he likely had a device that could scan the
room—but he decided against bringing him into it.

Back to the search.

Jake carefully looked at each object in the living room. He
thought of the wall outlets and switches, dreading having to
take them apart. He reasoned that Stafford would have placed
the bug as close as possible to the outside recording device in
order to get maximum reception. He looked at the east wall but
found nothing out of the ordinary. The ceiling smoke detector
leading to the spare bedroom caught his eye. It was near an
outside window, just a few feet from where Jake found the re-
corder.

Staring at the smoke detector, Jake's heart beat rapidly. He
got a step stool from the kitchen and positioned it, took one
step up and reached for the unit, twisting it firmly and removing the cover. He saw a small plastic device taped inside the
gutted smoke detector. Just then, Amy came through the bedroom door.

"Jake?" she said sleepily. "What are you doing?"

Jake's back was turned and he quickly slipped the bug into
his shirt pocket and placed the cover back on the smoke detector.

"Changing the battery," he said over his shoulder. He
folded the step stool and smiled at Amy. "Did you have a good
nap?"

"The best. Aren't you tired?"

"A little. Let me put this away."

Jake went into the kitchen, picked up the receiver from the
counter and took the photograph of Jason Stafford out of the

drawer, and he walked out the back door and went into the garage.

WHEN HE got back to the house, Amy was curled up on the couch reading a book. Jake made a show of doing some work on his laptop at the kitchen table, but his mind was on his discovery. He was sure that Bruce McAlister had set it up. Was he really *that* afraid of Jake spilling their secret from thirty years ago? As for Jason Stafford, Jake had visions of beating him senseless and cramming that bug down his throat.

There was a knock on the front door and Jake got up to answer it.

"Hello," Paige McAlister said when the door was opened.

"Uh…hi," Jake replied, startled by her presence.

Neither of them spoke for an awkward moment, and then Jake snapped to and invited Paige into his house. Amy had set her book down and was looking at them with a curious expression. Jake motioned Paige toward the sofa.

"This is my friend Amy," he said. "Amy, this is Paige McAlister." Jake paused. "Her father is an old friend of mine."

"Pleased to meet you," Amy said with a beaming smile.

She held onto Paige's hand and looked at her for a long moment, and then she turned and regarded Jake with intuitive eyes.

"It's nice to meet you," Paige said. She smiled, a little uncomfortably it seemed, and the three of them stood silently. Amy glanced from Jake to Paige several times before speaking.

"I was just about to take a shower. You don't mind, do you, Jake?" She gave him a conspiratorial look and he nodded imperceptibly.

"Not at all. When you're done, we'll figure out dinner."

Amy smiled and went into the spare bedroom and shut the door.

"You want an iced tea or something?" Jake said to Paige. "We can sit outside and talk."

"Water would be okay."

Jake got two bottles from the refrigerator and he led Paige out to the sun deck. It was dark now and he switched on the patio string lights. A neighbor was barbecuing, the breeze sending a tantalizing aroma wafting over, combined with the scent of jasmine and oak.

"This is nice," Paige said.

"It is," Jake replied.

They sat at the redwood table and drank their water. Jake wondered how Paige had found him. He was glad that she did, but he felt uncertain about her intentions.

"Do you own this house?"

"It was my father's. I inherited it when he died."

"I see." Paige seemed to gather her thoughts. "You're probably wondering how I got your address."

"The thought crossed my mind."

"I found it at my dad's church."

Jake nodded.

"Are you still close to him?" Paige said.

Jake hesitated, weighing his answer. He was on a slippery slope after the events of the last twenty-four hours, and while it had felt good telling his story to Amy, Jake knew that re-straint was still the best course. The fact that Paige might be his daughter added an emotional layer that was missing from their earlier encounter.

"No, I'm not close with Bruce," Jake finally replied. "The truth is, prior to last week I hadn't seen your father for some time."

"You saw him last week?"

"Yes, when I visited his church. I was impressed."

Paige's face lit up. "He's wonderful, isn't he?"

"Well, I'm not a churchgoer myself, but yes, I'd say that your dad has a definite talent when it comes to preaching."

"I'm glad that you went. The message is what's important, and if Dad was able to reach you, even a little bit, then he did his job."

Jake recalled the good feeling he'd had after hearing Bruce's sermon, the way it stuck with him and motivated him. Paige was right, it was the message that mattered most.

"How are his plans coming along?"

"They're moving forward," Paige said. "Slowly. Dad's been on pins and needles about it. Grandpa Bill even more."

"Is he involved in it?"

"Oh, absolutely. More than my father. In fact, the whole idea started with him."

"Interesting."

"Did you ever know him very well?"

"Your grandfather used to bend my ear back in the day. Mostly about religion, but sometimes other things. Bruce wouldn't give him the time of day, so Bill latched onto me." Jake laughed. "It used to drive your dad crazy."

"Sounds about right."

They sipped their water, an easy silence settling between them. Jake felt comfortable around Paige, and he sensed that she felt the same about him. He tried to imagine how it would go, broaching the subject of her paternity.

"I actually had a reason to see you," Paige said.

"I wondered about that."

"It's about your Jeep. I was able to resolve the situation and you can pick it up any time, and there won't be an impound fee."

Jake gave a look of surprise. "Thank you for that," he said. "How did you work it out?"

"A little old-fashioned string pulling," Paige said with a sly smile. "I know some people on the Orange PD—from church—and once I explained the situation, they were more than happy to help out." She gave out a cute giggle, her eyes bright. "Of course, I fibbed a little, told you were an old family friend, practically like an uncle to me. Is that bad of me?"

"Not at all," Jake replied with a laugh. "I certainly approve."

"I still can't believe Jason would pull a lame stunt like that."

"What makes you think he had anything to do with it?"

"It's pretty obvious there's something going on between you two. I won't pry into your business, so you don't have to explain. Suffice to say, I understand how he can be."

"And how's that?"

"Difficult. And pushy."

"I noticed some tension between him and you."

"I guess we have something in common," Paige said.

Jake nodded, and sipped his water.

"He went to high school with you and Dad, didn't he?"

"He was a few years behind us."

"Did you know him?"

"Not really."

Jake paused, considered elaborating on the matter. Paige might not have been prying, but Jake felt an urge to tell her more, to protect her from Stafford. Or something like that. He wasn't sure what he felt, it was all so mixed-up in his head.

"Stafford had a run-in with a close friend of mine recently. I got involved and apparently got on Stafford's bad side. Back in school I knew he had a temper, but that's all I really knew about him. Until the incident with my friend, I hadn't even thought about the guy for thirty years. It was kind of a shock to see him at the coffeehouse yesterday."

"For you and me both," Paige said.

"Do you feel threatened by him?"

Paige seemed surprised by the question. "I'm not sure. Do you?"

Now it was Jake's turn to be surprised. Paige kept him on his toes, no doubt about it. He thought about the surveillance device and Stafford's veiled threats. He supposed he *did* feel threatened, but that wasn't what Paige needed to hear right now.

"Naw," Jake said. "He's a punk."

"A punk with a badge. Which might spell trouble."

"If we let it." Jake smiled.

"I guess that makes us brothers in arms, then?"

"It makes us something."

Jake had an instant déjà vu flashback to the playful banter he used to engage Susan in all those years ago. The feeling knocked him back a step, and he smiled at Paige to mask it.

"Well, I'd better get along," she said. "I don't want to intrude on your evening."

Paige stood to leave. Jake briefly considered inviting her to dinner, but just as quickly decided against it. One step at a time, he told himself. Figure this thing out first.

"It was good to see you again," Jake said, rising from his chair. "Let me give you my number. If you need anything at all, call me. And if that fool Stafford gives you a hard time, you *better* call."

He smiled and gave Paige the number, and she entered it in her phone.

"Will do," she said.

Paige hesitated before leaving, seeming to consider something, and then she reached out and gave Jake a hug. He was stunned momentarily, before hugging her in return. She turned and walked away.

Jake stood alone on the deck, reflecting on what had just taken place. He heard Paige's car start, and the sound of it driving away.

"My God, Jake. She looks just like you."

He turned and saw Amy standing at the back door. Their eyes met, and Jake nodded in recognition.

Chapter 38

Bill McAlister grew impatient waiting for Bruce to arrive. It was past dark now and he took a moment to gaze out the window of his study, at the lights on the communication towers atop Saddleback, a moment of respite from more serious matters. He'd been in constant action since the phone call earlier in the day from Jason Stafford—full damage control mode—trying to mitigate Bruce's carelessness and blatant stupidity.

Bill always knew the potential existed for Stafford to wander off the reservation. The man was duplicitous, with a self-serving streak that Bill had tried in vain to eliminate through spiritual mentoring and a firm hand. The very qualities that made Jason Stafford so useful also posed a threat if not sufficiently controlled. The key was obedience, and absolute loyalty. Once that loyalty was breached, there was no turning back. Like right now.

It wasn't so much what Jason said during the phone call, it was more a feeling that Bill had, and if he had learned anything in his life it was to trust his instincts. You only know what you know, and swift action based on the facts as you understood them nearly always paid dividends. Conjecture was useless. Indecision was fatal. And if your decisions proved wrong, you simply regrouped and formed a new plan. The key was to keep moving forward.

Jason had stumbled onto information he should never have, and Bill had no doubts that he would attempt to use that information for his own ends. Even if it didn't happen right away, it would eventually, and there was no way Bill was going to live with *that* sword hanging over him. Bruce may not have the foresight to know better, but Bill damn sure did, and he didn't get where he was today by allowing any man to have leverage over him.

In all his dealings with Stafford, Bill had been careful to insulate himself, using various techniques to keep the trail of culpability a safe distance away in the event Jason decided to turn on him. Bill had set it up so others would take the fall long before he did. And Bruce was completely insulated, by design, which made this whole situation that much more galling.

There was a knock at the front door. Bill made no effort to get up. Let the boy come to me, he thought bitterly, Bruce's ignorance festering.

It would hurt to lose a man like Jason Stafford, and Bill did not relish the thought of finding a replacement. Maybe it was time to reconsider the need for such a man. They were so close now. Once the new church was underway, maybe Bill could finally rest. After all, when you've reached the top of the mountain, what more is there?

But that kind of thinking was foreign to Bill McAlister, fitting him like another man's clothes. He wasn't sure he could ever truly rest. If he stopped, he feared he would die.

Bracing himself for the task at hand, Bill settled into his chair and poured some whiskey. It was a three-finger night, no question. He added some rocks and a finger of mineral water and he was set. He drank deeply from the glass, savoring the smoky vapor and the mellow heat in his throat. After another deep drink, he freshened his cocktail.

Bill considered his only son, feeling equal measures of pride and disappointment. There was no doubt that he loved the boy. And he believed in what Bruce stood for. He knew that despite his shortcomings, Bruce was the absolute right man to lead the Canyon New Life Ministry into the future. But damn if the boy didn't continue to do stupid shit that confounded the hell out of his father.

It happened whenever Bruce fancied himself a planner and he attempted to chart his own course within the carefully constructed world Bill had set up. Bruce had his own special traits, his own unique skillset, and building empires wasn't part of it. That was Bill's department. They were two halves of the same whole, complementing each other beautifully. But whenever Bruce endeavored to act independently, it invariably threw a monkey wrench in the whole works. Like now.

Now it was up to Bill to pick up the pieces and repair the damage, and to keep the train chugging down that long track to glory. The fact that he secretly enjoyed the challenge of cleaning up after his son was irrelevant. He was good at this stuff, and in his declining years he found there just wasn't that much to get excited about anymore. Bill supposed that was the price for reaching the top of the mountain.

He expected resistance tonight and resolved to brook no argument. There would be no equivocating, no deviating from the plan. Bruce had put this thing into motion by his own misguided actions, and he would stand up and bear the consequences. They were set to lose a good man because of Bruce's shortsightedness, and if the boy wasn't reigned in, then the whole operation might collapse, a lifetime of work down the toilet. And that would never stand.

Bill would make sure that Bruce towed the line, and that would be the end of it. The chips will fall and order will be restored. There was no doubt about that.

Footsteps sounded in the hallway. Bill leaned back in his chair, closed his eyes, and waited.

Chapter 39

Jake and Amy made small talk as they prepared a light meal at home, neither of them hungry enough to go out. Amy kept the conversation light and she asked no questions about Paige McAlister's visit. Jake's head was filled with information and ideas, hard truths and conflicting signals pulling him in all directions. He remained pleasant with Amy, if not completely distracted.

After clearing the dishes and washing up, Jake asked if Amy minded him running over to Hector's house for a while. He was thinking about earlier in the day, when Hector said he had some information to share. Amy said she didn't mind, and after having coffee together out on the deck, Jake left.

"Your lady friend is very nice," Hector said when Jake entered his house.

"She liked you too. I'll be sure to pass along your approval."

"Have the seeds of romance been planted?"

Hector did not know of Jake and Amy's relationship in Truckee. He was vaguely aware that Jake had been involved with someone while living there, but he didn't know the circumstances.

"She's just a friend."

"For now, *mi hijo*."

Hector winked and took a seat in his easy chair. Jake let the comment go and he sat on the sofa across from Hector. Hector pointed to the paper sack Jake set on the floor.

"Something for me?"

"Later. First tell me what you wanted to talk about."

"As you wish. Do you remember the *campesinos*?"

"The ones abandoned in the desert?"

"Yes. Do you remember the man they spoke of, the one at Mr. McAlister's church, the hard man with the blue eyes?"

Jake nodded. "Go on."

"Yesterday I met with Father Ramón at his church in Santa Ana. When I was there, I saw our friend Mr. Stafford sitting in a car parked on the street."

"What was he doing?"

"I believe he was watching the church. It is not the first time I have seen him do this."

"Does he know that you know?"

"I cannot say for certain."

"What happened?"

"One of the *campesinos* has been working at the church. His name is Jose Chavez. He saw the car parked on the street and he recognized Mr. Stafford. He became very agitated and quite afraid. Father Ramón asked him what was the matter, and Jose told him that Mr. Stafford was the one he had met at the church in Mexico, the one they called the blue-eyed Devil."

"That's...interesting."

"There is more. Father Ramón insists on pursuing legal action against Mr. Stafford for his part in what happened to the *campesinos* in the desert. He has hired a civil rights attorney and has begun an investigation."

"Already? Seems kind of quick, considering all this happened yesterday."

"Father Ramón has been working with the attorney for some time, building his case, as the saying goes. I have my doubts about his chances for success, but it is not for me to say. When I told him that the man watching the church was a police officer, Father Ramón became indignant, and he insisted that justice would be served in the matter."

"Did you tell him that Stafford works for Bruce?"

"No, I did not."

"Why?"

"I did not deem it relevant at the time."

Jake raised an eyebrow.

"Let me explain," Hector said. "I do not know the true nature of Mr. Stafford's relationship with Mr. McAlister, therefore anything I say would merely be speculation. I do not want to fuel Father Ramón's anger with bad information. The truth will come out in its own time."

"You're a better man than me, Hector. I would have thrown Bruce under the bus in a heartbeat."

Hector smiled. "Do not sell yourself short, *mi hijo*. You are an honorable man."

Jake snorted. "Don't be so sure, old friend."

"So, I have told you my story. Now it is your turn." Hector pointed to the paper sack.

Jake picked it up and emptied the contents onto the coffee table. "I found this inside my house today."

Hector studied the items on the table. "Someone has been eavesdropping on you," he said, raising his eyes to Jake's.

"I'm pretty sure this was installed on the day you had your run-in with Stafford."

"I see. It explains much, does it not?"

"It explains what he was doing inside my house."

"How did you find this device?"

"My neighbor gave me a photograph of Stafford. It was taken earlier today when Bob saw a man at the side of my house acting suspiciously."

"Bob Jenkins?"

"Yes. His security camera captured the image, and Bob recognized the man as Stafford."

"I see. This is indeed an interesting development. And you believe this involves Mr. McAlister?"

"Of course it does. Bruce is afraid our secret will come out and it will ruin his plans for Limestone Canyon. He had Stafford plant this thing in my house to keep tabs on me."

"Your secret about Bahia de Cortez."

"Yes, Hector."

"The place where the *campesino* saw the blue-eyed Devil."

Jake nodded.

"And so we come full circle," Hector said. "It is odd how life works, is it not? Events separated by time, yet connected by a common thread."

"The common thread being Bruce McAlister."

"As it appears. But there may be more to the story."

"There may be, but I really don't care. Bruce's paranoia about the past doesn't concern me, and I have no desire to drag that sorry incident out into the light of day. But this thing with Stafford is getting out of hand. I'm afraid I'll have to force a resolution soon."

"Is that wise?"

"Probably not. But right now, I don't really care."

"I see."

Neither man spoke. The sounds of the canyon came through an open window, and Jake's mind drifted to memories of his youth, to times spent in this house and the sense of security he felt being in Hector's presence. It was here in this room that Jake told Hector about Mexico. He'd expected condemnation for his actions, but what he received was love and understanding, and in his darkest days Jake would remember the things Hector said to him that night and he would lean on those words to keep himself from falling.

"Look, Hector, I know there's no upside to starting a war with a cop. And there's no way I can report this officially, they'll never believe me. But I can't just let it go. Not with Bruce, and certainly not with Stafford."

"The things you say are true, Jake. I understand the position you are in. But you must understand that men like Mr. Stafford are not easily swayed, and they generally do not respond favorably to threats."

"Who's talking about making threats?"

"Perhaps I have misspoken. But I believe the point has been taken."

Jake nodded and Hector smiled warmly.

"Now," Hector said. "Tell me about your Jeep."

Jake told the story and Hector listened without comment. When finished, Jake waited for a response.

"I can see the reason for your feelings regarding Mr. Stafford," Hector said. "Although I still advise caution. I will say though, a younger version of myself would have likely wanted to kick the crap out of this *pendejo* policeman."

Hector's expression was stern, and Jake did a double take. He couldn't recall ever hearing a blue word—English or Spanish—come from Hector Santiago.

Hector smiled impishly. "My words startle you?"

"A little."

"Don't forget, *mi hijo*, I was once a young man too, full of verve and pride. I have not forgotten those days."

"I'll bet you were a handful."

"Possibly. But you must listen to my advice, and not start something you cannot finish."

"I'll take that on advisement," Jake said.

"Do you need help getting your Jeep back?"

"Funny you should ask. It's already been taken care of. By Bruce McAlister's daughter." Jake looked at Hector expectantly.

Hector studied Jake's expression, and then he said, "I sense you have a story to tell."

"That I do."

"First, I'll make coffee."

Hector shuffled off to the kitchen while Jake collected his thoughts.

A POT of coffee later, Jake finished telling his story. Hector asked no questions during the telling, and when it was finished he sat perfectly still, immersed in thought. It was late, after eleven o'clock, and Jake was wired to the gills from the coffee.

He felt restless, thoughts of Jason Stafford creeping into his head, dark thoughts tinged with malice. Everything was out in the open now. All that remained was for the other shoe to drop.

"Fatherhood is a wonderful thing, *mi hijo*," Hector said.

"Let's not get ahead of ourselves. None of this is settled yet."

"It is only an observation."

"Point taken. I'm not sure what to do, Hector."

"Why do you feel the need to do something?"

"Shouldn't I?"

"You have lived many years without this information. Now that you have it, I am sure you will be forgiven if you delay action for a while longer."

"Makes sense."

"I am a sensible man." Hector gave out a booming laugh.

"I'm still trying to sort it all out," Jake said. "I can't even begin to comprehend what it means to have a daughter. I feel a connection to her. It's hard to explain, but I know it's real. I just don't know what to do about it. And this thing with Bruce, this…I don't even know what to call it. How do I reconcile that? Where do I go from here?"

"You live for today, and let tomorrow take care of itself. I have found that in times of trouble, you must keep your focus on the present, and trust that your instincts are true and your spirit is strong. In this manner, you will persevere, and the answers you seek will be revealed in time."

"And if they aren't?"

"Then the questions you have asked are unimportant."

"Hmm."

"You are skeptical?"

"I'm tired, Hector. Tired of running from things that happened a lifetime ago."

"Then you must stop running and make a stand. Embrace your history in all its hideous glory, and rejoice in the life that you have been given. You are far from the worst man who has ever lived."

"Thanks. I appreciate the sentiment."

"My pleasure. And now we must call it a night. I have an early day tomorrow with Father Ramón, and after that, one of my sons requires my assistance with some home improvements."

"You're a good man, Hector."

"I try my best. So, you will heed my advice regarding Mr. Stafford?"

"I'll consider it, old friend."

JAKE DROVE slowly down the canyon road. He kept glancing at the paper sack on the seat next to him, thinking about Jason Stafford entering his house, violating his privacy. He gripped the steering wheel, anger bleeding inside him, caffeine stimulated nerves fogging his thinking.

Hector's advice was sound. Unfortunately, Jake was in no mood for sound advice. He was in the mood for retribution. He was in the mood for settling scores. Jake might not win this fight, but he could sure give it a hell of an effort. He pulled to the side of the road, grabbed his cell phone and dialed 911.

Chapter 40

At eleven o'clock on Wednesday night Jason Stafford sat in his patrol car at the turnout to Irvine Lake. Moonlight filtered through the tall trees ringing the parking lot, the gentle sound of lapping water drifted through the open window. Jason felt contemplative. Troubled was more like it.

It had been hours since his phone call to Bill McAlister and he'd yet to receive instructions. Surely there was some action required of him, some necessary task that only he could perform. But so far there had been nothing, only radio silence. And that troubled Jason greatly. It wasn't anything overt, just an intuitive sense of the natural order having been slightly disturbed—just one or two clicks off-center.

Bill McAlister had reacted strangely when Jason told him about the recorded conversation between Jake Donahue and Amy Watson. They spoke only briefly about it, Jason's excitement cut off at the knees by Bill's seeming indifference. That was red flag number one.

Red flag number two was Bill's lack of decisiveness. He usually had a quick answer ready no matter what the situation, and if he didn't have a plan seemingly mapped out and ready to go, he at least faked it with conviction. But not this time. This time he was…weak? Unsure? Something like that. Jason couldn't even put words to it, it was so foreign to him. But it was there, regardless of what you called it.

Bill had abruptly ended the call, saying he'd get back to Jason. And now, with each passing hour and no contact, Jason became increasingly concerned that he'd overplayed his hand. Maybe he should have waited, held onto the information for a while before acting on it. Maybe he should have strategized a little more. Bill had always taught him to think things through and not act impulsively, good advice that Jason had mostly taken to heart. Except this time. This time he shot from the hip, and it was looking like he'd miscalculated.

Jason considered it an even-money bet that Bill knew about what went down in Mexico. It was certainly possible that Bruce had never told his old man. But then again, thirty years is a long time to keep a secret. Bill gave nothing away, his words and tone of voice completely neutral, and Jason couldn't get a read on it. He almost came right out and asked but his intuition held him back.

It was true that Jason viewed the information as leverage for his own gain, but Bill McAlister had no way of knowing that. Not unless the guy was a mind reader. Jason played with that one for a moment. What if Bill *could* read his mind? Not literally of course, but what if he sensed Jason's intentions? A shudder literally went through him at the thought. Jason might be a badass, but he knew that to cross Bill McAlister was to invite grievous consequences.

Sure, Bill was a God-fearing man and all that, and he followed the Good Book diligently, but he was also a straight-up son of a bitch who could cite biblical chapter and verse to justify any action he deemed necessary. Which meant that Jason would most definitely have to tread lightly. He was still fully in Bill's corner, but this information was valuable, and Jason would be a fool to let it slip through his hands.

Jason had not divulged everything to Bill McAlister. He'd held back the part about Paige. He still hadn't come to terms with it, the possibility that Jake Donahue was her father. Whenever he imagined a life with Paige, Jason naturally pictured it including Bruce and Bill. But this little twist on the program cast everything into doubt. Did he still want her if it was true?

He wondered if Bill knew who Paige's real father was. Did Bruce know? Maybe that was skeleton number two hanging in the McAlister family closet. That's a hell of a one-two punch right there. Jason's instincts had told him there was dirt to be found between Bruce and Jake, and damn if he wasn't right about that. He thought about how Jake nearly got all weepy when he came by the church office last week and he saw the portrait on the wall, the one with Bruce and Susan and Paige. Was he still carrying a flame for that bitch? This thing had some angles to it, no doubt, and Jason had to carefully think it through before he took his next step.

Yet despite the tantalizing possibilities that arose from exploiting Bruce's secret, Jason couldn't get Bill McAlister's silence off his mind, and the notion that he'd made a critical mistake. He tried to think of a legitimate reason to call the old man, just to take his temperature, maybe suss out where he stood, but everything he came up with felt wrong. Bill would sniff out Jason's fishing expedition instantly. He'd told Jason to stand by, and no matter how agonizing it was, that's what Jason had to do.

All this thinking was doing a number on him. The night had been dead, leaving far too much time to run endless laps in his head. At eleven twenty a call came in about a suspected break in at the Silverado Canyon Market. Thank God, Jason thought, as he spun his cruiser around and headed down Santiago Canyon Road, hoping for some action to keep his mind off things he had no control over.

Chapter 41

S it down," Bill McAlister said when Bruce entered the study.

Bruce took a seat across the desk from his father. He noticed the drink, a stout one by the looks of it. Tonight's version of Bill McAlister looked sharp of mind and primed for action, as opposed to last night when the old man gave off the appearance of a whipped dog. What a difference a day makes, Bruce thought sarcastically.

He was agitated and impatient over being summoned two nights in a row. He kept it in check though, forcing himself into a submissive state of mind if only to appease the old man so he could get the hell out of here pronto.

"You fucked up, Bruce."

Bruce stared back at his father. "You must be angry," he said. "You use that word, what? One or two times a year."

"Shitcan the attitude, Son. I'm not in the mood."

Bruce held up his hands in surrender. "Considered it shit-canned," he said curtly.

"I got a call from Jason today."

"So?"

"He knows about Mexico."

Of course he does, Bruce thought dismissively. He's our man down there. What the hell is this anyway, is Dad losing his mind?

"I don't understand," Bruce said, playing dumb.

"I realize you don't understand, Bruce. That's why you're here."

Bruce's jaw tightened. He wanted this meeting over with, but he knew he had to play along. After all, this was the dance they did, he and his father, the steps unchanged for thirty years, the tune a tired old dirge that Bruce could never fully erase from his memory.

"You got me, Dad. What have I done now? What great transgression have I committed?"

"When did we put Jake Donahue under surveillance? And I use the term 'we' loosely."

"What do you mean?"

"Stop it, Bruce. You know exactly what I'm talking about. You put surveillance on Jake. And there was no 'we' involved, because you did it on your own."

"I wasn't aware I had to clear every little thing with you."

"Every little thing? That's what you think this is?"

"Why don't you tell me what it is, because I'm truly lost here."

"Jason knows about Mexico."

"I know, you already said that. So what? He's involved, so of course he knows." Bruce paused a moment, and then he said, "Are you drunk, Dad?"

Bill's face reddened and he visibly shuddered. He stabbed a finger at Bruce, his eyes bulging.

"Don't you dare condemn me!"

"Who's condemning?" Bruce shot back. "I just don't understand what's going on here."

Bill breathed deeply as he slowly regained his composure. Bruce could tell the old man wanted to hit his drink but fought against it. Bill slid the glass aside and leaned forward, his arms on the desk.

"Jason Stafford knows you killed that boy down in Mexico. That's what this is about."

Bruce was momentarily stunned.

"Sorry. I, uh…I thought it was about the other thing in Mexico."

"Well it's not. Why did you do it, Bruce? There was no reason to surveil Jake Donahue. He posed no threat to us. But now, Jason is the one who poses a threat."

"Jason? Why would he be a threat?"

"Because he's a corruptible opportunist. And you gave him an opening."

"An opening for what?"

"Come on, Bruce, use your head for once."

Bill's eyes bore into his son. Bruce tried to stand up to it, but after a minute he looked away—that steely gaze had always rattled him, from the time he was a child.

"How did you find out about this?" he said quietly, self-conscious for having wilted once again in front of his father.

"He called me today. He was transcribing recordings when he came across a conversation between Donahue and a woman named Amy Watson. Do you know her?"

"No."

"Well she knows all about you."

Bruce felt the color go out of his face.

"Unintended consequences," Bill said. "Bet you never stopped to consider that."

Bruce had no reply. He sat stiffly in his chair, waiting for a sign.

"What made you do it, Son?"

There was a note of sympathy in Bill's voice and Bruce latched onto it, reverting automatically to the small boy who would desperately try and win his father's approval. This was long before those defiant, troubled years in high school when every interaction was a battle and lines were drawn and re-drawn as the two of them fought to hold their ground.

"I was concerned he would talk. I thought I was doing the right thing."

"Why would he talk? The man has stayed silent for thirty years. Hell, he's been *gone* for thirty years. If he had a mind to make trouble for you, he would have done it a long time ago."

"Who knows what he might do now? Once he heard about the new church, maybe he'd decide to spill his guts."

"That's not likely."

"How do you know?"

"Jake's not that way."

Bruce flashed back to high school, the way Jake and his father would huddle together and talk, Jake indulging the old man's whims like a favored son.

"You always liked him more than me," Bruce said bitterly.

"That's not true."

"I remember it differently."

"We're getting sidetracked. The point is, Jake represented no threat to you or to the Limestone deal. You had no cause to go off on your own and do something like this. You know your role here."

"Yeah?" Bruce said, a little salt back in his voice. "Remind me, Dad, what's my role?"

"Damn you, lose the impertinence. This isn't an opportunity for you to air old grievances. We've got to move on from this mistake."

"Fine. Whatever. Just tell me what you want from me."

Bill stared at his son before speaking. If they got through the next few days unscathed, it would be clear sailing into the future. This situation would pass and the threat would be neutralized. All Bruce had to do was follow orders.

"I want you to leave town."

"What?"

"The final vote on the land deal is scheduled for Monday at a closed-door meeting. I don't want you anywhere around when it happens."

"What about the public hearing?"

"It's been canceled."

"I don't get it. What's going on here?"

"Damage control. That's my role. Yours is to follow instructions. You'll leave town tomorrow for the church at Bahia de Cortez. A press release will be issued announcing a new program you're initiating down there to feed and vaccinate orphans. You'll return after the vote, and after Jason Stafford has been dealt with."

Bruce looked at his father incredulously. Bill indulged his cocktail then, taking a deep drink, watching Bruce over the rim of the glass as if daring him to say something about it. He set the glass down and laced his hands together on the desk.

"Do you understand what I've told you?"

Bruce took in a sharp breath, suppressing his anger. "Yes, I understand," he said tightly, knowing full well that debate was useless. His father was an immovable object at times like this, and anything less than complete surrender was a losing proposition.

"Good. The plane will be ready for you at eleven o'clock at John Wayne. There won't be any press there, but if any reporters happen to show up, you'll have no comment. Do you understand?"

"Yes, I understand."

"Goodnight, then. I have work to do. You can show yourself out."

Bill McAlister picked up his drink and spun his chair around, gazing at the lights on Saddleback. Bruce stared at the back of the chair for a long moment, and then he got up and left the room.

Chapter 42

Jake sat in his rented Mustang in the driveway of the post office, across the street from the Silverado Canyon Market. He had a clear view of the canyon road and the market. Anticipation goosed his nerves as he waited. He knew he was edging toward a precipice but didn't care. It was time to force the issue with Jason Stafford and there was no point dicking around about it. Dude wants to rumble, well then let's get it on.

His cell phone rang and Jake ignored it. Then he glanced at the screen and saw Lucas Summerfield's name. He picked up the phone.

"Lucas, where the hell have you been?"

"Jakey!" Lucas's voice boomed. "How are you?"

Jake could hear what sounded like casino noise in the background.

"Where are you?"

"Las Vegas. And I'm losing my ass so bad I've got no ass left to give. Hell, I can't even sit at a table anymore, because I've got no ass left!" Lucas laughed uncontrollably.

"What are you doing in Vegas?"

"I had to come here for a deposition and decided to hang out for a few days. I got my clock cleaned at the Bellagio so I came over here to Binion's to try my luck with the lowlifes."

"Sounds like fun."

"I miss Big Ed. Hard not to think of the man when I'm here at the old Horseshoe. He was a shitty gambler but a damn fine person. And that's the truth."

Jake wondered if Lucas wasn't a little hammered. Or maybe a lot hammered. Whatever. He had to bring him up to speed and get off the line. Things were about to get hot.

"I have something to tell you, Lucas, and I don't have a lot of time. You aren't drunk, are you?"

"I'm fine. Fire away."

Jake started with the impounded Jeep and then he segued into the situation with Jason Stafford. Lucas didn't interrupt. At some point, Jake heard the background noise diminish, as if Lucas had moved to a quieter spot. Jake spoke quickly, keeping his eyes glued to the canyon road, glancing occasionally at the clock to check the time. After a few minutes, he'd spilled the gist of it.

"That's a lot to digest," Lucas said when Jake was through. "What do you need from me?"

"I wanted help with the impound thing, but that's already been taken care of. As for the rest of it, I just wanted you to know. That way, if something bad goes down..."

Jake hesitated. He hadn't thought it through, the possibility of something bad going down. He knew that after tonight, all bets would be off.

"Anyway, I just wanted you to know, that's all."

"Don't worry, I got your back. You just don't do anything foolish, you hear? You go up against a bent cop, things will turn ugly fast. Promise me you'll keep things copacetic."

Jake didn't reply.

"Jake, did you hear me?"

Headlights beamed eastbound on the canyon road. Jake saw the light bar and knew it was time. "Sorry, Lucas, I have to go. Something just came up."

"Answer me, Jake. Promise me you'll keep an even keel."

"I promise."

"Good. I'm heading home tomorrow. Or maybe the next day. But you sit tight and we'll strategize when I get back. Got it?"

"I got it. See ya, Lucas."

The cruiser pulled into the parking lot across the street and a minute later Jason Stafford got out. He slid his baton into his belt and stood by the cruiser, looking in the direction of the market. Then he started walking, his flashlight beaming in odd directions.

Jake watched from the front seat of the Mustang. He waited until Stafford went around the rear of the building before springing into action. He grabbed the paper sack containing the surveillance device, got out of the vehicle and took off running across the street. He sprinted to the public library next door to the market, taking position in a darkened alcove.

It was dead silent save for distant crickets and a small breeze swaying the trees. No cars came along the road, the canyon residents bedded down for the night, unaware of the drama playing out. Jake's heart thumped. He had no plan outside of aggressive confrontation.

Seconds and minutes ticked by. Jake heard footsteps coming from his right, saw the flashlight beam bouncing along the sidewalk. He stood tight against the wall. When the footsteps sounded right on top of him, he stepped out of the alcove.

"Find any bad guys?"

Jason Stafford stopped short and took in a breath. He shined his light into Jake's eyes, his other hand going to his gun.

"Easy there. There's no need for gunplay." Jake stared into Stafford's eyes, the flashlight blinding his own.

"That's a good way to get yourself shot." Stafford's voice was coarse. He clicked off the flashlight and slid it into a ring on his belt. Jake blinked stars out of his eyes.

"I have something of yours," he said, tossing the paper sack. Stafford flinched, grabbing the sack as it hit his chest.

"What's this?"

"Something you left at my house the other day."

"So, you're the one who called it in." Stafford looked inside the sack.

"Just doing my civic duty. I drove by and saw some suspicious activity."

"I'll bet." Stafford looked up. "What's your play here, Jake?"

"No play. Just a warning."

"About what?"

"About what's in that bag. About the dirty tricks you do for Bruce. About you staying the hell out of my life or I'm going to seriously fuck you up." Jake paused to let his words sink in. "I think that about covers it."

"How about I just shoot you instead?"

"You could do that. But it would be bad for you."

"How do you figure? I got a call about a suspected break in. It's dark, you went for a weapon. Case closed."

"I can see how that would go. But the people who know about what's in that bag might have a different story to tell, one that doesn't favor you too much."

"People? You mean like that little honey you've been shacking with?"

Jake's pulse spiked at the mention of Amy Watson. He took in a breath to steady himself.

"See, that's exactly the kind of thing I'm talking about. Just so we're clear, staying out of my life includes my friends. You have a beef, you take it up with me and no one else."

Jake smiled, staring into Stafford's cold eyes.

"But you're not going to have any beefs with me, because you're not that dumb. Having beefs with me is dumb. Fucking with me is dumb. Are we clear on that?"

Stafford stared in disbelief, barely containing his rage. The balls on this guy, confronting me on *my* turf, making threats, laying down terms. He started a mental countdown, each tick taking him further away from shooting Jake down. Ricardo Salazar had taught Jason well; what lines he could blur, what rules he could bend, what street justice he could dish out and remain insulated from consequences. This scenario fit none of that.

"It's good you're thinking it over. I don't have a lot to lose, except for my pride. And after the life I've lived, there's not a whole lot of that left either. But if you or Bruce think you're going to walk all over me, you better understand what you're getting into. Because I promise you I will fight with everything I've got. I'll *burn* you, no matter what it costs me. Are we clear on that?"

Jake got up in Stafford's face. If this thing was going sideways, now was the time. Stafford gave it right back, his jaw tight. The moment stretched out, neither man giving ground. And then Jason eased out a breath and he took one small step backwards.

"Smart move," Jake said, keeping his eyes locked on Stafford.

"Don't think you've won anything."

"You think this is a game? You think someone wins here?"

"Someone always wins."

"Whatever, Stafford. Just stay smart and stay the hell away from me. And if I find out you've been leaning on Danny Shaffer, I'll be at your doorstep so fast you won't have time to breathe. Are we clear on that?"

"Sure, we're clear. Now get the hell away from me before I change my mind."

"Nice doing business with you, officer." Jake turned and walked, his heart pounding. He stopped after a few steps and looked at Stafford. "By the way, you can keep the bag of goodies. I have photos. My lawyer is holding them. He had a fingerprint man go over everything. Did you wear gloves when you handled that stuff?"

When he got to his car Jake looked back across the street and saw that Stafford had not moved. He started the engine, turned right and headed out of the canyon. He needed to drive.

Ten minutes later he called Amy. He told her he'd be home soon, and to make sure all the doors and windows were locked. Then he clicked off the line and set the phone down, cranked the tunes and hit the gas, wondering what the hell his life had become.

Chapter 43

On Thursday morning Bruce McAlister boarded his father's private plane at John Wayne Airport and made the trip south to Mexico. He felt at ease, his anger having subsided to a tolerable level after a night of deep reflection. A new day always brings the opportunity for improvement, and when Bruce woke early and saw the sun rising bright over Saddleback, a smattering of clouds painted a golden hue, he knew that today would indeed be a good day.

Once he'd put his pride aside, Bruce began to see the situation more clearly. The dynamics of his relationship with his father had changed little over the years, and now that Bill was an old man and on the wrong side of time, there was no point in trying to bend him into something he was not. Let him have this moment, the final strategic push to the finish line of his lifelong ambitions. Bruce would be content to stay above it all, insulated from harm and free of heavy decisions, and more importantly, the chance of failure. He would spend time down in Bahia de Cortez doing the Lord's work, and then return home to a glorious new beginning, the messiness of the last few months firmly in the past.

Bruce could see now that it was a mistake obsessing over Jake Donahue, and that he'd let that obsession lead him astray. Bringing Jason Stafford into it was his biggest mistake, and Bruce cringed at the thought of Stafford knowing his darkest secret. He understood now why his father was so angry about it. It was a rookie mistake worthy of ridicule. If the roles had been reversed, Bruce would have kicked his own ass.

He wondered what would happen to Jason, feeling certain that he would never see the man again. The thought both shamed and frightened him, and he started the familiar process of blanking it out of his mind, just as he'd done with Richard Lawson, and with Susan. While some would call that cowardly, Bruce would disagree, viewing it simply as a practical approach to a situation he had no control over. He would say a prayer for Jason and hope for the best, and that would be the end of it. And if somehow Stafford survived and remained part of the team, well then it would be business as usual and Bruce would bear the man no grudge. After all, Jason was just following orders when he planted that bug in Jake's house.

There was one upside to Jason being out of the picture; the situation with him and Paige would be rendered moot. Problem solved. Not all unintended consequences are bad, Bruce thought with amusement as he recalled his father's admonishment last night.

The plane left the runway and became airborne. Bruce reclined his seat, closed his eyes and recalled how all this business with Jake had started purely by accident.

Over the last thirty years Bruce had been aware of only one other time when Jake had come back to Orange County. That was ten years ago, when a friend from high school mentioned it in passing. At that point the Limestone plans were a dream only his father possessed, and Bruce was content to build his little congregation in the canyon with no greater goal than to give a good sermon on Sundays. Memories of Mexico in '84 were distant and non-threatening.

But when Bruce saw Jake leaving the Silverado Canyon Market a few weeks ago, things were different. Limestone was close to a reality, the Canyon New Life Ministry had grown far beyond anyone's expectations, and Bruce had notoriety. More importantly, the murder of Susan was front page news. It was a precarious time, and the last thing Bruce needed was for Jake to have a crisis of conscience and start talking about the old days.

Bruce had gone to the market that day for an ice cream cone, after a long afternoon spent working on his weekly sermon at the church office. Pulling into the parking lot, he happened to glance at the front door, and that's when he saw Jake walking out with a sack of groceries. Bruce was stunned, and he sat transfixed as he watched Jake get inside a Jeep Rubicon and head into the canyon. It all changed after that.

Bruce couldn't stop thinking about Jake and the things he might say, and the more he thought about it, the more obsessive he became. Finally, he felt there was no choice but to act. He tasked Jason with keeping tabs on Jake, and soon after, he decided to put the bug in Jake's house. It all made sense at the time, but now...well, now Bruce could see that all he did was trade one problem for another.

But none of that mattered anymore. Thanks to his father, the ship would be righted and mistakes would be mended. And when Bruce returned home from helping those in need, his future would be secure. As it should be. For Bruce knew in his heart that it was preordained.

A warm feeling came over him as the plane banked over the Pacific and turned south. He thought of Jake in a different light. Perhaps someday soon Bruce could reach out to him and take the first step toward repairing past deeds, bear witness and bring him closer to God. They'd done a terrible thing all those years ago, and it was obvious that Jake had allowed it to hold sway over his entire life since. Unlike Bruce, who'd confessed his sin and repented, and was thusly forgiven. Maybe Jake could know that same peace.

A bold idea came to Bruce. In all his years of preaching he'd never attempted to use his experience in Mexico as a basis for his sermons. Not directly anyway. But now he began to envision telling that story. The names would be changed of course and certain other details altered, and a healthy dose of artistic license would be necessary, but it could be done. The bible was filled with stories of redemption and forgiveness.

Bruce's gift was the ability to share those stories in a way that drew people to the word of the Lord and made them believe.

It would be a series of sermons spread out over many weeks, told in a linear fashion, broad in its themes yet true to events as they happened. Properly done, it would be an epic achievement. But the story needed an ending, and the ending would have to include Jake Donahue. That part was absolute. Without it, the meaning would fall flat, the emotional impact rendered void. Bruce started jotting notes, the rough outline revealing itself. After a while he stopped in contemplation. The ending. That was the tricky part. The real life ending that had yet to be written.

Bruce set aside his notes and closed his eyes, knowing that it was within his power to shape the ending of the story. It was an awesome and humbling realization. He knew that Jake was brought to him at this critical point in time for a very specific purpose. It was so the ending could be written, and Jake could finally know some peace.

The plane hit a patch of turbulence, jostling Bruce in his seat. He bowed his head and silently prayed for guidance.

Chapter 44

Jake woke early on Thursday morning, feeling satisfied with how things had played out with Jason Stafford. He'd always gone out of his way to avoid situations like last night, but there comes a time in every man's life when he's got to stand up, and if it means fighting, then you go all-in and don't look back. Jake had taken proper care of business and he had no fear of reprisal. If Stafford was fool enough to come after him, so be it. Jake would never live under the heel of another.

He drove for an hour last night, sorting it out, walking through each step in his mind, firm in the belief that he'd done the right thing. When he got home, Amy was sleeping. He didn't wake her. Standing in the doorway to the spare bedroom, watching her sleep, conflicting emotions ran through him. He felt genuine warmth, and a feeling in his heart that might be love, or maybe just fondness. He wondered if he even knew the difference. If he would ever know the difference.

It was another hour before Jake unwound enough for sleep. He sat outside drinking a bottle of water, soaking in the aura of the canyon, the sounds of the night creatures, the slow passing of time. He thought about Bruce McAlister, and about settling scores. He didn't hate Bruce for the past and he had no desire to wreck the guy's future, and in a small way he understood Bruce's actions. He might even be willing to forgive, under the right circumstances.

Of course, if it turned out Bruce was culpable in Susan's death, there could never be any kind of reconciliation, and forgiveness was out of the question. In Jake's mind, some things in life are absolute.

Amy woke at nine. While she showered, Jake brewed coffee and made breakfast. They ate out on the deck. Amy seemed at ease, and she asked no questions about last night. The only awkward moment came when she told Jake that something had come up and she would have to cut her trip short. She insisted it was nothing serious. Her plan was to leave Orange County early tomorrow morning so she could be back in Truckee by nightfall.

Jake was genuinely disappointed by the news, but he had trouble expressing himself. His words came out haltingly, confused, and to his ears it sounded like he was relieved that she was leaving. That wasn't how he felt, although he knew it was for the best. He'd enjoyed the time they'd spent together and he looked forward to more of it, but it would have to come in small steps, without any guarantees given. The problem, as Jake saw it, was that Amy loved him too much. That wasn't his ego talking, it was simply the truth. And when Jake thought about it in those terms, he feared he could never love Amy back in the way she deserved.

He vowed to give it his best shot and remain open to all possibilities. He knew it was finally time to unburden himself, to break free of the guilt that had tethered him to the past. The idea that Paige McAlister might be his daughter, his own flesh and blood, filled him with undeniable optimism. Even if it turned out to be untrue, the mere possibility of it had opened the floodgates of Jake's soul, allowing decades of bad water out. He sensed that at nearly fifty years of age, he might be ready to start *living* his life, rather than watch it from the sidelines.

Drinking their coffee out on the deck, a glorious sun rising over the canyon, Jake and Amy plotted their final day together. An idea came to him.

"You ever been to Disneyland?" he asked.

"As a matter of fact, I haven't." Amy smiled. "Can you believe it?"

"How about we fix that?"

"Are you inviting me?"

Jake grinned and patted Amy on the knee.

"Go get ready, girl. We're goin' to Disneyland."

Amy giggled and went inside the house. Jake filled his coffee mug from the carafe on the table, leaned back in his chair and took a big swallow. He felt completely at ease, his mind free of worry and his heart light. Another idea came to him and he smiled at the thought. It was a long shot, but worth a try. He picked up his cell phone and dialed Paige McAlister's number.

Chapter 45

Jason Stafford spent his Thursday fighting off demons.

Images of his father came to him, all the fear and shame mixed with a deep yearning to please the man. But he could never please the man, and the enduring memory of his father's fist balled tight and ready to let go was burned into Jason's brain, forever negating any semblance of childhood normalcy, real or made up.

Jason's youth was a bad movie, taunting in its grotesque imagery, confusing in its disjointed narrative, a series of flashback nightmares that might be held in abeyance but would never truly be vanquished. Whenever that movie started playing, it might take days to find the switch and end the freak show.

This latest bout of reminiscence was brought on by Bill McAlister's continued silence, and Jake Donahue's brazen act of disrespect. Whenever Jason got to feeling inadequate the memories came. Whenever he felt like he hadn't stood up to a challenge the film would start rolling, a cavalcade of shame highlighting his inability to be a man.

He should have shot Donahue dead and lived with the consequences. In his mind, he could have done it. But Jason knew it would have been suicide. Had he killed Jake, he may as well have turned the gun on himself right then and there. There would have been no covering up something like that, and as much as he hated letting Donahue get one over on him, Jason knew that he'd done the right thing by allowing it to happen. Bill McAlister would be proud. *If* the guy would ever call him.

And that's what was really eating at Jason. He knew almost certainly now that he'd misfired when he called Bill yesterday. It came to him in his sleep, in a lull between the memories, and when he woke in the morning he could see it clear as day; Bill McAlister was deciding if Jason could be trusted to keep Bruce's secret. If the answer came back no, then Jason was in a world of hurt.

He'd never done anything disloyal to the McAlisters, nothing that would ever merit suspicion, but that mattered little. Men like Bill McAlister don't get where they are in life by being trusting souls. They succeed because they work the angles and keep their eyes open to all possibilities, and they understand that everyone has a price.

Jason's mistake was assuming that Bill knew about the surveillance of Jake Donahue. Bruce may have ordered it done, but Bill had his hand in everything. But maybe Bruce had acted on his own, and when Jason called Bill and informed him of the situation, he'd hit him with a double shot of reality check—Bruce's rogue actions *and* the fact that now Jason was in on the secret.

A panicked feeling rose as Jason considered his stupidity. No matter who knew what and when, the time to lay that news on the old man would have been after the land deal had gone through and the new church was under way, and more importantly, after the murders of Richard Lawson and Susan McAlister had faded from the news. Things were too hot right now and Bill McAlister was laser-focused and firing on all cylinders.

He recalled how the phone conversation went down. For one, he was too eager. He thought it was important for Bill to know that Jake and that woman were talking, but the unspoken meaning was clear; Jason was planting a seed that would later be cultivated into a little something extra for himself. And that's where he'd miscalculated, for Bill had surely figured out Jason's duplicity, and now he was going to fuck him royally for it. Jason tried to rationalize it another way, but all roads led to the same damn place.

HE PICKED up the tail later that day, when he was leaving the Canyon New Life Ministry. A silver Audi sedan with smoked windows. He'd gone to the church looking for Bruce after not reaching him by phone all day. The old lady who volunteered on Thursdays said that Bruce had gone down to Mexico on church business.

The news blipped Jason's radar. Why was Bruce *really* in Mexico?

He mulled it over while sitting in his car in the parking lot. He was scheduled to go down there in two weeks to arrange transport for another group of *believers*. That was the ridiculous code word they used for the illegals, as if it made the whole enterprise more acceptable. Bill had come up with the word and Jason felt stupid every time he used it. The truth is, he'd grown to hate the whole operation. Sure, he was paid well for his services, but he couldn't help but think about the damage he was doing. He was contributing to an epidemic, and it made him sick sometimes, to think how far he'd stooped for money.

Not that he would give any of it back, mind you. For money was power, and Jason was determined to get his share. And if he had to do some distasteful things to get what he wanted, well, that was just the cost of doing business.

So, Bruce was gone and Bill had gone dark. Hard not to read something into that. Jason pulled out of the church parking lot and accelerated on the canyon road. The Audi rolled up on him. He'd seen the car twice earlier in the day, once at his house and once in Irvine. That's not coincidence, that's a tail.

There were two men in the car, maybe a third in the back seat. Jason slowed his BMW and the Audi eased off. The sun was sinking fast and it would be dark soon. Jason had a choice to make; he could string these guys along, or he could throw down right now. His blood pumped, thoughts of the McAlisters freezing him out spiking his adrenaline.

Coming out of a curve Jason gassed it.

He hit ninety. Before the Audi caught up he slammed the brakes and skidded hard right, onto Black Star Canyon Road. The Audi shot past on Silverado Canyon Road and Jason floored it to the trailhead gate. He stopped sideways on the road, grabbed his holstered H&K 9mm from the glovebox and clipped it to his waistband. He jumped out of the BMW and headed for the creek that ran along the road, vaulting the barbed wire fence at a dead run. He landed in the dry, sandy bottom about four feet below road level, crouching and watching for the Audi.

It pulled up then and parked behind the BMW. The sun had dropped below the ridge to the west, the creek bed bathed in fading light. The doors of the Audi opened and three men exited; skinny white guys—shaved heads, ink on their arms, sketchy posture. Jason pegged them for amateurs. He watched for a minute, and then he turned and ran toward a stand of oak and scrub down creek.

The three men fanned out, walking slowly on the road beyond the trailhead gate, handguns at their sides. Hot wind blew from the east, static charging the air. Jason wiped sweat from his eyes and regulated his breathing, calculating odds.

He was thirty yards from the men. They talked in low voices, the gusts of wind masking their words. He figured he could take all three in a fight, but it might get a little dicey. Unless he just shot them down. But that was some heavy freight right there, and Jason wasn't sure he wanted to go that far. He could work his way down the creek and eventually he'd reach Irvine Lake, hide out until those dudes gave up. But running wasn't part of Jason's program. And if he ran, he wouldn't be able to find out who sent them, although Jason had a pretty good idea about that.

The shooters looked spooked. And why not? Black Star Canyon was spooky. People said it was haunted. Jason didn't have an opinion about that one way or the other. There wasn't much that scared him anyway. He supposed that was another thing his father had taught him. Thanks, Pop, Jason thought bitterly, as he prepared to make a move.

The men continued along the road, passing the spot where Jason hid. They walked single file, separated from each other by ten feet or so. Jason crept away from the oak and scrub, worked his way to the edge of the creek. It was dark now, but Jason had excellent night vision, and he mapped it out like choreography in his mind, his nerve steeled for the task at hand. The thrill of the fight had taken control, and Jason was ready.

The men stopped walking, still spread out in a line. Jason edged closer to them along the high bank of the creek. The timing would be critical. The men started walking again and Jason scrambled up the bank and slid under the barbed wire running alongside the road. He lay flat on the ground, watching. Then he eased the pistol out of the holster. The wind gusted and Jason took advantage, rising quickly and sprinting to the last man in line. He locked his forearm around the man's neck, using him as a shield. At the sound of the scuffle the other two men turned. Before they raised their weapons Jason squeezed off four shots and the men dropped.

The third man struggled and Jason holstered his weapon, put the guy in a chokehold. He squeezed, regulating the pressure. The man stopped struggling and Jason let him drop to the ground.

"Who sent you?"

The man gasped for breath, looking at Jason with dead eyes.

"Who sent you?" Jason repeated.

He waited two seconds and then kicked the man in the face, sending him backwards. He stood over him, put his foot on the man's chest. He pulled his H&K and pointed it at the man.

"I'm not gonna ask again. Who sent you?"

"Fuck you. I'm already dead."

"Yes, you are."

Jason put two rounds into the man's face.

"Asshole," he said, holstering his weapon. He noted the time and went to work.

He checked the man's pockets, found a cell phone, car keys, but no ID. The other two men were clean, not even pocket change on them. He collected their guns, picked up his brass, and put everything in the trunk of the BMW. He dragged all three men off the road and forced them under the barbed wire fence, sent them rolling down into the creek bed. He got a pair of surgical gloves from his car and searched the Audi. Paper plates and no vehicle registration. Nothing to indicate the identity of the three men. He started the car and parked it a short distance away, rolled all the windows down and left the keys in the ignition.

He checked the time. Fifteen minutes gone and the scene was as clean as he was going to make it. Time to get moving. The last thing he needed was for the sheriff on duty tonight to stumble across this mess.

Inside the BMW, Jason checked the dead man's cell phone. He scrolled through received calls. No names, just numbers. Including one he immediately recognized.

"Son of a bitch," he said under his breath.

He started the car and drove away.

LATER, HE sat in the darkness of his living room, staring at the lights of the Saddleback Valley through an open window. Black rage coursed through him like infected blood. He gripped his pistol, dark thoughts blurring his vision, constricting his brain. He had to fight through it. Giving in to this moment, acting on pure emotion, would only lead to his destruction. And Jason Stafford flat refused to let that happen.

It was time to lay plans. To take all that Bill McAlister had taught him and put it to use. He had options. Ones that would balance the ledger in his favor and teach those who'd dared to cross him that *he* was not a man to be fucked with.

He thought it through. Leverage is what he needed, and he knew exactly how to get it. As the plan coalesced, he thought about Bruce down in Mexico; it was as good a place as any to make a stand. After it was done, Jason could charter a boat to South America and lay low. It wasn't a life he'd ever envisioned for himself, but he always knew, deep down, that getting in bed with Bill McAlister might lead to something like this.

It all started to click, each step followed by the next. When he got to the end of it he went through it again. After an hour, he'd nailed it. He picked up his cell phone and made some calls. A day of reckoning was in store for some very foolish people. With any luck, they'll never see it coming.

Chapter 46

On Friday morning Amy Watson left Orange County. Jake woke her early and they walked to the Silverado Cafe for breakfast. The food was good and the conversation easy, and Jake began to regret her leaving. He resisted the urge to plan her next trip though, preferring to let things run their natural course. There would be a next time, of that he was sure. The thought pleased him, and he let the good feeling carry him forward.

Back at the house Amy collected her things and prepared to leave. When she was ready, Jake walked outside with her.

"Thanks for understanding," she said.

"Understanding what?"

"My ambush." Amy giggled.

"Oh, that. You're welcome. Just don't let it happen again."

Jake grinned and hugged her. She spoke into his chest.

"I had a good time, Jake. Disneyland was cool."

"Hmm."

"She's a wonderful young lady."

Paige McAlister had gone with them to Disneyland and the day was nothing short of magical. Their easy rapport cemented a feeling in Jake, and he was certain now, in his heart, that Paige was his daughter. Maybe that was enough. After all, to know in one's heart is the ultimate truth.

Amy pulled away, looking into Jake's eyes.

"I think you should talk to her about it, put it all out there. You owe it to her, Jake. And she deserves to know. Your life has been tragic. Please don't let it be tragic anymore."

"You may be right about that."

"I am, mister. And you better believe it." They both laughed. "Time to go now. I want to be home before dark."

Jake took Amy's hands in his and collected his thoughts.

"I'm glad you came. And I'm sorry for the wrong I've done to you. You deserve better, and I will try my best to deliver."

He paused and looked away. Then he went on.

"You've opened my eyes to some things, Amy. And my heart. For that I'm thankful. It's not easy for me to talk this way, but there you are."

He hugged her then, and she squeezed him tight. After a final kiss, she was gone.

Jake stood in his driveway, the canyon heat descending, a red-tailed hawk soaring overhead. He took in the moment, every detail, and then he went inside his house.

HE SPENT the day working under the sun deck. He searched under the house for a hidden trapdoor but didn't find one, reinforcing the notion that Big Ed was full of it when it came to the stories he told. After finishing under the deck, Jake washed and waxed his Jeep. He'd picked it up yesterday on his way to Disneyland. The Mustang was cool, but Jake was glad to have his wheels back. He saw it as one little step toward getting his life back on track after the last few days of tumult.

Dusk fell in the canyon. Jake showered and dressed, and he considered his evening. He thought about inviting Hector to dinner. After that he could reach out to Danny Shaffer, maybe get together for an hour or two. It had all the potential for disappointment, but Jake knew he had to try.

While puttering around the house, Jake happened to glance out the front window. He saw movement down at the end of his driveway. A moment later Jason Stafford came into view, walking toward the house. Jake went to the front door, ready for a confrontation. And then he reconsidered; it would be better to try and find out what Stafford was up to.

Jake ducked out the back door, removed the access panel from under the sun deck and crept inside, fitting the panel back into place just as Stafford turned the corner.

Chapter 47

Ricardo Salazar left his house in Santa Ana at five o'clock on Friday and walked to the *taquería* around the corner for an early dinner. He'd been waiting all day for word from the three dickheads he'd hired to take out Jason Stafford.

He was too old for this shit. One more year to go and he was set to pull the pin, move his ass down to Rosarita Beach and enjoy the good life; afternoon cocktails and señoritas by the sea, no more scumbags and their dirty deeds, no more trying to make sense of the depraved nature of man—not that Ricardo had ever spent much time pondering *that* specific topic. But the point was the same; he'd done his part, now it was time for someone else to carry the torch.

When he got the call about Stafford, Ricardo was *this* close to saying no. But when the price is right, it's right. And the unexpected windfall would be enough to pay off his beachfront retirement pad, a bonus he hadn't counted on. Making it an offer he couldn't refuse.

It didn't set right though, what he was asked to do, although he could see the reasons for it. Jason was a good kid at one time, reliable and accountable. Sure, he was wound tight, but he wasn't *loco* like some other cats Ricardo had known. Somewhere along the way, things changed. The closer Jason got to the McAlisters, the more uppity he became. Like he was a kingpin. The head honcho. Before long, the wide-eyed young disciple who had so eagerly soaked up Ricardo's vast well of knowledge had become a cocksure, strutting *cabrón*.

Ricardo pretended not to notice the disrespect, the way Jason had gradually cut him loose. Jason fancied himself someone special, on the road to a special place, surrounded by his special people. Foolish *cabrón*. The kid always had a problem seeing the big picture, and now it would cost him.

That is, if the lowlifes he'd hired got off the pipe long enough to get it done. Short notice had forced Ricardo to recruit from the B team. We're talking the benchwarmers on the B team. He figured it even odds they'd get the job done. If they didn't, he'd find some other dudes to take a crack at it. Keep going down the bench until he found the right ones.

Ricardo finished his dinner and got ready to leave. A text message popped up on his cell.

There's a problem. We need to meet.

What the hell?

That's what I get for hiring amateurs, Ricardo thought bitterly. He paid his bill and walked home, climbed inside his Crown Vic. He checked the address on the text, and then headed for Silverado Canyon.

IT WAS almost dark when he got there. Traffic was a bitch and the streets in the canyon were confusing as hell. Ricardo circled around a few times, following his GPS, wondering if the thing was working right. He finally found the address, pulled up to a clapboard cottage and parked at the end of the driveway, a few feet behind a Jeep Rubicon. The scene was hinky, and Ricardo's cop intuition pinged.

The hitters drove an Audi—a stolen Audi, but whatever—and there was no such vehicle parked in the driveway. Maybe they ditched it and stole the Jeep? Ricardo didn't think so, and he immediately regretted coming here. He should have met them in a public place, not at some random house out in the sticks.

He stepped out of the car and drew his service pistol, holding it down at his side. The neighboring houses were dark, the canyon as quiet as a church. It was a good place to get yourself dead. Ricardo moved forward slowly. He went up on the porch and looked through the front window. Lights were on inside the house but there was no one about. He could see through the front room to the kitchen, and beyond it, a patio area with lights strung overhead. He stood to the side of the door and knocked. No one answered, and there was no sound of movement from inside the house. He knocked again, waited thirty seconds, and then walked to the back of the house.

He stopped at the corner and carefully peered around it, saw a raised wood patio deck that backed up to a creek. There was no one on the deck, and Ricardo relaxed a bit. He still had to check the other side of the house, but it was looking like the hitters either never came here, or they split for some reason. So, what's with the text? Typical crackhead bullshit, Ricardo thought as he walked toward the patio deck.

A cat came up and brushed Ricardo's leg. He knelt and scratched behind its ear.

"Hey, buddy. Seen any crackheads around here?"

Ricardo chuckled and the cat scampered off. As he rose, something metallic was shoved behind his ear.

"How's it goin', Rico?"

Ricardo's gun hand stiffened.

"Drop it," Jason Stafford said.

Ricardo hesitated. Jason pressed the gun tighter.

"This can go easy or hard. Your choice."

Ricardo dropped his weapon, doubting there would be anything easy about this night. Jason moved him forward, up onto the deck. Ricardo always knew it might come down to this someday. Now that someday was here, he wondered where the hell he went wrong.

JAKE SAT upright under the sun deck, positioned almost dead center between the house and the retaining wall at the creek. He heard the men step onto the deck and sit down at the redwood table. He moved closer, the gaps in the decking big enough to see through. The two men spoke, and Jake concentrated on what they said. He caught a glimpse of the gun in Stafford's hand, pointed at the other man, and his heart thumped wildly. He steadied his breathing. He felt safe under the deck.

"YOU LOOK like you've seen a ghost," Jason said.

Ricardo stared back.

"What? You got nothing to say about that?"

Ricardo continued staring. He had lots to say about it, but none of it would make a bit of difference. All he could hope for now was a miracle. Maybe the cat would come back and save him.

"Tell me, Rico. What's my life worth?"

"I don't understand the question."

"Sure you do. How much did Bill McAlister pay you to take me out?"

Ricardo stiffened in his chair, considering what to say.

"Relax," Jason said. "You think I'm gonna do you right here? In some guy's backyard."

Jason grinned. Ricardo eased his posture.

"That's better. Now answer the question."

Ricardo saw the lights of a house in the distance. Others were nearby, which meant witnesses. He looked at the pistol in Stafford's hand. The weapon wasn't silenced, making it less likely that he would use it. Maybe he could turn this thing around.

"Forty thousand," he said.

"How much did you pay the hitters?"

"Six."

"You went cheap."

"It was last minute. Not a lot to choose from."

"Why didn't you do it yourself?"

Jason's eyes were stone cold. Ricardo stared into them. What do you say to a question like that?

"Believe it or not, I've never killed anyone."

"How long have I known you, Rico?"

"Eleven, twelve years."

"Let's call it twelve."

"Okay."

"Take your forty minus the hitters' fee, and you're left with thirty-four grand. Divide that by the years I've known you. What do you get?"

"I was never good at math."

"Twenty-eight hundred and thirty-three dollars. Give or take."

"If you say so."

"That's what my years of friendship are worth to you."

Ricardo shrugged. "What do you want me to say?"

"Nothing. There is absolutely nothing for you to say about it." Jason shifted in his chair, scratched the back of his head. Then he stifled a yawn. "By the way, your six grand is laying in a creek in Black Star Canyon."

"I figured something like that."

"Did McAlister give you a reason?"

Ricardo's heart hammered and sweat ran down his back.

"Come on, Rico. You can tell me."

"You know how this works, Jason."

"Yeah, I do."

Stafford reached behind his back and pulled a silenced pistol from his waistband.

"Vaya con dios, motherfucker."

He popped three rounds into Ricardo Salazar's heart.

Jason sat perfectly still and watched his friend's last breath wheeze out. He looked around, saw no indication that anyone had heard the shots. He took his cell phone out of his front pocket and made a call.

"Is she on the plane? Good. Sit tight. We're wheels up in one hour."

He ended the call. Then he stood and took Ricardo's cell from his jacket pocket. He dialed 911. When the call was answered he amped up his voice.

"I want to report a shooting! A police officer has been shot!" He paused, breathing rapidly. "Three twenty-four Shady

Lane. It's in Silverado Canyon. A man named Jake Donahue lives there. I think he did it. Hurry, please!"

Jason ended the call. He checked the time. Then he picked up Ricardo's gun from the walkway, grabbed a backpack he'd stashed nearby and put Rico's gun and cell phone inside, along with his two guns. He slung the backpack over his shoulder and walked calmly to the end of the driveway. He looked in all directions, saw nothing out of order, and started jogging to his rental car parked a short distance away. He drove out of the canyon slowly. On the way, he passed two sheriff's cruisers speeding by, lights flashing and sirens blaring.

Chapter 48

Jake removed the access panel and crawled out from under the sun deck, listening for sirens and hearing none. He figured he had only minutes before they arrived. He went up on the deck, looked at the dead man sitting in the chair at the redwood table—he could have been sleeping, if not for the blood leaking out the front of his shirt.

Jake went inside the house, grabbed his wallet and cell phone. He got a small duffel bag from the closet and went into his room, got a pair of hiking boots, a change of clothes and a jacket, stuffed them into the bag. He put a ball cap on and left the room. He heard the sirens now, and he forced himself to stay calm and think clearly.

In minutes this place will be crawling with police, and they'll think I killed that man out on the deck.

If he took the Jeep, Jake knew he wouldn't get far. He had to go someplace safe where he could think it through. The sirens sounded closer now. Jake took the only option available.

He ran out the back of the house and went over the retaining wall at the end of the deck, dropping down to the dry creek. The sirens were at the house now, car doors slamming. Jake ran upstream, in the direction of Hector Santiago's house.

IT TOOK him more than an hour to get there. The night was warm with no breeze, and soon Jake was sweat-soaked from the exertion. The creek bed alternated between a flat sandy bottom and more treacherous sections strewn with rocks and vegetation and debris carelessly tossed out of sight and out of mind by residents and passing motorists. He stayed in the creek most of the way, leaving for the paved road when he had just a short distance remaining. Once on the canyon road Jake kept his hat pulled low and his posture relaxed—just another citizen out for a Friday night stroll. He encountered no people, although a coyote stalked him part of the way. He figured the cops were probably locking down the entrance to the canyon right now, and eventually they would start coming this way, going door to door.

When he reached Hector's house he went around to the back door and knocked. A minute later the door was answered. "Come inside," Hector said.

He led Jake to the front room, lowered the shades on the picture window and dimmed the lights. He seemed to know something was wrong. When he sat in his chair, he regarded Jake with probing eyes.

"You were expecting me?" Jake said.

"I received a call from Mr. Critchfield at the market. He said the sheriff has put up a roadblock. No one can enter or leave the canyon. They say you killed a man."

"Jason Stafford did it. It happened at my house and I witnessed it."

"Tell me about it."

Hector listened without questions. When Jake was through, Hector remained silent, as if in deep thought. "This is quite unbelievable," he finally said.

"Well believe it, old friend. I'm in deep shit right now. No two ways about that."

"So it would seem."

"You look a mess."

"I hiked up the creek to get here." Jake laughed morbidly inside, thinking of the old joke about creeks and paddles. "I had to stay off the road. The cops were at my house when I left.

I had nowhere to go but here. I'm sorry to bring this to your home."

Hector waved a hand.

"I will not hear of it, *mi hijo*. You are my family, and you are welcome in my home regardless of the trouble you are in."

"I'm grateful, Hector. Thank you."

"I will make us some coffee," Hector said. "Have you eaten?"

"No. But I'm not hungry. Maybe later."

Hector went into the kitchen. Jake eased back into his chair and closed his eyes. He felt very tired, nervous energy pushing against the tiredness. He recounted what happened, disbelief clouding his thoughts, the whole thing too unreal to grasp. Hector returned with two steaming mugs of coffee. He set Jake's down on a small table next to his chair.

"Perhaps you can go to the police and explain the situation."

Jake stared at Hector. "I don't see that working out too well."

"I am merely suggesting it so we can cross it off the list."

"Consider it crossed off."

Jake picked up his mug and drank, savoring the rich flavor, the warmth inside him. Hector brewed a damn fine cup of coffee. He set the mug down and told Hector the rest of the story, starting with what happened on Wednesday night, the confrontation with Jason Stafford. When he was finished, the two men sat in a long silence, Jake's ears subconsciously tuned to the sound of police sirens.

"I am glad that Miss Watson has returned home," Hector said. "That is one less worry to have. As for the situation with Mr. Stafford, I am disappointed that you did not heed my advice."

"Whatever happened to loosen Stafford's screws has nothing to do with me."

"Perhaps. But I am sure it was salt in whatever wounds that man carries with him."

Jake nodded and drank some coffee. "Maybe you're right about that."

"What would you like to do about this situation?"

"I need to call Lucas Summerfield."

"How is that old scoundrel?" Hector said with a laugh.

"He's good. The same old Lucas."

"And why must you call him."

"I'm hoping he'll throw me a lifeline."

Jake finished his coffee. Hector went into the kitchen to refill his mug, and Jake dialed the number.

"I WAS just about to call you," Lucas said when he answered the phone.

"Are you back in town?"

"I got in late last night. Have you heard the news?"

"What news?"

"A man was found shot to death in Paige McAlister's condo. She's missing."

"What?"

"They suspect kidnapping. Get this, the dead man was in a wheelchair. Can you figure that? It's a cold world we live in, Jakey."

A feeling of dread rose inside Jake as he considered the news.

"Did you get the guy's name? The one that was killed."

"Schmidt or Smith, something like that. His first name was Danny."

"Danny Shaffer," Jake said numbly.

"That's it. Do you know him?"

"I went to school with him."

Jake went silent, the enormity of events consuming him. Hector came into the room with the coffee and set it on the table. Jake drank from the mug, collecting his thoughts.

"I'm in trouble, Lucas. You remember that situation I told you about the other day? About the cop who's been on my case?"

"Please don't tell me you did something stupid."

"I didn't do anything. But there's a dead man in my back-yard, and Jason Stafford set me up for the fall."

"How do you know this?"

"Because I was there. Stafford came to my house. I hid under the sun deck, hoping to see what he was up to. Another man showed up and Stafford held him at gunpoint. And then he shot him. He called the cops and pretended to be a witness, gave them my name and address. He told them I did it, Lucas."

"That's a hell of a thing. Where are you now?"

"I'm with Hector Santiago at his house. They've got the canyon sealed off."

"Give Hector my regards." Lucas paused, and then said, "You've got to turn yourself in, Jake. It's the only way to make this right. I can set it up."

"I can't do that. I need to get to the bottom of this, and I can't do it from jail. I need to see Bruce McAlister. He's in the middle of it."

"Bruce is in Mexico," Hector said.

"Hold on, Hector is talking to me."

Jake put the phone down and Hector handed him a copy of the OC Register, folded to a story about Bruce McAlister and his goodwill trip to Bahia de Cortez. Jake scanned the article. He set the newspaper down and picked up the phone.

"It looks like Bruce is down in Mexico, Lucas. I got a bad feeling about this. After Stafford shot that guy he made a phone call. He talked about a girl on an airplane. He said they'd be wheels up in one hour."

"What's your read on it?"

"Stafford is taking Paige McAlister to Bahia de Cortez. That's where Bruce is."

"Why would he do that?"

"It's complicated, but the gist is this: Stafford is muscle for Bruce and Bill McAlister. He does their dirty work. Something went down between them and Bill McAlister hired the dead guy to take out Stafford. But Stafford took out the hitters, and somehow he lured the dead guy to my house."

"Ricardo Salazar. That's the dead man."

"How do you know that?"

"It's on the radio right now. A special report." Lucas paused, the sound of the radio broadcast faint in the background. He came back on the line. "This is bad, Jake. Salazar is the lead detective investigating the murder of Richard Lawson and Susan McAlister. You're not suspected of killing some random guy. You're suspected of killing a cop. That's a whole other ball game."

Jake didn't respond.

"Listen to me, Jake. You have to turn yourself in, it's the only way. If you run, you're as good as guilty. And if they catch up to you, you're as good as dead. These guys take care of their own. If they get a crack at you, they'll take it. Don't make it worse than it is."

"I can't do that."

"Why?"

"There's another piece you don't know about, Lucas." Jake paused and breathed deeply. "There's a good chance I'm Paige McAlister's father."

"Whoa, that's some heavy stuff there. Can you explain?"

"It's a long story, one that goes back to high school. I can't get into it now but I promise when this is over I'll tell you everything. Right now, I need you to stand by. I might still surrender, but I've got to do it my way. Are you okay with that?"

"Whatever you need, Jake. Just say it."

"Good. Now, you wouldn't happen to have Bill McAlister's phone number, would you?"

"I don't. But I can probably get it. What've you got in mind?"

"Shake the guy's tree and see what falls out."

SUMMERFIELD CALLED back a short while later with the number. Jake went into Hector's garage to make the call; there were some things he didn't want his old friend to hear.

When Bill McAlister answered the telephone, there were no pleasantries, and he expressed no apparent surprise at hearing Jake's voice for the first time in thirty years. Instead, he was defiant and accusatory. Jake had barely gotten some words out before Bill launched into a tirade, railing on about God and destiny and retribution for evildoers and the agents of the Devil. None of it made sense, and Jake wondered if Bill was losing his mind.

And finally, when Bill McAlister had purged all of that from his system, he broke down and confirmed Jake's fears. Jason Stafford had taken Paige against her will to the church at Bahia de Cortez. Bruce was there too, and Stafford was holding them both for ransom.

And then, in a truly bizarre turn, Bill McAlister asked for Jake's help. He said he couldn't go to the police because of his complicated relationship with Stafford, so he had to find another way. That was how he termed it—*complicated*.

Bill offered money and whatever else Jake needed to get the job done. He said he would gladly pay the ransom, but he couldn't trust Jason Stafford to honor the deal. Stafford was evil and he was hellbent on revenge, and Bill feared he would kill Bruce and Paige. The only recourse was for someone to take Stafford out.

Jake was speechless. It felt like he was walking through a dream. Silence stretched out on the line, broken only by McAlister's heavy breathing. And then Bill played his hole card.

"Don't do it for me, Jake. Do it for your daughter."

Chapter 49

Jake found Hector in the kitchen preparing a meal for the two of them. Leftover homemade tamales and Spanish rice with a chopped salad and iced tea. Jake stood in the doorway of the kitchen and watched, the aroma enticing.

"I told you I wasn't hungry."

Hector finished preparing the dishes and carried them to the dining room table.

"Yes, you did," he said as he squeezed past Jake in the doorway.

"Then what are you doing?"

"Disregarding what you have told me, *mi hijo*."

"Who's the scoundrel now?"

Hector smiled. "Guilty as charged."

Jake's heart warmed. Hector's presence had a calming effect, and for a moment Jake could forget his dire circumstances. Hector finished setting the table and the two men sat.

"I have to go to Mexico," Jake said. "And I need your help to do it."

"First we will eat. And then we will discuss the matter."

Jake smelled the food. "Good idea."

"See, you are a sensible man after all."

AFTER THEIR meal, Jake laid it out for Hector, what Bill McAlister had told him. It was after nine o'clock and there was no sign yet of a police search. Hector called Sam Critchfield at the market for an update. The roadblock was still in place and the sheriffs were checking everyone coming and going. A group of canyon residents had gathered at the market and were trading stories and gossip, wild rumors fanned like brushfire by loose tongues. Sam said he would keep Hector posted.

Jake called his neighbor Bob Jenkins. Bob was shocked to hear from him, but he stayed calm and listened to the facts as they were laid out. Jake said he would be gone for a while and he asked Bob to look after his house. When he returned, this whole mess would be cleared up. He didn't say where he was calling from, telling Bob he was better off not knowing. And then he asked Bob to check his camera feeds, see if he captured anything that could prove Jason Stafford's guilt.

"One more thing," Jake said. "Don't tell the cops about Stafford or that photo you gave me the other day. Or any others you turn up."

"But it might help to prove your innocence."

"It might. But Stafford is on their side and they'll protect their own. He's twisted, Bob, and if he catches wind of your involvement it could spell some serious trouble for you. And for your family."

Jake threw in that last part just to ensure that Bob didn't get any ideas of his own.

"Wow…yeah, I didn't think about that. You're right, Jake. Absolutely. I'll keep a lid on what I know. I'm going to check the hard drive right now. My backyard cameras might've caught something useful."

"Thanks, Bob. I appreciate your help. And your discretion. It's good to know I have someone watching my back."

"You got it, buddy. Man, this is something else. They're all over your place right now. I can't believe it. It's like a movie, you know?"

"I know. A lousy movie. Let's hope it has a good ending."

After the calls were made and everything had been said, Jake and Hector sat in silence for a long time, each of them coming to terms with their own truth, deciding how far they were willing to go. It was Jake who spoke first.

"I need to borrow your truck, Hector. And I need your help getting it out of the canyon."

"You cannot do this by yourself, *mi hijo*."

"I know. But I have to try."

"I will help you. But on one condition."

"What?"

"I must go with you."

"No way, Hector. This is not your fight."

"Have you forgotten the *campesinos*? I have spent time with these men and listened to their stories. I have heard of their pain and the suffering endured at the hands of careless men. I have given my word to help in any way I can. The person responsible must be held accountable."

"That's Bill McAlister."

"Yes, he is the man at the top. But Mr. Stafford is our more immediate concern. He has taken your daughter. And he has done harm to people I respect. People who did nothing more than desire a better life, and in pursuit of that life they unknowingly entered into a deal with the Devil."

Hector paused, looking at Jake with determined eyes.

"So you see, *mi hijo*, this is indeed my fight."

Jake started to speak, but then hesitated. The resolve in Hector's eyes was unmistakable, and it was unshakable. Jake sighed. "You're a stubborn old buzzard, you know that?"

Hector gave out a laugh, his blue eyes brimming with emotion. "You may be right about that, old friend."

The two men shook hands, and then made their plans.

HECTOR STOPPED the truck at the gate to the Maple Springs trailhead. Jake got out, took a pair of bolt cutters and some tie wire from the bed of the truck. He cut the lock, swinging the gate open to let Hector pass. Then he closed the gate, wired it shut, and got back inside the truck.

They started up the fire road that would take them over the Santa Ana Mountains. With the police roadblock at the entrance to the canyon, the fire road was their only means of escape. Jake was surprised the cops hadn't thought of the same thing and posted men at the trailhead. He counted that as a good sign; maybe this wasn't a suicide mission after all.

Once over the mountains, they would pick up Interstate 15 south to Interstate 8 east, and cross the border at Mexicali. If the border agents were on the lookout for Jake, their trip would end right there. Or if they discovered the guns.

While preparing to leave, Hector took Jake into the garage and unlocked a tall steel cabinet. Inside was an arsenal. Shotguns, hunting rifles, revolvers, semi-automatic pistols, and enough ammunition for a small platoon. Jake had seen the cabinet many times before, but he never knew what was inside. He looked at Hector with a bemused expression.

"I thought you were a pacifist," he said.

"I am, *mi hijo*," Hector said. And then he added with a grin, "One who fervently believes in the second amendment."

Jake shook his head in wonder at the many facets of Hector's personality.

They loaded weapons and ammo into a long steel toolbox and strapped it to the bed of the truck. And then they piled old lumber and pieces of scrap metal from Hector's side yard on top of the toolbox, covering the bed of the truck with a heavy tarp and tying it securely. If the police pulled them over and looked under the tarp, hopefully they'd search no further.

It was a tedious journey over the mountains. The moonlight was sufficient to navigate by, and the road was well-graded, but sections of it were steep and sharply curved, with treacherous drop-offs going down hundreds of feet into ravines choked with vegetation. Not a good place to have an accident. It was nearly midnight when they finally emerged in the city of Corona, where they stopped for gas and coffee before getting on the freeway and continuing their journey south.

Hector took the first leg while Jake tried to sleep. But Jake's mind was too busy for sleep, and the apprehension he felt over returning to Bahia de Cortez fired his nerves. He tossed and turned in the seat, trying to get comfortable, trying to come to terms with everything that had happened. He thought about Danny Shaffer and felt an overwhelming sense of guilt. While Jake couldn't begin to know the circumstances of Danny's death, he felt certain that *his* actions had brought it about; if he had never sought Danny out, then Danny would never have gotten spun up in the McAlisters' dirty dealings. The logic was flawed and Jake knew it, but his emotions told a different story.

Hector kept his old Chevy steady on the highway, his speed just a few miles over the limit. They had many hours of travel ahead of them and what they were heading into Jake could only guess. Their immediate plan was to just get there. From that point, it was open to debate. It was crazy, what they were doing. But crazy or not, Jake knew it had to be done.

Chapter 50

Bruce McAlister sat in a locked storage room at the church in Bahia de Cortez. There was an armed man guarding the door, another one outside the room's only window. It was after dark on Friday, although Bruce didn't know what time it was. The armed men had taken his wrist watch along with his cell phone and wallet.

Bruce had recognized one of the men. He was part of a group that came to the church regularly, hard men with vacant eyes. They would meet with Jason Stafford and a day or two later they were gone, taking with them a group of men who had been staying at the church. Bruce knew what it was about but he steered clear of it, telling himself it was his father's business. He never spoke to Jason about it, although it hung between them like an unspoken truth. Anyway, Bruce only occasionally happened to be at the church when all this took place, and whenever he saw it, he made a point to pray for the group's safety.

Bruce had arrived at the church on Thursday and he'd spent the day tending to a variety of matters. At some point he'd driven down to the shoreline, to the old Reef Point 2. He pictured it as it was, thinking about Jake and Susan, and what had taken place there a lifetime ago. He rarely did that, saw no purpose in it, and now, standing on the bluff overlooking the sand, he wondered at the irony of it all, how those long-ago events had been resurrected at this critical juncture in his life.

I guess we can never really escape our past, Bruce thought as he gazed out at the waters of the gulf. We can atone for our sins, receive forgiveness from our Lord and Savior Jesus Christ, but the past remains, rearing its ugly head whenever it damn well pleases. And there's nothing you can do to stop it.

Bruce hadn't spoken to his father since their meeting on Wednesday night. He knew things were happening back home, and while he was curious about the outcome, it was better if he remained ignorant. He felt confident that everything would work out exactly as it should, and when he returned home, all this business of the past would be over.

But now he wasn't so sure. Something was wrong, that much he knew.

It was late Friday afternoon when the armed men came for him. He was in his office finishing up some work before heading into town to get something to eat. The men barged into the office and literally dragged Bruce down the hallway and into the small storage room. They took his phone and his watch and his wallet, not speaking, their faces expressionless. And then they left. Bruce knew they were guarding him; he could hear the man outside the door, barely see the top of the other man's head through the high window.

It had been hours since this took place, and in those hours Bruce prayed and fought back his fear. He felt certain it had something to do with events happening back home, but he had no way to be sure. Maybe it was something else. Maybe one of the drug cartels was targeting the church. Bruce had heard stories over the years of Americans being kidnapped and held for ransom, their homes ransacked. Maybe they were commandeering his airstrip, using it to move their drugs. There were a lot of possibilities.

Bruce had always known that their *business* arrangement down here had the potential for danger. It was that old saw about lying down with dogs and ending up with fleas. Is that what happened?

He forced himself to stay calm, to not let his mind wander. He listened for signs, some small clue as to what the hell was going on. He heard nothing, the room stone quiet, no move-ment from outside save for the occasional shuffling of the man's feet outside the door, and the faint smell of cigarette smoke. Anger started to mix with his fear, indignation rising over his treatment at the hands of men who were paid hand-somely by his father. Unintended consequences. Yeah, right. Choke on that one, Dad.

Bruce pounded on the door. The man outside did not re-spond.

"Baño," Bruce said loudly.

The man ignored him.

Bruce knew very little Spanish, an irony not lost on him when he considered how much time he spent down here. Now he wished he'd learned more than the handful of words and phrases he'd picked up over the years. He had to take a leak and wasn't about to do it in the corner of the room. He repeated the word and pounded on the door. The man outside continued to ignore him. Bruce finally gave up and sat down on a stack of file boxes, and tried not to think about pissing his pants.

Hours later he heard movement outside the door. He'd dozed off, his lower back strained from his awkward sitting position. He was painfully aware of his full bladder. The move-ment stopped outside the door. A key was inserted in the lock, and when the door opened Bruce saw Paige, her face red and swollen from crying. He reached for her as she was pushed through the door, embracing her tightly. When he looked up, Bruce saw Jason Stafford and two armed men. He knew then that he was in trouble.

THEY'D LET Bruce use the bathroom, and now he was back inside the locked storage room with Paige. His captors had also allowed two chairs to be brought into the room, along with some bottled water.

"What happened?" Bruce said.

"They took me from my house. They killed Danny."

"What?"

"Danny Shaffer. Your friend from high school. They killed him, Dad. They shot him to death in his wheelchair, in my living room."

Paige began sobbing, her chest heaving with deep breaths.

"What was Danny doing at your house?"

"He called me this morning," Paige said, regulating her breathing to bring the sobs under control. She wiped her face with a shirtsleeve and looked at her father. "He said he had something to tell me. About Jake Donahue, and about you and Mom."

She paused a moment. Bruce's heart beat steady thumps against his chest, nervous pinpricks tingling his skin. "Go on," he said. "What happened next?"

"I arranged to meet Danny at my house. After he got there, someone knocked on my door. When I opened it, a man pushed his way inside and grabbed me. He tied my hands together, said he'd kill me if I screamed. It happened so fast, I was in shock. Danny was in the other room and he must've heard something, because he came around the corner, yelling at the man to stop. The guy shot him, Dad. Three times. He didn't say a word, he just shot him."

Paige took in some breaths to collect herself. Bruce nodded, encouraging her to continue, the enormity of events overwhelming him, his heart breaking.

"After he shot Danny he put a hood over my head and took me downstairs. He put me into a car. I prayed someone would see us and stop him. But no one did. We drove for a while, and then he took me from the car, walked me a short distance and then up some stairs. When he took the hood off I was on an airplane. Like the one grandpa Bill owns. Jason was there."

"What did he say?"

"Nothing. He just stared at me for a long time. When I asked him what was happening, he said 'ask your father'. And then he went into the cabin and stayed with the pilot until we landed."

"Ask your father?"

"That's what he said. What does that mean?"

"I don't know. Who else was on the plane?"

"The man who shot Danny. And the pilot."

Bruce nodded, thinking. He wondered about his father; where was he in all this? Was he even alive? Something had obviously gone wrong.

"What did he tell you?"

"Who?"

"Danny."

Paige looked at her father for a long moment.

"He said that Jake Donahue was my father."

Bruce saw fear in Paige's eyes, and sadness too. But most of all, he saw a pleading innocence, like a child seeking the truth. All at once he felt the crushing weight of his carefully constructed world collapse upon itself, the weight of lies, a lifetime of denial burying him in despair. Tears came to him, and he made no effort to stop them.

"Dad?"

"Yes, honey?"

"What did he mean? Why did Danny tell me that?"

Bruce took in a breath.

"It's a long story."

Paige took his hands in hers.

"Start at the beginning."

Chapter 51

They crossed the border at five o'clock in the morning. The early Saturday traffic was light, and after thirty minutes waiting in line they were waved through by a sleepy-eyed border agent who asked a few questions in Spanish, and seemed satisfied with Hector's responses. Jake pretended to be sleeping, slumped in the passenger seat with his face obscured by his ball cap. As they drove away, Jake sat up and smiled at Hector; their luck was holding, and he began to relax for the first time since leaving Orange County.

They drove straight through Mexicali and stopped for breakfast at a restaurant at the south end of town. The morning air had a chill to it, the faint glow of sunrise visible in an eastern sky void of clouds. Jake took a moment to stretch, while Hector checked the ropes securing the tarp over the back of the truck.

"How are you feeling?" Hector asked after they were seated in a booth.

The waitress brought coffee. Jake slid his cup closer and added cream. "Better," he said.

"Have you given some thought to our plans once we reach Bahia de Cortez?"

"Not really." He drank some coffee; it tasted bitter, but it was hot, and it revived Jake's senses. "I was kind of hoping you'd have that all figured out by now."

Hector smiled. "I have an idea."

"Care to share it with me?"

"Later. For now, it is like a cake baking in the oven. We must wait for it to rise before removing."

"A cake?"

"You do not care for my analogy?"

"You just let me know when that cake is ready. Because I'm open to suggestions."

"As you wish, *mi hijo*."

They ordered their food and drank more coffee. They spoke little as they ate, Jake's mind preoccupied with the situation back home, and what lay in store some two hundred miles down the ribbon of asphalt running past the restaurant. After they finished, Hector excused himself to go to the restroom. Jake sipped his coffee, trying to clear his mind of troubling thoughts. When he turned to flag the waitress for more coffee, he saw Hector standing outside by the truck, talking on his cell phone.

What's he up to? Jake wondered. He was hardly gone long enough to use the restroom, and now he's outside, talking on his phone. Watching Hector, a wave of guilt came over Jake. What the hell was he thinking, agreeing to let him come along? Even though Hector carried himself like a much younger man, he was still eighty years old, and here Jake was dragging him into a potentially dangerous situation. He didn't doubt Hector's grit, and he'd heard enough stories from his dad to know that in his younger days Hector was a tough hombre, but this could well turn out to be life and death business.

Hector finished his call and came back inside the restaurant. Jake turned in the booth and drank his coffee, and he made no mention of the phone call when Hector sat down.

"Are you ready to continue our journey?" he asked.

"As ready as I'll ever be, I suppose."

"It will be fine, Jake. You will see. Let your conscience be clear in this matter, for you are doing the right thing."

"Is that how you see it?"

"Why of course. Do my words sound untrue?"

"You're a good man, Hector. Let's hit the road. I'll take the wheel."

THE HOURS and the miles passed slowly, the monotony of the journey unrelenting, the Sonoran Desert landscape alternating between majestic sections of pure beauty and desolate stretches of barren wasteland. Nothing looked familiar to Jake, although he was certain that little had changed in the thirty years since he'd last made this trip. Conversation between Hector and Jake was sporadic, the long silences filled with music from Mexican stations on the AM band. Hector's Chevy drove beautifully, and Jake thought that the old truck was a lot like Hector himself—reliable and consistent, a trusted friend to the end.

They passed several inspection points without incident, and encountered very little traffic outside of the few small towns along the way. They gassed up in San Felipe just after eight o'clock and Hector took over the driving. It was hot already and the truck had no air conditioning, so they kept the windows down. The rush of warm air was irritating at first, but soon settled into white noise that lulled Jake to sleep. When he woke, Hector was approaching the outskirts of Bahia de Cortez.

"Sorry," Jake said through a wide yawn.

"There is no apology necessary," Hector replied. "The prodigal son must be well-rested for what lies ahead."

Jake looked at Hector dully. "Are we starting *that* again?"

"I am merely humoring you, *mi hijo*," Hector said with a sneaky grin.

Jake looked around for signs of familiarity. Vague memories tickled his brain. "Turn left," he said, pointing ahead. Hector turned onto a road leading to the shoreline. "I remember this," Jake said absently, more to himself than to Hector.

The Gulf looked as blue and wondrous as Jake remembered it. In the distance, he saw the old pier where he'd rented the fishing boat, and a few outboard boats beached on the sand. But the bait shop looked completely different, and the beach cabanas were gone, and as they approached the old Reef Point 2, Jake saw that the trailers were no longer there, replaced now by two-story wood and plaster buildings that looked like condominiums, some of them with unfinished roofs and missing windows, as if abandoned during construction. Like boom times gone bust.

"There used to be trailers all up and down that bluff along the sand," Jake said. "I'd get my morning coffee at that building over there." He pointed to the left. "It used to be a bait shop with a little market inside. An old man named Esteban ran the place."

Hector turned and smiled.

"It is good that you remember these things, Jake."

Jake responded with a blank look and a slight nod.

They drove along the beach road and Jake's heart started a steady, rhythmic thumping, propelled by nerves and a different set of memories coming at him now. "Keep going along this road," he told Hector, his voice thick with anxiety.

They were heading south, away from town, toward where it happened.

The memories coalesced and came into focus; the curving beach road, Bruce driving too fast, a crazy, wicked look in his eyes, that damn song blasting on the stereo. The beach road was paved now—back then it was washboard dirt—the severe dips and sharp turns graded and smoothed. The town had developed too, scattered dwellings and businesses extending way out here, an area that was wide open desert in '84.

Hector kept the truck steady and his speed at thirty miles an hour, remaining silent as Jake remembered. After a few minutes, Jake told Hector to pull to the side of the road. He got out of the truck and walked a short distance, crossed the road and stood at some boulders surrounded by cactus. He turned and scanned the desert, then he knelt and took in some deep breaths. Hector watched this from the cab of the truck, and he crossed himself, something he had not done since Magdalena died.

Jake returned to the truck and leaned into the open window, his forearms resting on the door. "This is the spot," he said, his voice clear and unwavering. "The road used to curve here. The boy came from over there."

Jake stood straight and pointed. And then he noticed something—a sign fifteen yards down the beach road, on the right side. He walked toward it, stopping short when he read the words *Ministerio Vida Nueva*. He stood in that spot for a long time, staring into the distance. The sign marked a crossroad that led to the west, far into the desert, a development of some kind about a half mile away. Hector approached then.

"Is everything all right, Jake?"

"What does that sign say?" he said, his back turned to Hector.

"It says, 'New Life Ministry'."

Jake turned and looked at Hector, his face expressionless. The sun burned bright and hot, the asphalt reflecting the heat, enveloping the two men. Jake stood rooted, both physically and emotionally, his brain processing the moment. And then he spoke.

"This is it, Hector. Bruce's church." He turned and gazed beyond the sign. "He built his church where we buried that little boy."

Chapter 52

Jason Stafford hung up the telephone. He sat at the desk flexing his hands, regulating his breathing, walking himself back from the conversation he'd just had with Bill McAlister. Bill was a son of a bitch, no doubt about it. Jason knew that negotiating with him would be difficult, but this was ridiculous. The guy couldn't seem to get it in his head that he had no leverage here, and if he didn't straighten up and fly right, his preacher son was going to end up in a ditch in the middle of the Mexican desert. As far as Paige was concerned, Jason hadn't yet decided about her. He hoped it wouldn't get that far.

All Bill had to do was pony up the cash and everyone would go home happy. It's not like Jason wanted a pound of flesh from the man or anything like that. True, he'd played with the idea of demanding a signed statement from Bill admitting that he tried to have Jason killed—it would be a nice little insurance policy, just in case McAlister got it in his head to take another crack at it once the dust settled—but he'd decided against it. No, this was a straightforward business transaction. One million dollars in exchange for Bruce and Paige, the money to be wired to Jason's offshore account. Simple.

But nothing was ever simple with Bill McAlister. He made excuses, tried to buy time, said his liquidity had been compromised by the Limestone deal. Which was complete bullshit. Jason knew for a fact that Bill had plenty of money stashed in his own offshore accounts. The old bastard had probably dropped at least that much in the last few months alone, greasing the wheels, trying to lock down his land deal. Jason leaned back in his chair and closed his eyes, felt a blistering headache coming on. So far everything was going as well as could be expected, given that he'd planned on short notice. The thing with Danny Shaffer was unfortunate. Jason may not have cared for Danny, but he didn't want to see the guy dead.

Zamora came into the room then. Jason opened his eyes. "Yes?"

"What's happening," Zamora said.

It wasn't so much a question as a demand for information. Zamora was Jason's right hand man down here, his liaison in the smuggling operation, acting as a bridge between Jason and the cartel. Jason didn't like dealing with the cartel—they were a nefarious lot, with their shifty-eyed stares and dubious loyalties, none of them speaking a word of English, although Jason had long suspected they understood plenty. Zamora kept them in line and he kept the train rolling, like clockwork. He was a hardcore Santa Ana homeboy to the bone; multiple jail stints for assault and robbery, senior member of the notorious F-troop street gang, an overall bad citizen.

"I'm still putting it together," Jason said. "You in a hurry?"

"No hurry, *jefe*, just wondering what the fuck is going on. You call me up, short notice, and put me in the middle of something."

"I don't pay you enough?"

Zamora just stared.

"Speaking of putting people in the middle of things, why did you pop the dude in the wheelchair? Was that really necessary?"

"You said the girl would be alone. If I knew there was company, I woulda wore a mask. The gimp got a good look at me. I can't have that shit on me. One more felony, I go down for the count."

Jason didn't respond. Goddamn criminal logic, he thought spitefully.

"I took care of business. You got a problem with that?"

"Killing that man wasn't part of your business. Besides, the girl saw your face. What about that?"

"What about it? She ain't walking out of this."

Jason fixed his eyes on Zamora.

"What? Why you mad dogging me, *jefe*?"

"Nothing happens to the girl. Or her father. I decide what goes down here, not you, and not those assholes outside. Are we clear on that?"

Jason kept his eyes on Zamora, ready to take the man out if necessary. Zamora was a badass, a stone killer, but that mattered little to Jason. He'd rip the dude's heart out and not give it a second thought.

"Easy, *jefe*, ain't no reason for attitude."

"It's not attitude, it's how it is. And tell your crew to lay off the booze. I need people with clear heads. If they can't get it together, kick their asses out of here. Do you understand?"

"Sure, I understand. I'll do what you say, Stafford. But make sure you get my bread together. No matter how this goes down, I get paid. And that shit ain't negotiable. *Comprende, jefe*?"

Zamora walked out of the room. Jason watched him, thinking about how quickly things fall apart. He was tired of it. He wanted his money and he wanted out. He realized now that he was glad things with the McAlisters had blown up. It was kind of fucked the old man came after him like he did, but on a certain level Jason understood. It was part of the game, he got that. And now that it happened, now that the cards had been laid on the table and everyone knew where they stood, he was happy. Ecstatic, actually. Ready to be free of Bill and Bruce, and Paige. Especially Paige. He didn't want to harm her, and in truth, he thought he still loved her, but that was never gonna play and he knew it. And now that he knew about Jake Donahue, well there wasn't really all that much incentive left anymore. So, he was ready to be done.

But first I have to deal with asshole Santa Ana beaners shooting cripples, and Bill McAlister turning tightwad on me, surely just a ploy to buy time and try and fuck me another way.

Well bring it on, old man, because I'm ready for you. I got your family down here, everything that's important to you. I don't want to hurt them, but make no mistake, I'm walking out of this deal on top. One way or the other.

Chapter 53

Jake and Hector got a motel room at the south edge of town. It was a ranch-style place set on a sweeping rise that looked down at Bruce's church in the near distance. With its dusty plaster exterior, cracked barrel-tile roof, and general appearance of neglect, the El Adobe looked like the end of the road. But the room was clean and it was strategically located, and since this wasn't a vacation it would do just fine.

Their room was next to a patio with sun-bleached plastic furniture and a thatched cover. There were three cars in the parking lot, but their owners went unseen. After settling in and taking a quick nap, Jake sat in one of the plastic patio chairs, observing Bruce's church through Hector's field glasses. The sun blazed in a cloudless sky, the shade of the thatched cover offering scant relief from the oppressive heat. Jake wondered if it was this hot back in 1984.

Hector was inside the room, tending to the weapons—two Mossberg pump-action shotguns, a Colt Peacemaker that had belonged to Hector's father, a scoped hunting rifle, and three Browning semi-automatic pistols. It was a lot of firepower and Jake was leery, but Hector said it was better to be prepared. Besides, if they were going to risk bringing guns into Mexico, they may as well bring enough of them to do the job.

Jake was ambivalent about guns. He'd owned a few over the years and had become a fair shot while in the Navy, and he'd spent some time at firing ranges honing his skills, but he hadn't handled a gun in years. Still, he figured he'd be able to hold his own if it came down to it.

But that kind of violence seemed incomprehensible, and Jake walked through the events that had led him to this place, trying to make sense of it. He held to the belief that he was doing the right thing. Paige was in danger, and Bruce too, and Jake could not just turn his back on them. Jason Stafford was a bad man, a bully and a manipulator, and a killer. That alone justified Jake's actions. The key was neutralizing Stafford without anyone getting hurt. Jake had serious doubts it could be done.

He scanned the church again. The property was several acres in size, surrounded by a low block wall. The paved main road entered from the east, through an open wrought iron gate, ending in a courtyard at the center of the compound. There was some sort of monument in the courtyard—it reminded Jake of crypts he'd seen in New Orleans—and beyond, a long, narrow adobe building with a pitched tile roof that Jake assumed was the chapel. On the far side of the road there was a wooden structure that resembled a military barracks, and on the near side several cinder block buildings.

Beyond the chapel, another paved road led out of the church compound to the west. The gate there was low and made of wood, and it was closed. The road curved to the south, went on for a quarter mile before ending on a plateau. There Jake saw a paved runway with a wind sock at one end and light poles evenly spaced along the length of it. There was no plane on the runway.

Turning the field glasses back to the church compound, Jake noticed a man standing under a high window at one of the cinder block buildings. He was cradling a shotgun. He looked bored, several empty beer bottles littering the ground around him. Jake heard music and men talking, laughing. He repositioned the field glasses toward a stand of trees at the east end of the barracks, saw a group of men sitting on picnic tables, a boom box next to a metal tub filled with ice and bottled beer. Jake counted three tequila bottles next to the tub of beer. He also saw weapons—handguns, machine guns, a machete and several long knives. He lowered the binoculars and considered the implications.

Hector came out then. He took a seat next to Jake and handed him a cold bottle of water.

"Thanks," Jake said.

"You are welcome." Hector drank some water. "Have you seen anything of interest?"

Jake drank half the bottle of water before speaking. He handed the field glasses to Hector. "Look at the trees."

Hector adjusted the focus. After a few seconds, he extended the binoculars to Jake. Jake waved them off, said, "Now look over there, the block building to the right." He pointed the direction.

Hector zoomed in on the man who appeared to be standing guard. "What is your assessment?" he said, setting the binoculars on a small table next to their water bottles.

"You first," Jake replied.

"The man at the window is guarding Mr. McAlister and your daughter. The others are the ones who do the smuggling for the McAlisters. I suspect Mr. Stafford has brought them in to ensure that his plans succeed."

Jake nodded. "Agreed."

Hector grew silent, as if in thought. Jake drank the rest of his water and stared down at the church compound, wondering how they were going to pull this off. If he'd had any plan at all, it was only for dealing with Stafford, not a group of armed thugs. Drunk armed thugs, by the looks of it.

The dynamic had changed and Jake was concerned. Maybe they should seek out whatever passed for law down here. There must be a police station in town they could go to for help. They'd have to hide the guns, of course, and they'd have to convince the cops that their story was true, and there was always the chance they wouldn't believe them, or worse, think that he and Hector were up to some dirty business of their own. There were pitfalls, to be sure.

"How's that cake coming along?" Jake asked Hector, hoping the old man had some ideas of his own.

"It is still baking," he replied.

"Will it taste good after it's done?"

"We shall see," Hector said with a grin.

"So, humorous analogies aside, how are we going to play this?"

"The path forward is clear. We must confront Mr. Stafford and rescue your daughter."

"The odds don't favor us."

"This is true."

"Does that bother you?"

Hector drank some water. He stretched his legs and crossed them at the ankles. He looked down at the church, and then at Jake.

"No, *mi hijo*. I am not bothered by those men down there. I have faced much worse odds in my lifetime."

Jake nodded. He'd heard the stories of Hector's service in Korea, the Silver Star and two Purple Hearts, the eight months he was held as a POW. Most of the stories were told by those who knew Hector, as he was reluctant to discuss his war experiences. A few times Hector had opened himself to Jake. It was always a somber affair, whenever Hector spoke of that part of his life, and Jake knew that the time Hector had spent in service of his country had impacted him greatly.

"We can always go to the cops and tell them what's going on, resolve it that way," Jake said.

"We could, but it may very well backfire on us."

"How?"

"The law in Mexico is complicated, Jake. Criminal influence runs deep, and one can never be sure where the loyalties lie. It is entirely possible for us to go to the police with the best of intentions, and end up in a very difficult situation, with much explaining to do. Once that happens, the results may not be to our advantage."

"Is that a polite way of saying we can end up in jail?"

"Or worse."

Jake nodded. "So, we're on our own."

"For now," Hector replied. "There is still time for a change in our circumstances."

"A miracle?"

Hector laughed. "I would gladly accept a miracle."

The two men sat in silence. A warm wind blew from the south, the sun starting its slow descent in the west. The voices of the men at the church carried on the breeze, combined with the music from the boom box. Jake turned to Hector.

"Maybe if we wait long enough they'll all pass out. Make our job easier."

"Perhaps," Hector said. "Although I doubt Mr. Stafford is partaking. He has far too much at stake to carry on so foolishly. He is the one we must contend with."

Jake nodded. The waiting was driving him crazy. Part of him wanted to leave this place and never return, another part begged him to get to it, race down there with guns blazing and rescue Paige, kill them all, if that's what it took. He looked at Hector.

"Can I borrow the truck?"

"Certainly."

Jake took the keys and left.

Chapter 54

Twenty minutes later, Jake stood on the bluff overlooking the old Reef Point 2. The sun hovered low above the jagged hills west of town, the air warm and smelling of salt. Jake took in the wide expanse of the Sea of Cortez. Then his eyes moved along the shore, to a point south, where he imagined the trailer used to be. He pictured Susan that night, standing there with her, his skin electric from her touch. He saw himself making love to her, the clarity of his memory astonishing after so many years. Then he saw Bruce coming for him, later, after Jake had run from the trailer, feeling ashamed of his cowardice. He saw their wild ride along the beach road, the manic, deranged look in Bruce's eyes, *Eye of the Tiger* blasting incessantly from the stereo. Finally, he saw the boy's mangled body as he set him into the makeshift grave.

Jake turned his gaze back to the ocean. It was a beautiful sight to behold. Yet despite the beauty spread out before him, Jake had the overwhelming sense of being under water, of being pulled down by a force he was powerless to overcome. He felt like he was drowning. He'd been drowning in this place for thirty years.

Drowning in the Sea of Cortez.

This had been his penance for the foolishness of his youth.

And now it comes down to this. He could see it all laid out before him. It was time to balance the scales, to right the wrongs committed so long ago. There was no way to avenge the boy's death—except perhaps, to die in this endeavor. But Jake knew that was pure fatalism talking. He'd been serving a self-imposed sentence since that day in 1984, when he and Bruce McAlister committed their unspeakable act. And through that act, they'd set into motion a chain of events leading back to this spot, to this moment in time, standing on a bluff overlooking a place that had enthralled Jake for so brief a time, before consuming him in tragedy.

Jake knew he wasn't a bad person. Still, he couldn't escape the truth, how easily he'd succumbed to Bruce's twisted logic on that horrible night. Was that his true self? For years, he'd rationalized that he was just a kid, a scared kid who'd found himself in an impossible situation. But that was merely the first lie, the one that all the others were built upon.

He'd wondered often about that little boy. Who was he? Where did he come from? Did he have brothers and sisters? A mother who cried endless nights, wondering, what happened to my son? Jake never spent long pondering such questions. They'd come of their own volition, and Jake would swat them away by immersing himself in work, by ignoring them, by running.

But now the running was done. So much had been revealed in these last few weeks, the wellspring of consequences that had come from that stupid, senseless act. Jake knew he could never return to his old life. It was no kind of life, although in the twisted logic of fate's cruel hand, he knew it was the life he'd deserved.

Firm in his conviction, steeled in his nerve, Jake turned and walked down from the bluff. It was time for the final act. It was time to confront the wrong he'd perpetrated here, and had tried to bury for too many years. It was time to make a stand.

IT WAS dark when Jake returned to the motel. He parked the truck, shut off the engine, and sat for a few minutes collecting his thoughts. The light was on in their room, and he could see Hector moving about. He prayed for the old man's safety.

If someone should die here, let it be me.

Jake exited the truck and walked to the patio. It was quiet down at the church, the music turned off, the men unseen. The guard remained outside the block building, a light shining through the high window. Jake felt sure that Paige was inside, probably Bruce too, and he sketched a plan in his mind, focusing on getting inside the room.

Hector came outside and sat in one of the patio chairs. "How are you feeling," he said.

"I'm fine," Jake replied. "How about you? After all, you're the old man."

"Yes, I am. But I am a spry old man." Hector smiled warmly.

Jake sat down. "Gallows humor," he said. And after a moment, "I'm scared, Hector. Scared of dying. Scared of killing someone."

Hector looked into Jake's eyes for a long moment.

"But you will see it through."

"Yes. I will see it through."

"Fear is good, *mi hijo*. It means that you are human."

"If you say so."

Hector stared into the distance. Jake watched the side of his face, overcome by a surge of emotion, by how much he loved Hector and respected him. He knew with absolute certainty that he could never have done this alone. Hector's presence made all of this seem so…right, so honorable. And possible, too. Jake realized now, just how much he was counting on Hector's experience, his wisdom, his *courage* to see this through.

Hector spoke, his head turned, his voice somber.

"When I was nineteen years old the Army gave me a medal. They said I was brave, and because of my bravery I was deserving of recognition. I had killed men for my medal, Chinese and Koreans, many of them boys just like me. I did not feel like a hero. I felt like a scared child, too far from home, unsure of myself, unsure of why I was there. I certainly did not want to kill those men."

"But that was war. That was the job you were sent to do. This is different."

"True, it was a different situation altogether. But what I am talking about is fear, Jake. And morality, the concept of right and wrong. A rational mind knows that killing is wrong. But it also knows that killing is sometimes necessary. There can be no ambiguity about that. Assuming, of course, that the cause is just."

"And fear? What about that?"

"You cannot stop fear. It is there, or it is not. If it exists, you must first acknowledge it, and then control it."

Hector paused and put his hand on Jake's knee.

"Your cause is just, *mi hijo*. And your fear is real. Know this in your heart, and I have confidence that you will succeed. And if you should die, if *I* should die, then it is God's plan."

"I thought you didn't believe in God's plan."

Hector laughed. "If I have ever given you that impression, then I have been misunderstood."

"My apologies."

"We will make every effort to resolve this situation without violence," Hector said. "But if Mr. Stafford or those men down there choose a different path, we will react without hesitation. Of that we must be clear."

"I understand."

"Good."

"So, what's the plan?"

"Do you remember the story of the Trojan horse?"

"As I recall, that horse had men inside it. More than two, which is what we've got. So maybe you can explain that to me."

And then, as if on cue, a pickup truck drove into the motel parking lot and pulled up to the patio, its headlight beams blinding Jake as he looked. He shielded his eyes, saw two men in the cab, at least three more in the back. He turned and looked at Hector.

"What's this?"

"The cake," Hector replied. "It is finished."
He got up and walked over to greet the men.

Chapter 55

Hector drove the truck steadily along the main road leading to the church. Jake sat in the passenger seat, cradling one of the shotguns. Neither man spoke. They'd done all their talking back at the motel, when they finalized their plan.

Fifty yards before the wrought iron gate, Hector stopped the truck and Jake got out. He nodded to Hector, who whispered, "Good luck, *mi hijo*," before Jake shut the door and jogged away into the desert. Hector put the truck in gear and entered the church compound through the wrought iron gate.

Jake ran along the low wall surrounding the church, to the wood gate at the west end. He stopped for a moment, looked and listened, and then he vaulted the gate and walked slowly to the cinder block building where he believed Paige was held.

The plan was simple. Hector would distract the men out front while Jake freed Paige. They would escape through the desert and make their way to the motel, where Hector would join them and they'd leave that night for home. Bruce was on his own. Jake would help him if the opportunity presented itself, but he wasn't going to stick his neck out for the man.

The immediate problem was how to deal with the man standing guard outside the window, and whatever men were inside. Jake wasn't sure how to do that without using his shotgun. He imagined how they did it on TV shows and in movies, clubbing a man behind his head and knocking him out cold. He always thought that was bullshit, even though it made for good drama.

As he went down a narrow walkway, Jake prepared himself for a fight. The night was eerily quiet, the air deathly still, and he listened for sounds of Hector's truck. He should be inside now, making his play. He hoped things didn't go sideways, although he felt certain that they would.

Chapter 56

Hector stopped his truck a few yards in front of the stone monument at the center of the courtyard, the one that reminded Jake of a New Orleans crypt. In the beam of the headlights he read an inscription etched into the base: *Miguel Ángel Garcia 1974-1984*.

Staring at the inscription, a thought came to Hector, and then a moment of realization that touched his heart. He crossed himself, shut off the engine and headlights, and waited.

A man emerged from the darkness of the barracks building; medium height, stocky, dressed in baggy jeans, high tops, and a Raiders hoodie, strutting toward the truck like a man in charge. Hector reached down to the floorboard and adjusted a beach towel that was lying there, then put his hand back on the steering wheel.

"What do you want, old man?" Zamora said loudly as he approached. He stopped a few feet from the truck. Come a little closer, Hector thought as he smiled at the question.

"I believe I am lost."

"Lost?"

"I was looking for the Catholic church."

"You got the wrong place. Turn around and keep looking."

"Are you sure this is not the place I am looking for?"

"Are you hard of hearing? I told you to leave."

"I can hear you just fine," Hector said pleasantly.

"Well then what are you waiting for?" Zamora stared at Hector. And then the light of recognition came to his eyes. "Hey, I know you," he said.

"How is that possible?" Hector said with an astonished expression. "I have never seen you before in my life."

Zamora stared at Hector, putting it together.

"Yeah, old man, I definitely know you. You're not lost, *cabrón*. What are you doing here?"

Hector shifted his weight slightly, taking his hand from the steering wheel and resting it on the seat by his leg.

"I am sorry, but I believe you have me confused with someone else."

"Don't fuck with me. You're the one who works with that priest in Santa Ana. The one who talks shit about illegals. You been making a lot of trouble for the wrong people."

Hector's mind drifted from this disrespectful hoodlum to Jake, and he wondered if he'd found Paige yet. Zamora moved closer to the truck. Hector saw the other men now, stepping from the shadows of the trees, their weapons drawn.

"Get out of the truck," Zamora demanded.

"There is no need for belligerence."

"Listen to me, old man. Get out of the truck. Now."

Hector smiled. And then in a quick movement, he reached to the floorboard and grabbed the Colt Peacemaker from under the beach towel, swinging his arm around and pointing the gun at Zamora, pressing the barrel into the man's forehead.

"Please step back and make no sudden moves. This pistol has a very fine trigger."

Hector opened the door with his left hand, pushing it far enough to get out of the truck, keeping his right arm extended, the gun barrel pressed to Zamora's forehead.

"Take two steps back," Hector said calmly. Zamora hesitated. "Do it now, or I will split your skull faster than you can draw your last breath."

Zamora seethed, beads of sweat popping on his forehead. He stepped back. Hector moved away from the door of the truck, keeping the Colt pointed at Zamora's head.

"Fucking foolish old man. You're dead."

"We shall see," Hector said. "Tell your men to drop their weapons."

Zamora was about to laugh, to call Hector's bluff. But then he looked into the old man's sky-blue eyes, and he saw something that shook him to his core. He'll do it, Zamora thought coldly, he'll shoot me like a dog and not give it a second thought. He called out to the men to drop their weapons. Hector whistled a sharp, piercing note. The tarp over the bed of the truck moved, and then folded back to reveal five men standing and pointing weapons.

"Now," Hector said. "Where is Jason Stafford?"

Chapter 57

Jake had cleared four rooms when the shooting started.

He'd made his way down the walkway fronting the cinder block buildings, a total of three with several rooms inside each of them, picturing the layout as he remembered it from the motel patio. For some reason, he was confused. He thought the guard was posted at the first of the three buildings, but he'd just finished checking all those rooms and found nothing. And then he heard a shotgun blast, followed by loud voices and more gunshots.

He moved from the building into an open area, but he had no clear view of the church courtyard. The shooting was sporadic, the voices indecipherable. Jake felt the urge to run and help, but Hector had said to find Paige no matter what happened. He hesitated, knowing he would never forgive himself if Hector was harmed. But the same thing applied to Paige, and Jake didn't know which way to go. A flurry of gunshots sounded out, and Jake made his decision. He turned and headed for the second of the three buildings.

IT WAS Raúl who set it off.

As soon as he jumped out of the bed of the truck, he recognized Zamora. Angry words were passed in Spanish, and then all hell broke loose.

The five men were *campesinos*, from the same small town as the men Hector had been helping at Father Ramón's church, the men who had been left to die in the desert near Yuma. Hector had called these men as soon as he and Jake had entered Mexico—it was the call he'd made from the restaurant in Mexicali—knowing they would need help if they were to succeed in rescuing Paige.

Hector also knew that these men would be more than willing to settle the score with the blue-eyed Devil, Jason Stafford. True, it would be like throwing a burning match into a powder keg, but Hector's conscience was clear.

He'd had an agreement with the men that guns would be used only as a last resort, although Hector could see that Raúl was the wild card, the one he'd have to keep his eye on. Raúl's older brother had nearly died on the crossing, abandoned in the desert by these cartel dogs, and even in recovery the damage lingered; his brother would never be the same, the emotional scars as deep as the physical ones.

Raúl had planned to accompany his brother on the journey, but he fell ill upon arriving in Bahia de Cortez and was forced to stay behind. As soon as he heard what happened, he crossed the border on his own, going through the rugged country near Tecate. He'd only been in Santa Ana one day when he was rounded up in a raid and deported.

So now he was here, staring at the man who had nearly killed his brother, and he wasn't going to let the chance for retribution pass, regardless of any agreements he'd made with Hector.

The shotgun blast took Zamora in the stomach, knocking him back several feet. Raúl pumped the shotgun as the other *campesinos* scattered, firing their weapons. Hector took a quick look at Zamora and knew that he was dead, the man's blood seeping in a widening pool around him, and then he scampered to the rear of the truck as Zamora's men returned fire.

Well this is a fine turn of events, Hector thought as rounds winged past him, striking the truck and the dirt around him. He held his fire, watching as the *campesinos* engaged Zamora's men. Letting the other men do the fighting, Hector strategized.

He scanned the courtyard, looking for Jake. He knew that any minute now, Jason Stafford would show up. He decided to give Jake five minutes, before setting out to find him.

PAIGE WAS jolted awake by the gunfire.

"Dad, something's happening."

Bruce stood at the door, ear pressed to it, listening. He checked the lock. Then he moved to the window, standing on one of the chairs to look out. He didn't see the man standing guard outside.

"Dad?" Paige said. "They're shooting outside. What's going on?"

"I don't know, honey. But we have to stay calm. I'm sure there's an explanation for it."

As soon as he said it, Bruce knew how lame it sounded. He stepped down from the chair, grasped it firmly, and swung it overhead, shattering the window. He lowered the chair, stepped up on it and cleared the remaining shards of glass from the frame.

"What are you doing?" Paige said.

"I'm going out to see what's happening. I want you to stay here. You'll be safe if you stay here. I'll come for you when I can."

"Dad, please, don't go."

"I have to. Stay here and keep quiet. Jason won't hurt you."

Paige looked at her father, doubt clouding her eyes, and Bruce wondered if it was true, that Jason would not hurt her. He searched the storage room for a weapon, something for Paige to defend herself with, but there was nothing. He looked at a metal shelving unit.

"Help me move this," he said.

"Why?"

"Please, just help me."

They moved the heavy unit in front of the door.

"If anyone tries to come through that door, this will hold them off long enough for you to go out the window. If that happens you run, as fast as you can into the desert. Go into town, to the police station, and tell them what's happened here. You got that?"

"I can't leave here without you."

"If they come for you before I get back, you have to run, Paige. Do you understand that?"

Paige shook her head, and then she hugged her father tightly, the things he'd told her earlier running through her mind, the shock of his confessions stinging her heart and soul. She looked into his eyes.

"I love you, Dad. So much. Please be careful, and come for me when you can."

"I will. You just do like I said, and everything will work out."

Bruce didn't believe it, but he prayed it would be so. Then he stepped up onto the chair and hoisted himself through the window, falling awkwardly outside. He landed on his shoulder and rolled, a sharp jolt of pain shooting across his back. More shots rang out, and he took off running.

JASON STAFFORD heard the gunshots from inside the church office, located at the rear of the chapel.

He'd dozed off and now he was groggy, his head aching, a stabbing pain at the center of his forehead. He never got headaches, certainly not like this, and it was pissing him off. It was because of Bill McAlister, not agreeing to terms, and Zamora's attitude, and those fools outside, drinking and carrying on. And now they were out there shooting, like frat boys run amok. Assholes. He regretted ever bringing them in. It was a stupid move, as evidenced by this crap. He got up and started for the door, ready to kick some ass.

And then he stopped and listened more carefully, something about the cadence of the gunfire making him reconsider. He pulled his handgun and checked the load, returned it to his holster. He left the office and moved through the chapel to the front door. The gunfire intensified. Jason eased open the door and peered out.

It was the goddamn O.K. Corral out there.

Men running, firing, shouting in Spanish. And there in the middle of it, Jason saw a familiar pickup truck. It can't be, he said to himself.

Jason ran back through the chapel and into the office, exiting through a rear door. He crept around the side of the chapel and looked out to the courtyard. From this position, he could see Zamora's men back in the trees, firing wildly. Another group of men had taken cover throughout the courtyard, returning fire. And there, at the back of the truck, crouched low, Jason saw Hector Santiago, pistol in his hand, a straw hat perched on his head. What the hell are they, the cavalry?

Jason considered the situation. If that old man was here, it meant that Jake Donahue wasn't far behind. This thing was seriously going off the rails. He had to get Bruce and Paige out of here, pronto. If he played it right, he might still be able to salvage something. There was a Ford Bronco parked in a maintenance shed at the far side of the compound. He'd use that to make his escape, get to somewhere secure and regroup, and find a way to get Bill McAlister to come through with the money. He watched the gun battle for a few seconds, cursed his bad luck, and then turned and ran.

JAKE WALKED down the hallway of the second building, opening doors and checking rooms. The gunfire continued outside. He came to a locked door. After checking its sturdiness, he prepared to kick it in. And then he heard a voice from inside.

"Dad? Is that you?"

"Paige?"

"Who is it? Who's there?"

"It's Jake Donahue."

"Jake?"

"I'm going to force the door open. Stand back."

"Hold on a minute."

There was a sliding noise and banging against the door.

"Okay, it's ready now."

Jake stepped back, planted himself, and gave the door a hard kick with the sole of his boot, just above the doorknob.

313

Pain shot through his leg and into his groin. He changed position slightly and did it again, the door coming free from the splintered jamb. He pushed it open and saw Paige standing back in the corner, a metal shelving unit near the door opening.

"Where's Bruce?"

"He went out the window as soon as the shooting started. He said he would come for me when it was safe. He put that thing in front of the door." Paige pointed to the shelves. "Have you seen him?"

"No," Jake said. "Come on, we have to go."

"What's happening?"

"I have a friend with me, outside. We're going to take you home."

"He's out there, where they're shooting?"

"Yes, but it's okay. We have a vehicle and we have other men helping us. Follow me, I won't let anything happen to you."

"What about my dad?"

Jake stared at Paige. He didn't know how to answer. He wanted to say that he didn't care about Bruce, that he only cared about saving her and Hector. But he couldn't tell her that. So he lied.

"We'll look for him on the way. If we don't find him, after you're safe, I'll come back. But we've got to get moving, before Stafford finds us."

"He kidnapped me."

"Yes, I know all about that. I also know about Danny."

Paige's eyes watered and she reached for Jake. He set the shotgun down and embraced her, holding her tight as she sobbed into his shoulder. He didn't want to rush her, but he couldn't stand here all night, hugging while Stafford was out there somewhere and Hector was in danger. He broke the embrace, squared her shoulders and looked into her eyes.

"Are you ready?"

"Yes, I'm ready."

"You going to be okay?"

"Don't worry about me," Paige said, her voice steady now. "Let's go.

Jake picked up the shotgun.

"Stay right behind me. If I go down, you grab my shotgun, point and shoot. You got it?"

"I got it."

They left the room, headed for the church courtyard.

FIVE MINUTES later, Jason Stafford rounded the corner and saw the open door of the storage room. He looked inside, gun drawn. The room was empty.

"Son of a bitch!" he yelled.

He saw the broken window, the splintered door frame. And then he noticed that the shooting had stopped. He listened to the silence, followed by the rumbling sound of a truck's engine, and men shouting in Spanish.

What now?

Jason left the room, walked slowly down the corridor to an outside door. He stood alongside it, sweat running down his back, his head throbbing from the headache that wouldn't give up. He pushed the door open, waited a few seconds, and then stepped outside, ready to end this right now.

Chapter 58

The gunfire was sporadic. Bursts of shotgun blasts, pistol and automatic weapon fire, followed by short intervals of silence broken only by the moans of the wounded. Zamora's men were back in the trees, the *campesinos* spread throughout the courtyard.

Hector crouched behind his truck, planning his next move. And then the shooting stopped. Zamora's men yelled to each other, and minutes later a four-wheel drive truck barreled out from behind the barracks and tore down the paved road, men crowded in the bed of the truck, firing wildly. The truck drove through the wrought iron gate, disappearing into the darkness.

"They took off!" someone yelled in Spanish.

"Cowards!" another man yelled back.

Hector stood and saw the *campesinos* moving in the direction of the trees, weapons drawn, looking for stragglers. He turned and saw Jake walking slowly toward him, shotgun out front, Paige close behind. He went to greet them, made it just a few steps before he was jerked from behind by a strong hand. He nearly fell before being hoisted to his feet by Jason Stafford.

"Easy, pops. Drop the hardware." Jason had his left arm around Hector's neck, squeezing tight. Hector immediately dropped his pistol. "That's good. You listen, do what I say, and maybe you'll walk out of here."

Jake stopped when he saw Jason grab Hector.

"Stafford!"

Jason put his pistol to Hector's head. "That's good, Jake. Stay right there."

Jake aimed the shotgun, standing twenty feet away. The weapon was no good for this, he thought, sweat seeping from his scalp. If he tried to shoot Stafford, he'd blast Hector too. He needed a pistol.

"Stay behind me and don't move," Jake whispered to Paige.

"Where's Bruce?" Jason said.

"He took off. I don't know where he is."

"Doesn't matter anyway. Here's what's going to happen. You drop the shotgun, round up those other assholes over by the trees, and drive out of here. Paige stays. You can come back in an hour and pick up the old man. You got all that?"

"I'm not going with him," Paige said into Jake's ear, her voice low and panicked. "I'll die first."

"Easy," Jake replied. "No one's staying, and no one's dying."

"You want to share that with the rest of us?" Jason said.

The *campesinos* started moving toward Jason and Hector. Raúl held his left arm, bloodied at the shoulder, and two of the men helped another, his leg bloody and dragging.

"Tell your men to drop their weapons and stay where they are," Jason said to Hector. "Tell them, or I'll blow your damn head off."

Hector told the men in Spanish. They stopped, eased the man with the wounded leg to the ground, and dropped their guns.

"That's good," Jason said. "So, what's it gonna be, Jake?"

"I'm not leaving without Paige."

"You want me to kill your friend here? Because that's what I'll do. I don't have a lot of options, and Paige is my only bargaining chip. You take that away from me, I'm pretty much screwed. You never want to negotiate with a desperate man, Jake. It never turns out well."

"Don't do it, Jason," Bruce called out, emerging from the shadows of the barracks. He walked with purpose, stopping midway between Stafford and Jake.

"Hey, Bruce," Jason said. "Been waiting for you to join us."

"What are you doing, Jason?"

"I'm getting ready to haul ass out of here. I'm taking Paige with me. I was going to take you too, but now I'm thinking it's better to travel light."

"You're not going anywhere," Bruce said.

"Really? Are you going to stop me?" Jason laughed. "How about I just shoot you right now, put an end to your crazy hero notions."

Bruce moved a few steps closer to Stafford. "It's time to end this."

"Dad, please, stay back," Paige said, her voice quavering.

"Listen to her, Bruce. Because I *will* kill you."

"I don't believe it," Bruce said. He reached out his hand. "I don't believe that's what's in your heart."

"What?"

"Your heart, Jason. Despite what you've done, you know that it's wrong. You know it in your heart."

"What the fuck, Bruce, are you going to preach to me now? Are you going to *save* me?" Jason laughed disdainfully.

Jake held the shotgun steady, sighting down the barrel, looking for a shot. Bruce edged closer to Stafford, motioning with his hand.

"Put the gun down, Jason. We can fix this. We can fix it so everyone gets what they want."

"Shut up, Bruce."

Jason's head was splitting, his vision blurred.

"Feel the love of Jesus in your heart, Jason. Put the violence aside."

The headache throbbed, Bruce's voice grating, driving the pain.

"God loves you, Jason. He forgives you. He wants you to—"

"I told you to shut the fuck up!"

Jason raised his arm and fired at Bruce. Hector jerked sideways, throwing Jason's aim off. Bruce collapsed and Paige screamed. Hector threw his elbow into Jason's stomach, once, twice, with the strength of a man half his age. Jason released his arm and Hector dropped to the ground. Jake pulled the trigger, taking Jason Stafford high in the chest.

Paige ran to Bruce. Hector stood, looked at Stafford and then at Jake, nodding his head slowly. Jake lowered the shotgun, his ears ringing.

Epilogue
The Lord Giveth

Six months later, Bruce McAlister was sentenced to fifteen years in prison.

He'd agreed to a plea deal, accepting full responsibility for the conspiracy that had led to the death of Susan McAlister and Richard Lawson.

Jake knew that Bruce was not directly responsible for the murders, that he was a minor player at best, but since Jason Stafford was dead and Bill McAlister had been rendered incapacitated by a massive stroke a month after Bruce was released from the hospital, where he'd been recovering from the gunshot wound that had nearly killed him, no one remained for the authorities to charge with the crime. That left Bruce to take the blame. He seemed to welcome it.

The Limestone deal was in shambles, the Silverado Canyon congregation disbanded, and the church at Bahia de Cortez had been taken over by another ministry. In Bruce's mind, he had nothing left.

After much reflection upon the evil that he had allowed to enter his heart, Bruce decided *he* would accept responsibility for the things that were done in his name, for his willingness to turn a blind eye, for the pain and heartache he had caused others. He would accept responsibility, take his punishment, and ask the Lord for forgiveness.

Despite all of Bruce McAlister's shortcomings, the many aspects of his life that were pure charade, his faith was genuine. Jake nearly admired him for it. It was comforting to know that his former friend wasn't a complete fraud.

In the immediate aftermath of the shootout, a doctor was summoned from town to treat Bruce and the other wounded men, and paid cash for his silence. The *campesinos* buried Zamora and Jason Stafford in the desert, and dumped the weapons in the ocean. Jake called Bill McAlister and arranged for Bill's private plane to be flown to Mexico to bring Bruce and Paige home. Jake and Hector drove, Hector's trusty pickup sporting several bullet holes, yet none the worse for it.

Jake did a lot of soul searching on that long ride home, coming to terms with the fact he'd killed a man. He had no regrets for his actions, and he knew with certainty that he'd done the right thing. But death is an absolute, and killing, regardless of the reason, goes against the grain of basic humanity. *That* is what Jake struggled with.

Hector was a faithful companion through it all, giving Jake the space he needed, providing the right words at the right time, his intuition pitch-perfect, his wisdom invaluable. Jake thanked God for sparing Hector Santiago's life, and he looked forward to many more years spent in the company of his old friend.

Jake wasn't sure what to expect when he got home. How would he clear his name, now that Stafford was dead? He needn't have worried. Bob Jenkins's security camera had captured images of Jason Stafford shooting Ricardo Salazar, and once they were presented to the detectives handling the case, Jake was cleared of all suspicion.

As soon as Bruce and Paige arrived in Orange County, Bill McAlister started his propaganda machine, shaping the narrative of Jason Stafford's evil doings and the steps Bill was forced to take to save his family. He kept Jake's name out of it, claiming to have hired a private security team—mercenaries, one newspaper called them—to go to Mexico and rescue

Bruce and Paige. He claimed that Stafford got away, his where-abouts unknown.

It didn't take long for the narrative to fall apart, a few dog-ged reporters digging into the story, finding the holes and ex-ploiting them. They began to look more closely at Jason Staf-ford and his relationship with Bill McAlister. When the bodies of Stafford and Zamora were discovered, the roof caved in on Bill McAlister. And then he had a massive stroke, leaving him all but dead. Bruce took the fall, the reporters lost interest, and the story faded from public view.

Jake saw Bruce shortly before his sentencing, when Bruce was out on bond and confined to house arrest, monitored by an ankle bracelet. They didn't spend long together.

Bruce apologized to Jake, said he was sorry for Susan, and for Danny, sorry for the things Jason Stafford had done to Jake. Most of all, he was sorry for Miguel Ángel Garcia, the boy he'd killed in 1984. He told Jake the story of how he'd found the boy's family not long after establishing the church in Bahia de Cortez. He was not brave enough to admit to killing Miguel, but to assuage his guilt, he secured the family financially, com-ing up with a plausible excuse for doing it. And he interred the boy's remains at the new church, in the crypt-like monument that stood at the center of the church courtyard. It was all a little morbid for Jake, and he didn't know if he should forgive Bruce, or pity him. In the end, he just listened, his feelings re-maining unspoken.

Finally, they talked about Paige.

"How long did you know?" Jake asked.

"I'd always suspected, after what happened in Mexico."

"What happened in Mexico?"

Bruce smiled. "Really, Jake?"

Jake didn't respond.

"Susan told me about you two. I wasn't surprised. I would have bet money that night, after I picked you up, that some-thing happened. She used to bring it up, whenever we fought. She'd use it as a wedge, hammer me with it. The more she drank the worse it got."

"She was sick. She needed help."

"She really admired you," Bruce said, ignoring Jake. "She was drawn to me in a purely self-destructive way, but she respected you." He paused, his expression distant, almost wistful. "I think she would have ended up with you, if you'd stuck around."

"I couldn't stay. Not after what we did. Not after that night."

"I understand, Jake. And I'll admit that you leaving made it easier on me. Unfortunately, that's not what I needed then. If you had stayed, a lot of things would have turned out differently."

Jake nodded, but said nothing.

"I knew for sure that I wasn't Paige's father when I had a DNA test done five years ago. Like I said, I had my suspicions. Susan finally admitted to me a few months before she died that you were the father."

"Is that why she was killed?"

"Maybe."

"Christ, I can't believe it," Jake said, his voice breaking. "Why, Bruce? Tell me why. Tell me something that makes sense."

Bruce sighed.

"There is no 'why', Jake. It just is. My father was always driven by blind ambition. Once he settled on a goal, he would stop at nothing to achieve it. If it's any consolation, Richard Lawson was the real threat. He was the target."

"Did your dad know about Paige?"

"Yes."

"And about Miguel?"

Yes. I told him the year I was saved. Nineteen ninety."

"So all those plans, building you up as a pastor, the new church, all of it was done with full knowledge that you'd killed someone, and covered it up?"

"Yes."

"And you were willing to go along with it?"

"Yes, Jake, I was."

323

The men went silent. Bruce breathed heavily.

"I told Paige everything, that night in Mexico. When we were locked in that room."

"How'd she take it?"

"I'm not sure. She was shocked, of course. But in her heart, I can't say. She sees me often, but we don't talk about it. We're not ignoring it exactly, but we're not talking either. I suppose in time we will. What about you two?"

"What about us?"

"Do you talk about it?"

"Yes, but it's awkward."

"I imagine it is." Bruce looked away, his eyes watering. He sighed deeply. "So, Jake Donahue, where do we go from here?"

"I don't know, Bruce."

"Neither do I," Bruce said, and hung his head to cry.

JAKE PULLED up to Paige's condo in Newport Beach. After a few minutes, she came outside and Jake got out and opened the back of the Jeep, putting Paige's small suitcase inside. They got into the Jeep and drove to the freeway.

"I'm excited," Paige said.

"Me too," Jake replied.

"I've never been to Truckee."

"I think you'll like it."

Paige smiled, her hair pulled back, her eyes clear and full of life.

"I'm looking forward to seeing Amy," Paige said. "I think she's good for you, Jake."

Jake nodded. She *is* good for me, he thought. Thank God I was finally able to see it.

They had a week planned in Truckee; skiing, relaxing, getting to know each other. They were going to stay in the small house Amy rented near the Truckee River. Jake looked forward to revisiting his old haunts, seeing friends from his time spent there. He looked forward to going back to Squaw, maybe have a beer with the snow cat operators. He looked forward to seeing Amy.

He wasn't much of a skier, certainly not Amy's caliber, but he could get down the mountain in one piece. Paige said she hadn't skied in years, and Jake figured they could help each other when the inevitable spills came.

It was January, the beginning of a new year, and Jake's life was finally whole. He didn't know what tomorrow held, but he knew that today was good, and that was all he was entitled to. With the open highway in front of him, his past reconciled, and his beautiful daughter beside him, Jake dove headlong into the future, eager to embrace the life he'd been given, and to never again waste a precious minute of it.

www.ingramcontent.com/pod-product-compliance
Lightning Source LLC
Chambersburg PA
CBHW032141190626
46814CB00005BA/1790